Juliana Lopez Is Fu*king Fire

Dori Aleman-Medina

21 Boys Later…

Juliana Lopez is Fu*king Fire

This is a work of fiction. Any names or characters, businesses, or places, events, or incidents, are fictitious. Any resemblance to an actual person, living or dead, or actual events is purely coincidental.

Copyright © 2022 Dori Aleman-Medina

Cover Art Created by Kristina Wyatt

All rights reserved.

ISBN: 979-8-3546-5695-0

This book is for those girls, trouble, and the ones with a past.
You, who are not your typical romance novel, types of girls.
The kind of girls you can't take home to meet your mom.

For those who think you don't deserve it.

You do.

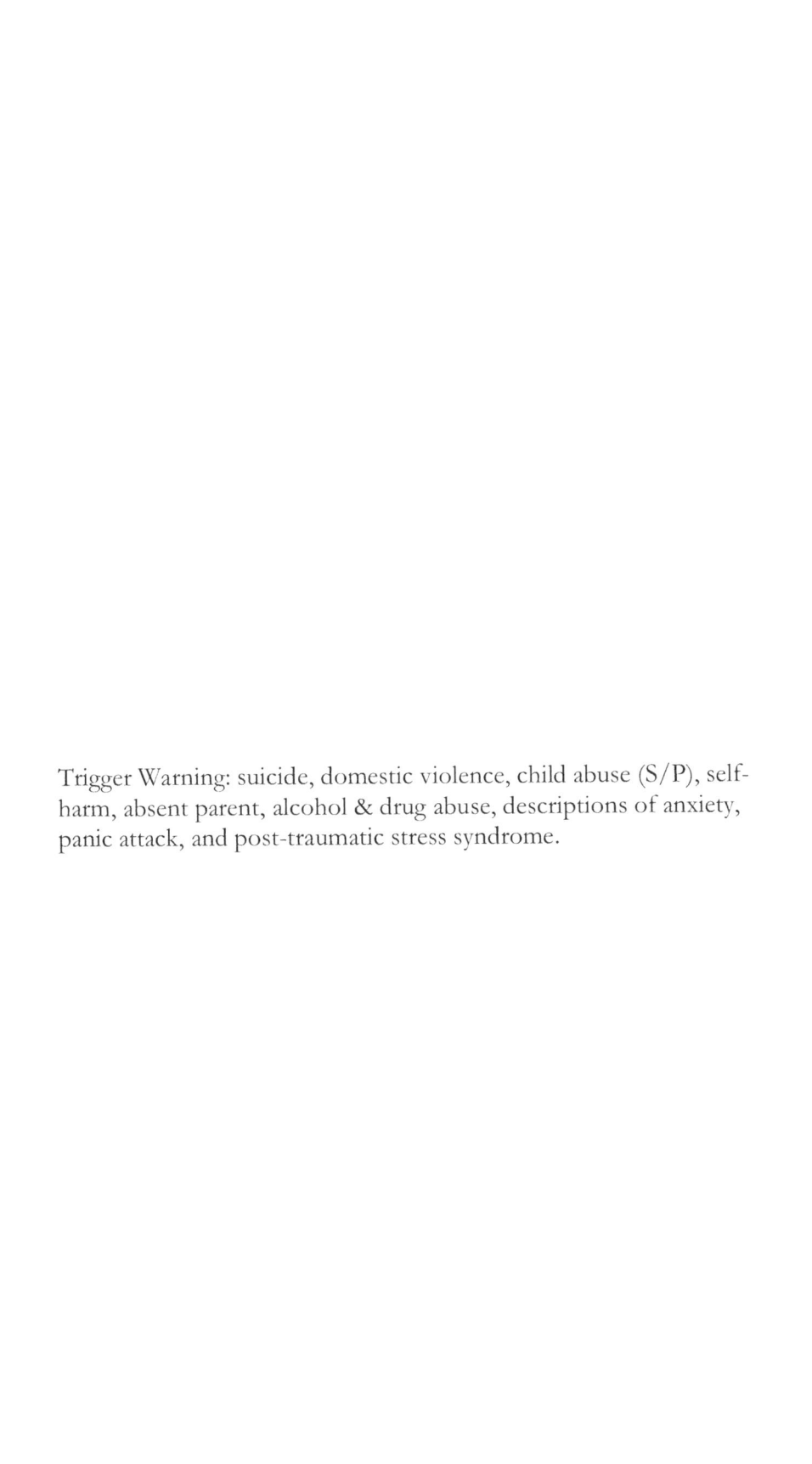

Trigger Warning: suicide, domestic violence, child abuse (S/P), self-harm, absent parent, alcohol & drug abuse, descriptions of anxiety, panic attack, and post-traumatic stress syndrome.

Part I

18

Two brothers: one of them wants to take you apart.

Two brothers: one of them wants to put you back together. ...

Richard Siken

I wanna be saved.

E-40

Dori Aleman-Medina

JULIANA
After
August 23

"Is this Matt Lopez whose dad is also Matt Lopez? You're both cops?" I'm purposely being evasive. It's taken me two months to work up the nerve to finally make this single phone call. The past few times, I dialed and let it ring only to hang up before he had a chance to answer it.

I hope he hangs up but, at the same time, I want him to give me a reason to keep talking. This is a reckless, bad idea, but Susan, my therapist, thinks it's a good one. What hell does she know?

Matt says nothing for a second. He hasn't heard from me in 18 years. I wonder if he even remembers who I am.

"Who is this?" He sounds like a cop, just like our father. Fucker.

"Who is this?" I sound drunk but I'm far from it. Like always, when I perceive power over others, I get this weird surge of adrenaline that makes me feel invincible and I say the stupidest things. "Well *Detective* Matt Lopez, this is Juliana Lopez, your sister."

He's quiet for a few breaths. I wonder if he even remembers me. "No shit? Where the fuck have you been? I thought you were dead."

He's almost right. I'm still alive even though I wouldn't consider this living. "I'm not dead. I'm not alive, but I'm not dead."

"Is this you, Juliana?"

"Of course it's me. I highly doubt anyone else is running around Fresno pretending to be me," I snort. Seriously? "Your mom teaches Spanish at Saint Paschal High School. She made you quit soccer because you had to go to catechism classes instead. You have a little brother; we have a little brother named Adam."

He's quiet. I know he's thinking about this.

"Where have you been, Juliana? I haven't seen you in years. Where are you now? I want to see you in person."

"I can be at the Daily Grind Coffee Shop in 20 minutes. Do you know where that is?"

"Off Olive and Wishon? I can be there in 30. Give me 30 minutes to get there." Matt asks, "Are you going to show up?"

"Text me, here's my number. I'll meet you there. I will be there."

******

I knew I would arrive first. Hell, I only work across the street. Although Fresno has grown, another victim of urban sprawl, I live a small-town life. I rarely wander out of the Tower District. It's on the older side of town but has a cool vibe. Lots of locally owned businesses mixed in with the occasional overpriced franchise. It's kind of retro, kind of hipster, kind of kitschy but mainly bohemian and totally gentrified. The local community college isn't far, so there are a bunch of young kids walking around a lot. Parking is a pain in the ass most of the time.

I have little need to travel to the more recent construction neighborhoods in the city. Everything past the imaginary line of Shaw Avenue is brand new and shiny. All across the far north side, Fresno is littered with strip malls and new oversized track houses. If people need me, they come to find me here. It's better that way. I keep my bubble small.

It's scorching hot every Fresno summer, even this late into September. The heat travels up through my ratty old Vans from the smoking hot asphalt. It's hotter at 5 pm than at 1 pm. I still ordered a hot coffee, never iced. Iced coffee is a sin in my humble opinion. I need caffeine and sugar to make it through this conversation. My brother, my little brother Matt, is coming to see me. What the fuck have I done now?

On the small patio outside the coffee shop, I sit near the water misters knowing full well my hair will be a frizzy mess but the outdoor fans are on and it feels so much nicer outside than in the super-chilled AC air inside. I'd rather be warm than cold. I'm always cold.

I have a few rules in my head. One, I will not rant about his fucking father. I don't need him. He didn't want me and that's that. I can't be chasing that anymore. Two, I won't mention how much his mother is a bitch. I will hate her in private. I never considered her my stepmother. Three, under no circumstances will I mention my mother. She's a wasted life too. I just want to know what happened to Matt and Adam, my two little brothers.

I know it's a cop's car the second he pulls up. It's the kind my father would drive when he was off duty. It's not literally a Fresno Police department car with all the logos but it's a flat black Suburban, with no stickers on it. Dark tinted window, the kind I would get a ticket for having but he won't. He parks in the open spot right in front. In a land of no parking, he finds an empty spot in just a few seconds.

My phone buzzes on the table with a new message alert. My fingers are trembling, so nervous to finally be in this moment. My brother, who I have not seen since I was a kid, is right over there. All the adrenaline in my body mixes with my diet of too much coffee. I want to throw up.

Text to Matthew Lopez Junior: I'm right out on the patio.

No one else is out on the patio. This is a good spot. Most people are inside the air-conditioned building. I don't need other people to hear our conversation. My fucking heart hurts, it's beating too fast. I'm going to have a heart attack one of these days.

This is a stupid idea. I shouldn't have done this. I should have just, I don't know, I shouldn't be doing this. That's for sure.

Matt gets out of his car, with cop-like shades on and a dark gray suit. He's just like my father, tall and unapproachable. Suddenly that old Carly Simon song pops into my head, but not her version, the Marilyn Manson version.

This is a bad idea. This is all wrong. I managed to create a situation I'd rather not be in, again. That's my superpower, maker of fucked up messes. Now I have to talk to him?

Matt leans against the front of his car for a moment, checking his phone. It's weird to see him all grown up. He's tall for sure. I guess we share that chromosome. He was maybe twelve years old the last time I saw him. He must be around 30 now. Damn, where does the time go? How did I miss my whole life?

My heart is beating out of control, I'm lightheaded. I should just leave, but I'd have to pass him to get out of here. I have to remind myself to breathe, that everything will be okay. No matter what happens, I will have closure, won't I? There won't be any more "what ifs." This is my "what if." I know how to play the confidence game; pretend I know what I'm doing.

He gestures to the guy with him, and they walk toward me. It's like a weird episode of COPS or The First 48. I do have an unhealthy relationship with reality TV police shows. Daddy issues I guess. He sees where I'm sitting. I won't make eye contact with him. Pretending to be busy with my phone, I only look up once he's reached my circle table. He's my brother for sure. We're not nice people.

I'm a hot mess, sloppy and confused. I struggle with people. My social skills suck. This is the stupidest idea I have ever had. Power, Juliana, focus on your power.

"Juliana," he says, approaching my table. He's visibly shaken up by my unexpected arrival into his life. He looks bewildered, another reminder that I really don't belong in his family. "Where have you been?"

"I was never hiding Matt," I say, trying to sound flippant. I don't want to remind him that his fucking father never looked for me. "I have always been right here."

"I thought you were dead." He doesn't sit, just has that cool cop vibe, watching me. He stands tall, trying to stare me down. He doesn't scare me.

I hate when people study me. I have to fake being calm. I am not calm. My heart is racing; I know that this coffee is not helping. I don't bother giving him a response.

"Sometimes I'd ask Adam if we just imagined you. We had a sister. One day she was gone."

"I was never your sister. I remember things a little differently than you. There was nowhere for me to stay when I turned 18. I needed to be gone." I stare at my fingertips, my nails all bitten to the quick, sloppy, messy.

"That's bullshit," Matt scraps the chair back and takes the seat across from me. He's struggling to keep his emotions in check. He's angry? Not sure what he has to be angry about. He had a perfect life, I'm the one no one wanted.

He's not what I expected but he is. We look alike. We have the same almond-shaped eyes but where mine are dark, his are hazel. I remember so little about him. It's more of a feeling. I liked him being around, but jealous that his home was never really mine. He was born when I was 5 years old. He got the good version, the dad who wanted him after he figured out his life plan. Matt is not the result of the bad high school hookup gone wrong.

"Why did you leave?" He stares at me with a strange intensity. I would hate to be the offender on the other end of that gaze. I know that look. I have mastered that look myself. It doesn't work for me.

I can't really give him an answer that will make sense to him. I move my empty coffee cup from one hand to another. There are parts of my story no one needs to know.

"I didn't want to be home anymore." Does he know, does he remember I left on the day of my eighteenth birthday? Yes, I got myself to school every day for the last two months of high school but I didn't live at home anymore. I didn't even attend my graduation. "My mother needed me to leave."

"Why didn't you come back to our house?"

"Seriously, your mother hated me."

Broken rule number two. I hold up my hand before he has a chance to defend her, "No, we are not going to do that. We are not going to argue about the semantics of what happened. I want to know who you are now. The past is gone. We can waste all our time arguing about parents we have vastly different opinions of or you can tell me who you are now."

I pound on the table to get his attention and point at him, "We are here right now. Don't waste our time thinking about the past."

He leans back in his seat, crossing his arms and not saying anything. He just studies me from the other end of the table. I have totally fucked up his day. Good, let him be moody and pissed off.

"I'm so tired Matt." All the results of my past bad choices press against me all the time. I cannot escape as much as I'd like to. There are things I can't change. Resting my head against the table for a minute, trying to get my thoughts straight again, I am that confused. This was not supposed to go like this. I was prepared for a big fight or a happy reunion, not strange gaps of silence. I should have expected silence.

Leaning back in my chair, I check out his partner. He's said absolutely nothing this entire time. He's all wide-eyed and lost. He has no idea what's going on here. He's cute. I know, I shouldn't be thinking about that, but hell, that's who I am. I judge on fuck-ability first, then ask questions. Yup, I'd fuck this one.

He's not too tall, taller than me, but not by too much. He's got that little boy hair thing going on, combed over to the side. It's cute on him and makes him seem lost. He's like the good little boy next door type of guy. He's wearing glasses, the thicker, black-framed type. It makes him seem approachable. I love a guy in glasses.

"Are you the good cop or the bad cop?"

He gives me this cute, shy smile, "I'm the good cop. He's the bad cop."

"Figures," I say, gazing at Matt, who is still visibly angry. Fuck that. He doesn't know shit. He knows only what he wants to believe.

"Do you have a name, Mr. Good Cop?" I gesture to his partner, all my black gummy bands moving on my wrist.

"I'm Daniel, Daniel Fernandez. I'm his partner."

"Partner, like," and I close my eyes and make an "ump" sound. I give him a pointed look. Leaning toward him, tapping the table as I speak, "Be more specific than that, clarify partner for me."

The handsome guy blushes just slightly, giving a knowing look. When he smiles, I notice he's got a cute little dimple on his left cheek. Hot, just so hot. "Cop partner."

"So it's not a life partner huh," I say, sarcastically, "My father is a cop too."

"I've heard."

"Dad said you had some mental health issues," Matt finally blurts out.

"He's not my dad," I snorted. Anger flushes through me. Is that how my father explains my existence away? Mental health issues? So everything is my fault? "That man might be your dad, but he sure isn't mine."

"Hey," the owner of the coffee shop pops out of the door, "Are we good, Jules? "

"I'm fine," I called to him, dismissing him with a lazy wave.

I guess Aaron doesn't like these two men sitting with me. He comes out of the door and over to our table. Aaron is an older African

American man with a deep voice and a flat sense of humor. He is my dad. He cares about me. "Do you need more coffee?"

"Always," I say, shaking my empty paper cup at him. "What kind of establishment are you running here, sir?"

He snorts, making a disgusted sound at me. Aaron looks at Matt and Daniel, "Do you need anything gentlemen?"

"They're cops AA-Ron," I always say his name wrong on purpose, not Aaron like it should be, but Letter A, Letter A-Ron like he's a rapper. He pretends to hate it but he loves it.

"Gentlemen, don't be fucking with my girl," he sasses at them. He legit puts his hand on his hip and glares at them.

"It's cool AA-Ron," I lean forward and gesture, "I'm kind of related to that one," I say as I gesture to Matt. "He's my half-brother."

"Well, Lord, have mercy," Aaron laughs, "I thought for sure they were harassing you. Do not take shit from men, Jules."

"I'm not."

"Brother huh? You're really him? I've heard a little about you, but I heard a lot about your father." Aaron crosses his arms against himself. "You're Matt Lopez Junior?"

"I am," he says, giving Aaron that cop look, sizing him up.

"Stop that, I say to Matt. He has no right to make judgments about Aaron. Aaron is the best kind of person. Matt is not allowed to look at him like that, with that cop look, investigating him. Asshole.

"I thought you were immaculately conceived to give me nothing but shit," Aaron tells me, grabbing my empty cup. Aaron knows me well, too well. "So brother man, do you need something? Coffee?"

"Plain coffee please," Matt tells him, giving him an honest smile. Aaron must have passed his policeman test. I guess he likes Aaron way faster than me but that is Aaron. He's uniquely likable.

Then he looks at Daniel, checking him out too, "You want the Juliana special, sugar?"

"What the fuck is a Juliana special, AA-Ron?" I swear sometimes, Aaron will be the death of me.

"A cup of black coffee with no sugar, just like your soul, maybe a dash of cream to make that pretty Latina color."

Aaron looks back at Daniel, "You need a Juliana special."

"Stop saying it like that, Aaron," I tell him, blushing. "What the fuck?"

"Don't be so sensitive." That damn Aaron, he's a punk ass sometimes.

"I take no shit from any man," I say, throwing my balled-up napkin at him, "Even you."

Aaron explodes into one of his body-shaking laughing spells.

"Girl, you'll do alright," he sings, swinging his hips and vanishing back inside. "I'll be back."

"Your buddy," Matt asks.

"Aaron is my dad." Aaron helped me build myself up when I had my accident. I've never wanted to disappoint him since. He's been there for me, for a long time. We have a unique relationship, sometimes parent and child, sometimes just friends, and sometimes just flat-out enemies. It's been a minute since we were enemies.

Matt rolls his eyes but doesn't question me about Aaron.

"You, Detective Fernandez," I say, slowly stretching all the syllables of his name while pointing at him, "Do you know him? His father?"

Daniel looks between us. He looks around and then looks back at me. "I do."

"Did you know he had a daughter?" Rule one is broken. Entrapment is to trick someone into committing a crime, or in this case, to confess something they did not want to. I'm going to make him say it. Matt needs to remember, his father didn't want me. I just steered this conversation in a way I didn't want it to go. Creating a fucking mess, it's what I do, maker of messes.

Daniel looks alarmed like he can't admit he had no idea. "No."

"Whatever," I am instantly overheated even under the fan. He doesn't know the whole story. I don't feel like telling him. It's rising in me, the urge to scratch my skin and bleed. The coffee and adrenaline hit my stomach. I am sick but I breathe through it. I count to myself, struggling to keep calm. Think of the color blue, ocean waves crashing, Susan said that should help. I have to stay calm even if I'm jealous that he knows my father while I don't. "My therapist says I need friends. She says I need to develop healthy adult relationships."

"Therapist? I thought you didn't have mental health concerns." Matt's teasing but it's not mean. The anger he had earlier is now gone. It's a different tone all of a sudden.

"I'm totally ADHD, but no Adderall for me."

"I do not want to hear the fucking word Adderall come out of your mouth, Jules," Aaron says as he saunters back with coffee. He dishes out three cups and a bag of cookies. "Not today, girlfriend."

"I don't do that, AA-Ron, I'm a good girl."

"Good girl, my ass," he makes a sound, like a huff of air to pointedly stress his statement, setting coffee cups on the table. "If you need me, you know where I am. Love you girl."

"Love you AA-Ron."

It's quiet for a minute, only the sound of busy traffic passing. It's time for people to get home, five o'clock traffic.

"These cookies are not good," I say, taking one and breaking it in half, noticing how stale they seem since my early morning delivery. I toss the broken cookie onto a napkin. Peanut butter cookies will be the death of me. I can't seem to get it right.

My brother is what I expected. Matt is a cop. I knew that. There was an article about him and our father that popped up in my social media feed once. It was one of those feel-good, happy stories that make other people sick. All about how Matt Lopez Senior and his son both became cops. His other son became a paramedic. No mention of a lost daughter who just vanished. Assholes. Matt, looks like him, tall, but Matt Junior wears a suit and tie. Last I heard, the last time I trolled his social media, my father is still a patrolman with the typical cop uniform.

His partner, Daniel, is the stuff of my nightmares. He too wears a suit and makes it look good. He's taller than me, but not by much. If we were standing, I'd be almost even with him. He's handsome for sure. He has that fucking cop persona and all cool attitudes, but there is an undercurrent of nervousness. It's almost like he's playing dress-up. He's not the tough guy out of these two. It's really cute. He's attractive for sure.

Detectives, what does that mean? I've watched The First 48, they don't look like this guy. It's the black-framed glasses that do it for me. It makes him seem smart, and I've got a thing for men that seem smart.

"Do you have a wife? A girlfriend?" I stare at him, forcing uncomfortable eye contact because that's what I do. I make people nervous. I hate it and I love it at the same time. I crave power over people. "A sweet girl who you think about and want to text but haven't because you're too chicken shit?"

"Me? No." Daniel glanced at my not-hot outfit, "Do you have a job?"

That's what he thinks of me? I'm homeless?

Tattered old checkerboard Vans, ripped-up black skinny jeans, and a faded black t-shirt that once upon a time had Green Day stamped on it. My hair is always up in two messy pigtails because it's too short for the messy bun look. My left wrist has ten thick rubber band bracelets paired with my smartwatch. My only make-up is my MAC Marrakesh lipstick, an orange-brown shade. "As a matter of fact, I own my own business."

They glance at each other. Cops, ugh, judgy much?

I smack my hand down, flecking cookie crumbs across the table. I'm instantly angry. Life is not fucking fair. Who the fuck are these people to judge me? "I made that. I make wedding cakes. I'm a baker. I don't need shit from you. I don't need anything from your father. I called you because I wanted to know what happened to you. You and your brother, where are you now? I talked about these memories I have with my therapist and she thought it would be," air quotes, 'healthy for me to call you.' There are things that happened at my mother's house that…"

I pressed my hands to my forehead, not letting those thoughts crowd me. Visualize ocean waves, picture calm seas. This moment is not about that. This is me being an adult. I have to force air into my lungs. Now is not the time to fall apart. "It doesn't matter. Your fucking father, my father, the cop? Never figured out what was happening at my mother's house. He left me there. How could he not know? He didn't want to know. He didn't care. I never fit into his perfect life with his perfect wife and perfect children."

I wipe my eyes. They're dry, but they burn. I no longer cry at those memories, ugly, hurtful, and horrible. I won't cry about it anymore. I lost too much to the past to allow it to control me now. I'm being erratic again. Susan would not be pleased. Breathe Juliana, control what you can, and let it be with what you can't. Control the future while acknowledging the past. We are creatures of our actions. Now is reality. Everything else is simply a memory with no control. I have control. My reactions are my own. My power belongs to me.

I am not ready for this.

"This was a mistake. I need to go. Be good. And you," I point at Daniel, "You are dangerous."

As soon as I say it, I know it's true. He makes my blood thick in my veins, a fire burning through me. It's more than being embarrassed but not enough to cause me to act like a total idiot. Beautiful men have always been my weakest point. This one, I want to take him home with me. It's been a minute since I had to fight that feeling. "I need to go."

"Jules," Aaron calls after me, from the door, "You good girlfriend?"

"Yeah, I'm good."

And I leave the coffee shop as ungracefully as ever. I might even trip over my Vans to get away.

DANIEL
August 23

I'm not dangerous.

I've never been so confused by a woman. I have no idea why I asked her if she had a job. I work with erratic people daily. I'm a good judge of character but this one? I have no idea. She's this weird combination of way too tough and very breakable. Scared? Maybe she's already broken and is trying to rebuild herself. She said rehab and therapy.

She called me dangerous.

Matt didn't talk to me on the way back to the station. He asked me to drive and got on the phone with his brother Adam. The entire ride back to the station was, "dad said," and, "she said."

I believe her. I know Matt Lopez Senior. He does have a picture-perfect life. He's practically a father to me. He was my mentor when I first finished the academy. He's stood by me during some of the worst times of my life. His son is one of my closest friends. I've had dinner at his house too many times to number.

I didn't know he had a daughter. A beautiful, intense daughter who thinks I'm dangerous.

******

I look her up. Criminal record-none. I hope the whole Adderall thing is just some overblown joke. She doesn't look like a typical party girl but that doesn't mean much. People are more than stereotypes. She had more of an emo vibe, wearing all black and all those black bracelets. I feel sneaky doing it behind Matt's back, but he's still talking to his dad. Such a major crisis, the kid no one talks about called home. Senior's wife is going to lose her shit. She is a prima donna.

5150, involuntary commitment due to a mental health crisis; that happened a couple of years ago. It sounds like she had a serious suicide attempt. Pills, lots of pills, and there were indicators that it was not her first attempt. There is a mention of cutting scars, but no images. She refused the crisis intervention team's permission to allow pictures. Sounds like her roommate found her and called 911. The roommate's name, Aaron Johnston. AA-Ron? That's all. Not even a clear report.

What she said rings through my brain, things that happened at my mother's house. Things that happened and Senior didn't figure it out. It doesn't take rocket science to figure out what she is talking about.

Opening a new window, and a Google search, her bakery. It's all these dark-themed wedding cakes and cupcakes. It's not my style, but I can see how people would like this stuff. It's dark and gothic. Everything is black, red, and burgundy. It's such a weird twist on the traditional white and ivory I would expect people would want for their celebrations. Her work is amazing. Even the name, Midnight Vanilla, suggests a dark aura. Clicking on one cake, the image fills my screen, four layers, the bottom black, the next layer checkered black and white, the third up white with a black damask pattern, and the tip top deep purple with a shocking green teacup on the top.

It reminds me of Alice in Wonderland, a wild tea party. Eric. Eric would have liked this.

"Getting married, Fernandez," Matt says, startling me.

"That's your sister's cake," I say, rolling over in my chair so he can see her work. "That's her bakery. She makes wedding cakes."

"I feel like shit that I didn't believe her." He looks at all the dark designs. It's not like Matt to admit he's wrong. His parents have always treated him as if he was perfect. Typical firstborn boy Mexican shit.

"What the fuck? You never told me you had a sister."

Matt rests back in the rolling office chair. "I stopped believing I had a sister. She was the one weekend-a-month arrangement kid. One day she was just gone. My parents never talked about her. Everything she said is true. My mom hated her. Probably still does. I was just a kid then and I didn't see it until later, once I became an adult. I figured out why she left.

You know my mom. She's a princess. My dad doesn't help by giving her everything she wants."

"How do you lose a whole person?" I've known Matt forever. He has a sister he never told me about? People, you think you know them, and then you don't.

"How do you figure out how to vanish when you turn 18?" Matt clicks through more cakes, all dark, magical. "She's the reason I never left Lexi."

Lexi is his daughter, who isn't his biological daughter. She's about 13, or 14 years old now. He dated her mom a long time ago. When they broke up, he didn't walk out on Lexi. Matt is the only father she has. They share custody, he pays child support. Lexi spends more time with Matt and his wife than with her mom.

"But you never told me? That's not weird to you? I'm not your boyfriend, but shit."

"That's not what Juliana hinted. She's funny."

"She's a smart ass," I remind him, "Just like your brother. Man, she's just like Adam."

"My mom is going to lose her shit."

"It didn't sound like she wanted to see your dad."

"The last time she left our house, she told him to fuck off and die. Said that she hated him, or some shit like that. I thought she was crazy or something. Seeing her today, dude, she was just a little kid. She still looks like a little kid."

"You never saw her again?" It's comforting to know that other people have drama. I'm not the only one.

"Just gone, at least, from what I know. I think she's five years older than me. I think, maybe six? I'm not exactly sure."

"She is about 36?"

"Something like that. You're not dangerous," he snorts, clicking out of the cake images. He turns to me, "What the fuck was that? You're the good guy."

"Hey, she's your sister." I hope I know what that means. I can't stop thinking about the way she just stared at me. "We should go back and shake down AA-Ron, get him to tell us her story."

"AA-Ron seems to know something, doesn't he?"

"He definitely did not like us talking to her," Matt states.

AA-Ron asked if I wanted the Juliana Special. What the fuck does that mean?

"I don't want to know her story."

"What do you think happened to her?" I think of the way she spoke, measured, and tried to be funny about things that are not funny. The way she just bolted once he decided she was done with us. "She said..."

"I know what she said." Matt leans forward, talking more to the floor. "I don't want to know what happened to her."

JULIANA
August 24

Sitting in the corner of the Daily Grind, I am an idiot. I only have myself to blame. I should not have met up with Matt. I rushed into it. I should have just stuck to having a phone conversation until I could figure out all my shaky emotions. I overreacted and said things I should not have said. I made foolish mistakes. I didn't stick to the script in my head. I am a fool, typical.

Waiting for Aaron to come over to me, I wallow in self-pity. I'm a child; I don't bother ordering anything at this point in our relationship. I just wait for him to bring me coffee when he's not busy. I normally take the far table inside, closest to the back exit. This is my spot. Everyone who's a regular knows this is my spot. No one fucks with my spot.

I have my stupid journal in front of me that I'm supposed to write in, to help sort out the details that confuse me, but it's just too much sometimes. So I fill it with cake designs, words, small pictures, and swirls of pencil lead giving an image to my confusion. Sometimes it is a single word with scribbles around it. Today's word: inconsequential. My meeting today was filled with inconsequential comments that had no bearing on my objective. Yup, community college dropout. I really made a mistake with all this.

"You good girl?" He saunters up with a cup of coffee.

"Yep," I say, not bothering to look up at him. My art therapy needs my devotion.

"Brotherman seemed like an okay dude."

"He's an asshole." Tears are there but I refuse to cry. I have to keep blinking to get rid of them. "Like his father."

"Well, girlfriend, most men are. Take no shit, Jules." He bestows the coffee onto my table and sits with me. He glances towards my left wrist. "You good girl?"

I pull my long-sleeved shirt down, "I'm not going to do anything stupid if that's what you mean."

He glances over at my latest sketch. A three-tiered cake, all black with an open umbrella on the top, the word inconsequential scribbled across it. "That's a lot of black, like your soul."

"I don't like it. It's not what I'm seeing in my head." I'm picturing an elaborate swirling design with a black umbrella and some sort of glitter falling. I've developed this weird obsession with umbrellas.

"Make some more vagina cupcakes, that always clears your head, girlfriend."

"Shut up AA-Ron," I say, laughing. It was an unusual request, that one.

When I first started making cakes, someone ordered two dozen cupcakes with vagina tops. I didn't tell Aaron what they were, but only showed him the final product. His flat response was classic, "I don't mean to be rude Jules, but are those vaginas?"

"I did not disappoint." The memory makes me smile. Everything is fine. So I fucked up, so what.

"You look tired."

"I can't sleep." He knows a lot about me. I don't have to hide the ugly parts with him. He knows what haunts me at night.

"Stop drinking so much coffee." He laughs, another whole-body explosion of laughter, "Girl, you need a date. Who was the other guy? Not brother man but the other one? He looks like he could help you out." Aaron laughs, he sings, "He seemed to like looking at you."

"No," I say, holding my palm up to him, "We are not having this conversation about some guy I don't even know."

"Isn't that your preference?" He's teasing, swatting the back of my hand as he talks, "Men you don't know. Even better if you don't know their name."

"Shut up."

We're both quiet for a minute. It's so nice when it's the end of the day and the coffee shop is closed. We can just sit and be still for a moment. My brain doesn't feel so heavy when it's quiet. Aaron knows that sometimes I need him close but quiet. He is my dad. Aaron and his partner, Quinn, are my family.

"Talk to Gabriel lately," he asks me.

"No."

Gabriel was once my best friend. He moved to DC years ago. He was the reason I got out of my mom's house. Then one day, I realized I was holding him back. He was my parent instead of my friend. When his boyfriend invited him to move to DC with him, I made sure to encourage him to go. When he insisted I go with him, I didn't, I stood my ground and stayed in Fresno. Once he was settled and happy in DC, I let him go. I stopped answering his texts and calls. Slowly, so he wouldn't get crazy on me, but eventually, he was just another person on my social media feed. Sometimes we try to talk. It's just not the same now. Nothing is.

"They had another baby." I know that Gabriel and Aaron talk. I'm sure they talk about me. This is a boundary I need. Aaron knows this. "One boy, one girl, fucking perfect."

"Um," he says, "Tick tock, Juliana."

"No one wants my used-up shit, AA-Ron." Aaron knows my obsession with time. I'm running out of time. Isn't that the most fucked up thing? Women spend their 20s avoiding pregnancy to just turn 30 and start chasing it. I'm 36 years old and hopeless. I'm running out of time.

"I'm telling you, girl, that cop was looking at you. He wanted the Juliana special."

"Definitely not the cop, he thought I was homeless."

"Girl, you're the prettiest homeless woman on the street," he laughs, his whole body shaking, "Men are simple. Give them a blow job and he'll do whatever the fuck you want."

"AA-Ron, I am not sucking a man's dick for a baby," I sighed at him. "Fuck it, if someone wants me, they're going to prove it. Someone needs to pick me for once."

He leans forward, "You don't need a man to have a baby. You can do this on your own if you want. You know Quinn and I will love up on that baby, pretty girl."

I say nothing to him. He means well, but that's not what I want. I want a life partner. I want someone to hold me when I'm having a moment. It's so much more than just having a baby. It's the life that goes with it. "That's just not the way I have it pictured."

"Life is not a picture," he says, "It's a moving river. You can't predict what's going to happen. You have to let it be. Stop pushing everyone away from you. You gotta trust sometime. Now, get your ass home."

"Fine, night dad," I say, dragging myself out his front door. "Love you AA-Ron."

"Love you too, girl."

DANIEL
August 25

    Juliana Lopez owns a bakery in the heart of the Tower District. It's almost too easy to miss, nestled between a consignment shop and co-op plant and household goods store. Next door is one of those places where you need to bring reusable bottles to buy detergent in bulk. I hate that kind of environmental crap. It's all so Tower District. This is not the place I like to be. I can't believe I've come here twice in two days. I normally avoid this part of town.

    Fresno is a huge place. The Tower District is an area in the city. From the 180 freeway up past the community college, and then to Roding Park where the Fresno Chaffee Zoo is located, it's filled with progressive people who use phrases like *gender-fluid* and *carbon footprint*. It's a bunch of shit as far as I'm concerned. It's not a place for me. There are too many old buildings with neon lights. Not for me at all.

    Midnight Vanilla in a tall script, cake designs by appointment only, gluten-free, allergy-free option available; the outside doesn't look inviting, but it's interesting. Sort of like Juliana herself, she gives off a vibe, don't mess with me. Smoky paint blurs the edges of the window, so you're forced to look at the beautiful deep burgundy wedding cake sitting in the window. Ivory orchids cascade from the top to flood the bottom layer of the square cake. It's a style I've never considered, but then again, men don't care about wedding cakes. At least, I don't.

    It's a small shop. It's more of a counter and table than a full-blown shop. She has old-school rap music playing, so loud you can feel it when you walk in. Exposed brick and dark display cases, even the baked goods in the case have a dark aesthetic. Everything is dipped in dark chocolate. It feels like a secret, like an old-fashioned speakeasy.

She's singing some dirty rap song I vaguely remember while pressing forward on fondant. I don't think she even heard us come in. It's small, for sure, but it smells like sugar and icing.

Her black hair is twisted into two messy pigtails on either side of her face, and her cheeks are flushed a lovely pink shade. It's only now that I notice she has a multitude of midnight blue highlights peppered in her hair.

Matt has to knock on the counter to get her attention.

"What?" She glares at Matt, turning the music down. She doesn't look happy to see him. "Did you run a background check? Credit report?"

She scowls right at me, "Am I homeless?"

"Adam wants to meet you." Matt touches all the different items on the counter, packages of cookies, and black and gold birthday candles.

Hum… not a word but a sound. She busies herself with a complicated coffee machine. She's mesmerizing, I can't stop watching her. She is like music. Her hair, the blue and black locks, even the way her black shorts squeeze at her hips, the cropped top she's wearing peeking out. Since she's so tall, they seem almost too short on her. Her legs are covered with fishnet stockings.

She's back to singing the song, ignoring us. It takes me a few seconds to place it. It's really old. I think my oldest brother once got grounded for playing it when my mom heard it. Old dirty rap from the 1980s?

She hands each of us a foamy coffee drink with a cinnamon heart on top of the foam. "Vanilla or chocolate?"

"Chocolate." Sipping my coffee, it's surprisingly good. I'm not a fan of fancy coffee drinks, but this is not sweet at all. It's dark and has a strange smoky taste.

She hands each of us a thick slice of decadent cake. "Try it."

She leans forward against the counter. I can see right down her shirt, noticing how round her breasts are. She's still Matt's sister, sort of. That's the unwritten Latino rule; don't look at your buddies' sister. Does she count? I didn't even know she existed last week. Shit. She's definitely a solid handful. What the fuck is wrong with me?

Opposite the counter, our foreheads almost touching, I watch her. She seems like she doesn't like me being so close to her, but she refuses to move. *You are dangerous.* Without breaking eye contact, I tried her cake. She stares at me, blinking quickly. This close I can smell her soap, something like mangoes. No makeup but dark shadows under her eyes, like she can't sleep. What haunts her?

She licks her lips, and I want to bite her. I want to touch her. I want to know what she tastes like if I licked her. Would she taste like chocolate? Fuck, she's beautiful.

I want to see her wrist; what she did. Does she still cut? I want to kiss her wrist and convince her that life is better. What made her so ready to just end it all? I want to know all her demons. I don't want to be right.

Matt finally speaks; somehow I forgot he was even there. "I'm impressed. You know what you're doing. I don't even like cake."

"You don't like cake? Maybe we're not related. I have doubts now." She rolls her eyes, pulling away from the counter.

She's too far away now. She never stops fluttering around like a hummingbird, moving and being busy. Her mind must be so busy.

"Adam wants to meet you."

She ignores him, back to being busy wiping the counters.

Matt goes on, taking a more humble approach with her. "He's the bad brother. He's the troubled one. He caused my parents so much drama."

She's listening but not still. She has this faraway look, I see her, she's right here but she's not. She's removed, distant.

Matt seems nervous now, not sure of how to repair the damage he has caused. He insulted her yesterday. He needs to make this right. He turns around, back against the counter, staring out the window. He struggles with the good cop role. "Adam barely made it out of high school and had his first kid at 19. Never got married, but calls her his wife. They live together. He wants to meet you."

"You were always the golden child, Matt." She watches him, lost and tired. She wears this shield of toughness that breaks when she isn't actively protecting herself. Like she's been alone for so long, she doesn't have the energy to keep up the act. She's so focused on talking to Matt; she forgets I'm watching her. "Even as a kid, I knew that."

Matt doesn't turn to her, keeps talking towards the window. "Well, maybe, but he likes the idea that there is someone like him running around."

"You mean we're both fucked up, crazy?" She sounds hurt like she's tired of this. She looks like her brothers, but where they are all hard angles, she's soft. With big brown eyes and black hair with peppered blue streaks, she seems lonely. I want to protect her, even though she gives me a "don't fuck with me," vibe. I wonder if she would go out with me.

"You both have your act together now. You have all this. He's a paramedic now."

"He has emo tendencies," I say. "Like you."

She gives me a heated look, "I'm not emo."

I gesture at her tight overalls and a black t-shirt. She has a metal studded belt on, Converse on her feet, and all the black bands on her wrist. She isn't wearing black eye makeup, but she has that look. All black, all the time. Even the look of her baked goods, they're all dark. "You could have fooled me."

She notices me again, and looks at me from head to foot. Maybe the whole suit and tie thing isn't her style, but she notices me. For some weird reason, I want to impress her. I want her attention.

"Are you used to women falling all over you?" She falls into that ghetto fab stance, sassy and mean. She glares and steps toward me, challenging me, "Are they helpless? Are they hopeless? Do you need to be needed to be valuable? Is that your kink, Detective Fernandez?"

Matt snorts and nudges me. She's right. Matt's wife calls me Captain Save a Hoe. I'm always mixed up with the helpless type. I don't have an answer for her.

Juliana continues that glare. I can't look away from her, but she's not looking at me like she likes me. "Is that your type? Lost girls who need to be saved?"

"It used to be." Honesty, it's a little uncomfortable how quickly she summed me up.

"Until?" She crosses her arms against her chest. She continues that unrelenting stare, like I've wronged her somehow like she hates me.

"Until I met this woman who seemed like she'd stab me before she gave me her number. She might have called me dangerous."

She rolls her eyes and bursts into laughter. Her dark eyes crinkle and she beams. It's the most genuine smile she's had since I met her. She is bright, like sunshine. She starts twisting the ends of her left pigtail. "Who the hell are you? You give me total stalker vibes. You scare me."

"He's harmless," Matt tells her.

I could smack Matt. Thanks.

"Harmless? They say it's always the quiet ones." Juliana studies me, her brown eyes look at me like they see more than just what's on the outside. She's intense. When she talks, she purposely over-enunciates each syllable of my name. "What's your deal, Detective Fernandez?"

"Isn't that my question? What secrets are you hiding?"

She leans forward again, her hands resting on the counter, "I have no secrets. I am completely honest about my shit."

I want to reach out and touch her. Does she know she scares me? Can she tell I want to take her home? Does she know I can see right down her shirt?

Matt interrupts, "Adam wants you to come to his place for dinner tonight. I guess he wants you to meet his kids and wife."

"I thought he wasn't married?"

"He's not, but calls her his wife. Says he doesn't need to conform to the rules of society to make what he has real."

"Wow, I like him already." She stops moving around, talking to Matt but still looking at me.

"I'll bring my wife and you can meet her too."

"I'm going," I say to her, purposely not making a gesture to Matt. "But I don't have a wife."

"That's too bad." She glances at me, clearly, obviously checking me out.

"Maybe you'll bring a cake?" I lean towards her, both palms flat against the counter. Will she move to me? Will she back up more? I still can't tell if she likes me or hates me, or maybe both.

"Baking is my love language." She seems lighter now like she's over the anger she had earlier. Again, she stands in front of me and slides her hand over, the tip of her middle finger pressing against mine. I swear it's the fucking sexiest thing I've ever experienced. It's an electrical shock. "Vanilla or chocolate?"

I don't think she's talking about cake.

"Vanilla," Matt answers this time, smacking me against my arm, "We need to go. I'll text you the address."

*****

"Dude," Matt's tone clarifies my thoughts. I wasn't imagining it. She was flirting with me.

"What? Give me a break Matt."

"She's my sister," he reminds me as if I could forget that one damn fact.

"Now she's your sister? Last week, I had no idea you had a sister, and now I'm not allowed to talk to her?"

"Just leave her alone," Matt falls into that whole Mexican, don't fuck with my sister mode, just a little too easy for someone who just found her. "She's not your type. Go mess with that new dispatcher."

"Fuck off, Lopez," I say to him, picturing the new dispatch chick. She is my type. She's petite with long dark hair and helpless. She wandered into our department last week looking for the cafeteria that's two floors below us. I was toying with the idea of asking her out until I met this woman who bakes. "Shut up."

"She seems like trouble. I can't figure her out."

Juliana is taller than what I'm normally attracted to. Her hair is all messy, most likely wavy when it's down. It's not too long, maybe just to her shoulders. The two times I've seen her, she doesn't have make-up on. Just that lipstick, some deep orange-red brick color. She's curvy, nothing like the women I've dated in the past. She's got a strong goth vibe, well not goth, more of an emo thing, all the black and moody. I'm normally attached to the girly types in floral patterns. "Maybe she's not yours to figure out."

"What the fuck does that mean?" Matt's got a bad temper, must be a Lopez thing now that I think about it. Juliana has that same, turn on a dime, temper. "Don't fuck with her Daniel."

"What makes you think I'm going to mess with her?"

"Are you lying to me or yourself? I can see how you look at her. She's not your type."

"Is that because she's your sister?" Matt's my best friend, yeah, I know, he hates it when people don't do what he expects them to do.

"I don't need this shit right now." Matt sighs when his mother's name flashes on his phone. "What's up mom?"

"I just spoke with your father." Matt always has to take care of his needy mother, always. "Did you see her, Matthew?" She's sobbing, barely understandable over the speakers in his Suburban.

"Mom, she's my sister."

"No, she's not. She's your father's daughter. You don't even know her, Matthew. You don't owe her any loyalty."

"Mom, she didn't ask me to do anything for her, she's not asking me to pick a side. She just wanted to meet up."

"Matthew, you don't remember what she's like. She was always in trouble. Always, Matthew, she caused so many fights."

"You guys forced her to go to Catholic school."

"That was your father. I had to deal with her every day, Matthew. She was almost kicked out three times for doing things she was too young to be doing. Do you have any idea what that's like? Your stepdaughter is the talk of the school? And Adam wants to meet her? Your brother," she's off on another rant about what Adam had done wrong.

No wonder Adam wants to meet up with the more fucked up version of Senior's kids.

JULIANA
August 26

    It's a beautiful house, nothing I would pick for myself, but it's beautiful. Brand new construction, on the far north side of Fresno, Adam seems to have it all. He's got a brand-new truck in the driveway and a picture-perfect front lawn.

    North Fresno, everything in North Fresno is shiny, even the people. This is not my side of town. I love old houses with character, not mass-produced, master-planned communities with cookie-cutter charms. No thank you, I'll stick to living in the 'hood.

    Adam, I don't really remember Adam. He's younger by a lot, at least by kid standards. He's about eight years younger than me. I think. I'm not sure. He was maybe ten years old the last time I saw him.

    Adam swings open the door before I have an opportunity to knock. It's so quick and startling, I almost drop the cake. I'm holding.

    "You," he says, with authority. He's way taller than I expected and lanky. He has the same almond-shaped eyes too, beautiful hazel, just like Matt's. He's wearing no shoes but has painted black toe polish on, tight black jogger pants, and a t-shirt. He does have emo tendencies. His dark, golden brown hair is pulled back into a wispy bun. It's a good look for him. "You're not dead."

    "I'm not dead. Did you think I was really dead?"

    "No, I knew you were alive. Matt thought you were dead. Matt is an asshole. Ignore him." Adam opens the door wide, "Welcome home Juliana Lopez, missing sister."

"Oh my god, you look just like Adam," says the blond girl standing just off to the side of Adam in the entryway. She's one of those lost-looking girls with big blue eyes, all cute and tiny in a petite box. She walks over, grabs my pink cake box, and sets it down on the entryway table. She squeezes me like we're long-lost buddies. "I'm your sister-in-law, Kim."

Oh lord, what the fuck am I doing? I don't even know these people.

******

"So what's your story? Where did you go? Why did you leave? Why are you back?" Adam doesn't seem like the type to beat around the bush, he just flat-out says shit.

In the super white kitchen, I don't even know where to start. I move my cold San Pellegrino from one hand to the other, leaving a trail of moisture on the granite countertop. What is my deal? I don't even know anymore.

"I'm positive that what comes out of your mouth is no worse than what's gone in it," Adam says flatly.

Oh my god, I'm totally related to this guy. He's handsome and he knows it. He's got an older, bad-boy skater vibe. It's unnerving how much we look alike, even though we have different moms. The force must be strong in Matt Lopez Senior, we all look like him.

"Why did the long lost daughter come home?" Adam flips off the cap of his beer bottle, letting it fall to the floor and right under the space beneath the sink.

I need to pick up that cap, I can't leave it there. I have to pick it up and put it into the trash. Damn ADHD, I can't leave it there. "My therapist thinks I need to develop healthy relationships with people. This is my next step after rehab. Repairing bridges or some shit like that. I'm trying to repair it."

"Rehab? Were you a drunk?" Adam shakes his beer bottle at me. Not in a, too bad you can't have this way but a little annoying brother way. I like him.

"Tequila, lots of tequila, sometimes pills." I allow only small snippets of my party days to move into my memory bank. Some of the times were the best of my life. Some of my memories are not haunted, but most of them are. I try to appear casual as I pick up that cap. Damn it. "I should be dead."

"Should be?"

"Totally dead."

"What do you want with us? We're pretty fucked up too. Matt can't get out of dad's shadow. He's a people pleaser."

Matt huffs but doesn't argue with him. He just quietly leans against the counters. He's different this time, more relaxed. He's wearing jeans and a hoodie. He seems more like a person now than when he was in his cop suit. He's approachable now.

"I say all the shit everyone else is afraid to say. I call everyone out on their bullshit. I'm the black sheep," Adam snorts, messing with the bottles on the counter. He moves around a lot too. I do that. I wonder if he's ADHD too. "At least I was until you showed up."

"I just want to know you. That's all. I just want to figure out where I fit." I'm so confused right now. I wanted to meet them and now I'm mixed up. It's like I've always known them, but I have no idea who they are. "I don't fit anywhere."

"You fit here," Adam answers quickly. He moves to me, "You're my sister. I don't give a shit about anyone else, anyone's opinion, my fucking parents, no one. You're my sister *por vida*."

"Are you for real?"

"Fuck yeah I am. Am I clear Matt?" Adam moves towards Matt. He sounds slightly angry but more annoyed. I can tell they've argued or two about me. This argument might have started earlier but it's ending right now. Adam has a large presence. He owns the space he stands in. "I don't give a shit about what mom and dad are saying to you. In my house, in my presence, she's my sister, my little sister."

"You realize I'm older," I remind him.

"Not anymore." As tall as he is, I'm sure most people wouldn't judge twice that he's not older.

"Don't bother arguing with him," his wife Kim smiles, "It just means he likes you."

Adam sets his beer bottle down, "I could use some Molly now too. I miss those days. Remember that time at Javier's house?"

"Shut up Adam," Matt smiles as he says it. He seems lost in a memory of the "good old days." I know that feeling. Right now, those feelings are all I have left. I wonder about the trouble my two little brothers might have caused as teenagers. I missed that whole part of their lives.

Kim instantly holds her hand up, "No Javier's house stories. No." Her blue eyes flash at Adam. She doesn't sound angry.

Adam grabs her hand and kisses her fingertips. He pulls her close into a big hug. "There is no one but you in my heart, baby mama."

"Javier is one of my old high school friends. We all went to Roosevelt together," Matt explains to me.

"Wait, you didn't go to Saint Paschal's?" I'm instantly flushed with anger. Catholic school, I have nothing against people's choices when it comes to religion, but the amount of guilt and shame worked into the school day was insane. The only thing my father made me do was to go to Catholic school. I went to Saint Paschal, a small, strict high school in the middle of Fresno. Senior's wife works there. She made sure everyone knew I was not her family. "What the hell? I suffered through years of Catholic school."

"Not for high school. They sent us to public school," Matt explains.

I'm furious. Stay in control. It's not that big a deal to them. Breathe, relax, and put the feeling in a box. Don't overreact.

"I had to wear a stupid ass uniform to school," I say, "I had to deal with your mother. She was my freaking Spanish teacher. She failed me. I had to change electives because of her."

"After you, they didn't force us. We went to Roosevelt." Adam is laughing so hard, he's shaking. He pushes Matt, "Can you imagine the shit we would have pulled if we had to go to private school?"

"They would have kicked us out," Matt answers. "We weren't good kids."

"Nope, not at all. We lived up to the typical 'our dad's a cop so we're as bad as fuck' stereotypes and did everything we could to piss him off." Adam gestures to me, "So I guess you saved us from that torture. Thank you for taking one for the team."

"Hey," Daniel says, "still got that uniform?"

This guy's going to be the death of me. Daniel is covered in tattoos. I mean, he's covered in them. I never imagined that when he was in a suit and tie but now in shorts and a shirt, I see all the thick swirling black ink covering both arms and his leg. Star Wars and Alice in Wonderland images decorate one arm and down another. I want to run my fingers along him, feeling his skin. He's beautiful. He's just so hot. And he wears glasses? Thick black frames paired with those tattoos? Fuck, he's killing me. My breath catches for a moment, almost as if he can hear my private thoughts.

"Why? Do you think I'll let you spank me? Asshole." It's instantly awkward. Yep, that's what I do, make things awkward.

Matt's wife, Echo, real name Esperanza, only giggles. She probably knows I'm all up in Daniel's Kool Aide. Bitch. Breathe, just breathe.

Don't look at him. I have to fight the urge to openly stare at him. It's all the tattoos mixed with his lost boy feeling. Jesus, it's not cool. This is not fair. He's so pretty it hurts. The weight of his gaze causes me to be electric It's a static charge. This is not good. I need to change the energy in this room. I turn my attention to Adam and Kim instead, "How did you meet?"

Adam gives his megawatt smile, "At a party, Kim showed up with some guy she claims was her boyfriend but went home with me."

"He was my boyfriend," Kim smiles at Adam, "He got drunk so Adam offered to take me home, to his house and I just never left."

"I think I sort of held her hostage. I was kind of obsessive in those days. I pissed my parents off by making them grandparents 9 months later. We fought a lot."

"And made up a lot," Kim smiles, giving him a sideways glance.

His gaze on her is intense, he doesn't break her gaze. "And our children are 16 months apart."

"*Aye papi*," she purrs against him.

"Stop," he pulls her closer, pretending to whisper into her blond hair, "We have company."

She just laughs and I get it, that's what I want. I want someone who can love me unconditionally. They're the cutest couple ever.

I gesture to Matt and his pregnant wife Echo, "And you guys? How did you meet?

"Nothing special, my mousy cousin set us up," Echo shrugs, twisting her wedding ring around her swollen finger. "Then he called me a hoe."

"I didn't mean hoe," Matt's blushing.

"Matt Lopez," she sasses, hands upon her hips, "You called me a hoe. He didn't like my ex so he called me a hoe."

"I didn't mean hoe," Matt returns leaning against the countertop, "She didn't want to date me because I had a daughter."

I'm surprised, "How many kids do you have Matt?" I guess I expected him to be the perfect child. I didn't expect him to have another kid.

"Two, one daughter from before and we have a son. This is another boy, so almost 3. My daughter Lexi is almost 15 now."

"Just like dad," Adam teases. "Perfect, you fucking asshole."

Tic tock, I'm 36 and running out of time. I'm a total fuck up.

"His daughter freaked me out," Echo explains. "I gave him a chance. Now, I can't imagine not having her."

There's that feeling again, slow burn, slow cut. Someone else's daughter, forcing those thoughts away, I watch Echo instead. She is super pretty, all curvy, and with soft edges. With big chocolatey brown eyes and a round innocent-looking face, I can see why Matt was attracted to her. She's sweet but fierce. She looks at him like he's a freaking god. No wonder he married her.

Echo sipped her bubble water, "We dated, broke up, and then dated again. Somehow he tricked me into marrying him."

Sure, right, that is not what happened, I'm sure. He's so wrapped around her finger, not what happened at all. It's kind of nice to know that this side of Matt is in there. He's not a total dick all the time.

"Why are you not married?" I gesture towards Daniel. He's always around so I might as well figure out his deal. He seems nice enough. "What is your deal, Detective Fernandez?"

"You can call him Daniel," Echo laughs.

"No, she can't," Daniel says, giving me that sideways smile he has. He looks at me through his thick lashes, "I like the way you say, Detective Fernandez."

Don't look at him, don't look at him, and don't look at him. Oh my god, he's killing me. He knows I think he's hot. I need to be mindful. I hate being responsible. I can't fuck this up already. I hate being an adult.

"Okay, sure, whatever," I say, rolling my eyes, "Detective Fernandez, what's your deal?"

"Just haven't found the right person," Daniel shrugs.

That's all he's going to tell me? After all that, he's going to give me such a simple answer. Jerk.

"He's the save-a-hoe type," Echo teases, "He likes to be the hero."

Daniel only makes a gesture with his hands. What the hell does that mean?

"Like the E-40 song?" I ask as the song I love burns through my brain. I love that stupid song.

I love E-40, the Bay Area rapper with a knack for making up his own vocabulary. One of my old friends introduced me to his music when I was a kid. It was a special moment, well, not that special, but that E-40 was playing. I still love E-40.

"Like the emo girl knows who E-40 is," Daniel teases.

"Fuck you. You don't know shit about me." I roll my eyes. I'm still for a second, "Why? What's in it for you? To have some sort of power over her? Be the hero?"

He seems to think, "No, that's not it."

"He wants to be the only one," Echo continues to tease him, "Kind of young, kind of dumb, always with some drama. He needs to be needed. He does want to be the hero."

I want to burst into giggles, but I don't want to make fun of him. I don't even know him. She might be telling the truth. It feels true. Well, if he wants to be the only one, we are not a good fit. Glancing at Daniel, he shrugs.

"He's always the rebound guy," Echo says, pointing at him while touching her round stomach. She looks like she's about to pop any moment. "I told you, stop being helpful. Stop being the nice guy."

"Nice is good," I say. "Sometimes, nice is good."

"Bad is better," Echo laughs, "Bad is way better."

"Excuse me," Matt smiles when he says it. He's totally messing with her but she doesn't seem to care. She knows she's the center of his universe, and she likes it. If I had friends, we could be friends.

"Bad is so much better Matt, you're bad."

"Um hum," he murmurs, "I'm not bad."

"You might not be very bad, but you're not very good," she says, playfully nudging him.

"Oh, I'm very good," he tells her.

This is such a different side of him, I'm pleasantly surprised. I am happy for them. They seem to have strong, healthy, adult relationships. They seem normal. Susan would like them.

"See the shit I have to put up with," Daniel tosses his empty beer bottle away. "Why haven't you gotten married? Where's your loser emo boyfriend?"

"I'm the kind you can't take home to your mother. Maybe I should find that uniform so... you know, I want to be saved."

Matt spits out his drink. Adam starts laughing. Damn that Susan. I feel at home. I can stand in the light of what's true and know they're not going to judge me. Well, maybe Matt will, but not Echo, not Kim, and certainly not Adam.

"Is your number higher than 20? 30?" Echo asks, giggling.

Matt playfully swats at her, "Don't ask her that kind of shit."

"I'm not going to make excuses for myself. I am who I am. I have done things I am not proud of. Take it or leave it, but don't fuck with me."

"Fuck people and their notions of what's socially acceptable." Adam points in the air as if defending my honor against the world, "Be a hoe if you want to but don't do it to get people to like you."

"It wasn't that." I'm not ready to give the real reason. "I stopped after rehab. It's not the same anymore. Nothing is the same anymore, and I don't like people anymore. Life isn't fun anymore. I'm not sure if it was really fun before, but at least I was drunk and it was tolerable."

"It doesn't matter anymore. You're home. We like you." Adam doesn't touch me, but he sets another San Pellegrino in front of me. "We're not going to judge you. You're a fucking Lopez, Juliana, and you belong with us."

Tears, real tears flood my eyes. Nope, not today, I cannot be emotional. I'm in charge of myself. I'm not going to start crying. I don't even know these people. "Where's your restroom?"

DANIEL
August 26

I don't want to watch her leave the room, so I watch her beat up Vans march out of the kitchen. She's not like any woman I've ever been attracted to, but I can't seem to stop watching her. Those damn ripped-up skinny jeans and crop tops she wears are fucking infuriating. Sure, she's got an oversized yellow flannel shirt over it, but it's not buttoned up. It's so easy to imagine her naked. Something about her makes me want to take care of her or have sex with her. I'm not sure which, maybe both.

"Quit looking at my sister like you want to eat her." Adam snickers, lowering his voice just enough that she can't hear us. The bathroom isn't that far off the kitchen.

"Dude," I say, resting my beer bottle on the counter. I have no excuse. He's right. She's fascinating.

"You are." He grabs another beer and pulls Kim back to him. "She's pretty. I get it but back off her. She's a little on the edge right now. Be her friend, give her time. Then once she trusts you, fuck her."

Matt slams his hand against the counter, that temper is back, "Adam, what the fuck?"

"Dude, they're grownups, knock it off," Adam rolls his eyes at Matt, "She deserves to feel valued. She has zero real confidence. It's all an act."

"You're not an expert on human behavior." Matt is annoyed by Adam, but hell, when is he not? Matt and Adam are like oil and water.

"We are Matt, we know behavior, I'm a paramedic, and you're a cop. That's literally our job. What's wrong with her? You know what's wrong with her, all behavior is communication. What's the function of her behavior?"

"You're making a wild guess."

"A wild guess," Adam sets his bottle down and lowers his voice, forcing everyone to take a step toward the center island of the kitchen. "Facts, one she ran off at 18. Two, she hates dad because 'he left her there.' You said that's what she said. Three, you can tell she's hiding cutting scars on her wrist. What happens to little girls with no dad, Matt?"

"You don't know that," Matt glares at Adam. "We don't know that."

"Don't be ignorant." Adam leans against the counter, continuing in a quiet voice. "I don't want to be right about this, but it makes sense." He looks at Kim, and pulls her closer, "Rachel used to cut."

"Who's Rachel?" The name is familiar, but I'm not remembering the story.

Both brothers look at each other. They both glance at Kim. I kind of remember this now, Adam's ex-girlfriend.

Kim answers, "Javier's sister, Adam used to date her."

"It was before you baby mama, you know that. You're the only one for me." He kisses the top of her head, "All behavior is a result of an unmet need. What was Rachel's need? She needed to be loved. Fucking Mike Castillo dumped her, right after her parents died. On the day of her parents' funeral, he told her she was a mistake. All behavior is communication, Matt."

Matt doesn't speak.

"I don't want to be right. I don't want to imagine what has happened to her, but what is the function of Juliana's behavior? Why is she lost? Why is she alone? What made her…"

"Feel like she needed to die?" Both Lopez brothers glance at me. "She had a 5150 a few years ago. I looked her up. She took a bunch of pills."

"She tried to kill herself," Kim asks, shock displayed on her face. "When?"

"About four years ago, there was a 911 call. There's not much in the report."

"They just locked her up," Echo asks, "Nobody looked for her family?"

"She's an adult," I say quietly, as I glance toward the bathroom. I don't want her to hear me sharing this with them. "After the hold, there's little we can do."

"No one called your dad," Echo asks, "Where's her mom? Why didn't anyone tell us?"

"That's not how this works."

"So all this time, she's felt unwanted? Not cared about," Echo scowls at us as we did it. She glares at me, "You're sure she tried to kill herself?"

"That's what the report said, I want to be wrong, but that's what it said."

"What kind of parent leaves his only daughter? He knew something was wrong. He just let her suffer," Adam drops his head. "What kind of dad just leaves his kid?"

No one has an answer for Adam. It's just quiet.

"He treated her like she didn't even matter. We had a fucking perfect childhood, Matt. The whole time, dad forgot about her. Who does that kind of shit?"

"Daniel, what did she say?" Matt asks, "She said something weird, what did she say? I had to leave home? Something like she had no choice but to leave home?"

"My mom needed me to leave," I answered, trying to remember exactly how she phrased it. "She said, 'my mother needed me to leave'."

Echo sighs, "This conversation needs to stop while she's here. Don't run her off so soon. I like her."

"Finally someone in this family who isn't pretending to be perfect," Kim sighs. "She owns her shit."

"Daniel has a crush on her," Adam sings softly, nudging me, clearly teasing about it. "Don't blow it, Daniel. I wouldn't mind you being my brother-in-law. Fucking, 'do you still have your uniform, call me Detective Fernandez.' Asshole."

"Shut up." It's the only answer I can give without lying. I do have a crush on his mystery sister. What the fuck is happening?

"She called him a stalker," Matt laughs. "She already got him figured out. Oh wait, she said, dangerous."

"She's trouble Daniel," Echo sings quietly, "She's like real, next level trouble, like locked up in jail trouble. She's the kind of trouble you might not know what to do with."

"You guys are getting way ahead of yourselves," I protest, knowing I'm lying to all of them. I need to figure out what's going on inside my head. I need to get the image of Juliana in those fucking schoolgirl uniforms out of my freaking brain. Shit. "I just met her."

"What's in the box?" Echo asks, louder than needed.

Juliana's back, her eyes all rimmed in red. She might have cried, but she wouldn't want us to mention it. That I can tell. She is simply the most beautiful woman I've ever laid eyes on.

DANIEL
September 1

My mom is confused. She puts her coffee mug back onto her dining room table and looks at me like I'm the one who should be confused.

"Wait. Say that again, you're telling me that Matt Senior has a daughter? And she's an adult?"

"Yes, she's an adult." Sunday mornings mean visiting with my mom. I'm her only son left, so it's my job to take care of her. Is that a Latino thing? I don't know, but it's definitely a Fernandez thing. My dad made sure I knew this is what he needed me to do for him once he was gone. I don't miss this unless it's a fucking emergency. My mom is strong, but she's had too much loss in the last few years. The least I can do is be a good son and take care of her.

"Did Matt know?" My mom gestures, "you know?"

"Yes, he was aware she existed."

My mom refills her coffee. It's a cool morning, but it feels like it's going to be hot later. Fresno mornings start cold, and the high will be near 99 degrees, typical late September weather, hot.

"She's older than Matt."

"How much older?"

"Matt said she's 36," I say, thinking back to Juliana. She feels younger than Matt, but Matt has a ton of first-born Latino shit going on all the time. Matt takes being the oldest seriously, he can't help it. He was raised to be that kind of person, responsible for taking care of everyone. "She's from a high school relationship. You didn't know? Dad didn't know?"

"I didn't know. If he knew, he never told me, but your dad didn't keep secrets from me. He would have told me this."

"Well, I'm telling you, Matt was not surprised." Thinking back, he was only surprised she called, not that she existed.

"What did she want from him? Money? Is she a drug addict? Homeless? Is she hooked on meth?"

"No mom, give me a break. It's not like TV. She seems nice. She makes wedding cakes."

My mom scrunches up her face, "Wedding cakes? Does she have kids? A husband?"

"No. That's the sad part. I think she's alone. She doesn't seem to have anyone."

"Where's her mom? Who's her mom?"

"She doesn't talk about her mom." Juliana never says, mom. She always says mother. *My mother needed me to leave.* "She's private about that."

My mom studies me. "What does she look like?"

"Well," I have to stop. She's a fucking angel. She called me dangerous. I can't say that to my mom. She'll try to marry me off in five minutes flat. She is like that, always looking for a wife for me. She's a Latino mom, that's what she does. "Well, she looks like Matt and Adam, but at the same time, she doesn't. She's really pretty."

"How pretty," she asks. "She's about your age."

"Stop," I say to her, refilling my coffee. "She might be crazy. You don't know her. I don't know her."

"A little crazy might be okay. How pretty? Next level, crazy pretty? Restraining order pretty, or just normal Latino crazy?"

"She's, I've had too many boyfriends, pretty," I tease my mom. I know her goal is to marry me off to a Latino woman. Wait until she sees Juliana, she's just that type, at least physically, what my mom would want me to marry. Juliana looks like the late fashion model Anna Nicole Smith. Damn.

My mom stops her coffee cup midway to her mouth. She gives me a smirk. "Um hum. She's pretty, huh?"

"She's Matt's sister." I know where she's going with this. I know how she can be. We have this in common. "Besides, I don't know her.

I've met her, and I've talked to her. She seems nice but she's guarded. She seems like she doesn't like people."

"Like Tomás, Tia Maria Elena's son?"

"No, she doesn't strike me as autistic. She's intense. She stares at me like she can read my brain. I don't know, maybe she does has autism."

"She stares at you," my mom sings. "Explain stare."

"Not like that mom. She does it to everyone. She questions everyone, she stares at everyone. She's like a cop. She calls me Detective Fernandez. She doesn't say, Daniel."

"Detective Fernandez?"

"That's my fault. I told her she could only call me that. I was just messing with her."

My mom watches me over the top of her coffee mug, "How were you messing with her?"

"Not like that, I was just kidding with her."

"How many times have you seen her?" My mom acts like I'm keeping secrets. Maybe I am.

"Just a few, Adam and Matt are trying to get to know her, but as I said, she's guarded, she keeps everyone at a distance. She's studying all of us all the time. It's weird."

"What do you think she wants, with Matt and Adam?"

"A family." It's the truth. I think she wants to belong somewhere. Juliana seems so, I don't know, lost? She needs a hug, as simple as that sounds, she needs a hug.

"Is she lonely?"

"She seems sad. I don't think she wants us to see that."

"And Matt Senior?"

"He doesn't give a shit."

"Daniel," she says, in that "don't curse in front of your mom or talk bad about adults," tone. I'm an adult, but I will always be her baby.

"I know, I know. Come on mom, he hasn't said one word about her. He doesn't talk to her. He hasn't even asked about her. She said he left her. And Celine? She lost her shit."

"Well, she is crazy. We all know that." My mom has no love for Matt Senior's wife.

"According to Matt, she left home at 18. That was the last time he saw her."

"18," my mom is quickly doing the math in her head, "That's almost 20 years ago." She taps her fingers on the table, "This poor girl."

"Matt said she told her dad to fuck off and die, and then they never saw her again." I'm surprised she doesn't mention the language. "She just left."

She presses her hands against her forehead, trying to figure this out. "Wait, I need to write this down, I need a timeline. Your dad met Matt Senior about 20 years ago. So, I can understand how we never heard about her. Maybe she had already left?"

"But to not look for her," I remind her. "Would you let a child go missing like that?"

"No," my mom says with authority.

"Me either." Juliana deserves something. I don't know what, but more than what she got, which was a dad who pretended she didn't exist. I don't tell my mom about the 5150. I think, I know, I regret telling everyone else about it.

"This is so strange," she pushes her coffee away. My mom smiles again, "How pretty is pretty? Ms. Too Many Boyfriends?"

"Stop." The question makes me blush.

"I'm just asking," she continues to tease. She knows me way too well.

"She's very pretty," I say, imagining Juliana for a moment. Her intensity and energy, the way she always twists her dark blue hair. The way she listens to me when I'm talking to her, and the way she bites her lip all the time. That fucking lipstick she wears. I can't explain why I have this weird protective feeling about her. "She's beautiful."

"What does she look like?"

"Like a girl version of Adam," I say, which is true, but such a fucking understatement. She's fucking gold. "She wears orange lipstick. It's a good color for her, and she knows it. She looks like Marilyn Monroe but Latino. Not Marilyn Monroe, the other one, what was her name? Anna Nicole Smith, that's who she reminds me of, Anna Nicole, but with black and blue hair."

"Anna Nicole Smith?" My mom is obsessed with 80's and 90's pop culture. She knows exactly who I'm talking about. She grins, "So she's sexy?"

"Stop, no."

"I'm just asking," she giggles.

"Well, let me just say she is a beautiful person. She's got a touch of sexy. I can say that, but she's got some issues for sure. She's lonely. She's sad. She might need real friends, not a boyfriend. I'm not going to ask her out."

She pats my arm, "You could change your mind."

"Mom, stop."

"I'm just saying, *mijo*," my mom has a sing-song tone, "If she's lonely, needs friends, you could be nice and ask her out. You're a nice man. You were raised right. Maybe Ms. Too Many Boyfriends hasn't met a nice man."

"She doesn't need pity." That's the last thing Juliana needs. She would see through that in a heartbeat and then she'd hate me. I barely know her, but I know that.

"I didn't say, feel sorry for her," my mom teases, "Maybe Ms. Too Many Boyfriends needs to meet a nice man."

"Maybe Ms. Too Many Boyfriends needs to be left alone." Juliana needs some quiet in her life to figure out what she wants next. "Let her figure out what she needs. She needs to be heard."

"Heard?"

"I think she wants to talk about something but she's not there yet. She doesn't trust people. Ms. Too Many Boyfriends needs a place to belong."

"I want to meet her." My mom sets her mug down with authority, "You need to figure out a way I can meet her."

"Why?"

"If she looks like Anna Nicole, you know I love Anna Nicole." She studies the inside of her mug, most likely debating if she wants another cup. "I was supposed to be Anna Nicole in a past life."

"Anna Nicole died of a drug overdose. You were supposed to be her?"

"You know what I mean, Daniel. I was supposed to look like that too, but I had three kids instead." She laughs at her joke.

"You're beautiful mom." My mom is the strongest woman I know.

"But I don't look like Anna Nicole Smith. You should bring her over one day."

"We're not friends," I say, thinking about Juliana again. "If we become friends, I'll bring her over, but you don't get to make it weird and try to get me to marry her."

"Marry her?" My mom smiles again, that mom knows more than I do, look. "I didn't say one thing about marrying her. I said you should ask her out."

"I know you." I need to get out of this house. I am saying shit I don't mean to say to my mom. Juliana Lopez takes up too much of my brain space. She's simply stunning and mysterious. I should not be thinking of her so much. I don't even know her. "If we become friends, I'll bring her over. Come on, are you ready? Let's get all your errands done."

JULIANA
September 9

    Adam has a nice backyard. It's the newer housing section on the Northwest of Fresno, with big houses, and smaller lots. The designer made the most of the space. By having a built-in pool and BBQ kitchen, it feels larger than it is. Nothing more would fit, but it backs up to open space. The house itself is huge. Must be nice, but all I can think of is who has time to clean this place? It takes me an hour to clean up my place. I can't imagine how long it would take to clean up after 5 people and five bedrooms. Damn, that's a lot of laundry. I'll stick to my tiny old duplex.
    "Are you okay, Detective Fernandez?" I'm pretending to watch all of Adam's daughters screaming and playing in their pool. He seems distracted, thinking.
    "You can call me Daniel," he says, giving me a slight smile, highlighting his dimples. He looks tired. "I was just fucking with you."
    "Nope, too late, you're always going to be Detective Fernandez now." He must be close with Matt and Adam, he's always around. He said he knew my dad. I wonder how close they all are. So strange, he's closer to them than me, and I'm their real sister.
    Since he's next to me, I can check him out. He smells nice, limes and shea butter. It's not too strong, just a faint hint. And that perfect little boy hair and glasses, damn. Daniel has this charming, schoolboy vibe, but he looks like a total bad boy with all those tattoos. He's like a dark Superman, good guy to bad guy. It's so freaking hot.
    "My day sucked. How was yours? Did you have any cake emergencies?"

"Don't hate on my job." That's exactly what he thinks of me, useless. Fuck him. I'm a waste. He doesn't have to remind me of it. "Are you okay? I'm not good for much but I can listen."

I want to know what he's thinking about. He is certainly lost in some thoughts that have him removed from this moment. The funny thing about Detective Fernandez, he might be around a lot, but I haven't really gotten to know him.

When I'm hanging with them, Matt, Adam, and their families, yeah, Daniel is here, but we don't engage. He thinks he's sneaky. I see him watching, just absorbing what I'm doing. It doesn't feel stalker-ish, but it's a little strange, flattering maybe? I can't remember the last time someone noticed me like that. I'm only good for one thing.

"Just a bad day," he tells me, looking off towards the view from the house.

It's later in the afternoon, the sun has turned the sky a bright pink color, and the clouds have a touch of gray. It's magical really. The sunset in the Central Valley can be stunning. It's from all the wildfires in California. Yeah, the air quality might suck, but we have these golden sunsets.

"We arrested a kid for killing her abusive boyfriend. She's 19 years old. She's just a little kid."

"She killed him?" My blood runs cold, that's a leave of despair I can relate to. Hopeless, lost, broken. I may not have killed anyone, but that level of desperation is not lost on me.

I don't pretend to understand the weight of the job he has. I have a cake life. My life journey is not one of helping others. I can't imagine what it's like to have a real job like that.

"She shot him," he starts to tell me, looking at me and scooting closer on the outdoor couch. Daniel's talking low so the kids don't overhear, "But the thing is, she's been abused by him, raped. She won't talk. She won't tell us anything that happened. She just sits there."

"You know that survivors relive the trauma every time they have to retell the story. Every time they have to tell the story, it hurts like the first time all over again." This is making me anxious, him telling me about his job, and sharing about his life.

"I want to help her." He reaches over like he wants to touch my knee, but stops himself. "How do I help her?"

"What do you want her to say to you? Honestly? How is that going to help her?"

"I want to know why."

"You know why. You just told me. That is her reason. You know he did something, something awful to her. Maybe she can't get the words out. Maybe saying the words out loud makes it real. You said she's just a kid right? She probably loved him."

"She did love him. I think you're right about that."

"She probably believed he was her whole world. He violated her trust, most likely more than once. Maybe she blocked out that she really killed him? What good will it do to tell you what happened? Why can't everyone look at the evidence and figure it out for her? You said it looks like domestic violence, like rape, why isn't that enough?"

"It doesn't work like that."

"But it should. That's the hardest part for some people, having to articulate, to explain to other people what happened. And then, sometimes you tell the wrong person and they use that information against you."

He's watching me. I realize this is the longest conversation we've had without Matt or Adam hanging around. It makes me uneasy to have his attention. I want it, I crave it, but now that I have it, it makes me nervous. Even though we're discussing this heavy topic, it makes me skittish for him to be so close to me. What the hell is wrong with me?

"Maybe your girl was drowning," I say, imagining how she must have felt. She couldn't find a way out. I get that. "She had no one to help her, no one to turn to for help. She took care of it her way. It was the wrong way for sure, but now he can't hurt her anymore. Maybe she didn't see any other way out."

"She could have called the police."

"Do you really believe that? What would have they done? She's an adult, right? She most likely had nowhere else to go."

"We could have gotten her some help."

"Are you trying to convince me or yourself? What kind of help? Social services for adults take forever. Who is going to help a 19-year-old kid? Legally, she's an adult. Who is going to help her?"

"There is help for people. She just needed to ask for help."

"You believe that? I guess you do or you wouldn't be a cop." I'm being a defensive brat. Sometimes my mouth won't stay shut. I'm making a fool out of myself. I'm taking all of this super personally. Just shut up, Juliana, stop. "In the meantime, some asshole was beating the crap out of her. Where was she going to go?"

"I don't know."

"Do you know how hard it is to be that age and have no resources? Do you know what it's like to try to escape something and have no one to help you?" I have to stop talking. I can't make myself stop talking. "You know the hardest part of trauma is that no one believes you. When people take your trauma and twist it into what they want to hear, to make your story irrelevant. They make it seem like it was your fault. Who believed her? Did anyone believe her? Have you ever been in an abusive relationship, Detective Fernandez?"

"Have you? Did anyone believe you?"

I've said way too much. I don't know him. I shouldn't be talking to him about this. I'm making a huge mess.

"Why did you just disappear when you turned 18?"

"Why are we talking about me? I thought we were talking about your case?"

"Were we?"

I stare at him. He is making judgments about me that he has no right to. "Don't pretend to know my shit, Detective Fernandez. You know nothing about me. I am not having this conversation with you."

Leaning back on the couch, I pretend he's not there. I need space. I don't think he's really trying to be an insensitive asshole, just like I don't mean to be a know it all. I think the opposite is true. He doesn't strike me as a total dick. He seems like a nice guy. Why he's a cop is a wonder. He's almost too nice to be a cop. Granted, I have issues with cops because my father is one and such an ass.

Once, they locked me up, the cops. I didn't deserve to be locked up like that, 5150, mental health crisis code. They made me stay in that damn hospital room for 72 hours and tried to figure out what was wrong with me. They made me feel crazy and untrustworthy, a danger to myself. Took all my stuff away, and made me wear a stupid hospital gown. They stared at me for hours. Nothing is wrong with me. I just made a mistake. It was just a mistake.

"Do you know what that feels like? To love someone so much and then have to realize that he's the enemy?"

"No."

"It fucking sucks. Your brain knows it's wrong but your heart keeps saying, it's okay just one more chance. You have to fight yourself."

"But you left?"

"People make mistakes." I'm not going to correct him, that's what a guilty person would want to do. I don't need to defend my actions to him. He doesn't know me. "At that moment, she probably thought there was no way out. She needed to get out. She just couldn't figure out how to do that. She just panicked."

"And now she's going to prison for manslaughter."

"Yeah, well, that sucks."

"Sorry about the cake comment. I didn't mean it," he reaches over, and this time he does put his hand on my knee.

Like a dorky ass teenager, my freaking heart starts racing. Give me a break, he's touching my knee. It's not sex. "It's cake, cake isn't special."

I'm fucking useless.

"What did you want to be when you grew up? Cake isn't your life plan?"

My life plan? Wow, I guess he hasn't figured out I don't even have a daily plan. What did I want to do when I was a kid? "A flight attendant, that's what I wanted to be. I wanted to go far away and never come back here."

"Here in Fresno? You don't love Fresno? What changed? You're still here."

"I don't know. I hate Fresno. I don't know how I got here," I take a deep breath; this is not what I planned to talk to him about. All of this, it's too much for someone I barely know. "My best friend moved to DC a few years ago. Sometimes I wish I went with him. Sometimes I'm glad I stayed. Why are you a cop?"

"I wanted to help people."

"Do you? Do you help people?"

"I like to think I do. Why do you hate cops?"

"I don't really."

"My dad was a cop too. I wanted to be like him. He passed away."

"I'm sorry." I'm a little afraid of the answer but I ask anyway, "At work?"

"Oh, no, nothing like that," Daniel smiles again, "Sorry, didn't mean to make it sound like that. He was sick. He passed away. Why do you make cakes? What led you down that road, emo girl?"

"Dude, I'm an adult with a job. Stop calling me that. I'm not a kid. I'm just a girl who likes black." I watch one of Adam's daughters climb out of the pool. She comes over and drops herself next to us, dripping sprinkles of pool water all over us. Nice. Adam has the cutest kids ever. Tick, tock, my time is running out.

"Uncle Daniel, come play with us," she starts pulling on his hand.

"Leave Uncle Daniel alone, heathen," Adam calls after her. He picks her up and just tosses her back into the pool like she's all of five pounds. She giggles uncontrollably once she breaks back to the surface of the water.

Daniel does get up and moves towards the pool. He goes to the other side, sits at the edge, and talks to the girls, tossing a pool toy to them. He's super sweet with them. It makes me feel wistful, like the things I haven't admitted could happen.

Detective Fernandez would be a good dad.

My heart fucking skips a beat. I have problems. Shit. I'm so stupid.

Wistful, a word meaning a longing for something that never existed. I need to call Susan. I'm being all weird again. Maybe this, creating relationships with Matt and Adam, is taking up more energy than I realize. I need to be proactive. I have to protect my power. I might need to see Susan sooner. I'm feeling all girly. This sucks.

Adam takes the now empty seat next to me, purposely sprinkling water onto me. "I've known Daniel forever. It feels like forever."

"I've known him for all of five minutes."

"Do you think he's a nice guy?"

"He seems okay." I cannot tell Adam that I think Daniel is the hottest thing ever. He's nice to the kids? What the fuck? "Why? What does it matter?"

"It doesn't. I was just wondering."

"Wondering what?" Is this Latino brother shit? Wow, I've never experienced it myself. I wonder if he's about to tell me not to be messing with his friend. Or is it the other way? He'll tell Daniel not to talk to his sister? I thought for sure that would be a Matt thing, not Adam's.

"Nothing, just wondering."

"I think you know what you want to say. Just say it." I've got no time for these games. This conversation is making me anxious. My heart isn't racing, just beating a tad too fast just enough to make me notice, but not enough to be worried. Chill out, just be relaxed.

Adam makes a smirk, "Has he asked you out?"

"No." I'm so embarrassed. I'm never embarrassed about shit like this. Hell, I can have a whole conversation about sex with Aaron, no problem. My brother, my real brother, asking me if his friend asked me out, makes me feel like a child in five seconds flat. Has he asked me out? No. Detective Fernandez has been nothing but nice to me, asshole.

"Maybe he has a Matt problem?" Adam turns his attention back to his daughters.

"Do they have some weird perverted shit going on?"

"Perverted shit?" Adam starts laughing, "No Jules, I don't think so. Maybe Matt has some, 'don't fuck with my sister' shit going on."

"If you can't be an adult, fuck off, I don't have time for that shit. We're barely related."

"Alright then, are you good? I mean, how do I say this?" Adam's gaze returns to the pool, watching his children splash Daniel. It's sort of cute.

"Just say it, Adam, I'm not good with suspense. That's what gives me anxiety. All this, let me think about how to phrase it, shit. Just ask, what do you want to know?"

"Where's your mom Jules?"

"I don't know, at home I guess. We're not cool, but it's not a big deal. It's been a very long time. Trust me. I'm good."

"And dad? Are you okay with that? He's being a total asshole."

"That's nothing new, not to me." I have to remember to breathe. My heart rate is increasing but not too much. I've dealt with this. I've talked to Susan ad nauseam about this. I'm over this. "He's not my dad, Adam. I need you to understand that. That's why I go to therapy. I've got nothing to be ashamed of. I go to therapy because my parents were assholes. It's not me, it's them. Really, all this is cake, you know? If we can be cool, I've reached my goal. I just want us to be cool. Honestly."

"We're intense people," he says to me, "We might be those kinds of people who take over everyone around us. We're way too close for a family."

"As long as you're not into pervy ass shit, I'm cool."

"Pervy ass shit? Damn dude, what the fuck kind of friends do you have?"

"Before rehab doesn't count, but just know, I wasn't that bad. No pervy ass shit in my past." Rolling my eyes, I shove him, brothers, who knew? "Honestly, I'm good with all of this. I knew what I was getting into. Fuck your father. I don't need shit from him."

I need everyone to believe that, to understand that. I really don't need my father. I need all of this, brothers, nieces, nephews, and even a sister-in-law or two. This is what I want. I might even need a hot family friend they call Uncle Daniel.

DANIEL
September 11

"I have so much guilt. How could we have let this happen?" Adam keeps hounding Matt with this question.

They ended up at my house this time. We're out in the backyard and sitting around my Death Star replica propane fire pit. It's cooler tonight than the previous night. Fresno nights can be like that. Tonight it's warm, but that slight breeze blowing through is downright chilly. The weather is so unpredictable here.

"You were ten the last time you saw her Adam, we were kids," Matt sounds like he's tired of this same conversation. Adam can be relentless at times. He doesn't let shit go.

"But we grew up into adults, we never looked for her. We just bought into mom and dad's bullshit about her. Why didn't we ever look for her? Not them, us?"

"I don't have an answer for that," Matt tells him, switching his beer bottle out for a full one.

"You kept Lexi," Adam reminds him, "She's not your biological daughter, but she's yours, Matt. You knew she needed a father."

"Yeah, but Lexi became my daughter when I was older. I chose to be her dad. Juliana was born to two screwed-up 16-year-old kids."

Lexi, Matt's daughter, she's almost fifteen now. She knows Matt is not her biological father, but he is her real dad. No one questions that.

"She seems so lost. We didn't help her."

"Adam, you're forgetting she's older than us. You see her and think she's our age. That we missed it and should have done something. She's eight years older than you."

Adam continues, ignoring everything Matt just said, "You know Rachel was my best friend. The fucking shit she did to herself because of Mike Castillo. She was destroying herself."

"Who's Rachel again?" I know the name, but I'm not as clear as I should be. Too many drinks after a long day, I need to quit drinking.

"He's my high school friend's sister," Matt clarifies, rolling his eyes, but sort of smiling. "Adam used to not be her boyfriend. Those were the good old days."

"Rachel had the same kinds of issues. How old would she have been then? If I was 18, she was 25?"

"Something like that."

"And we didn't take five minutes to think about her?" Adam rubs his face. "Do you think it was physical or sexual?"

Matt is quietly thinking. "Does it matter?"

"You think it was a stepfather? Her mom? Who? You're a cop, figure this out."

"I don't want to know," Mat tells him, staring over the fire. "Do you want to know? You can't unlearn that kind of shit. Something bad happened to her. I know that and that is enough."

"Has dad brought her up? Asked about her?"

"No." Matt looks up at the dark sky. He carries the burden of being the oldest son in a Mexican American family and all the shit, good and bad, that goes with it. "After mom lost her shit, he hasn't asked."

"Do they know she came over to meet the kids?"

"I didn't tell them. I feel like we're keeping secrets, but I also feel like they don't want to know. Who's right? She doesn't want to know them. She wants to know us."

"What would you do Daniel?" Adam asks, "What would you do if some surprise sister appeared out of thin air?"

"Truthfully, I always wished there was a niece or nephew that would pop out of nowhere. My mom would love that. Eric or Juan Carlos never had kids."

"How is Juan Carlos doing?"

"It's prison." My oldest brother is a convicted bank robber. He's been in prison for eight years and has at least ten more to go. "Hella sucks."

"How's your mom dealing with Eric?" Adam asks quietly, "How is she doing with that?"

I don't talk about Eric. I miss him. I think about him all the time, but I normally don't speak about him out loud. It's too painful to know he's gone. He was two years older than me. He was the life of the party. Everyone loved Eric.

Eric got involved with some trouble after high school, but nothing serious. Then he started messing around with drugs, but again, nothing serious. There were no life-changing clues to let on what was about to happen.

Sometimes he would have these intense philosophical discussions with me about the afterlife, but I was just out of the police academy and struggling to be a good cop, helpful, and community-based, and I didn't have time for him. I wasn't a good brother. I kind of blew him off. I just didn't realize what he was fighting. I figured there would be more time and then he was gone.

I think he was fighting bipolar issues. He had a lot of manic episodes. And then he would fall into these depressing moments that we didn't comprehend as being that serious. One day he was just gone. Remembering the events of that single day, red flags were only noticeable after it was done. He was already gone. I wasn't even home.

"She's managing," I tell him. "I wish we could have seen it. You know? We can't let that happen to her."

I need Juliana. Fuck, this is not good. I don't even know her and I want her for the rest of my fucking life? What the hell is wrong with me? I need to stop drinking so damn much.

"Her? Do you think my sister is pretty, Daniel?" Adam kicks my foot, laughing, "Don't fuck with my sister."

"Now she's your sister? Dude, I had no idea you had a fucking sister and now you're all, don't fuck with her. It's a little late, don't you think? She's an adult."

"We're full of shit, ignore us," Adam laughs. "I'm fucking with you. You do think she's pretty, right?"

"Your sister is beautiful," I tell him honestly. I'm done trying to act like she doesn't have all my attention, all the time. "I have no idea how she's related to you two assholes, but Matt said I can't mess with her."

"Fuck Matt," Adam says. He had too much to drink too, "Matt doesn't know shit. I think she likes you, *Detective Fernandez*."

"She called him a stalker," Matt says, laughing.

"No, she called me dangerous. Get it right, Lopez. What the fuck that means, I have no fucking idea."

Adam scrutinized me, "You're not dangerous. Honestly, you're a nice guy."

"You know who would have asked her out?" Matt snaps his fingers, "Eric. Eric would have asked her out. Eric wouldn't have even waited. He would have told me to fuck off, and then barged right into that coffee shop and ordered the fucking Juliana Special. Isn't that what, what was his name again? That's what he said?"

"AA-Ron," I say, picturing my lanky ass brother making his way through life with that long dark hair, wearing skinny jeans and a faded-ass band t-shirt. I wouldn't have stood a chance with Eric around. The thought is funny and painful at the same time. I miss Eric. He was my fucking hero. "AA-Ron asked if I wanted the Juliana Special."

"She was pissed when he said that. Whoever he is, they're close, but she was ready to kill him."

"Who said what?" Adam is confused and looking for clarification. "What?"

"Her friend, AA-Ron, works at the coffee shop," Matt says to him, "He asked Daniel if he wanted the Juliana Special. She told him to fuck off."

"Who? AA-Ron or Daniel? Who needed to fuck off?" Adam is confused and buzzed. This is who we are. We need help. Maybe we need rehab too.

"Both of them," Matt answers. "She told Daniel he was full of shit."

"She's not wrong," Adam says with a smile.

"Yeah, well Eric would have just walked right in and would have stolen her right from you," Matt says. "I wouldn't have been able to talk to her, he would have just noticed her and done that Eric thing. You know what I mean. They'd be married by now and have emo babies."

"Yeah, you're right." Eric had a natural charm that everyone fell for in five seconds flat. Eric was the one all the girls wanted to go out with. That was Eric, always the charmer. God, I miss him.

Eric. It's hard to remember him and hard to not think of him. I don't want to forget him, but it's fucking torture to talk about him, to think about him. I failed him. We all failed him. I just miss him so much. I wish he was still here.

"What was she like as a kid?" I ask, "What do you remember?"

"It's fucked up now, but I just remember thinking all she did was cause problems," Matt answers with a deep sigh. "My parents would fight when she was around. When she wasn't, I just pretended she didn't exist. We all did."

"I really don't remember her," Adam says. "I don't think there is one single picture of her in my parents' house. They're fucked up."

"It's hard to judge them without knowing their part of the story."

"No, don't do that, 'make it better Matt shit.' They're at fault. They're fucked up. Dad is full of shit and you know it."

"You can ask her out, but don't fuck with her," Matt says as if he had any authority. Like she's not an adult who has already lived a whole life without his help. "Don't mess with her, just to mess with her. I know you're not like that, but still, I have to say that. She's still my sister. Sort of."

"Don't forget how she described herself," Adam says, pointing at me with his beer, sounding sober now. "Think about that before you do anything. She said she's done bad things. I wouldn't give a shit, but that's me. That kind of stuff doesn't bother me. I know people are allowed to make mistakes. I don't pretend to know what she meant by that, but I wouldn't just overlook it and then later realize you can't live with it."

"Name one person without drama, self-made or not," I say to him, thinking of my shortcomings. I'm not a perfect person. I don't expect anyone else to be perfect either.

"Yeah but we're Latino," Matt is full of that smug tone again. Matt is cool most of the time but sometimes he thinks he knows more than everyone else. "We can make mistakes, not our girlfriends."

Adam starts laughing. "No comment."

"Shut up. It wasn't a mistake. We weren't together."

"And it wasn't easy to move past it," Adam reminds him.

"No, it fucking hurt. I won't lie, but I'm glad I did," Matt says, "I can't be married to anyone else. Echo is the only woman for me."

I know what they're talking about. I know the whole story about how Matt called Echo a hoe. He did that because he caught her out with another person. They weren't technically together at the time so it shouldn't have mattered but it did for a while. Eventually, he knew he needed to move past it or he was going to lose her for good. She wasn't in a relationship with him when it happened. He just happened to run into her while she was on that date.

"Just really, be careful," Adam says, "I don't think you would purposely hurt her, but I don't think she could take any more hurt. She seems so, I don't know, I don't want to say sad. She seems so guarded."

"Fragile," Matt adds, "She's had a lot to deal with. We might not know exactly why, but she sure doesn't need more shit dropped on her. We just got her back."

Matt's quiet for a moment, and Adam too; even though Eric wasn't their brother, they were friends too. There were moments, a lot of them, where Eric was with us. I'm not the only person who misses Eric. This grief is not only mine. We all miss him.

"Eric would have liked her."

I like her.

And yeah, Eric would have liked her too.

JULIANA
September 12

Echo is one of those girls. Pretty and curvy, she's beautiful and she knows it. Even pregnant, she wears the cutest outfits, flowing short dresses with leggings. Her son, Matt Lopez III, is sound asleep on the couch in the corner of the room, worn out from a hard day of kindergarten.

Echo's a princess, but she's not completely full of herself, just half full. I hate her, but I love her at the same time. My Sister-in-law, she's the closest thing to a girlfriend I've ever had.

"Why didn't you want to date Matt?" I keep grilling her on this topic because my ADHD brain can't seem to understand how Matt and Echo can just accept some random kid as their own. It makes no sense to me. "Why did his daughter freak you out?"

"I don't date baby mama drama. At least back then I didn't. But Matt's hella fine so there's that."

"They look alike," Kim says, studying me again. She gestures to me, "You look like both of them."

"We don't look alike." We totally look alike.

"Yes, you do." Kim watches her daughters run down the stairs, "Hey, knock it off. Get a juice box and go play in your room."

"When did you know it was Adam you were going to stay with?" I ask Kim once she sends the girls all back upstairs with a juice box.

"He told his mom to fuck off. She didn't like me. One day, she was getting on my case about something stupid. She really hated that I was living there. I knew he was the one for me after that. I may have cried."

"She's a bitch," Echo says. "Dude, she's like, your stepmom."

"No, she's not. He's not my dad." Looking back to Kim, I keep at my fact-finding mission, "You guys lived with her? Them?"

"Well, yeah, Adam was getting his paramedic license. He went to Fresno City College. Once he was done, his dad gave him the down payment for the house and we moved out."

"You too, right?" I gesture to Echo. Matt already told me this. Their dad gave them the down payment for the house they live in. "He bought you a house too?"

"He didn't buy us a house, he gave Matt the down payment," she corrects, inspecting her perfectly manicured bright pink nails. I'm sure her toes match.

"Do you want that too?" Kim's so innocent looking, with those big clear blue eyes. She rests her elbows against the counter, her hands against her chin.

"No. I don't want anything from him. Besides, I have a dad. I have two. They take care of me." I think of my Midnight Vanilla. All of their crap will one day be mine. The coffee shop, Midnight Vanilla, and the duplex, all of it, mine. Me and Gabriel have to split it. I have a copy of the trust stashed away in my apartment. Aaron and Quinn insisted we created a trust about a year after my accident. Just in case they said. I honestly don't need shit from anyone, not anymore. They got me.

"Does it bother you? That he wasn't there?"

"No. I talked to my therapist about that. I've worked through that. I really don't care about that anymore. I care about the other stuff."

My phone buzzes. Glancing at the screen, I can see it's an image from Enrique Sanchez, Ricky. It's a picture. I know it is. There won't be any text to it. He's not dead. If he's alive, I can be alive too. I tap a quick reply, heart emoji. Ricky gets weird when I don't respond to him. He can ignore me, never the other way around. He'll text me a million times unless I respond immediately.

"What other stuff?"

"This," I say to her, gesturing around. "I need this, people."

"You have friends," Kim asks, "Outside of us?"

"Yeah, of course." Thinking of my close circle, it's small, it's tight, but it's mine. I trust mine with my life. "It's just complicated. My friends, I've known them all a very long time, too long in some ways. They worry about my bad choices."

"What? The drinking?"

"Yeah, drinking, men. I dated losers. They worry about all my choices. They forget I'm an adult. I've left too many messes for them to clean up."

"Describe the biggest loser," Echo says, raising her eyebrows. She's a total gossip and I know it. I guess gossip isn't the right word, *chismosa*, that's what she is. Echo just likes the details. I have to be careful of what I say to her.

Sitting back on the barstool, I shake my foot. I have too much energy for this space. The biggest loser, that's a tough one. Because of my text from Ricky, I can only think of him. Every story I can think of involves Ricky. Ricky's not a loser. He just has loser-sounding stories.

"Once, my neighbor had to call the cops because one broke into my apartment. We had a big fight. Then he broke into my apartment."

"What," Echo's eyes grow huge, "He broke into your house? Why? Jesus, what was he going to do?"

"It wasn't like that." Ricky isn't a bad guy, not really, he's impulsive. Besides, what really happened is too difficult for me to put into words. Only Ricky and I know the truth. "We have that kind of relationship. I answer when he calls, he answers my calls."

"Wait, present tense," Echo presses her hand against her head, "You still talk to him?"

"Well, no, this is hard to explain. It's hard to explain what he is. We don't talk. We just argue. He texts me just to let me know he's alive. He's my other friend's brother. They never talk. I let them both know how the other is doing. I'm a peacekeeper."

"But he's not your boyfriend? Or wasn't?"

"No."

Echo leans closer, giggling, "But did you hook up with him?"

"Pre-rehab doesn't count."

"Yes, it does."

"Then under 18 doesn't count."

"Fine, under 18 doesn't count. He broke into your apartment, that's not normal," She stops and thinks, "Is he cute?"

"Cute is not the word I would use for him." Nervously, I bite my nail, "He's interesting. His brother, Gabe, is very handsome, but very different from Ricky. Gabe is pretty. He's tall and just the most charming guy ever. Ricky, although they look alike, he's not pretty. Ricky is the bad boy version."

"Oh, he's bad? He's a criminal. Tell me more."

"I haven't seen him in a long time. He's kind of like a skater boy but not. He's tall and skinny. He's got a ton of tattoos. His lip is pierced right here," I explain, gesturing to the side of my lip. I don't say he's got a tattoo of my name or that he's got a tongue ring too. It sounds worse than it really is. "He moved too. He doesn't live here anymore. He lives in the Bay Area. He's in a band, a punk rock band."

Echo gives me a look. She knows I'm not telling her something. It might be my guilt. "Who else did you date?"

"I dated a teacher once. He was a cheater."

"Oh yeah, Matt knows a lot of teachers, he works at the high schools north of Clinton. Maybe he knows him."

"He didn't teach high school. He taught 5th grade." I studied Kim for a second. "Who was the guy you dated before Adam?"

She smiles, and a flush tints her cheeks. "My high school sweetheart. I was just about to graduate when I met Adam. I just went to prom with my boyfriend and then we went to a party. He got drunk, and Adam took me home. I never left. We've been together since we were 18, 19."

"So you know Daniel, he's like that too," Echo smiles over her coffee mug. She toys with the tea bag tag. "I hate tea."

"He's like what?" The snake plant on the counter looks like it needs water. I move it towards me. Feels light, maybe it needs water.

"He likes to be in a relationship but he has a bad habit of choosing dumb women," she sings. "You're not dumb, teen mom. I don't mean it like that."

"Don't call me that," Kim says, laughing and grabbing a juice box. She throws the straw wrapper at Echo.

Sliding off the stool, I take the snake plant off the countertop and move to water it. "I'm not sure why I need to know but tell me, how dumb is dumb?"

"So, so, dumb," Echo laughs, holding her stomach, while giggles spill from her, "That plant is fake."

"Oh shit," spilling water all over the counter, I start giggling uncontrollably, "I'm not normally this dumb. Don't get any ideas."

"You're not dumb." She's laughing so hard, she's shaking. "You might be too smart for him."

"You're damn right." I wish he wasn't so attractive. Hunting for paper towels, and a kitchen towel, I avoid making eye contact. A fake plant, dork, I have moments, that's for sure.

"A powerful woman who can seek help when she needs it," Echo states, looking me over, "Damn, I wish there were more people, more Latino people, like you out there."

"Are you really going to be a therapist?" I haven't told her the truth, therapy found me. She doesn't know why I had to start therapy. That's my business. It was just an accident.

"Yep, I need to do my clinical hours after the baby comes," she beams. "I've been in school part-time for a long time. Will you see me?"

"Hell no, that's not a good idea. You don't want to know my shit but maybe you should have Daniel see you. Maybe you can help him work through his issues."

"I know what's wrong with him. He is trying to fix things. His family life, I can't really go into it but he just wants to fix people."

"I am not a project."

Echo gives a knowing smile. "I don't think he thinks that. He doesn't see you as a project."

"Never mind, that's not what I mean." I need to change the subject. Shit, I just said way too much. I gesture towards her stomach. She looks ready to pop at any moment. "Are you going to work soon? After the baby?"

"No, just a few hours here and there." She touches her stomach again, "I'm not in a rush to get out of the house once the baby is here."

"What are you going to name the baby?"

"Joseph, he's going to be named Joseph."

"That's a nice name. Are you ready?"

"No, I am, but I'm not. I am not looking forward to labor, but I miss having a baby to hold." She gestures toward her sleeping kindergartener, "He's already so big. I can't wait. Would you go out with Daniel?"

"No. It's too weird," I tell her, watching her son. He's a sweet kid and looks just like Matt. "This is weird enough."

"Yeah, maybe you're right," she says in that tone like she doesn't believe me. "You just keep wandering through life with your texts from a guy who broke into your apartment. He sounds like a stalker."

That's what Aaron calls him. Aaron doesn't like Ricky either. "He's not. Trust me. I know him very well. I've known him for a very long time. He's harmless."

"Daniel isn't a stalker. He's normal. He's cute too if you like those nice types of guys He's a nice guy."

"My therapist wouldn't approve," I say, trying to dry the plant with a paper towel. Avoiding eye contact with her because I know I'm lying. My heart beats a little faster. Daniel isn't cute, he's hot. It's the whole package, the sweet, nerdy guy look, mixed with tattoos. He's unlike anyone I've ever had a real chance with. He's not dangerous, not really, and that's what makes him so dangerous.

"She approves of the breaking and entering guy?"

"She doesn't know." Using the damp paper towel, I get most of the water up off the counter. A fake plant, really?

"You lied to her?"

"I wouldn't call it lying. I just selectively tell her the truth. I get it, that situation is strange. It makes no sense. We're very good friends that don't talk. I've known him forever. Do you know what he's like? He's a touchstone," I shake the damp paper towel at her before tossing it into the trash. "When I feel like no one cares, I know he will pick up the phone. He will always care."

"He was your first love," Kim says. "That's who he is."

I feel myself grow warm. I don't love Ricky. I didn't love him. My fingers start to tremble. Ricky wanted to take care of me. My blood pools right under my skin, "We can't talk about that."

"Is he?"

"No, no more," I say, hopping off my stool again.

Echo taps her hand against the counter, "Just tell me it was consensual."

"It's not that. Just, no more. I need to just go for a walk."

I turn and leave the room, heading for their front door. I just need a moment, just a moment.

It's not Ricky. He's not hard to remember. It's the why. He wanted me to feel better. That's pathetic. He just wanted me to feel important. Who does that kind of shit? He just wanted me to feel wanted. He knew what terrible things my mother would say when I was in the way. Ricky, just wanted me to feel pretty.

    I should go home.

JULIANA
September 15

"Aunt Juliana," Lexi is full of questions. "How come we didn't know you before?"

Before I can answer, Adam interrupts, "She came from a magical, heavenly place called a rave."

"A rave?" I can't help but laugh, "A rave?"

"Yup, she fell from the sky as commanded by the rave gods," he nudged me.

Adam is like that, he makes me feel like I belong here. Everything about him, it's just all, here, you belong here. I should have called him instead of Matt. Not to suggest Matt isn't as accepting but he seems to have more, "What does my dad think," kind of crap happening in his head. He hasn't said it out loud, but I think Matt has family guilt about talking to me. Adam doesn't.

Lexi doesn't buy it. She has that flat tone only a teenager can muster. "What's a rave?"

"You don't know what a rave is?" I ask while looking at Echo. She has party-girl vibes so I'm surprised. "I'm totally questioning your parenting skills. A rave is a dance with the best music ever."

I pair my phone with the speaker on the TV stand and turn up the volume. "This is a rave. Throw your hands in the air and close your eyes. The music has to be so loud, you feel it in your toes. It's so loud, your heartbeat changes."

I won't mention the need for some E, drugs, and alcohol. I miss that sometimes, that lovely floating feeling. I hate being an adult. Tick tock, Juliana, tick tock.

"Your toes," Lexi rests her hands on her hips, glaring at us like we're too old and not cool at all.

"Just try it," I say while deciding on an old 2 Unlimited song. The synthesized music pours from the speakers, shaking the whole speaker. There is no way to stand still with this song playing. I turn up the music and start jumping around. This song, this album, I loved this CD when I was a kid. I loved the loud, pounding party beat it has.

Adam dances around too. "This song is lit. I remember this song."

Lexi huffs in the way only an affected fourteen-year-old can, but she gives a slight smile. She totally wants to dance.

Echo starts laughing, "This is like, way old-school techno." She joins in our mini rave but only grooves slightly. She's too pregnant to move much.

With hands in the air, we're singing along with the lyrics, acting like total fools. Lexi is still indigent. She snorts but stays near us. She wants to dance with us but refuses to move closer, teenagers.

"Flip the lights off," I command. "It's better with the lights off."

Lexi does that and once it's dark, she starts to rock with music.

This is my music. I hate remembering and love it at the same time. All those nights of partying with Gabriel, we had the best times but we also had the worst times. The party times were good. It was all the social crap around us that brought us down. If we could have just stuck to the dancing, maybe the drinking, we would have been okay. Instead, we both engaged in self-destructive behaviors, looking for connections in all the wrong ways. We both made so many mistakes.

"Why are the lights off in here?" My father calls through the house, flipping on the lights, immediately ending our dance party.

He notices me, but there are no words from him. I haven't seen him since I was maybe 24. I ran into him once, at Target. We talked that day. It was a fake conversation. My boyfriend at the time told him he was full of shit, and then that stupid ass man called my mother. She left me a rant on my phone. She cussed me out for being alive. I changed my number after that. She can't call me now. He can't call me.

The wave of nerves flows through me. I grab my phone and turn off our party music. I refuse to speak to him. Breath, I knew this might happen. He has none of my power. I don't need him. Fuck him. In this situation, I am allowed to be a child. Even Susan would agree with me.

"Aren't you going to say hi?" Adam questions him, crossing his arms against his chest. "You know her right?"

"No, fuck that," I glare at him. I do look like him. I hate to admit it, but I do. Pointing at him, I continue, "Don't let anyone force you to do anything. Just keep pretending. I'm cool with that."

I need to be away from here. Isn't he the dad? It's his job to look for me? This man, who is supposed to be my father, acts like I'm a bother. I am an intruder in his perfect life.

I do not take shit from any man, especially him.

JULIANA
Halloween Party

    I regret my Halloween costume choice. I regret coming here. When Matt invited me over to his house for a Halloween party, it sounded fun. I haven't been to a real Halloween party in years. I forgot what it's like to be an outsider. I used to be the girl at the center of attention, but that's because I was drunk and doing outlandish things, like wearing barely anything and touching all the beautiful men around me. Back then, I didn't need to know anyone to be the center of attention. I made my attention. Now, I don't want any attention at all.

    When I was a kid, my father made me go to a private school. I had to wear a school uniform every day for my whole childhood. I hated those stupid outfits. I never saw the man, maybe for a weekend here and there, but he insisted I go to a private school. Now, I think he just liked to fight with my mother about it. He thought he could control her, or us, but really he is full of shit.

    When the other girls in the neighborhood became friends and shared secrets outside on the sidewalks, I didn't fit in. They never included me. I never knew who they were talking about. Kids can be mean if they don't like you. They never liked me. Luckily, Gabriel, my best friend all through my childhood, fell off his bike in front of my house. He cried. He was maybe seven. I remember I went out there. My mother was asleep inside. She always worked nights.

    Gabriel's family was new to the block. They moved in a few weeks before. A whole bunch of noisy boys my mother complained about. Then she became friends with their mom. They were close in age, the two moms. His mom offered to watch over me a few times. Gabriel's mother used to make cheese sandwiches for us.

When he fell, I went outside and told him to quit crying or I'd give him something to cry about. He called me mean. Then he sat with me on the curb in front of my house. My house must have seemed like heaven to him. He didn't know what happened inside. For a long time, it was just me and my mother. She would be asleep inside, so we hung out on the front porch.

Every day, out on the porch playing make-believe, as we grew up, talking. He told me he was gay after he tried to kiss me when we were about 12 years old. I pushed him. I asked him then why he tried to kiss me, and he said because he thought I was pretty.

*****

From outside Matt's house, I can already hear the music, old-school hip-hop. It must be nice being a cop. You get to make your own rules. It's loud, too many people and so much booze. There are people everywhere in silly, seductive, and scary costumes. Everyone looks so carefree and happy. It's freaking Halloween. It's supposed to be fun. Everyone seems like they are having so much fun. That is, everyone but me. I don't belong here.

At home, it sounded like an easy, funny idea, dressing up in a Catholic school uniform. I just wanted to fuck with Daniel. I don't like that I think about him so much, but I like to think about him. I opted for a real uniform, not a cheap polyester oversexed Halloween costume version. It's not too small, not too short, or overly revealing. I even wore my favorite, black tights to keep it safe. But when he notices me, he responds like I'm naked.

Even if he's across the first floor, Daniel stares at me as he can see through all my clothes. He checks me out, starting at my Doc Marten boots and slowly moving up to my skirt, then my snug white dress shirt. There are butterflies in my stomach. I'm glad I wore a blazer. Fresno nights start warm, then cool off fast, this time of the year. His gaze makes me uncomfortable. I don't like when people look at me. I lived for that when I was drunk, but now it makes me feel too vulnerable. I lose all my courage. I wish I could just take a shot of tequila. I need liquid courage. But, fuck it, I'm here. I've made my choice. I will do this.

DANIEL
Halloween Party

    Watching her come into Matt's house, Juliana looks afraid. I want to protect her. Matt's house has one of those open floor plans that make most of the first floor open to all the different rooms. We can see her come in the front door from the kitchen.

    Women like Juliana never notice men like me.

    But Juliana is wearing a fucking private schoolgirl costume. She's all curves and sexiness, but it's not overt, showing off her body type of sexiness. She is the most beautiful woman in the room. She's completely covered in that uniform. It's paired with black tights and Doc Martens which give her that emo vibe that I normally don't like, but on her, it's a fucking turn-on. She straightens herself, shaking off the edginess, and stands tall. She's wearing a ton of black eye makeup and deep red, almost black lipstick. And she's carrying a large black umbrella.

    Adam looks at me, somewhat evil-looking, and his devil costume makes him more intense than normal. He gives me a knowing smile, "Dude, I told you. You better be nice to my sister."

    "She's not wearing that for me." Echo's eyes are huge, playing into her magician outfit. She looks at Juliana and back at me. "I don't think you need to save her. We might need to save you. That's a lot of real girl there."

    "Don't talk shit about my sister," Adam says, obviously teasing Echo. "She's beautiful."

    Echo laughs, shaking her magic wand at me, "Abracadabra."

    "Shut up before she hears you." I need them quiet. I want to look at her. I want to memorize this moment. She's perfect. I'm not stupid, I know she's wearing that for me. Echo laughs and nudges me, "Tell her she's pretty. Make sure you tell her you think she is beautiful."

"She is beautiful," I tell them, sipping on my beer. I cannot stop watching her. She's magic. She's slinky and graceful but seems just a bit lost like she doesn't want anyone to notice she's not as confident as she tries to seem. But I see her. She needs something, maybe a place to rest, to be still with her thoughts. I don't know, maybe she needs a home.

She needs to feel safe.

We're all quiet as she makes her way toward us. She comes into the kitchen where we're standing. Dressed like this, she does look more like a moody teenager than a cake baker. She seems almost fragile. She glares at us accusingly like she knows we were talking about her. I can feel the animosity behind that gaze. She's confusing for sure.

"What?" She is skittish, maybe she regrets her choice. She takes a deep breath and stands tall, scowling at us.

I'm not that tall. I normally date petite women, so it's unnerving that she is so tall next to me. "I thought you weren't emo."

"I may have emo tendencies," she breathes, sounding raspy and embarrassed, but trying to hide it, touching the loose ends of her hair. She circles the ends of her hair against her thumb.

Is it me? She called me dangerous. I'm the nice guy. Women like Juliana don't notice men like me.

"Hold up," Adam bangs his hand on the countertop. "I have an announcement."

Someone turns the music down.

"I'm Adam, a lot of you know me, and I'm Matt's brother. I need to introduce you all to my little sister, Juliana." He tugs her towards him, introducing her to the group of 50 or so people inside the house. I wonder if she knows most of them are cops. "No one is allowed to talk to her. You know how Mexican men are. Don't fuck with my sister or you'll have to answer to Matt."

"Yeah, make my husband the bad guy," Echo calls out to him. "You're full of shit, Adam."

Juliana starts giggling as she spins around and looks at us, everyone still watching her. She holds up her finger as if signifying for us to be quiet and wait. She gives us all a glance over, looking from Adam, to Echo, and finally to me while she ignores all the people behind her. She twists the end of her pigtail. Only then, did I notice she has an empty prescription bottle tied to her hair. She takes the umbrella and holds it over her head.

Echo warns, "Don't open that inside, you'll have bad luck."

"If it wasn't for bad luck, I'd have no luck at all," she tells her, giggling. She takes the huge black umbrella and holds it over her head. She closes her eyes. As she opens the umbrella, at least 20 empty prescription bottles rain down on her head. "Cops suck."

"You fucking drug addict," Adam starts laughing as if she was the funniest person ever. She is so much like him. "Where were you ten years ago?"

"Be glad we're not close in age. We'd both be dead." She drops to her knees to pick up all the bottles that are scattered everywhere. "I prefer beer and tequila but I could use some Ecstasy."

The music returns to normal. She's crawling around on the floor, picking up the bottles. Adam grabs a few and hands them to her. She's laughing so hard, stops picking up the bottles, and sits on the floor with her knees to her chest, leaning against the kitchen island.

I should be happy. She seems weightless. It's a playful side of her I've never seen before. None of that initial hesitation is there. That stressful, lonely look she normally has is gone. She's happy.

I march over to where she's sitting. I don't know why I'm furious with her. She just fucking pissed me off. This surge of rage fills me. I want to take all her bottles and throw them in the trash. I want to yank that damn bottle out of her hair. I want her to change outfits. I don't want anyone to look at her dressed like this.

"What?" She stares up at me while stuffing the pill bottles back into her now-closed umbrella. "Why do you look mad?"

"You need to value yourself more than that."

"You're not my dad," she huffs at me. She sounds hurt like the words catch in her brain when she says them. She avoids looking up at me.

"Thank god." I instantly feel like shit.

"Don't try to stand there and judge me. Who the hell do you think you are?" Her face darkens and a look of absolute pain crosses her features for a second. Then she gets that mean look again. "You don't know shit about me."

I don't have a response for her. I don't know why I'm so angry with her. I'm fucking jealous. That's what this is. I don't even know why.

"It's a joke. It was supposed to be funny." She scrambles to her feet, brushing off imaginary dust from the front of her coat. She touches the bottle in her hair, making sure it's still attached to her hair. "Hell, it was all for you anyway."

"For me," I ask. I'm so close to her that I can smell her mango soap. She's backed into the corner of the kitchen, close to the sink, but in the corner. "Why?"

"It was supposed to be funny." She looks like she didn't mean to say that to me, "That's all. It's Halloween."

I continue to glare at her. I'm being irrational, but I can't stop myself. I've had too much to drink. I'm standing too close to her. I'm way too close to her. She keeps glancing at me. Maybe she's trying to decide if she's going to push me out of her way and take off or not.

She gestures to me, "Don't you dress up? Don't you like Halloween?"

Juliana is afraid of me. Someone hurt her, and she's scared of me now. I've got her trapped in the corner of the kitchen, and I'm being a total asshole, just watching her, instead of moving back.

She's moving around, touching the counter, holding her umbrella, but I can see she's trembling just slightly. She's so shaken up by me she's shaking? What the hell am I doing? All the weird anger I had with her just vanishes. I never want her to be afraid of me. I never want her to be afraid of anyone. Who hurt her?

"I am dressed up," I tell her, taking a step back, trying to reset this weird moment. I toss my empty beer bottle into the sink. "I'm a psychopath. I'm a serial killer. They look normal. Just like everyone else."

She's still moving around, still touching her hair. I feel like shit that I made her feel bad. I didn't have a plan, but I didn't plan for that. I need to take care of her. I'm acting like an abusive asshole too. I'm not.

I lean too close to her again, "And do you know what I like?"

She got a faraway look about her, detached. "What?"

"Pretty girls dressed in a school uniform. I'm going to kill you, but first I'm going to tie you up and take you home. Try to figure out what you're good for."

She smiles, pushing me away. She's back, and her whole personality changes to be present with me. She grabs a Diet Coke off the counter and starts to leave the room. "Wouldn't you like to know what I'm good for? Fuck off."

    I have to follow her. I don't want anyone else to look at her. Not unless I'm right next to her.

JULIANA
Halloween Party

Okay, maybe the prescription bottles were one step too far, but it was funny. I know for a fact he likes my costume. He's acting all jealous and following me around the house. He's standing too close when another person even glances at me. It's a shame, I know that, but I'm more valuable when I have his attention. I need his attention.

"I didn't know Matt had a sister," this random guy says to me, "I didn't know Senior had a daughter."

"We have different dads." I don't glance at the guy, he's not who I want. I rest my hand on Daniel's shoulder, his warm skin under my cold fingers. "Tell him, Detective Fernandez, we don't have the same dad."

"Juliana popped out of thin air," he says, taking my hand from his shoulder and holding it, as a boyfriend would. What the fuck? He is so confusing. "She's here for one thing only."

"And what's that?" I guess the hole he just dug himself into is evident because he isn't answering me. He just shrugs.

"What the fuck am I here for Daniel?" I want to yank my hand free but it feels nice having him hold it. I'm waiting to hear something utterly stupid, maybe even mean. I wish he would say something sweet, but in my life, men are never nice.

"You're here to have my baby," he says, looking right at me as he says it, while he squeezes my hand.

I completely forget how to breathe. My heart instantly starts racing, I can feel my blood thickening and pounding through my veins. What the hell did he just say? Shit, he must be hella drunk.

Tick tock, Juliana.

It wasn't a shitty thing to say. It's probably the nicest thing any guy has ever told me. I can barely glance at him. I can't form a coherent smart-ass comment. He's fucking hot.

The other guy laughs and wanders off, "See you later Fernandez, I don't want to be the one to tell Lopez I heard that."

"Leave me alone, you stalker." Pulling my hand free, I need to get away from him, or I'm going to do something stupid. Moving out the door and into the backyard, I call over my shoulder, "Like I would have your baby."

"You know you would." He tells me, following me again.

I just give him a playful shove. He's so warm. I want to take him home with me. He's so cute.

******

Matt has this beautiful oasis in the backyard. Where Adam has a small yard that ends at a view of the open space behind him, Matt's house is like a fish bowl, house and yard at the bottom, with the backyard having high space around, almost like a secret garden. It's not a big space for people. The slope up is filled with tropical trees and green shrubs. It's romantic with garden string lights and oversized outdoor furniture.

There are two distinct sitting areas. One is a large sectional couch type of setup with a fire pit in the middle. Someone, Echo, set up a cute s'more-making cart there. Most of the people outside are over there, all having a loud, great time.

The second sitting area is set off to the side, with a small loveseat and two oversized chairs. No fire pit. Instead, it has an outdoor heater. That's where I go. I'm cold now. Inside it's warm, outside, the temperature has fallen and it's cold. That's the thing about Fresno; the temperature changes are fast and drastic.

There is an outdoor speaker next to the couch. Pairing that with my phone, I drop myself on the couch. Emo love songs play. There, let him keep thinking I'm emo. I'm not emo. I'm not a little teenager running around in black feeling sorry for myself. Nope, I'm a 36-year-old person running around in all-black feeling sorry for myself.

Sitting crisscrossed on the couch, I pat the spot next to me for him to sit with me. I don't think he wants to move away from me, but then again, he doesn't know me very well.

"I have questions for you," I announce as if he needs to grant me an audience. I sit up on my knees, tucking my feet under my butt after I kick off my boots. I should have worn my Vans instead.

"What kind of questions," he asks, still messing with the bottle in his hand. He's had way too many beers for me to keep track of. He's not looking at me.

"Who do you trust to do your tattoos?" I openly gaze at him, inspecting his skin, just not touching him. This is way hotter than I ever imagined. This is not what I expected him to look like under his detective uniform of suit and tie. This makes my blood thick.

"Why?"

"Because I want a tattoo, an umbrella."

"More emo shit?"

"No, just an umbrella, right here." I point to the spot on the back of my left leg, just high enough so my socks wouldn't cover it but not too high up my calf.

"An umbrella? Who do you think you are? Rihanna?"

"No, Helena," giggling because that is emo shit. Maybe I'm more emo than I'm willing to admit. "I have risen from the dead."

He's not sure if I'm serious or not.

The breeze makes all the trees around us sound spooky, like a haunted night. "It feels like the Blair Witch. Have you ever watched that movie?"

"Part of it," he says, resting his beer bottle on the coffee table, "that movie made me sick. The camera was moving too much."

"I love that movie. We should watch it. May I touch you?"

He looks at me as if he isn't sure he heard me clearly, "What?"

"I mean, your tattoos," I say, leaning closer to him, openly studying his arm. "May I touch you?"

He's a nice guy, but Daniel does not look like one. I swear, each of his arms, starting right above his wrists, up to his shoulder, and down under his shirt, is inked. Everything is placed so that when he's in a long sleeve dress shirt, everything is covered. Concealed, isn't that a police word? His body is a concealed weapon. Oh shit, he's fucking hot.

He doesn't answer me. He only shrugs like, yeah.

"Is that a yes or no, Detective Fernandez?" Lowering my voice, leaning to him, "I need you to give me your consent."

"Is that important to you? Consent?"

"Critically, I will always ask you for what I need."

"And what do you need?"

"I need to touch your arm." He makes my heart beat too fast. I have to keep biting my lip to keep from saying something ridiculous, like, would you please just have sex with me? "May I touch your arm?"

"You can touch whatever the fuck you want."

Daniel Fernandez is hella drunk.

My heart is beating so hard I have a pulse in my fingertips but I reach out and touch him anyway. This is such a bad idea. He's so warm under my cold fingers. His skin is so soft and silky. It's not what I was expecting. I was expecting that the ink would somehow feel raised like the edges would be traceable. Or maybe his skin texture would feel different. It's not. He's like silk. I don't want to stop touching him.

"When are you going to get one?"

I'm studying him like he's some Greek god. He doesn't even trip off my behavior, which means he must be drunk. At least he's not a problem. He's not making a move toward me like he thinks I'm a hoe. Like this is some sort of invitation for something more. He's just watching my fingers.

"I'm not sure. I have commitment issues. I want one, but I'm afraid."

On his forearm is a Star Wars one, four circular images; a Rebel symbol, Jedi under that, Imperial badge ending with the Mandalorian brand on the end, each one about three inches in diameter, stacked and placed so the whole thing ends before his wrist. I keep running my fingers around each circle, making lazy figure 8's.

"You're afraid," he gives me a look, making eye contact with me. "You don't strike me as afraid, at least, not of a tattoo."

"You don't know me very well, do you? I'm terrified. Let me see your other arm."

He takes my hand, stopping me from touching him and pulling me towards him. "What are you afraid of? Tell me that first."

"Life is scary."

"You don't need to be afraid. I'll protect you." He says it so fast that I almost believe him. It's not a pickup line. He's been drinking, it's Halloween. He doesn't mean it. They never mean it.

I have to pull away from him and sip my Diet Coke. Do not read into this Juliana, do not. I'm sure he's all buzzed. I miss that feeling. Not clear, but not sharp. I miss being fuzzy with bubbles bursting deep in my brain. I have to bite my lip to keep my focus. He's way too dangerous for me right now. I really want to take him home.

"I want an umbrella or maybe that really thin print down my spine; you know what I'm talking about?" I have to create space between us. There is no us, and I can't get lost in the night. It's a beautiful night. We're sitting together, but we are not an *US*. We are two people just hanging out, and that's all. Yes, I wanted to mess with him, but that's all. I am not taking him home with me. I need to protect my power. I have the power. "With the phrase 'Love yourself first.' Or maybe, 'Stop that shit, Juliana'."

"Stop what shit?"

I'm doing it again, going on and on about nothing. I need a stop sign on my freaking forehead. I cannot decide now to take him home with me. Who am I lying to? I already decided days ago.

He glances at my wrist, "Tell me what happened, and I'll take you to my guy."

"That's too high a price to pay." Sipping my Diet Coke, I wish it would turn into a beer. He's drunk. This is funny. "Fuck off, I'll figure it out myself."

DANIEL
Halloween Party

Dead puppies, dead puppies, dead puppies.

Fuck.

I'm too drunk for this shit. I am not clear anymore. Juliana's right next to me, and I can't stop looking at her, imagining her naked. I want her with only the private school blazer on. That's the teenage boy fantasy I'm having. A sexy ass Juliana naked with only that stupid blazer on. Fuck. I need to get away from her. I don't want to be fucking turned on by her. I'm looking at her way too hard. She doesn't seem to notice or she's being polite, I am not sure which.

"Let me look at your wrist. I'll even pay for the tattoo." I don't know why I want to see it. I know people cut. I know self-harm is a manifestation of pain, of hurt. Who would hurt her? Who could hurt her? She is a fucking angel, a lost emo angel to drag me to hell. She's not my type, she's not, but I'm obsessed with her. If I'm being honest, I've been thinking of her since the day at the coffee shop. I can't stop.

I want to tell her about my brother Eric. I never talk about Eric with people, and I never bring him up on purpose, but since she doesn't know about Eric, it must seem like I've got some fetish about her cutting. I just want to understand that level of pain. I don't understand how anyone could choose death over life.

"Is that your kink?" She sneers at me, "Is that what gets you off? Damaged girls?"

"Nope, it's just you," I tell her, watching for her response, just watching her. She's been biting her lip this whole time. Now her bottom lip is swollen, fuck. I want to stick my dick in her mouth. I wonder what she'd say if I just flat-out asked her for a blow job? What would it feel like to have her lick me?

I have to think about dead puppies.

When I was a kid, going through that awkward stage all boys go through, my body responding in ways I couldn't control, my older brother Eric told me to think about dead puppies to stop myself from getting a hard-on. Juliana has me so fucking turned on, touching me in that stupid costume. I have to think about dead puppies. I haven't thought about that since middle school. Shit. I need to tell her to stop touching me. I don't want her to stop, she's giving me a fucking hard-on. My damn jeans are tight. I want to fuck her right here on this couch.

She doesn't talk for a few minutes. She only bites the tip of her short nails. She needs to stop biting her fucking nails. I don't want to look at her lips. I've got something she can put into her mouth.

Dead puppies, dead puppies, dead puppies.

"It's not what you think." She's talking, but not looking at me. "It's never what you think. There is no real answer, but every answer makes perfect sense."

I need to get away from her before I do something stupid, like jump up on her right now. I want to hold her down against this couch, right here. My fucking heart is racing. What the hell is wrong with me? I want to pull the bands out of her hair and let her hair fall around her face. I want to watch her, make her lose her breath, and say my name. Let her call me Detective Fernandez. I'll show her dangerous.

I want to take her home with me. She won't say no. I think she wants me to ask her. I want to take her hand and press it against me, show her how hard she's making me. Maybe she'll give me a hand job?

She glances at me. She might know what's racing through my brain. Does she know I want to hold her down? That is my kink, isn't that the stupid ass phrase she said? That's my kink, Juliana Lopez. I want to fuck you, but I want to hold you down when I do it.

She bites her lip again, staring up at the sky, watching the stars. She looks lost. She's not sure of what to make of me. Does she still think I'm the good cop? She called me dangerous. Does she know what I'm thinking about her?

Eric.

My brother Eric killed himself.

All my perverted ass feelings disappear instantly. That's it, she reminds me of Eric. Not that they look the same, but there is a feeling that reminds me of my brother. She feels like him. That's why I was so angry earlier. She reminds me of Eric. She might not know it, but she needs to be saved.

I feel guilty for even thinking that shit about her.

She touches her wrist. A dozen bangles jingle when she moves. "I don't let people touch me," she says quietly. She avoids looking at me. She seems so much younger all of a sudden, unsure of herself, vulnerable, "I hate the way it feels. I just need to remember that I am still alive, drowning, but still alive."

She pushes the bracelets up and shows me her wrist. Faint, thin lines, layered, decorate her wrist.

"No one notices me anymore. Do you know what that feels like Daniel? Invisible? Like no one cares if you're there or not? No one to see you?"

"I see you, Juliana."

"Do you?" She leans closer, "Daniel, are you sure you want to see my shit? You can't save me, Detective Fernandez. I don't matter to people."

"You matter to me."

I run my fingers over her wrist, thin skin scarred with barely noticeable, raised, fine lines. I press her wrist to my lips, kissing her wrist. I want to lick her.

Dead puppies, dead puppies, dead puppies.

"Let me take care of you," I didn't mean to say it, but I do. I mean it. I don't want to fuck her. I want to make love to her. I need her to have my baby.

Her breath catches and she pulls from me. "Don't do that." Her eyes fill with tears she blinks back, then that tough girl persona is instantly back, "I'm not a charity case. I can afford my own therapist. I am not homeless. Don't feel sorry for me."

JULIANA
Halloween Party

    I want to tell him everything. I want to open my soul and tell him how lonely and hopeless I feel all the time. I just want to be important to him. He kissed my wrist. I can't remember the last time someone touched me, not expecting sex. I just wish I were someone else. I hate being me. I just want to be someone worthy of being wanted. I want to be someone kind of dumb, kind of young, and helpless.

    And then, there she is. It's like she manifested out of thin air and into Matt's backyard. Some girl dressed in a Halloween superstore cheerleader outfit approaches us. She's bouncing up and down in her white Nike shoes and twirling her long straight hair in her fingers. She's a beautiful shade of golden caramel, just like the images of Aztec goddesses on a bakery calendar. She's simply stunning. She looks at him with her doe eyes, with perfect winged eyeliner. She's already picked him.

    I wonder if he knows she already picked him to have sex with tonight.

    "Hi Daniel," she sings, slightly intoxicated. She's got that slightly flushed look. She glances at me but instantly ignores me. She does not see me as her equal.

    This is her. Whoever she is, this is the girl. This is the kind of girl he wants. She's super cute and itty bitty. She's got her long dark hair in a high ponytail and her big boobs stuffed inside her stupid costume. Her skirt is so short, I can see her white boy shorts under it. I fucking hate her. She's holding one of those seltzer alcoholic drink things, lightweight.

    "Who's that Detective Fernandez?" Leaning super close to him, I am so going to fuck with him. Daniel is uncomfortable, glancing between us. Fuck that, he doesn't get to pick. "Is that your girlfriend?"

"That's," he starts to say, but then she starts that stupid-ass giggling girls do when they think, when they know, they're cute. She bounced up on one foot and then on the other. She moves like a hyper puppy.

"No, we work together," she says, sipping her can.

"No way." Leaning towards her, crossing my legs, and resting my elbow on my knee. I want to only focus on her. I direct all my attention to her. That usually gets this type to start talking. They like to hear themselves talk. "How fun? Omigod. So do you know my brother too?"

"Matt? Yeah, I know him. He's like, intense, right?"

"Totally," I roll my eyes at her. I want to kick Daniel. Are you kidding me? He would pick her over me? I deserve this shit.

"Yeah, well, I just wanted to come over and say hi," she says, clearly not amused that Daniel hasn't responded to her the way she was expecting. She sort of huffs and crosses her arms against her chest while shifting her weight to one hip. She's giving him a chance.

"Well, hi," I say, being slightly louder than necessary, "So what do you do? Are you a cop too?"

"Well, no, I work in dispatch. What do you do? You're Julia right?"

"Juliana, I don't have a job. I'm homeless."

"Stop that," Daniel tells me.

I dismiss him with my hand, I can't tell if he's mad or annoyed. I don't care.

"I'm just messing with her. You know that right? I'm not homeless." I take my Diet Coke can from the coffee table in front of me and sip it. God, I wish it were a fruity alcoholic beverage with extra salt.

"Yeah, sure, totally," she says, rolling her eyes and giving me her flat palm, "Totally kidding."

Does she speak in whole sentences? Seriously? This is his type? Oh my god, this is freaking cake.

"So, do you have a name?"

"Zoey," she says. She looks me over and seems to decide I'm not a threat to her. I'm not. We are not the same kinds of girls.

"Zoey," I say, seriously? She's totally Latina, but her name is Zoey? I'm sure it's not. It's probably something like Zurina or some shit like that that she had to make cute.

She continues to bounce around, "What do you do Juliana?"

"I make wedding cakes."

"That's so cool!" She takes the chair near us and pulls it over, pushing her way into our circle. She sits close to me too like we're best friends or something. "Like, are you one of those hopeless romantic types? Working at weddings, I mean."

"Not exactly, it's just a job. It's fun, I love what I do, but I honestly hate weddings."

"Right? Bridezillas and stuff. Got ya. Women can be so catty, right?"

No answer for her, she just wants to gossip about someone, "What do you do for fun, Zoey?"

"Me?"

"Yeah, you, what do you do for fun?" She is a total idiot.

"Well, um, I like um, work out, the gym, and you know, um, hanging out, watch dumb stuff, and chill. You know. So what do you do in your free time?"

"I like to read." I glance at Daniel. He's just shaking his head at me, like stop it, but not really. He can take her home. They deserve each other.

"What do you like to read?" Zoey is just asking questions to be polite. She doesn't give a shit about what my answer will be. She wants Daniel's attention. "My friend loves all those smutty novels, you know, like 50 Shades, but I don't have time to get into them."

"Yeah, no, I read real books," I use my Diet Coke can as a prop, emphasizing books. "Like with a lot of pages."

"You're funny. Anything good," she asks, not listening. She's just messing with her phone.

"The last book I read was called 'What Happened to You,' it's about childhood trauma and how to survive it." It's only a second later that I realize what I said. Sometimes I forget to think before I blurt things out. ADHD. Daniel sits up and looks at me. Not today, you don't get to know my secrets. I changed the subject, "I read a lot of stuff. I read Twilight."

"Oh, I love those movies. I didn't read the books, but I watched all the movies," she straightens up and takes a selfie. She starts scrolling through her social media, posting it. I am positive she gets a lot of likes. She's that perfect type of girl. I loathe her.

"You don't think the vampire in those movies is a controlling stalker?" I'm so glad I have a cold soda in my hand. I want to smack her. "Like, he is totally controlling her life and she lets him."

"I would let him," she says loudly. Maybe she's drunker than I first thought. I miss that feeling, drunk, and stupid. She closes her eyes for a second, "He's hot."

"Interesting, I would never want anyone to control my life. I don't give a damn how hot he is," I say flatly. "But really, he's not hot. The hot guy was the wolf guy. That guy was hot, not the vampire. He has a tattoo. Men with tattoos are hot as fuck."

Then I remember Daniel is covered in tattoos. Shit. Oh well, ADHD, I said what I said. He's too drunk to care anyway.

She starts giggling again, "He's hot too. I like you, Juliana, you're funny. Do you have a boyfriend? Matt never talks about you. I feel like I know Adam but I don't know about you. Married?"

"Nope," I say, "My happily ever after had a fiancée he forgot to tell me about. He was a liar and a cheater."

"Oh I'm sorry," her eyes get all wide like she cares. Bitch. She just wants to hear the details. "That's so sad."

"I'm not. I could have been stuck with him. He built me a dog house. My mother said that a man has to be able to do three things," I sit up and count on my fingers, "One, change the oil in your car, two, I can't remember what two was, but three, he had to know how to build a dog house. He built me a dog house. But he wasn't the one."

"Men suck," she announces profoundly.

"They do."

"Did you keep the dog house?"

"No, I don't have a dog. I didn't even really want a dog house."

"Who built you a dog house?" Daniel asks, "What's his name?"

"It doesn't matter. Are you going to build me a dog house? Or are you going to change the oil?" I glance at her, "Which one is it? One takes work and the other is 15 minutes tops. You might even find a coupon."

She starts laughing. She has no idea what I mean. Daniel does. He has a surprised expression on his face. Drunk ass fool. He just looks at me.

I don't give him a chance to answer. He doesn't get to pick. I get to pick. I am no one's second choice. I take no shit from men. "I need to go."

"It was nice to meet you, Juliana."

"It was so nice to meet you too," I get up to leave. Daniel can just stay there with her. They fucking deserve each other.

"Wait," he called, pulling my hand, "Who built you a dog house?"

"What do you care?"

I feel it. It starts in the pit of my stomach, then the flash of intense panic and adrenaline pressing up towards my heart. My heart starts pounding so fast I'm lightheaded. It's like my brain explodes, fire burning through my veins. I need to go before I fall apart right here.

I can't get out of this space fast enough. I shouldn't have talked about Christian Garcia. I know the rules, don't talk about Christian. He built me a dog house. He promised to love me, but then he didn't. He's a cheater and a liar. I loved him with my whole soul. He destroyed my heart. He promised me forever, and then he left me. He made me feel like shit like I was crazy.

I'm itchy and want to start pulling my hair, but I'm not in my car yet. Shit, I'm not even out of the backyard yet. My body is on fire. I'm hot and burning out of control. He didn't mean it when he said he loved me. He used all my secrets against me. I can't feel where my body is in this space, my edges feel blurry. I can hear my blood pounding through my veins.

There are so many people inside. I have to push my way forward and get to the front door. I hold my wrist and pinch the scarred skin, digging my thumbnail into my skin. This is pain I can control. The music is so loud, I can't think where the fucking front door is.

He made me trust him, but he lied. I should not have trusted him. My head is throbbing and I am sick. Everyone can tell I'm breaking down. Everyone is staring at me. He said I was crazy. I have to keep moving. My heart is racing. I can't catch my breath. I can't let this happen here. I'm biting my lip so hard I start to bleed. I'm trying to navigate through a dark funhouse, but this is not fun. He lied to me. He told me it was all my fault. Christian Garcia broke my fucking heart.

My face feels so numb, it's going to happen. I can't stop it. I have to get to my car. I'll be safe inside my car.

DANIEL
Halloween Party

It takes me a minute to catch up to her. She's running away. It's only once we're outside in the front yard that I catch up to her.

"Stop Juliana, where are you going?"

I yank her by her wrist, forcing her to stop. I push her up against Matt's suburban. She is terrified. I don't even think she sees me. It's something in her mind. I catch her face, to keep her still and lean into her. I kissed her, her mouth against mine, pulling her closer to me. She feels like home and she shouldn't. I don't know what the hell I'm doing.

Juliana doesn't fight against me. She closes her eyes and leans forward. She kisses me. Running her tongue against my lip, she relaxes for a second. Then she shoves me off her.

She screams at me, "Don't treat me like that. I'm not a slut."

She is crying, hyperventilating, and walking in a circle. She's holding her wrist. She might be hurting herself. She is chanting something to herself, over and over. She stops moving and hugs herself, her eyes are closed and she's rocking herself.

She's having a panic attack. That is what this is.

I grab her by the waist and hold her against me as tight as possible. Sensory input, that's what she needs. With deep pressure and weight, I have to struggle to hold her. She's fighting against me, but I grab her other wrist and squeeze her still. In our stupid crisis intervention training, they said sensory input and cross the mid-line, what did that mean again? Cross the midline, to move her hands to opposite sides of your body. Holding her, get her arms crossed in front of her. It takes a few tries, but I finally catch her other wrist. She fights against me, but I refuse to let her go.

"Breath Juliana, just breathe baby girl, I got you," I whisper in her ear, "Breathe with me. You're okay."

She keeps pulling. I don't let her go. I practiced this on Matt, we had to hold each other. It felt stupid when we did this. Now I'm glad Matt didn't fake it with me. She's so much stronger than I would have guessed.

Using Matt's Suburban as leverage, I lean back and get her to sit on the floor with me, sliding down the side of the car to get to the ground, never letting her go. I hold her tight. When I wrap my legs around her, she softens. Sensory input, pressure. She's not fighting anymore. Her breathing is more rhythmic now. She's quiet. She's not pulling away from me as hard. I don't remember what I was supposed to do next.

Juliana just leans against me. Her tears fall onto my arm. She doesn't make a sound. I want to say everything is okay. That's the last thing she probably wants to hear. I stay quiet so she can think. No one needs a million questions.

"You can let me go now," she says, sounding exhausted.

"Are you sure?" I don't want to let her go. She's so warm and soft. I like the way she feels. She smells like mangoes.

"Let me go." She sounds angry, maybe embarrassed. "I'm not crazy."

She scrambles to her feet as soon as I let go. Her makeup is smeared and she seems exhausted. "Don't tell anyone what happened, I got this. I'm fine."

I'm not ready to get off the floor. "You sure, baby girl?"

"Don't call me that," she stamps her foot, glaring at me. She looks at me like she hates me again. "I am nothing to you."

She's embarrassed. It's basic human nature. I am not supposed to see her so vulnerable, so she needs to push me away. I get it. I don't like it, but I understand. Her reaction is not a surprise.

But I'm not going to stop looking at her. She's still the prettiest woman here. Hell, she's the prettiest woman ever. She's wiping the tears from her eyes. The uniform makes her seem so young. She needs someone to take care of her. She is nowhere as strong as she pretends to be. I wonder if she'll let me figure out what she's good for.

She turns and leaves me there.

"Juliana," I called to her, "You need a ride home?"

"Fuck off, Detective Fernandez," she responds. "You leave me alone."

It kills me to watch her go.

JULIANA
November 7

"I'm so humiliated," I say, watching Susan. I've known her for about four years now. She's my therapist. I need her. "I made a fool of myself. I'm an idiot."

Susan is quiet. She's a tall person who wears hippy, baggy, breezy clothing and a lot of makeup. Sometimes I wonder if she's transgender, but since it's none of my business, I don't ask her. I don't care if she is or not. I'm just nosy. She reminds me of Mrs. Roper from that old TV show about the three people who live in an apartment. A really old show, my mother used to watch it.

Susan's looking out the window and not responding to me. It's dark outside already. It looks like it might rain. I hope it does. I like the sound of falling rain. Everything feels so fresh after rain and smells like wet dirt. I love that smell; earth, soil, rich and dark, almost like coffee.

Susan is good at what she does. She listens and doesn't get shocked by the outlandish things I say. She's a good match for me. She seems to be watching the early holiday traffic going by, but I know she is listening to me. She likes to give me space to figure out if what I say is true or just something shocking to say to fill the quiet.

"Do you think I'm an idiot?" Twirling my hair around my fingers, her answer worries me. Maybe it's me. It's always me.

"I don't," she says quickly, turning back to me. She has a softness about her that feels like a grandma. "What I think shouldn't matter to you. What do you think? Do you think you're an idiot or are you embarrassed you needed someone to help you?"

I don't have a quick answer for her. It's been a week since my panic attack. I've avoided both Adam and Matt. They text and invite me to their lives. I'm hanging back a little bit. This is too fast for me. I hold the power. No one has power over me. I own my power. "I don't need people."

"Everyone needs people," she says, shifting her weight in her oversized green crushed velvet chair. She moves her coffee mug closer to her. "We are social beings."

I want to argue with her, but I know that's just because I want to engage with her about stupid details and not face what's the problem.

Real problem? I had a fucking panic attack. I let Detective Fernandez kiss me. I haven't forgotten that. I let him. "How can I face them?"

"Panic attacks are normal parts of life. People have them. In their lives, considering what they do, it probably happens more than average. I do not believe they would judge you for having an unexpected human reaction," she says with such authority, I want to believe her. "People, all kinds of people, have panic attacks."

"My brother's stupid friend had to hold me." I'm embarrassed about that the most. I'm ashamed that it was nice to let him hold me. I cannot remember the last time someone, aside from Aaron and Quinn, who don't count, held me like that. I haven't admitted to her that I wanted to take him home with me. "I don't think anyone saw. He had to hold me."

"What did that make you feel like, now, not then, not when it was happening, but now as you reflect?"

"He probably thinks I'm crazy."

"Do you think you're crazy?"

"I'm not normal, that's for sure." I want to have a big fight with her. I want to have a reason to stomp out like a toddler, yell and say mean things. "I'm so embarrassed Susan, I had a freaking panic attack at a Halloween party. Who does that kind of shit?"

"Why does it bother you so much?"

"I want to be like everyone else. I don't want to deal with this. I hate this. I feel out of control and crazy. I don't want to feel like this."

Susan watches me, thinking about my comments, I'm sure. She knows me. She probably suspects I'm trying to fight with her too.

"Do you think that you are building walls again? You're looking for a reason to pull away from people?"

"No."

"So my question is," Susan moves her mug around. "Do you need space?"

"Yes."

"Then claim your space," she says, this time, looking directly at me. She taps her well-manicured finger against the coffee table as she speaks, "Claim all the space you need, but do not pretend to claim space when you're pushing people away. Do not confuse embarrassment with boundaries."

Damn that Susan.

DANIEL
November 10

It's not enough we work together, but now I'm roped into helping him build crib number two for his child. Great, just what I wanted to do on a Saturday. He promises me a beer. It's not a total loss. I wonder if that bothers Juliana. She doesn't act like it, but I'm learning that she hides things.

We're close, yes we're partners, but we're also friends. It's a strange relationship between cops. At work, my life is in his hands, and vice versa. We have strange downtime and extreme adrenaline moments. We've known each other for years. He's closer to me than my brother. Adam is like my little brother. These are my people.

I want to know if Matt's heard from her. She vanished again. He told me she's not answering his texts, or if she does, they're quick answers. Sounds like she's upset about what happened. I haven't admitted to him what happened. I caused her to have a panic attack.

I want to talk to her and apologize, but I don't want to be a stalker. Maybe I am dangerous? She needs space. Honestly, she said fuck off. She's most likely humiliated. I want to tell her it doesn't matter. I doubt she'll listen. For her, it's not okay.

If it was Eric, what would I want someone to say to me? I would want someone to tell me. I would give anything to have my brother back.

"Think she's done with our shit?" Matt asks, twisting the frame that's supposed to magically join part A to part B. It's not working. "We might be those people."

"You should have just paid the guy to put this shit together for you."

"No cussing in the baby's room," Echo says. She's getting tired. Her due date is close now. She's busy folding baby shit and putting it into the closet. Like this kid even cares about blue onesies and t-shirts.

I haven't mentioned the panic attack to him. It doesn't feel right for me to tell him what happened to her, but isn't that what got her here in the first place? Do people know what happened? I wish someone had told me about Eric.

"She had a panic attack at your party." I'm betraying her, but someone should go check in on her. Just not me.

"What do you mean she had a panic attack?"

I shrug at him, really, seriously, all in one look without words. Matt can be obtuse sometimes.

"You know an involuntary loss of emotional rationality. You heard me."

"Maybe we gave her too much shit," Echo says, setting the baby stuff down. She looks at both of us.

"Hey, no cussing in the baby's room," I say to her.

"What did you guys tease her about?" Matt rolls his eyes as he trips over the word tease. He'd rather say "give her shit" but is being good for Echo.

"I don't think it was that," I say before Echo can bring up that damn costume again.

I won't tell them how the dog house story seemed to be the trigger. I liked the way she felt as I held her, even when she was fighting me to get away. Hell, I can't even admit I held her at all. I kissed her. I'm fucking everything up.

"I'll go see her," she announces. "I'll go see her and order peek-and-sip cupcakes. She makes cupcakes right?"

"What the fuck is a peek and sip," Matt asks.

I'm glad he said that. I have no idea either.

She stops and gives both of us the dirtiest look, "What the hell have I been talking about to you guys for the last 15 minutes? Do either one of you listen to what I'm saying?"

We glance at each other and start laughing. I have no idea what she was saying. Neither does Matt.

She is annoyed, "A peek and sip is a mini party to introduce the baby to our friends. Not a baby shower, this is for once the baby is born. You have wine and cupcakes."

"Do we have to do that?" Matt does not want to have this party. The look on his face is priceless, he's trying not to make faces at her, but he is not happy about this.

"Matt Lopez, I already bought a dress. Yes, we're having a peek and sip," she says to him.

He can fight it all he wants, but Matt is more like his dad than he wants to admit. He will do whatever Echo tells him. She knows that. She definitely knows it. They will be having a peek and sip, whatever the hell that is.

"I'll go order cupcakes." She glances at me, giving me that sneaky smile she does when she's playing matchmaker or asking Matt for something ridiculous, girl crap. "Maybe Daniel can give me a ride. I shouldn't be driving now that I've met my due date."

"I better not. I think I'm the last person she wants to see right now."

"What the fuck did you do to her?" Matt asks.

"Dude, I just told you," I roll my eyes and look over at Echo, "He just doesn't listen to us when we're talking, does he?"

She starts giggling, holding her stomach, "Dude, he just told you he saw her have a panic attack. You're asking what the fuck he did to her? He saw her moment. Are you serious Matt? She won't want to see him because she's probably embarrassed. She strikes me as a very private person."

"I think she's just mad at Daniel," Matt tells us. "What the hell did you do to my sister?"

"Me? Dude, really?" I told them her personal shit, all about the 5150. I should have just kept that to myself.

"Give me a break Matt," Echo says, "Come on, she's just like you. Certain things, she's got no problem sharing about, but her moments? Times when she's scared, times when she perceives herself as weak? She hides that."

"I'm not like that," Matt tells her, finally getting part A to join part B. "Stop reading all those self-help books."

"Yes, you are." She laughs, "You hide all kinds of crap from me. You and her, you're just the same, moody-ass people."

"Help me pick this shit up," he says to me, ignoring Echo's comment. "This next step says this needs to be upright. Fine, go order peek-a-boo cupcakes and have your stupid party."

JULIANA
November 13

Echo is pretty. If I didn't like her so much, I'd hate her. She's everything I'm not. She has everything I want. She walks into my bakery with Kim in tow. I guess they're the search party. They're girls, and that makes me jumpy. They act like girls. It's kind of scary.

They're dancing around to the dirty rap music I always have on. I should have music along the lines of 30 Seconds to Mars or Fall Out Boy but old-school dirty rap, 2 Live Crew, and Too Short, somehow makes everything better. They're both lip-syncing to the song and laughing their asses off.

"May I help you ladies," I say, turning the music down. I sneer at them, very mature. I'm tired. I'm not sleeping. I don't have the energy for this today. I hope I look as annoyed as I feel. I cannot with them today. I just want to sleep one night, just one night.

"Where have you been?" Kim blurts, hopping up on the counter.

"What's wrong? Why are you avoiding us? Is it Daniel? I say it's Daniel. He said something stupid right? He's a great guy, truly. I love him like a brother, but sometimes he's too helpful. He does not know when to stop being nice."

I am not ready to talk about Daniel or anything to do with that Halloween party. I made mistakes. I let him in too far. I can't stop thinking about how it felt to be next to Daniel. He felt safe. He wouldn't hurt me or pressure me to do something I wasn't ready for. I cannot admit how much I needed him. At that moment, I needed someone to just hold me still. I hate that I needed that. I don't need anyone.

"No, it's just peak cake season for my clientele." I hope I sound as flat and unaffected as possible. "It's autumn. Halloween to Christmas is my busiest time."

"Teach me how to do this," Kim is staring at all the different baked goods in the case. "I want to try that. What is that?"

I find what she's pointing at, "Dark chocolate tiramisu. I just used red velvet for one of the layers."

Kim is quick to grab a fork and try the cake. Her response is the kind that I live for. She closes her eyes and savors the cake, slowly eating it. Nice, check mark, one good thing today.

"Do we do coffee or is that a no?" I've read conflicting things about pregnancy and coffee.

"It's supposed to be no, but I need coffee and chocolate. Give me a slice of your best chocolate cake. My freaking doctor is over the top. She's great, don't get me wrong, but she's a little too granola for me sometimes."

"De-cafe, heavy cream, no sugar," I asked her, shaking a paper coffee cup at her, "I have a really good sugar-free vanilla syrup I like to use."

"Yes, please to all the things," she gestures, trying to get seated on the green crushed velvet low chairs I have at my table. Her baby belly seems to be preventing her from truly being comfortable. She must be due any day now. "I'm so over this."

"When exactly are you due?"

"Two days ago."

"Walk a lot and have sex," Kim tells her, "That's what you need."

Echo looks at Kim with a flat expression, "Have you met my husband? He's afraid of me right now. He thinks he's going to hurt me."

"Ooow," Kim sings, still dancing around to the music while eating her cake, "Hurt me, baby."

"Shut up," Echo laughs. "You know how he gets."

Echo gets coffee first. Hers has more steps, and Kim is eating cake. I'd rather listen to them talk anyway. They are funny, these two. Circumstances made them sisters-in-law, but I can tell they are friends too. They hang out a lot, it must be because of the kids. They're nothing alike. Maybe that's why they get along.

"I love this," she breathes the smell in when I hand her a cup. "Juliana, please make this every day."

"I'm open 5 days a week, right at 7 am," I say, starting up on Kim's drink.

"You should let me work here," Kim says, "I would love to learn how to do that. Could you teach me?"

"Sure, I could sure use help sometimes."

"I need to order cupcakes," Echo says, "We're having a peek and sip."

"You want emo cupcakes for peek-and-sip?"

"No, *sangrona*," Echo laughs, "I thought you weren't emo? You can use blue right? It's not going to go against your capitalistic views to add light blue to your frosting, is it?"

Sangrona? No one has called me *sangrona* in a lifetime. It's a strange word; stupid, sassy, back talker all rolled into one that can be used as a tease. Gabriel's mom used to say that word.

"This cake is gorgeous," Kim says, studying the final black umbrella cake I have been struggling with for weeks. "Is this for someone's wedding?"

"Yes," I say, laughing because I know what I'm about to say isn't true. "Mine. That's what I want, at least today. Really, it's for the front window. It took me forever to get the shade right. The red powder kept sticking to the fondant, all clumpy."

"Do you want to be married?" Kim turns her attention back to her cake. "Do you like Daniel?"

"Which question do you want me to answer?" Tapping my finger against the counter, I don't have the capacity for this juvenile shit. Daniel, that's why they're here. They must be close family friends, the Lopez Family and the Fernandez Family. Cops, ugh. Bitches. "You get one question."

Kim stops and sips her coffee, making the same face Echo does when she's thinking. "Do you want to marry Daniel?"

"What are we? Thirteen," I ask her, crossing my arms across my chest. I'm instantly defensive. Who are these women to judge my worth? They don't know shit about me. "No."

"Is he your type?" Kim's hard to lie to with those big blue eyes.

She seems so sweet.

"I don't have a type," I say to her truthfully.

"No?"

"Nope," I say, thinking about that. Easy men, that's my real type. "Not really. I like jeans and a hoodie."

"That's like, all men." Kim makes a sour face at me.

"How about hot? Is that good enough? How about hot and wears glasses, maybe has a tattoo." Oops, dumb ass, I blame my headache.

"That sounds like Daniel," Kim says, using her fork as a pointer. "Daniel is super cute."

I pressed my hand to my forehead. I have a migraine coming on. It's always hard for me to tell. Is it anxiety or a real migraine?

Kim hops up on the table, crossing her legs and leaning back on her arms, "Tell us, mystery sister-in-law, what are you looking for? Who would be your perfect fantasy man?"

"Are you serious?" I'm entertained by them, but nowhere stupid enough to tell them anything real. They are friends, I get that. I am not their friend. I'm the outsider sister who appeared out of thin air.

"You're no fun," Kim sings. "Daniel can make your life fun. He's kind of needy, but he's fun."

"Teen Mom," Echo calls, totally enjoying her coffee. "Shut up. You're making him sound desperate. He's not desperate. He's just a bad judge of character."

"He's a bad judge of character? Wow, that's a fatal trait for a cop."

"Yes, he likes, or thinks he likes girls with drama."

I remember Zoey, yep. "So why would I want to get involved with that? I've had enough drama for a lifetime. I am not looking for a relationship but if I was, I need a nice guy."

"Well, he's nice. Seriously. He's a nice guy. I think you scare him."

"Me? I'm harmless." It's me, always me. I just need to go to a freaking sperm bank.

They look at each other and then burst into laughter.

Echo looks at me, gesturing her hand towards me, "Really? Look at you."

"You look like a porn star," Kim laughs, "All sexy and shit."

"I have a t-shirt that says that," Echo laughs, gesturing like she has large letters against her chest, "Porn, with a star. I should give it to you."

"I don't know if I should be embarrassed or flattered," I say, gesturing to my faded, ripped-up skinny jeans and oversized Radiohead t-shirt that I've cut the sleeves off. It's a men's size t-shirt, so it fits me more on the baggy side. "Yes, this is the latest in porn fashion, homeless."

Echo ignores my comment, "And the Halloween costume? Dude, come on now, you scare him."

"Okay, I honestly do not follow this whole conversation. It sounds to me like maybe Daniel has issues. He's looking for a girl to fix. He has a kink about helpless, lost women."

"Well," Echo starts.

"No, wait," I say, stopping her, "but he's looking for superficial problems like, oh no, I lost five followers on my account or I have a broken nail. When he meets someone who isn't afraid of themselves, he's scared of them. Like, you can't own your shit because he wants to own it for you, but it needs to be easy shit."

Echo stops, "Yeah. That's exactly right. He wants to be the hero."

"I don't need a hero."

"We all need a hero." Echo gives a knowing look, holding that cup of coffee a little too tightly. I should make her a second one.

"So seriously, shouldn't he be here then? We're not children. Tick, tock ladies, I don't have time for this shit."

Kim squinted her eyes at me, studying me, "How old are you, Juliana?"

"Thirty-six."

The two women give each other that look. I don't need them to remind me how much time I have left. I already know this. This is why I don't deal with women.

"What?"

"You want kids," Kim asks.

Tick, tock, Juliana. "Maybe." Lies, I'm contemplating going to a sperm bank and I say, maybe when pressed by them.

"People can have kids after 36 Kim, knock it off," Echo tells her. "Your teen mom drama doesn't mean anything."

"Dude, shut up," Kim says, scraping the last of her tiramisu off the plate. "I thought we were here to talk to her?"

"I'm telling you. I'm an adult. I don't do this shit," I say as I gesture to them, then change the music. "Whatever the fuck this is, I don't do this shit."

"Knock it off," Echo tells me, clearly not intimidated by me. It must be a side effect of being married to Matt. The Lopez temper doesn't affect her. "You are not as strong as you want to pretend. You need us."

"I don't need shit."

"We need you and you need us," she says. "Face it, this is what families do. We mess in your shit, you mess in ours. That includes knowing what you want with Daniel."

"I don't want shit from him," I spit the words out at her. "Fuck Daniel."

"I think he likes you," Echo says, not alarmed by my irrational level of anger. She sits there, all in my business. *Chismosa*, that's what she is. She's here for all the dirt, the gossip. "I think you like him."

"I'm not five." I slap my hand down on the table. This whole conversation has me angry. I'm fucking furious and I'm not 100% sure why. My blood is just boiling under the surface. I legit want to kill her. "I am not a child."

Echo ignores my temper tantrum. She remains unnaturally calm. "What happened at the party?"

"What does it matter?"

"He doesn't like Zoey," she says like it's a fact I need to hear. She leans back in her seat, sipping her coffee, watching me have a whole temper tantrum over the top of her coffee cup. It's a gaze filled with judgment.

"Fuck Zoey."

"Why were you arguing? Why were you fighting?"

I glare at her. I wasn't arguing with him. I was having a panic attack. From a distance, that's what it must have looked like. She thinks we were arguing. Shit, I hope she didn't see me kiss him.

Echo is a fucking bitch. I love her for that, but right now, I want to smack the shit out of her. Too bad she's so fucking pregnant. If she wasn't pregnant, I could beat the living shit out of her.

"I did not fight with him." I have no energy for this today. My head is pounding with blinding heat right behind my right eye. I have to press that spot with my fingers, hoping that will alleviate the pain. I need my migraine medication. This petty teenager shit, I haven't got the energy for this.

Echo sits there, like a queen on her throne. She only adjusts herself so that her swollen belly is in a more comfortable position. She lifts her finger to Kim, and without a word, she tells her to shut up. She watches me, waiting for me to say something.

A switch is flipped, like instant clarity. This isn't a fight for dominance. Echo, Kim, they're not here to judge me. That's where I am wrong. I'm reading the wrong signals. I'm defensive. It's me. I'm bringing unneeded emotions into this and leading them into a fight. This is what I do. I push people away, back outside of my imaginary bubble.

I have to just say it. Susan keeps telling me to say it. If I say it, it won't be this scary thing. Panic attack. It's just two words. I am okay. I can just say it. We are not the best of friends, but we are the same kinds of girls. I know it.

"I had a fucking panic attack. There, that's my shit. I had a panic attack at the party. Flip the closed sign, Kim, we're closed. I need a fucking drink."

"There is nothing wrong with having panic attacks," Echo says, much more kindly than a second ago. "We are your family. Talk to us."

My eyes fill with tears, I'm not sure if it's from her kindness or my migraine. I have it all balled up right there under the surface. Families are supposed to talk. I know that. I have Aaron, I have Quinn and Ricky. Sometimes I even have Gabriel. But I lie to all of them, even myself.

Susan says to say it, kills the stigma. If I say it, it's not a scary thing in my brain. It's just four letters. I just blurted it out, "I have PTSD."

"PTSD means," Kim asks quietly.

"Post-traumatic stress disorder," Echo says. She reaches forward, "Is it okay that I touch you? I want to hug you."

I can only nod yes. I can't form words right now. If I talk, I will start crying. I don't cry. I am not supposed to cry.

Her hug is solid, even with the baby in the way. She pulls me forward and I start crying. I don't mean to, but tears press out anyway. Tears, quiet sobs, release. Kim joins our little huddle. I'm crying and I'm hugging someone. Is this friendship? What kind of mess is this?

"Please tell me it wasn't a stupid ass boyfriend," Echo cry laughs. "It wasn't Mr. Breaking and Entering, was it?"

"I can't talk about why," I whisper. "I'm working through that in therapy."

Echo lets me go. "Kim, run across the street and get her an iced coffee."

"No, I'm good. I can make my damn coffee, myself."

"*Ay sangrona*, let me help you. Family, remember? Go, Kim. Just get her an iced coffee."

"No ice. Only hot," I say to Kim, digging in my pocket for my phone. "Use my Venmo card."

"I got it," Kim says, hopping off the table and bouncing out the door. Right before it closes, she pushes it back open, "Don't lock me out Echo. Bitch."

Echo laughs after her, "She knows me too well. Do you want to talk?"

"No," I tell her, taking the seat across from her. "I can't."

My crap is for Susan. I don't need to discuss it with anyone else but her. Even with her, I can't say it yet. She knows, but there are no words for what it was. I can't say it. When I'm ready, she will be too.

"You know, Matt loves you. When I couldn't get over the whole Lexi situation, he told me a story about his sister, his missing sister who just vanished. He told me how his dad just let her go. It broke my heart to think that some kid was out there. I gave him a second chance. If he could care about his sister so much he would adopt his daughter, I knew he would be a good dad, a good husband." Echo breathes deeply. She stands and stretches, "So it's your fault I'm pregnant and stuck with him."

I just smile at her. She's a liar. That is such an oversimplified version of their story, I can't even. She loves him. She looks at him like he's fucking perfect. I've been around them. She's not fooling me.

"Why are you here?"

Echo shrugs. "I wanted to be sure you're okay. I saw part of what happened. I thought for sure Daniel did something stupid. I just wanted to be sure you guys didn't have some weird fight."

My stomach is turning in knots. My headache is still pounding against my skull. I need an answer to a question I shouldn't even have. I don't even know why it matters. "Did he sleep with Zoey?"

"No," she says, quickly. "He passed out on our couch."

"He's not mine," I remind her, reminding myself. I might have kissed him and I like to look at him, but he's not mine. I'm behaving like a freaking, jealous child. I need to be an adult. "He's not my boyfriend. I'm being completely irrational about something that isn't mine."

Echo gives me a pointed look, and a knowing smile. "Make him yours, you know he wants you."

"I don't need your permission."

"Yes, you do. He's a nice guy. You don't think you deserve that."

I have no answer. I have no response to that. I only cross my arms over my chest. She's infuriating for sure.

Echo sighs, "Daniel is complicated. His family life, his mom, it's not what you think. He has a lot going on in his head too."

"Crazy people make crazy babies."

"He's not crazy." She smiles like I've shared a secret with her. Maybe I have. Fuck, I've said too much. "Do you want kids?"

I don't have an answer for her, I mean, I know the answer, but it's none of her business. I know what I want, but I don't want her to know. Words have power, if I say it, it won't happen. Tick tock, Juliana, tick tock.

I just want one fucking baby.

"Why did Matt call you a hoe?"

"*Sangrona*, you would bring that up. I wasn't bad, but I wasn't good. I used to be a little bit too drunk and stuff. Matt did think I was a hoe. But then, I told him he couldn't fuck me. He took my challenge literally," Echo leans back, laughing and rubbing her stomach, "He caught me with another person."

"Another person? Explain," I order her.

"You want me to tell you my shit? Then you have to talk too, Juliana," Echo glares at me. "I love you girl, I understand you more than you think."

"Fine," I say. I love her too, but can't tell her yet. I hope she knows.

"I left him. No, not left him. We were not together. He told me about his daughter and I lost my shit. I didn't want to be second, not even to a child. I didn't want to be second. So I broke it off and went out with this person I used to hook up with. And who do we run into? Matthew Lopez Junior. I thought for sure he was done with me."

Leaning against the counter, I wish I had a drink. My head is still pounding, I'm hurt for her. She looks so sad. I can feel her hurt. To finally meet your happy ever after, and then find out he has a flaw? The one flaw, imagined or not, that you thought you couldn't live with? I love her.

"He caught you on a date?"

"No, it wasn't even a date. I was drunk off my ass and we were at some liquor store. I was humiliated. Didn't stop me from going home with the other person but we had to work it out. We had to talk. You have to talk too. You run away. Why do you push everyone away?" Echo studies me, her dark brown eyes searching me. "Were you a hoe Juliana? Are you a hoe?"

No one understands. I can't make people understand what I can't explain. Kim knocks on the door and returns with a cup of coffee for me. Honestly, coffee tastes better when someone else makes it for me. Taking a sip, the hot fluid touching my tongue, this is what I need. My head is throbbing and I want to run. I don't want to have this conversation.

"A few months ago, I made a mistake. Normally, I take them to my place. I've got resources there."

"Resources?"

"A baseball bat under my bed. I can handle any kind of man there. I let some guy talk me into going to his place. I don't do that. I made a mistake."

It's quiet for a few minutes, only the tones of the last playlist I started, old 1980s music.

"This guy smacked me around a little and wouldn't let me leave. After that, I stopped. He could have killed me. I don't want to die like that. I don't want to die."

"You know where he lives?" Echo leans closer, her eyes wide. "That's rape. You need to tell Matt. He can do something about it."

"Don't call it that. It's not. It's a mistake." Tears press forward, spilling from my eyes. "Don't say that."

"Juliana..."

Interrupting her angrily, I smack the table again, "No, you listen. It's a mistake. That's what it was. You want me to call it that, but it's not that."

"Matt can help."

"Oh yeah? Then someone will ask me about all the other ones. I will have to explain that I don't even know who the other ones are anymore. There are so many fucking men. I don't know. People will judge me. I am not a nice person. I deserve this shit."

"No one deserves this shit."

"Trust me, I deserve this shit. I have fucked up my life from the first moment. Why would anyone, including Daniel, want a part of this?"

It's an impasse, I know she wants to argue about it, but she doesn't. I refuse to break my eye contact with her, making it a staring contest. She sighs deeply and moves her coffee cup around. I am being difficult.

"We all have secrets. Some of us have little secrets and some of us have big ones. The thing is, you don't need to carry yours alone anymore. You need us more than you realize. You're my friend, Juliana. We are here to be your friends, your family."

I can't say anything out loud to her. I can't give her a response. I needed to hear that, but I can't say thank you.

"And you look like a porn star," Kim says, interrupting the silence. "There's that."

We both look at her, before cracking up into laughter.

"Shut up." I can't breathe, I'm laughing so hard. It's such a ridiculous comment, but so perfectly Kim.

"I'm just saying if I were all curvy like that," Kim goes on, trying not to laugh. "Daniel isn't stupid. He knows you're hot too. We can see him pretending not to watch you."

"You've got this Juliana. You are our family."

Oh my god, I love them. I hate them, but I love them too. I guess this is what family must feel like.

"I think I love you guys," I say to Kim and Echo, pulling them to me for a hug. They might be the first people I've willingly hugged first in a long time, where I was the initiator.

"We love you too. Now, what are we going to do with your Daniel problem?"

I know. I'm not about to tell them, but I know. I've already decided the next time I see him, I'm just going to ask him. I think he'll say yes. Fuck dating, the next time I see Daniel Fernandez, I'm asking him to come home with me.

"Don't worry about Daniel, I don't." Lies, lies, lies.

JULIANA
November 20

"I called Gabriel." It's so close to Thanksgiving. It physically hurts how much I miss Gabriel. He has left a huge hole in my life, in my heart. I love him. I miss him so much. I hate that all we do now is fight. Everything, all our conversations, always end up in arguments.

"And how did that go?" Susan looks over her notes. It doesn't bother me that she takes notes and reviews them when we are talking. It's a lot of details. Sometimes, I'm purposefully vague to confuse her.

"We argued again." Digging through her candy dish, looking for an orange Starburst, it's disappointing to find only red. Maybe because of Christmas? Christmas will be here before I know it. I hate the holiday season. "He wants me to move to DC. I told him no. He thinks talking with my brothers is a bad idea."

"Did you give him an answer that made sense to him?" She moves across the room to her bookcase. She pulls out a plastic shoebox and hands it to me.

"No." Opening the box, I know what's inside. Susan keeps an emergency stash of orange Starbursts for me inside that shoebox. I only eat orange candy. "Gabriel said I'm being stupid and naive. He thinks talking to them is a replacement for him. He wants me to move over there with him."

"Do you want to live with him? Move to DC?"

"No," I say, as I unwrap two Starbursts. I just need two. "I don't want to be an afterthought in his life. Gabriel used to be my best friend. He was the only man I ever believed when he said I was pretty."

"Why did you believe him?"

I take my time chewing my candy. I love the flavor of the orange, tart, and sweet. I have to think about that question for a few moments. "He never wanted anything from me. His house was an escape. We would hang out on his roof. We were stupid. We figured out how to climb up there, and watch the stars."

"Did you tell him in words, Juliana?"

"No." Being friends with Gabe was my lifesaver. I needed him growing up. "He figured it out. We sort of hinted at it, but never said it, at least, not when we still lived at home."

"Do you think that words have power? I've noticed there are things you hint, at but do not say."

"Words are powerful when you say them out loud." Even now, four years into therapy, there are things I do not tell Susan. There are half-truths, but not all the details. I want to be healed, but there are things I cannot say out loud. When you say it, you can't take it back. It's real. "There are things I am not even ready to hear out loud. Yes, you're damn right words have power."

"Since you didn't have to tell him in words, how did Gabriel figure it out?"

"Well, it was obvious. I had bruises. Private school uniforms cover more than a pair of shorts and t-shirts."

"Did Gabriel's mother ever figure it out?"

"She was a single parent too. If she ever figured it out, I never knew about it. Don't get me wrong, she was very nice. I liked his mom. She would joke that I could marry Gabriel or his brother, Enrique."

"Enrique? Ricky? Can we talk about Ricky?"

I don't answer her. Enrique Sanchez, Ricky. I can't even look at Susan. I can't give her an answer. That is my answer. Ricky is an idiot too, but at least he got me something I couldn't get myself. I would rather be with Ricky than that stupid ass man.

"His mother joked you could marry Ricky, didn't she? Did she do that before or after?"

"Before, just a few times after but I think she figured out something happened since he was such a dick to me all of a sudden. Then Ricky moved out, and Gabe moved out. I never went to see her after Gabe moved out."

"Did you want a romantic relationship with Ricky?"

"No. I wanted him to take me with him. That's all," I get up from her couch and move to the window. It's foggy outside. It's going to be a cold walk home. I didn't drive. I should have driven to Susan's office. It's less than two miles from my house. It's a nice walk in the afternoon. Now, dark, the fog has dropped. It's cold, but I have my bulky jacket with me.

"I have a lot of empathy for Ricky, you know? He's misunderstood. We're the same."

I don't tell Susan that I text him. Ricky is mine.

"Aaron doesn't like him."

"Aaron overreacted. That's all. Ricky is just Ricky. We were friends. I don't want to talk about that. How do I fix things with Gabe?"

"Do you miss Gabe?"

"I want to just hang out with him and his kids, but every time we talk, we get into these huge arguments. He thinks I'm making stupid choices. He thinks I should leave Fresno and go live with him."

"Why? I'm not suggesting he's right or wrong, but what's his motivation for you leaving? What does he think will be different there?"

"Because that is what worked for him. He met Sam and his life changed. And when they moved? He became an adult. That's all. He thinks I'm still a child."

"Do you still feel like a child?"

I make a spiral in the moisture of her window. Do I feel like a child still? I don't think so. I have moments of acting like a child, but I don't see myself as stuck as a child. I feel empty. I feel unseen. I feel invisible. I am not here.

I don't want to answer that question.

"I have goals for the new year. I am going to have a baby next year. I've decided it's time."

Susan gives me a surprised look, "I am not judging, but how do you plan to accomplish that?"

"I am going to have sex with nice men. I'll have an accident," I give a small laugh. "I'm stupid, I know. That's the plan. Find some random nice guy and just have an accident. I don't need a father Susan, I need a sperm donor."

She crosses her hands across her chest and studies me. "Have you spoken to Dr. Cohen?"

"Not yet. I have an appointment with her in December. I need to decrease my meds. I'll be fine. I'm ready to do this. I've read articles, as long as you and I keep this going, I'll be fine. I'm ready."

"I think you are too. You can do this. I believe that. Have you spoken to Aaron and Quinn about it?"

"Aaron suspects, I haven't said it to him but he suspects. I've told him, no, but you know Aaron. He can tell. I think Aaron wants it to happen as much as I do. Quinn, he's going to be a problem."

"Quinn is the more protective of the two."

"You know Quinn, he'll lose his shit. He thinks he's my dad. He wants a more traditional life for me like he's an expert on social norms."

"Does it bother you that he has assumed that role in your life?"

"No. I love them. Really, I'd be dead without them. I'm not stupid about that. I know what I did."

"You know, that is another thing we don't talk about. Do you ever want to discuss that, your accident?"

"It was a mistake, Susan. I know that. I just made a mistake. I'm okay now. I promise. I don't want to talk about that." I'm over that. I'm going to have a baby.

JULIANA
December 10

"Oh good, you're here." Echo forces the tiny baby into my arms. She might have just pushed this baby out of her body, but this damn woman still looks stunning, with long dark spiral curls and nude lipstick. I hate her. "Hold him right, you dork. Don't drop my son."

The baby entered the world only 24 hours after a certain cup of coffee. I'd like to think our argument that wasn't an argument helped nature along. A healthy, eight-pound baby boy named Joseph, Joseph Lopez.

I barely have a moment to set the cupcakes down. I've got several boxes of beautiful basic blue cupcakes in my hands. Nothing babyish, just some ombre blue frosting with white pearls sprinkled on top. When it comes to my work, I take no prisoners. I know my shit is good. Do not fuck with my cupcakes.

"Excuse me, ma'am, slow your roll, baby mama drama. Take those boxes to the kitchen. Don't leave my cupcakes on the floor."

Baby Joseph is practically weightless. I don't know how to hold a baby. As much as I want one of my own, I don't have much experience with them. I don't have friends with babies. I'm sure I look as awkward as I try not to smash this little person. He's weightless, but how to hold him is a mystery.

"Matt, help me." How do you move with a baby? Aren't you supposed to hold them a certain way? Gabriel's baby was already 6 months old when I met him. He smiled, he made babbling noses. He was easy. This is a newborn.

"It's easy, Juliana, it's just a baby." Matt takes his son from me. He seems to hold him right. What the hell? Am I missing that gene? What if

I'm not baby material? "Go sit down, I'll teach you."

Sitting on their mahogany leather couch, Matt hands me his son again, this time, he helps me get it right. He puts a pillow under my arm and shows me how to hold him. Okay, dork moment, this is not nearly as hard as I first thought.

He's so tiny, all cute. He smells like a baby, like powder and freshness. He's fast asleep and dreaming, I think. He's moving his little pink mouth around. He's just beautiful. He has a head full of dark hair. I want one of these. Tick, tock.

"Well, it might be easy for you, but I've never had one, or even held one, not this small." Hide my fear behind humor, I hate to admit I'm a failure as a person. Add no baby gene to my list of failures.

"Really," Kim sits next to me. "He's so cute."

"Yeah, they're frowned upon in a nightclub setting." I share him, leaning over just a tad so Kim can see him. He doesn't even move. Little Joseph stays asleep. He's so beautiful with his long eyelashes.

"Dude, you're like a child," Kim laughs, "You're just like Adam, although Adam can change a diaper in the dark and still be asleep."

"Don't get any fucking ideas, Kim, no more babies!" Adam yells from the other room, "I mean it!"

"Don't listen to the mean man," she coos to the baby. She sighs with that misty look. "He knows he wants one more."

I know that look, I feel that too. This is hard for reasons I didn't expect. My want for a baby is visceral. I want to cry, I want one so badly.

"Yeah, you want one more girl, Kim? You want four girls?" Adam strolls in, "We'll have four girls, girls."

"Oh come on, one more," Kim takes the baby from me. "Look at him. He's perfect. Don't you miss this?"

It's displayed on Adam's face. He's totally smitten with this little bundle of joy. That's such a stupid contrite phrase, but it's true. It's pure joy. I have a nephew. What magical power do babies have that makes you want to throw all caution to the wind and have one? I desperately want one too.

Kim and Adam need one more baby. All his protesting is just a show. He takes the baby from her and starts unbinding all the blankets. "You guys know how to bundle this baby right, amateurs."

"We could have a boy," she tells him, leaning towards him, still looking at the baby. "It might be a boy."

"Nope, we only seem to have girl luck. Odds are, we'll have one more girl. I'm not paying for that many *quinceanera*s. Let's just steal this one."

"Yeah," Kim turns to Echo, "Just give us that one. All these damn kids look alike anyway."

"Nope, that's my kid," Matt says. "He looks like me."

"You look like dad, just like dad." Adam adds, "We all look like dad. What the fuck is up with him? He must have super sperm."

I have the urge to insist I don't look like him too, but I know I do. I keep my freaking mouth shut for once. I look just like my father.

I want that baby back. Kim stole him from me, and then Adam stole him from her. I want that baby back. The level of jealousy I have is unneeded. I'm stealing that baby and taking him home with me.

"Give me back that baby," I say to Adam.

I'm almost surprised when he does. He moves over and hands the baby back to me.

Then Adam stands there and gives me a look, almost a smirk. "You need a baby."

"Oh shut up, I don't need shit." Tick, tock. Lies. All I want is a baby.

Daniel pops into the living room with Matt, moving some unneeded tables into this room. They make so much noise, banging things against the wall, and everyone looks at them. Oh shit. No.

Adam starts laughing and looks at Kim. She starts giggling and glances at me. It's so much harder when people are fighting laughter. It's making it so much worse for me. I can't help it either. I have to not look at them. My foot is tapping, that damn ADHD, it doesn't seem to bother the baby. He's still asleep. They're going to make me start laughing. I know what they're thinking. They're wrong.

"What's so funny," Matt looks at all of us. "Why are you guys laughing?"

Echo starts laughing too. She's not even trying to be sneaky. It's a horrible chain reaction, she starts laughing, and we all start laughing harder. It's not even funny, but I can't help it. Giggling like an idiot, I can't even look at them. It's fucking humiliating.

Daniel looks at Matt and shrugs. For being cops, they totally missed it. They have no idea why we're laughing so hard. The two of them are confused. Good. No one offers to clarify it for them.

"Come take the baby." I need to get out of this room. I'm a total idiot with a stupid ass crush on this guy? I'm helpless. "I have to go fix the cupcakes."

Matt does take the baby, giving me an escape. I don't have to fix the cupcakes. I need a moment away from these crazy ass people.

DANIEL
December 10

"Who's that girl?" Chris seems nervous. He's staring through the window as he fidgets with his baseball cap. Juliana is the only person outside in the cool weather, arranging cupcakes on a table.

I'm being a total stalker, I know it. I study her when she doesn't know I am. At least, I hope she hasn't figured it out. Maybe she has. Maybe.

She's all bundled in a black North Face coat and wearing leggings with black Uggs. Her black and white checkered dress peeks out of the bottom of her coat. I was just thinking she looked over-bundled for this weather but it's so her to be that cold.

Echo insisted on setting up the cupcakes outside to get people to wander around the house. Echo's all about parties and creating a "party story" whatever the fuck that means. I think it's code for, get these damn people out of my house.

When Juliana shared the story about the dog house, I knew it was Chris. He told me something once. I can't remember all the details because it wasn't important at the time. He has a dog house at his house and no dog. Something about building it for some girl he used to date. It didn't end well. In his version, she cheated, she was a slut. He may have even called her crazy. I'm instantly jealous and I'm never jealous. Why the fuck did she have to date Chris?

"That's Matt's sister."

"Juliana Lopez is Matt's fucking sister?"

"Relax dude." I want to know what he did to her. She called him a cheater.

Lopez is a common last name, super common. Hell, even Garcia and Fernandez are common names. Just because Latinos have the same last name doesn't mean that we're all related but in this case, sometimes we are.

"You built her a dog house."

"She told you about that? What else did she tell you?"

"You told me. I didn't know it was her until right now. She's the girl you built a dog house for."

"It was a long time ago. We broke up a long time ago."

We don't say anything. I can hear people in the other room, cooing over the baby. It's strange, standing here, watching Juliana outside fixing up a cupcake table, standing next to her ex-whatever he is to her. She said he had a girlfriend. I'm not completely clear. I might have been more drunk that night than I'd like to admit.

"We were young, a lot younger. It was years ago." He's still watching her but he has a look of disdain. "She's a total slut."

"Don't call her that." I'm instantly defensive of her. I want to knock Chris on his ass. Just not right now, here at Matt's party. "Dude, really? Don't ever call her that again."

"She'll destroy you. That's what she does." He stops and takes a long drink of his beer. Chris glares at me, "You're not hitting that are you?"

"That's none of your fucking business."

"You better watch out, Fernandez. That girl will make you sell your soul before you can figure out what she is. She can make you do things you don't want to do."

Chris suddenly goes out the door. I follow him. There is no way in hell I'm leaving him alone with her.

Juliana looks at him, instantaneous recognition. Her energy changes in one second. She seems she's ready to murder him but at the same time, she seems afraid. She glances at him and then at me. I shake my head no at her, not saying anything. I hope she understands we're not friends. I didn't bring him to her. It's this weird, there is nothing to say, type of moment. I don't even know what is happening here.

She looks at him, nervously. She must be wondering what the hell we're doing together. Her energy is palpable, furious. She stops and focuses all her attention on Chris. Her icy stare could cut metal. I'm worried she's going to punch him, but I kind of want to see her do it.

"What are you doing here?" She does that strange, no-breaking eye contact thing she does. She stares at him without blinking. She's such a different version of herself.

"Do not start with me." He crosses his arms across his chest after adjusting his baseball cap.

"I am not starting anything with you. You came out here. Leave me alone Christian." She stops, never breaking eye contact with him. It's almost like she's not there like she's playing a role in a movie or something. "You can fucking die for all I care."

"You're so dramatic. You haven't changed at all."

"You are nothing but a cheater and user," she says, not loudly, not yelling, flat and even. I doubt anyone inside has any idea of what is happening out here.

"You're not any better."

"You lied to me." She seems heated and angry, but her words don't burst out of her. It's a slow burn, measured and deadly. She's a scary sort of calm. "All of it was nothing but lies, Christian."

Chris looks over her head. Juliana is tall but she is nowhere near as tall as Chris. He's built like a football player. "Where are your fuck me shoes? Skimpy ass outfits? You think I did something to you? You want to talk about all that?"

"That's what you came out here to ask me?" She points her finger into his chest, "You used me."

"You liked it," he says to her, not breaking eye contact with her while grabbing her upper arm.

"Chris, shut the fuck up," I say, stepping closer to them. I think they forgot I was even here. "Let her go. Don't talk to her like that."

He drops his hand instantly. I'm not sure he even realized he grabbed her arm. She doesn't even move. They're both so angry I can feel the animosity pouring off both of them in waves. The temperature around them has to be ten degrees hotter.

"What the fuck is wrong with you?" I move closer to them, but in a way that I'm protecting her, at a 45-degree angle to her, almost in front of her. I know he wants to say something fucked up to her, but won't because I'm standing here.

He gestures to me with his beer bottle, "You're sure you're not doing her, Fernandez?"

"Shut up, Christian. Leave me alone. Just leave me alone."

He laughs dryly, glaring at her, "Seen any good movies lately?"

Juliana turns into a different person. She doesn't move but she's instantly stone. It's a physical change I see happen. Her eyes turn watery, reminding me she has deep feelings right under the surface. She's right on the edge, this time I can see it.

"Fuck you," and she shoves him. She just pushes him with all her might.

He's a big guy, but I guess he didn't expect her to lash out at him. He steps right up to her. "Get the fuck away from me, Jules, or..."

"Or what?" She steps up right to him, super close like she is daring him to do something to her.

Pushing between them, she doesn't back up, but he does. She shows no fear, but I fear for her. I haven't known Chris for a very long time, but this version of him I have never known. He's a nice guy. He's the principal of a high school for fucksake. This version of him makes me worried for Juliana. I never figured him as someone who would hurt a woman, but her response to him makes me think differently. Her whole vibe toward him is scary.

"Hey, look at me, I tell her, pressing my hands up against her shoulders. Pushing between them, I need to get this to stop. What the hell kind of insanity is this? She doesn't stop glaring at Chris. "Juliana, look at me."

She blinks and then looks at me. She sees me. Her eyes focus on me. Whatever battle is going on, her energy breaks from it.

"I got you," I say to her.

I can feel her physically relax under my hands, her eyes close and that glossy glazy is gone. She's back with me.

"Are you good?"

Nodding yes, she blinks, over and over, hiding her tears, big cleansing breaths. She finally wipes them away. She looks heartbroken. Whatever happened with Chris, it's still there. That hurt is just under the surface.

Pulling her to me, she clings to me. She starts crying. It's not a total breakdown, just quiet sobbing. I don't know how she can be so quiet.

I only hold her close, keeping her pressed to me. I never want to let her go.

I hear Chris leave. I don't know if he went inside or he left the house completely, but I don't care. I hate hearing her cry. She needs to let it out. I saw what bottling it up does to her. The last thing that needs is to have another full-blown panic attack.

"Baby girl, listen to me, we're going, let's go for a walk," I grabbed her hand. She is always so cold. She is my focus. I need to get her away. "You're coming with me."

When I tug her away, she follows. She doesn't fight me. Matt gestures from inside the doorway, like what the hell was that but I shake him off. I have no words for him. Let him deal with Chris. Let him be her brother.

She is my priority. She needs me.

There is a small, tot lot type of park a few blocks from Matt's house. No one is outside in the cool weather. She doesn't say a word the whole walk, but she isn't crying either.

At the park, we sat on the only picnic table. There are no kids, just an empty climbing structure. It's nice and quiet. Unlike a real park, this one belongs to the homeowner's association and is surrounded by houses. It's nowhere as big as a traditional park, more of a glorified backyard play structure.

Juliana has a lost, faraway look to her. That look is the one I hate to see. I know she's fixating on her past.

"What was that about?" I almost expect her to tell me to go to hell and that it's none of my business.

"He doesn't matter." She has that distant sound again. I can tell she's caught up in memories that have nothing to do with me. "Just know there are two sides to every story. I'm sure he'll make me the bad guy in his version. That's what Christian Garcia does. He makes me the bad guy every damn time."

I wrap my fingers around her wrist, turning it to me. These scars she tries to keep hidden from the world.

"No. It's not because of him." She pulls free from me. "I don't owe you an explanation, but it's not because of him. It wasn't over some stupid guy, that's not why."

"What happened?"

"Some things you can't unlearn," she says quietly. "Are you sure you want to know? And I don't mean him. I mean, it's me. My shit is real."

I can't answer that. Truth is, I don't want to know, but I don't want to watch her struggle with demons I can't help her with. I can't walk away from her. I'm turning into a borderline stalker. I want to know everything about her, even if that includes learning something I don't want to know about Chris.

Juliana got that lost, looking through me, expression again. She doesn't face me as she speaks, "Do you know I used to be beautiful? I was pretty before."

"You're pretty now." She has an internal beauty that shines. The hardest part is that she doesn't even know it. Whatever vision she has of herself is simply wrong. She's amazing. Out here in the cold, the sun starting to set, she lets me hold her hand.

"I was the life of the party. People liked me," she whispers, voice filled with disappointment, and tiredness. "I was the girl everyone loved."

"Is that what you want to be now?"

"No," she quickly says, "It was all an act. It was pretending. I know that. I don't know what I want anymore, but I don't want to feel like this."

Her fingers are so cold. Why is she so cold all the time?

"You want to know something stupid? I'm not really an alcoholic or drug addict," she says, measured and hesitant. "I mean the dictionary definition I am. I did go to rehab, but that's not my problem. It's a symptom of what's wrong."

"What's wrong?"

"There are memories that haunt me." She continues to talk, looking at the floor, "I'm a total fuck up. I've ruined my life."

"It can't be that bad."

"It's bad. You need to believe me when I tell you that. You saw. Christian thinks it's okay to treat me like a," she stops, wiping at her eyes again, "I've done bad things. I tried to cover the memories with self-destructive behavior. How can anyone move on from that? Everywhere I go, it's always there."

I'm not sure she wants an answer from me.

"It was a long time ago." She touches the concrete table, brushing the dust off. She takes a deep breath and it comes out, "He made a pervy video. Then he showed his friends."

Seen any good movies lately, fuck. My heart fucking breaks for her, fuck Chris Garcia. I can't imagine being a woman and that happening to you. It is such a violation of trust. I hear about it all the time, it's very common. There are websites dedicated to that kind of shit. It's different when it's the girl I want to talk to, the girl I'm interested in.

"So, for revenge, I fucked his friend's girlfriend," she gives an embarrassed-sounding laugh, almost a sob. She leans forward and rests her head in her hands against her knees. "I did some stupid shit."

"Girlfriend?" Am I hearing her right?

"Yep, that's what I did. I fucked his friend's girlfriend. It didn't end well."

It didn't end well? I think I just witnessed the continuation of that fight.

"I was never his girlfriend. Don't get my story confused. I need you to know it was my fault. It was me. I let him be an asshole to me."

"Are you okay?"

"I'm fine."

She doesn't look fine. The war she must be having inside is evident on her face. She's not sobbing, but her tears haven't stopped falling from her eyes. She just keeps wiping them away. There is so much she is carrying inside. So much she is hiding from everyone.

"You are going home. I'm taking you home right now."

This time she listens to me. She doesn't argue with me about it. She lets me drive her home. She doesn't say another word to me the whole drive home.

JULIANA
December 13

I cannot believe of all people, how many freaking millions of people on Earth, Christian Garcia shows up at Matt's house. He's a loser and there is absolutely nothing I need from him. Whatever chemical that was in my blood that made me crave him when I was younger has now shifted to hate. I hate him as much as I used to love him. He broke my fucking heart.

I planned this out. I had a whole script in my head of what I was going to say. Now I have to focus and figure out if I'm still going to ask Daniel. I do not want pity sex. Or maybe I do. I don't know what I want.

The whole drive to my house, do it, don't do it, don't do it. I wonder if he feels sorry for me. I don't want that, but I want it. I need it. I have to quickly sort through these random heated emotions and stick them back in a box in my head. I don't think about Christian Garcia. I have to let this go. I know what happens when I think about him too much. I gave him too much power.

Daniel doesn't act like he wants me to leave, to get out of his car. He is not in a rush to get away from me. He just sits with me in his Jeep. We're right outside my place, a small, well-lit duplex in the heart of the Tower District.

"Can I touch your hand?"

My hand? What I need from him is not on my hand. I reach over to his knee, placing my hand on his leg. His warmth comes up through his jeans. He's so warm.

"Are you okay? You're so quiet."

Daniel's tracing the back of my hand with lazy circles. It's just enough to remind me he's there, but absolutely no pressure to do anything. I'm about to fuck this all up. I don't care. I have to ask. I need this.

"I have a proposition for you. No strings attached." I have thought about this. This is another bad idea, but I don't care. Nothing else matters. That's how I get, once I make my mind up about something, I have to do it. "Come in with me. I'm tired of dating apps and small talk. I just need a sure thing. I won't get weird and fatal on you. I know I'm not your type, but I'm good in bed."

He doesn't say anything. He's looking at me, studying me like I'm fucking crazy. Maybe I am.

"Does this have anything to do with Chris?"

I knew he would ask. The timing is really bad, but now, I need this more than before. I need someone to squeeze me and make me lose my breath. I need that high, that surge of energy and release that only sex will give me. I need to be valuable.

"I knew I'd see you tonight. I was planning on asking you. I picked today because there's a full moon tonight."

Please don't say no, please, don't say no, please don't say no.

"You're not emo at all." He continues to touch the back of my hand, "Are you sure?"

"Don't make me sound desperate, just say yes or no. Don't ask me a bunch of questions. Give me an answer."

He takes my hand and gently licks the tip of my pointer finger. Shit. All the heated emotions I have inside flood under my skin. He's going to say yes. He wants to say yes, but he's probably fighting those Mr. Good Cop emotions. Fuck that shit, I need this. I need him.

"I wouldn't ask you if I wasn't sure. I'm not clingy and psycho. I'm asking you for a sure thing, that's all."

"If you're sure," he squeezes my hand. "If you change your mind, we can stop."

Echo's comment pops into my head, "He wants to be the hero." I need him to be my hero.

Opening the door, I can't remember if I left a mess on the couch. I have lived in the same spot for years now. It's a duplex that I once shared with Gabriel. When he moved, I took over the whole place. Aaron owns it and lives in the front duplex. He lives there with his partner, Quinn. I just need to avoid him figuring out what I am doing and getting the wrong idea. Yes, it's a hookup, but it's not the old-fashioned random guy and hating myself later kind. This is a "he's a nice guy" kind of hookup. It might not even count.

Inside, I kick off my Uggs. "No shoes in my house," I tell him, pulling off my sweater and totally missing the hook so it falls to the floor. Whatever it can stay on the floor. I'm about to have sex.

DANIEL
December 13

It's a small space. It's a 1930's duplex, typical of the Tower District. Juliana has organizational containers and little piles of stuff that she hasn't quite put away yet. Her place has bright, big windows. Everything is gray, light, dark, medium, and gray. The walls are a light gray with bright white molding. Her couches and dining chairs are deep dark gray. Oversized framed prints of the ocean hang on the walls. No family pictures, but she's got an Xbox, the Minecraft version.

"You game?"

"Fortnite." She stops moving around and studies me, her hands on her hips. "You're here to hook up and you're asking about my Xbox? Should I turn that on instead?"

"How about after?" She's calm again. Whatever that was, with Chris, it's gone. This is Juliana. This is the girl I like to hang out with, sassy and a smart ass.

"Since I'll be asleep," she rolls her eyes, "Have at it. Sit anywhere, but don't touch my crap."

She starts rummaging through her white cabinets. Even inside the cabinets, I can see all her dishware is white. It suits her. I guess I thought everything would be black. Not this, it's all very simple and calming. It's unexpectedly her.

"You like basketball?" She has a Warriors mug on her coffee table. I really don't know anything about her. At least, not the little details that make her a person. My dad and oldest brother, Juan Carlos, both liked the Lakers. My brother Eric and I were Golden State Warriors fans.

"No, but I like E-40, he goes to all the games. I just watch enough of the game to spot him in the crowd, like Where's Waldo, then I turn it off. I have a friend and we both have this obsession with E-40. Stop looking at my crap." She pours me a shot at the counter that separates her kitchen from the living room space. "You look like you need a drink first."

"You have alcohol in your house?" She has piles of books on her bookshelves, stuffed into every available space. She said something about reading to Zoey. She does read a lot. Self-help, romance, thrillers, all the titles are so random I can't see a theme. Anne Rice? She has a huge collection of Anne Rice novels. "Isn't there an alcoholic rule about that?"

Juliana has a collection of LEGO Minifigures on a shelf. They're dusty. She has at least 40 of them crowded together. Some of them are posed in an action pose, but most are just lined up. Most are Star Wars characters. LEGO? I need to show her my brick tattoo. We have strange things in common.

"It's my E-40 tequila," she starts laughing, "I love E-40. I told you, I'm obsessed."

"He's not emo shit." When did she tell me something about E-40 before? I know she talked about him before.

"Dude, I'm not emo." She stops moving and rests her hands on her hips. She looks down at her outfit, black with a touch of white, checked dress. She laughs again and shrugs.

Turning on a speaker, she pairs her phone and twangy acoustic music plays. It's not emo or hip-hop. I'm not sure what it is. Maybe it's folk alternative or something. It's turned too low to make out what it is.

"I don't drink it. I just stare at it and remember what it tastes like. You need a shot, maybe two."

She raises her hands in the air and dances around her kitchen for a moment, singing the words of a slow song I don't know. I like seeing her like this. The weight of all the emotions she carries is gone. She's nervous, but she's not afraid that something bad will happen; it's me. I am making her nervous. She called me dangerous.

There's a picture frame lying face down on her table. It's of her and some guy. It's old. She's no more than 20, maybe 21, in the picture. She looks so different, with long straight hair, too much makeup, and that outfit, wow. It's some way too short black dress with these super high heels. Chris said, "Skimpy ass outfits and fuck me shoes." This is what he must have been talking about. The picture is of them sitting on the hood of a car, hugging each other, and posing with their beer cans as props. Honestly, she's more beautiful now.

"Give me that," she says, pulling it from me, seemingly embarrassed that I saw it. "I meant to put that away."

"Who's the guy?"

"That's Gabriel. He saved my life. He was my best friend when I was a kid. He lives in DC now." She puts the picture in a drawer and sits with me on the couch. "I had a different life when he was around. It's better now that he's gone."

"I like the way you dress now much better. You're not a coupon."

"Shut up." She pushes the shot glass towards me, "I wasn't sure you were smart enough to figure out that one. Drink it, Detective Fernandez."

I take the shot, warm fluid burning down, tequila. Shit. What the fuck am I doing?

"Do you miss it?" I want to know her whole story.

"It's complicated." She pushes back against the too many pillows, tossing two onto the floor. Then rests her feet on the coffee table. "I just want to be seen. That's all. I just want someone to notice I'm here."

"I see you."

She sighs, then looks at me. "Did you have party days, Detective Fernandez?"

"No, my mom says I was born an old soul." The heat of my drink is still burning down, alcohol sloshing through my veins. "You would think I was the bratty bad kid, but I wasn't. I'm the youngest of three brothers and I'm the only one my mom has left."

"Only one left?"

"It's a long story."

"What are your brothers like?" She's watching me. She's interested in what I'm saying, not playing with her phone while we talk. "Are they cops too, like your dad?"

"No, actually," I almost don't want to say it. I normally don't share these details with people, "My oldest brother is in prison for armed robbery."

"Oh, wow, I'm sorry. That sucks," she leans against me, her back up against my arm. I reach over and take the hair bands out of her pigtails, letting her hair fall free. The blue streaks are fading to a light green shade.

"Yeah, it's not my favorite subject. I'm the cop with the criminal brother. It was when I first started. I was still a patrol officer, you know, in the cop car with a uniform."

"I'll bet you were cute in a uniform." She puts her hand on my leg, and my blood pressure rises. I'm not a stupid ass teenager. What the hell?

"I still have it, the uniform."

"Oomph," she laughs. She traces a lazy circle on my thigh. "That uniform and you wear glasses? That's hot."

"Maybe you'll let me search you?"

"I'm going to let you do more than that, trust me, Detective Fernandez. Just promise you'll be nice to me. Don't hurt me, for real."

"Someone hurt you before?"

"Tell me more about your brother," she says, ignoring my question. "What's his name?"

"Juan Carlos, a lot of people just call him JC. He robbed a bank, a few banks. I felt other cops were judging me. Then an older cop, a family friend, helped me through it. He kind of helped me build that wall around me so I could ignore what other people might have been thinking."

I can't admit it was her dad. I can't say my dad knew her dad, not yet. I feel guilty knowing her dad was there for me so many times and not there for her. He just pretended she didn't exist. She had to deal with assholes like Chris Garcia all by herself? "I moved on to detective work. I'm better with that."

"Where's he now? Juan Carlos?"

"He's up in Northern California. He's in a maximum security prison." It's comforting, the way she looks at me, and listens to me. She's not judging me.

"Do you go visit him? You don't have to tell me. I'm just asking."

"I take my mom once a month."

"Are you a good son, Detective Fernandez?"

Am I a good son? I don't know. "I try to be. I'm all she has left."

"What happened to your other brother?"

I realize she doesn't have any bracelets on her left wrist. She must have taken them off when she was in the kitchen. I take her wrist gently in my hand and turn her scars to me. She doesn't fight me about it this time. She doesn't try to hide from me.

The scars are there, faded, light lines across her wrist. Some go across, but most are smaller cuts. All the ones closer to her hand are fading. The ones higher up are more recent.

"Don't judge me for making mistakes." She doesn't pull away from me, not this time. "I made mistakes. That's all."

"I don't. I won't."

"What's his name, your other brother?"

"Eric. I honestly can't talk about him, but he's not here anymore." I can't say he's dead. I can't tell her what happened. If I say it, it's real. I don't want it to be real. I can't tell her that I miss him so much. I have so much guilt for not noticing what was happening to him. "Is that okay?"

"Yes, of course." She takes my hand. I'm acutely aware this is the first time she has taken my hand. Normally, it's me who takes her hand. She studies my palm, her finger tracing the lines. "You have a long lifeline."

Juliana stops talking. Again, I can hear that song, it feels familiar. She must have set it to repeat. She doesn't ask me more questions about Eric. I'm grateful to her for not pushing it. It's too hard sometimes to think about him, let alone explain it to someone else. It's not lost on me that both she and he must have had to fight their demons within a few years. One of them lost, and the other survived. I need her to keep surviving.

It's rare to have a quiet, no-talking moment for me in these situations. I admit that I've dated immature women. I'm aware that's been my problem in the past. It's definitely me. I don't know how I got so lucky this fascinating woman picked me. She doesn't have to fill space with small talk. I like that about her. It's just quiet for a few minutes.

"I don't normally tell people all this." I don't know why I'm sharing all this information with her. The last woman I dated didn't know and we dated for months.

"I'm good with secrets."

I know her secret. I need to tell her I know. Damn, I told Matt and Adam she tried to kill herself. I don't think she's going to be happy when she finds out. I need to tell her soon. I'm the last person to judge her for that. I can't say I understand it, but I can empathize.

"I used to cut in high school. It was so hard. Some things were going on at home that I struggled with. I started cutting. Once I moved away from home, I stopped." She doesn't pull her arm free. She touches the spots higher up, the scars that seem more recent.

"I turned 30 and kind of fell apart. Gabriel already left. My party days were so bad. I didn't know what day it was. Sometimes I would wake up and not know where I was. I made a lot of mistakes. I don't pretend to be innocent. I know what I did, what I was doing. I'm sorry for making bad choices. I wish I could change it. I don't like myself."

"I like you," I tell her truthfully, holding her wrist, pressing my thumb against her scars, hoping nothing is hurting her now. "Do you miss your party days?"

"No. Yes. I miss feeling pretty. I don't feel pretty anymore. I'm just here now. It sucks, I'm too smart to let it happen again, but I'm too stupid to move past it. I'm just so stuck right here."

"Stuck is better than hurting."

"That's true. I don't hurt like that anymore. I'm so tired."

"Change your mind? It's cool if you did."

"You don't want me, Detective Fernandez?"

"I'm not stupid Juliana, of course, I do."

She sits on the coffee table in front of me as she does that weird girl shit when she gets her bra off without taking off her dress. Fuck. This is going to happen. This could be a good idea or the stupidest thing I've ever done.

JULIANA
December 13

He's nervous. I scare him. Daniel smells of shea butter and lime, very faint, but this close, the scent is so strong. He's going to taste like tequila. This might be a bad idea. I just don't care. I desperately need this. I need to feel seen. I'm sick of just being. I want to be seen. I need a hero.

"Full disclosure," I say, let him make his own choices. I am not about to try to trap anyone into anything. "I'm not on birth control, but there are condoms in my bathroom."

Daniel chuckles at me, "You have condoms in your bathroom?"

"I'm not stupid either, Detective Fernandez." My heart is beating out of control, and all the blood under my skin thickens.

"When was the last time?

"None of your business. Shut up and kiss me. Then go get a condom. They're under the sink."

I kiss him softly, just a gentle press against his lips. This close, I'm sure he can feel my heartbeat. He tastes like tequila. Then I reach over and turn off the lamp, leaving us in the dark.

He runs his hand up my thighs, sending chills up to my stomach. Just let this happen. Let him make me pretty.

Daniel takes my wrist and looks at my scars, running his thumb against me. Heat builds under his touch.

"Why do you do that?" I'm afraid of what his answer might be. I am aware some men have a fetish for women who cut. I don't want him to notice the scars on my hip or the bruises on my thigh. I'm trying so hard to stop.

"I want to erase it for you," he says, licking my wrist softly. "I want to make you all better."

"You can't do that. You can't fix me. There is nothing to fix. This is who I am. Just make me feel pretty."

"You are pretty. You're beautiful." He tucks an unruly lock of hair behind my ear for me.

"Make me believe it." I lean away from him and pull my dress off. I manage to wiggle out of my underwear with very little grace. I don't care. I'm finally having sex with a hot guy. I'm sitting on his lap naked and he's dressed. I want to be beautiful, even if it's just for tonight and totally pretending.

With his hands squeezing my hips, he licks the fullest part of my bottom lip and then bites me gently, causing my skin to break out in goose pimples. "I've wanted to bite you since the first moment I met you."

Everywhere he touches me is electric, tingling. My heart is beating too fast. I'm light-headed and slightly dizzy. I have to close my eyes so I don't cry. I don't want to cry. I just want to breathe. I want to be alive.

"I want to watch you. I'm going to make you feel pretty right here."

Watch me? What does that mean? My stomach clenches. This is happening. My blood is rushing through my veins. I want to lean forward and let him touch me. I have to bite my lip to keep from gasping.

Daniel wraps one arm around my waist. With his other hand, he pushes two fingers into me. Chills cover me, finally, finally. It's a lovely stretched feeling, alleviating that freaking burning need. I'm already so wet, his fingers slide in. He moves his fingers so slowly I'm going to fucking burst. I am finally alive.

"Let me make you feel good," he whispers, his breath against my ear, sending shivers through my body. "Just relax, let me do this for you."

Pressed against his chest, his hoodie is rough against my naked skin. I can't get closer to him, but I'm still not close enough. I'm so fucking turned on. His fingers feel so good inside me. My thighs are quivering. It's so much, all the pressure building in my body. I can't stop making little gasping sounds, shit. I can't catch my breath. Closing my eyes and resting my forehead against his shoulder, I need to relax to come. My body is clenching tightly. I'm about to pass out.

"I'm super close, just don't stop."

He takes his thumb and circles my clit, and then brushes against it.

"Shit," is all I can manage. I'm burning from my core.

"Like that," he asks.

"Don't talk, I can't." I have to wiggle over just a little bit, to get him to push deeper into me. My orgasm is building deep pressure. My stomach is in knots. "Don't stop."

He's holding me close to him, running his free hand up and down my back, and pressing his tongue against my neck. Stong, wet kisses trail up to my ear while he's sinking his fingers into me.

All my muscles clench up and it hits, waves of built-up pleasure pulse through me. Gasping, I can breathe. I'm not dead yet. I hug him, sorta embarrassed, but not really. I don't give a fucking shit.

"Feel pretty now? You look pretty."

"No, now I need you in me. Come on Detective Fernandez, come to my room with me."

He strips off his hoodie and shirt, and damn, he's fucking hot. He's got more tattoos on his chest and down his whole left side. Tribal symbols with the Death Star mixed in. He obviously works out too. Damn. Maybe I'm not good enough for him.

"What?"

"You're gorgeous. This whole tattoo thing you've got going on is hot. You're beautiful."

"That's my line." Daniel reaches over, takes my ankle, and slowly licks one of my toes, sending fire down my leg. "You're beautiful, baby girl."

Every time he calls me that, I legit get soaking wet. No one has ever called me that. It makes my stomach cramp and my vagina wet. He finally takes off his jeans, and damn, fuck me. All I can do is watch him. He's fucking huge. Now I am scared.

"You are dangerous." I'm terrified, but I need this. I desperately need this.

"I'll show you dangerous," he teases. "Turn around, lay on your stomach."

Trusting him, I do as he orders. I need this so badly. I'm so turned on, my body is clenching up in anticipation. Daniel is about to fuck me, finally. He takes a pillow and pushes it under my hips.

My heart is racing out of control, pounding super hard. Just the anticipation is killing me. "Oh my god, Daniel, what are you going to do to me?"

"Oh, now I'm Daniel? No more Detective Fernandez? I won't hurt you, I promise," he tells me, climbing between my knees. "Tell me if you want me to stop."

He runs his hands down my back, sending chills to my toes. His fingers stop right on my left hip, the other spot where my cutting scars are evident. He runs his fingers over that spot quickly, and then grabs my thigh before nudging my knees apart, wider.

"You have a nice ass, baby girl." He gives me a firm slap on my butt. Oh shit, I'm dying.

He finds my opening and pushes into me while pushing me forward. I'm still so wet from the couch. He easily slides in, filling me. It's so fucking good. One of his hands reaches down to touch my clit. With the other, he grabs my hand.

"You're so tight, damn you feel good." He's fucking holding my freaking hand. His fingers are in between mine. Don't read into it, this is just a hookup. He's holding my freaking hand. "Be good and just relax."

"Stop talking." Who talks like that? He's not calling me all kinds of nasty ass shit? Sometimes I have to stay shut up to men, they call me ugly names. Not Daniel. All I can do is gasp. He fills me so perfectly, maybe too much. I'm so stretched. It feels so freaking amazing. My stomach is in knots.

"You good, baby girl?" He whispers into my ear. His warm breath sends chills down my spine. This is happening. "You're fucking amazing, you're so hot."

"Uh huh," it's all I can muster. My body is on fire. "Stop talking."

He thrusts in and out, making my mind go blank. My fucking brain stops working. It's a holy hell hot meltdown. Everything is on fire and burning in the best way. With my free hand, I grab the edge of my bed to stabilize myself. It's a deep thrust, but so excruciatingly slow. It's fucking amazing. He's amazing.

He takes his hand and wraps it up my arm, and loops it through to grab my shoulder to pull me as close as possible to him. He takes the hand with my hand and wraps it up against his hip. I cannot wiggle free from him. I'm trapped under him. I can't get any closer to him, but I can't get away from him either. I can't move.

Panic creeps up for a fleeting second. My whole body tenses up and my breath catches. I'm trapped under him, the way he's holding me. I cannot move. I have to remind myself he's not going to kill me. I know that. He's a nice guy. He won't hurt me. I have to remind myself not to panic.

"You okay?"

"I'm fine," I breathe as chills run through me. I have to remind myself to breathe. He's not going to hurt me. He's just not.

He lets go of my hand and holds my other shoulder instead. I can move. I don't feel trapped anymore. I take a deep breath.

"You have to tell me the truth. You need to trust me," he whispers. "I won't hurt you, I promise you."

I wish I could believe that. I close my eyes and take another deep breath. That fleeting panic dissipates, instantly replaced by the intensity of this moment. It's all good. Focus on this moment, focus on the good stuff.

I'm so freaking hot. Remember my goal.

Nothing is crowding my brain except pleasure. I focus on this moment, the wonderful feelings washing through me.

Finally, my brain is quiet. Instead, it's filled with euphoric pulses coming from my heated core. I'm free from all my negative thoughts.

*****

"You want me to leave?"

"No, you can stay. You can go play Xbox." I'm so tired. I need to sleep tonight.

He doesn't make a move to leave but twists the ends of my hair in his fingers. This could be forever. This is what I need, someone who won't leave. Someone who can see my shit. I need someone who isn't afraid of me. I can't get ahead of myself. This is one and done. This is not a relationship.

"This is not a relationship. You don't have to pretend," I tell him in a whisper. "You don't have to stay. It won't hurt if you leave."

He's quiet for a moment. "Did someone hurt you?"

"No." I'm sure he knows I'm lying. "I avoid relationships."

"Are we in a relationship?"

"No." He can't have my power, not yet. I cannot fool myself. It's sex. I set the boundaries, "We barely tolerate each other."

"I like you, baby girl," he says, talking into my hair, "I don't want you to invite any other men over. If you're going to have anyone's baby, it better be mine."

He makes me feel at home. Isn't this what I've always wanted to hear? Isn't this Daniel picking me? "Isn't this just a friends-with-benefits arrangement?"

"We could have a whole fake relationship if you'll have my baby."

"Don't mess with me. I have an out-of-control biological clock. I'm running out of time." He said it, fake relationship. Don't get ahead of yourself, it's not real. None of this is real.

He leans closer than he needs to, "I'll get you pregnant, seriously. You can have my baby. I mean it."

"I guess you missed the part where I need to be married. In my sad, pathetic life, I need to do one thing right."

"I'll marry you too. You tell me when. You can be Juliana Fernandez."

He doesn't mean what he's saying. Men say stupid shit after sex. It's got to be the dopamine; all the pleasure receptors open equal, saying dumb shit. How many men promised they'd be the one, and then later sneak out? No, he's saying what he thinks I need to hear. It feels good, but it's not true. He doesn't mean it.

"Shut up and let me go to sleep."

DANIEL
December 13/14

    I'm a light sleeper, a perk of the job. Juliana's tossing, turning, and murmuring something. She is having a bad dream. Her nightmares must be horrible. She carries so much inside. I hope one day she can trust me with her shit.

    "Shhh," I'm not sure she can hear me. I pull her closer, "You're okay, baby girl."

    "Daniel," she breathes, "Don't leave me."

    I trace the scars on her hip. "I'm not going anywhere. You're the one."

    I'm positive she's not hearing me.

    When I wake up, I'm not sure where I am. Then I remember. Juliana Lopez is the most amazing woman I have ever met. She's funny, she's a smart ass, and she listens to me without judging me. It doesn't hurt that she's beautiful. She's not lying, she's damn good in bed, but she's not in bed anymore.

    Juliana is sipping coffee and watching something on TV. She's wearing a light olive green dress. It's the first time she's not wearing black.

    "Are you good?" All of Juliana's tough girl attitude is gone. I want to see her look like this all the time. Safe? She's not fighting her demons. That's what it is. She's comfortable.

    "I'm good, are you good? Was I good?" I'm trying not to be nervous but she's so calm, it sort of freaks me out. I'm not a one-night-stand type of guy. Usually, this is the part where the girls I date get all weird on me, all needy and sensitive. They want to cuddle and talk, and make plans for the future. Juliana's just watching murder documentaries on

TV.

"Yeah, you were great," she says, biting her lip.

Juliana has that glow people talk about in rom-coms. She's rested, she's relaxed. She is brighter than I've ever seen her.

"Are we still cool?"

"We're cool. There is coffee. Creamer is in the refrigerator."

"What are you watching?" There's blood and crime tape all over the screen.

"The First 48, I swear, cops are the worst. These damn detectives never tell these people they need a lawyer. Cops suck."

Hanging out with her makes me feel like a dork. Sounds stupid like that but it's this level of comfort like I can just be me and she's not going to trip out. I like it when she gives me shit about being a cop or makes fun of all my Star Wars quotes. I can just be myself. I don't need to impress her.

The metallic buzz of a phone goes off.

"Your phone is on the counter. Someone's trying to get a hold of you, Detective Fernandez. It might be the police."

I grab my phone. She doesn't even ask me who it is.

******

In her bathroom, I check my texts. Seven missed texts from Matt. Shit. Matt hasn't figured out his role in her life. He wants to be the protective older brother, but he's younger. She's made it this far without his help. Latino shit, sometimes it sucks.

Text message from Matt: What happened with Chris? What the fuck was that?

Matt: Where did you take her?

Matt: Dude, that's my sister. Don't.

Matt: It's midnight and her car is still here.

Matt: Dude, don't sleep with my sister.

Matt: Fuck you Fernandez, don't fucking mess with my sister.

Matt: Just tell me she's okay.

Me: Dude, I can't even articulate what that was.

Keep it simple. I just gave him a quick response. Forget all the others, don't sleep with my sister shit, it's too late now.

Matt: You or Chris? What are we talking about? Fucking ass.

Me: Chris

Matt: Chris looked like he wanted to kill her. Did she tell you why?

Me: maybe

Matt: Fuck you, Fernandez. Where did you take her?

Me: Really, this is what we're going to do? She's an adult. Knock that shit off. You're not her dad.

I won't remind him that his dad hasn't said shit about her.

Matt: Her car is still here.

Me: I'll take her to pick it up later. I'm taking her to my mom's.

Matt: Your mom? She'll think you're getting married. Echo thinks that's funny.

Me: What? Me marrying her or my next-level mom?

Matt: Both.

Me: What if I did marry her?

Matt: No.

Matt: Echo says yes.

Me: We both know who wins that argument.

Matt: Echo wants to know what the hell? Those are her exact words.

Echo, Matt: What the HELL? What the fuck Daniel?

Me to group text: I'm just messing with you.

Echo, Matt: Messing with me or her? Don't fuck with my girl Daniel.

Me to group text: Since when is she your girl?

Echo, Matt: Dude, she's my best friend.

Me to group text: Since when?

Echo, Matt: Since when are you her boyfriend?

Me to group text: I'm not her boyfriend.

Echo, Matt: Don't be an asshole and tell her that. That even hurt my feelings.

Me to group text: That sounds fucked. I didn't mean it like that.

Matt, Echo: How do you mean it?

I don't have an answer for them. I have no idea what I'm doing. I'm hiding in her bathroom and texting her brother and sister-in-law like a fucking bitch.

Me: I have to go see my mom. It's Sunday. I'm taking her with me.

    Echo, Matt: Is she with you now? Kissy Smile Emoji
    Me: You know she wouldn't want me to give you an answer.
    Echo, Matt: That means yes.
    Echo: Damn it, Daniel! Don't fuck this up. Make her feel special. Don't be a dick.
    Matt: Echo is going to marry you off to her too now. You're fucked now, Fernandez. She's planning your wedding. Between her and your mom, you're a dead man. LOL
    Me: Why would that be a bad thing?
    Me: Upside-down smile emoji
    Echo, Matt: Don't ask her a bunch of questions, Daniel. Just let her be. Let your mom ask, not you.
    Matt: Is she okay? Really?

    I don't have a textable answer for that. He wants to hear she's fine. What I want to say is that whatever happened in her past, she carries with her every day. We need to be aware of that. We have to watch her and make sure she's okay.

    Or maybe me, I have to watch for her. I don't know what the fuck I'm doing.

    Me: She's fine. She was just mad. She's good now.
    Me: She's fine.
    Matt: Don't hurt her.
    Me: It's not like that. But to be clear, I wouldn't hurt her.

Next text thread:
    Mom: Are you coming over? What time?
    Mom: Child?
    Mom: Are you busy?
    Mom: Text me you're alive.
    Mom: You are alive, right?
    Mom: Daniel, answer your mother.
    Me: I'll be there in 30 minutes. I'm bringing Ms. Too Many Boyfriends.
    Mom: heart emoji
    Me: Stop.

Me: Stop. Don't make it weird.
Me: Be cool, okay?
Mom: heart emoji

******

"Come with me to my mom's house."

Juliana looks at me over the top of her coffee mug, making a sour face. "Is that a good idea?"

"It's fine. Stop overthinking it. Come on, I don't even know you. Come hang out with me today. I'll take you to get your car."

"Oh shit," she holds her hand against her forehead. "My car. Damn."

"Are you ashamed of me, Juliana Lopez?"

"Maybe just a little bit," she teases, pulling all her bracelets off the coffee table and onto her arm. "I don't know what to say. I don't do this normally."

"Do what?"

"The next day, I don't have next days," Juliana says to me, sounding nervous.

Now she's nervous? About just hanging out?

"Welcome to the next day. People talk the next day. They get to know each other."

"I thought men didn't call on the next day?"

"I would call you. Ignore my mom, she's next-level crazy."

"Mom," I called, walking into my old childhood home. She refuses to move from here even if it's not the best neighborhood to live in. All her memories are in this house. We grew up here, in a small house, with three boys. It has two bedrooms, and one bathroom and there were a lot of boys fighting. I'm not sure how they did it.

It's an older 1940s bungalow-style home. Close to an old mall, Manchester Center, where the huge transit center is located, my childhood home is in a well-maintained, quiet area. It's a strong family neighborhood. Everyone here knows everyone else. It's generational families, I know your grandmother who babysits the neighbor's baby. Neighbors yell at each other's kids, and it means something. Everyone is a cousin, even if they're not. People watch out for each other. I get why my mom won't leave.

My mom is blasting old freestyle music. She might be in her mid-sixties, but she doesn't let that slow her down. I turn off the music, and she comes rushing out of the back room.

"That was my song, Daniel! Don't touch my music." She rushes over to her smart speaker, "Level 3, freestyle." She turns to me and looks over at Juliana. She gets that smile like I know a secret. She knows perfectly well who Juliana is. "Who's that?"

Juliana has her black and blue hair twisted up like Princess Leia. She has all the black rubber bracelets back on her wrist and is wearing her beat-up Converse. And that lipstick she wears, she looks amazing.

"Juliana, this is my mom, Rosario."

"Just call me Rosie," she says, and rolls her eyes, "Rosario is a name for a grandma. I'm not a grandmother. Daniel, she's too pretty for you."

"We're not on a date," Juliana tells her.

My mom moves towards Juliana, obviously looking her over like a mother would, judging her and sizing her up, "Juliana, do you know who Anna Nicole Smith is?

"The model? She died right?"

Juliana has the toughest demeanor. She holds her own against Matt, and Adam and gives me nothing but shit. She stood up against Christian Garcia and refused to back down, but minutes after meeting my mom, she is blushing. *I'm not the type you take home to meet your mother.* She's fidgeting around, touching her hair, picking at her nails.

"Anna Nicole was extremely beautiful." My mom smiles at me. This might be a bad idea. "Way too pretty."

"Mom," I give that, cool it, look, but my mom pretends not to notice. She just busies herself with setting coffee on the table.

"You're Senior's daughter," she asks while handing Juliana a mug of coffee. She studies her like Juliana is an alien, watching her. My mom is totally interested in this strange story. She's known Matt Senior for a long time. I'm sure she has no idea what to make of this situation.

"I am. Sort of, I'm not really his child, but he's my father. It's not much of a story."

"You need to sit down and tell me this story, Juliana. I don't mean to be rude, but I had no idea Senior had another child. I've known your dad for a long time."

"He's not my dad. He pretends I don't exist. Most people in his life don't know I'm alive."

"I had no idea."

"That's the way he likes it," Juliana is talking more to her coffee than to us. Her words are measured, and careful, "He likes to pretend his life is perfect. He met up with my mother in high school. That's about it. I don't know him. I saw him like once a month or so but not much, not enough to count."

"Once a month?"

"Sometimes less, sometimes he'd just leave me with his parents. When I got old enough, I refused to go. I am not his daughter. We don't have a relationship."

"Are they high school sweethearts?" She asks, "Your mom and dad?"

"No, they weren't even friends. They ended up in detention together. I guess he walked her home after, and here I am," Juliana gives an embarrassed laugh. She won't look at my mom. "At least, that's the story I was told. My mother said 'You're So Vain' by Carly Simon was playing on the radio."

"That song, from the '70s?"

"Yeah, that one," Juliana smiles as she touches the ends of her blue-streaked hair, twisting it against her finger. "That's my favorite song, but the version by Marilyn Manson, not Carly Simon."

"Marilyn Manson, the devil singer?"

"Mom," I gave her another look, to keep it in check.

My mom ignores me, patting Juliana's hand. "My son Eric liked Marilyn Manson too."

"Your son, Eric," Juliana moves just a fraction from me, towards my mom, "What was he like?"

My mom takes a deep breath, fiddling with her wedding rings. She looks at Juliana, taking her hand and squeezing it. "Eric was my middle child. He was the easiest of the three until he wasn't."

"You don't have to tell me anything," Juliana says to her, quietly, "You barely know me. I totally understand."

"It's not that," my mom tells her, still holding her hand. She sighs, the stress of the years evident for a fraction of a second, before she smiles again, "Sometimes I forget there were more good times than bad. I miss Eric."

"We both miss Eric." My mom's heartbreak is still clearly there. She has not gotten over Eric. I doubt she ever will. I won't.

"What was he like?" Juliana looks at my mom.

"Eric liked to dance. He liked all kinds of music, but his favorite was R&B love songs. No one knew that." My mom is lost for a moment in memories of easier times when Eric was still here. "His favorite color was blue, light blue. He liked to read Anne Rice."

"Anne Rice? I love her," Juliana says.

"Of course you do, emo girl."

My mom is watching us. I hope she doesn't figure out why we're together so early in the morning. Latino moms, next level, I want her to like Juliana as much as I do.

"You're a weirdo." Juliana smiles, shaking her head. She studies my mom before saying, "Tell me more about Eric."

"Eric was a good son. He was the kind of son who would dance with his mom in the kitchen. He was a good kid."

"He only drank Diet Dr. Pepper." My brother Eric was my best friend. I missed all the signs. I let him down. I failed him. "All day long, gross."

"He wanted to be a nurse." My mom smiles at the thought. "He was in nursing school. He liked basketball, the Warriors."

"The Golden State Warriors? E-40?"

"I don't think he had an E-40 obsession like you, but yes, them." I move to the couch where Juliana's sitting. I want to be closer to her. I want to share everything about Eric with her. I've never shared about Eric before, not in a long time. "He stole my girlfriend in the 7th grade."

My mom starts laughing, "Daniel, I don't think that girl knew you were alive."

"Well, once she figured out I was alive, she would have been my girlfriend."

My mom turns to Juliana, sharing the story with a touch of excitement, "She lived across the street one summer. Her grandmother lived there. She came to stay with her. What was her name again?"

"Something with an S, Sophie?"

"Sonia," my mom corrects. "It was Sonia. She was staying with her grandmother."

"She had long brown hair. She wore a red bow in her hair. She was my first true love, but she didn't know I was alive."

"Daniel had a crush on her and would go sit outside with her but she would only follow Eric around like a little puppy. She had a huge crush on Eric."

"It was the hair. Eric had long, dark hair that girls liked." I nudged Juliana, "She liked the older, bad boy types. Eric was already in high school and didn't have the time of day for her."

"Until he did," my mom says. "Right before she was sent home, he kissed her. They fought."

"Over the girl," Juliana giggles, looking from me to my mom. "Like, for real?"

"Like their dad had to get involved," my mom laughs, pressing her hand against her forehead.

"Well, I guess it worked," I say to Juliana, "She kissed me on my cheek right before she left."

"Must have been your one shot at true love," she says, giggling more. "Did you guys ever see her again?"

"No, her grandmother moved later that year. She, Sophia, and her family lived in San Diego or something like that."

"Sonia," my mom corrects, "her name was Sonia."

"Get your story straight, Detective Fernandez," Juliana smiles, "At least get her name right. I mean, come on, it was your one shot at true love."

My mom glances at me, *Detective Fernandez?* She just raises her eyebrows.

"He liked Marilyn Manson too," my mom continues, "He wore black all the time. He wrote poetry. He was a sensitive person. He loved Alice in Wonderland."

Juliana glances at my tattoo, Alice in Wonderland. She's putting pieces of truth together. I can't remember the last time we, my mom and I, talked about Eric. Not like this. This hurts differently. These are good memories of him. I miss Eric, we both do.

"Daniel hated Alice in Wonderland," my mom tells her, refilling her coffee mug. "He was afraid of Tweedle Dee and Tweedle Dumb as a kid."

"I wasn't scared." I shudder at the thought of those two creepy ass things, "They were just spooky."

"Eric would force him to watch it. He would pin him to the ground and sit on him, making him watch. And they would fight about that."

"Did they fight a lot, your boys?"

My mom looks at her, "Do you have siblings?"

"Not really." Juliana seems sad for a moment, then brushes it off. She kicks her shoe off, but only her left shoe. "My mom has daughters. They were born way later. We're not sisters."

"Well," my mom gives a deep, happy sigh, "Mine fought all the time, always two against one, never the same two, but always fighting. But don't mess with one, then the three would gang up and defend each other. My boys took care of each other."

"They sound happy." Juliana wrestles with her left sock and then slips her shoe back on. "Like a mad tea party."

"It was the best time. It's too quiet now." My mom leans back in her seat, looking around her small living room that was once filled with wild boys, "Well, now Daniel has a few Alice in Wonderland tattoos too."

"For Eric," Juliana asks, looking at my tattoo. She moves like she wants to take my arm in her hand and study me as she did on Halloween. She doesn't. She is aware that my mom is watching her. It's of the Mad Hatter's top hat and the phrase, "We're all mad here."

I nod, but can't look at her. I fucking miss Eric.

"Who liked Star Wars? Daniel or Eric or Juan Carlos," Juliana asks my mom.

"That's a tough one. I think they were about 50/50. All three of them fought over who could be Luke or Darth Vader, depending if they wanted to be good guys or bad guys."

"They made me be R2," I say to her.

"Beep beep." She laughs. "Does Juan Carlos have tattoos too?"

"You might have liked Eric, he and Daniel were very similar. Juan Carlos, you might be afraid of," my mom tells her, fishing a picture out of the arranged frames on the side table near her, "Here, that's Juan Carlos. He's not mean. He's not nice. He was the most difficult, still is the most difficult."

Juliana studies the picture. I know which one she gave her. Juan Carlos is at least 6"3' and 250 pounds. He's a fucking beast. He is mean. The picture is of him and my mom at the prison visiting area. I think I took it last Mother's Day. My mom still has pictures printed and puts them into frames, even if she has several digital frames.

"He would rather let you think he's mean than let you know he's funny. He was always in trouble. Juan Carols is not a bad person."

"Sometimes people play a part to hide themselves away," Juliana says. "Like a movie."

"What about you? Tell me about you." My mom looks at her, "Do you have a favorite movie?"

"Favorite movie? I guess Pretty in Pink," Juliana tells her, "Do you know that movie? It's old, really old."

"The girl is that 80's girl," my mom answers, "Molly something. She makes dresses."

"That's my favorite, when the guy sings, Jon Cryer, he comes in and makes a fool of himself for the girl. I love that part, but the ending is wrong. She picked the wrong guy. She should have picked Jon Cryer."

"He was a nerdy boy."

"He was nice. I don't know why the movie ends like that. Normally, I just watch the song part and that's it."

My mom asks her, "What's your favorite song?"

"That's too hard to answer. I love music. I can't live without music."

"She likes the 2 Live Crew, mom." I need to mess with her. This is too weird for me. It's nice, but it hurts. I miss my brothers. I miss my family, what we used to be.

"The 2 Live Crew," my mom stops, thinking, trying to place the group.

"You know, the song Juan Carlos got grounded for having. You broke the CD. That song."

"Stop, I remember now," she looks at Juliana, "You like that song?"

"No, I don't. I just know the song," she says, blushing again. "I have a bad habit of remembering all the lyrics of songs I hate, including that one. I don't like rap."

"Lies," I tease.

"Maybe," she giggles. She bites her bottom lip and leans against her leg. "Okay, maybe I like some rap but only old rap. I only like E-40."

"Juan Carlos likes all that rap stuff," she says to her. "But I'll tell you this, Juan Carlos is not a bad person. He's still my baby boy who likes LEGO."

"Juan Carlos was born angry," I explain, "He's five years older than me. He should have been an only child."

"I'm an only child, it kind of sucks."

"Be nice Daniel, he made a lot of mistakes, but he is still my baby boy, just like you. They made him sound like, like, I don't know, like he was evil. He just made mistakes."

"Cops suck."

"*Mija*, you know my son's a cop right?" My mom teases.

"I'm just messing with him. I like messing with him," Juliana smiles, just a hint of a smirk. "Which one is your favorite?"

"Daniel is my favorite kid," she teases, "He knows it. He's my baby."

"Out of your kids, I think I like him best too," Juliana laughs, "Oh, sorry, that doesn't…"

"Just stop now." It's funny when she says stuff that she doesn't mean to say. I think she means it but doesn't mean to say it. I playfully lean against her, "I know I'm your favorite. It's okay, you can admit it now."

"You need to stop it," she blushed again. She avoids looking up at my mom.

My mom stops and studies her, "You don't think Daniel has too many tattoos?"

"No," Juliana says to her, avoiding eye contact but trying to be polite. "It's a good look for some people. It makes him, him. I like him like that."

My heart skips a fucking beat, what the fuck? I like hearing her say she likes me. Fuck, what is wrong with me? Am I in middle school? I'm positive I'm blushing now. Get it together.

"It's an addiction," my mom tells me. She doesn't approve of the tattoos but we avoid the topic usually. We avoid a lot of things I'm beginning to realize. "I saw a show on TLC once."

"There are worse addictions," she tells my mom, glancing at me. She toys with the black bands on her wrist. "He could be an alcoholic or something. Tattoos are not that bad."

"Do you have tattoos?"

"No, my dad, my real dad, he would kill me."

"Who's your real dad?"

"My neighbor, Quinn, I call him dad. He's known me since I was 18. A few years ago, I got sick, really sick. Quinn, him and his partner, Aaron, had to sign forms for me. I had to give them power of attorney for me for a little bit. They helped me get well."

"*Ay mija*, what did you have?"

"I just got sick." Juliana bites her nail. "It wasn't a big deal really. I'm better now."

5150, I want to know what happened. She hasn't trusted me with that. I haven't earned her trust. What the hell is wrong with me? I'm fucking this up, all of it. I told Matt, all of them. Fuck, I wish I could take that back.

"Your mom, she didn't help you?"

My mother needed me to leave. I want to protect Juliana. I need to protect her. I need to stop my mom from asking her questions about that. "She makes wedding cakes."

"Wedding cakes," my mom asks, "That's what you do?"

"Yes, I'm good at making cakes. I don't have a lot of talent. I'm kind of useless."

"You're not useless."

Juliana looks at me and then at her nails. I think she wants to bite her nails but she's trying not to.

My mom studies Juliana and makes judgments. My mom gives me a genuine smile. Something about Juliana, she likes her already. That thought makes me nervous. "You look like you would make beautiful babies. Do you want kids, Juliana? Do you want to get married one day?"

Juliana blushes again, that pretty pink flushed look she had last night, "I want to be married, have a happily ever after, you know, all the things."

"Would you leave her alone? No wonder I don't bring anyone over here to meet you."

"Are you dating my son?" She leans closer, watching Julian's response.

"No." Biting her bottom lip, she glances at me nervously, "We're just friends. Sort of friends, we just met."

I don't normally bring women home. I know my mom has no chill. She's nosy, bossy, and overprotective. It doesn't matter to her that I'm an adult, to her, I'm always her baby. Just great, maybe this wasn't a good idea.

"Are those more of your family pictures?" Juliana walks over to the walls. She's looking over all our family pictures.

"That's Daniel's father." My mom follows her, pointing out one of the pictures, "I miss him. He passed away about five years ago. He was sick for a long time. It hasn't been easy."

"I'm sorry." Juliana leans toward my mom and hugs her.

My mom is a good foot shorter than Juliana. She squeezes her and starts sobbing. Juliana only rocks her slightly, holding her, letting her cry. She's singing something so low I can't make out what she is saying. I know she struggles with something.

I've put her into a situation she doesn't need to be in. I don't know what kind of pain Juliana carries, except that it's there. Now she is taking care of my mom? What the fuck am I doing? My mom is still sniffing, obviously trying to stop herself from crying.

"*Ay mija*, I am so sorry. I'm not normally like this." My mom moves, taking a box of tissue off the table, and wiping her eyes. She offers the box to Juliana.

"I don't judge other people," Juliana tells her, wiping tears from her own eyes. She takes a shaky breath, "I have no idea how deep your grief is. I am the last person on earth who would judge you. I have no right to judge you."

Juliana stops and looks at me. "I don't judge you either. I have no right to judge anyone. I understand grief, and trauma, even if it's not the same kind."

Juliana steps closer to me and whispers, "I see you, Daniel."

I stare at her, this beautiful woman who looks at me in a way I don't deserve. I lose my thoughts for a moment. I believe her. She does see what I hide. She doesn't need me to explain it to her. She just trusts that's it there.

That's what she needs from me. That's what she needs from everyone around her, someone to just believe her. Trust, just blind trust that it's there, her pain is real, to honor it, even if I don't know why. She needs me to believe her. "Do you?"

My mom pretends to not notice me pulling her closer and kissing her hand. She stays busy and wanders just out of the room where I can't see her. I know she's not far and nosy AF but she's giving us some privacy. I'd rather kiss Juliana like I mean it, pull her close and hold her tight, but Latino moms are not cool with public displays of affection, especially my mom.

"I see you too. I see you."

Juliana blinks back tears. The pain she hides is right there at the surface. She takes a deep breath, still aware my mom is watching, "Which one is your favorite picture?"

"This is my favorite picture of them." My mom shows her an old picture of us when we were younger. I'm sure I'm about seven in the picture. Nice move mom.

Eric and Juan Carlos are there, and so is my dad. It was a lifetime ago, back when we were a family. My father was a stoic, traditional Mexican American man. My mother seems so much younger then. She didn't have the burdens of having buried a son, a husband, and a son who is still alive but locked in a cage. The weight of those battles is evident within her, I don't even want to imagine what my being a cop is doing to her. She worries for me too.

"That's his father. He was such a good man," My mom sounds misty.

"How did you meet him?"

"Well, back in the old days there used to be a dance hall called the Rainbow Ballroom. They used to have dances there on the weekends. They had a huge break dancing, freestyle music dance one night and that is where I met him. I lied and said my name was Fabiola. Turned out he lived around the corner from my family and he knew who I was."

"You know, I've heard stories about the Rainbow Ballroom," she tells her, "It was supposed to be haunted."

"Haunted?"

"Yes, the story I was told was about a girl who went out of her house to go to a dance that her mother told her not to go to. She didn't listen and went anyway. At the dance, she meets the man of her dreams. He's handsome, he's charming, and he knows how to dance. She's dancing with him and she looks down and he has cloven feet. He's the devil. He vanishes. The girl runs away and gets hit by a car. The end. That's what my mother told me, never sneak out of the house or something bad would happen. I'm not good at telling stories. I think my mother just used that story to try to scare me not to sneak out."

"Did you sneak out a lot?"

Juliana laughs, "Not really. I mean, I did but I just went to my friend's house down the street. I didn't sneak out to go to a party or anything like that. I wasn't a bad kid."

"You don't talk now?"

"No. We just don't." Juliana looks out the window for a second, watching a car drive by slowly. "A very long time ago I had this not-great boyfriend. He wasn't even a boyfriend really, but he noticed how much guilt my mother would lay on me. If he, this guy, could see it, I knew I wasn't imagining it anymore. After that, I just stopped trying. She stopped too."

"You don't miss her?"

"I used to but when I talked to someone, a friend I really trust, she helped me realize I didn't miss her, I missed the idea of what I wanted her to be. After that, I just let her go."

"Now you're alone."

"Alone is better than in pain. I mean, it's hard to explain," Juliana sits up, looking nervous, "It doesn't make much sense. I know where I am and where I'm going, I just don't know how to get there. That's where I am right now, just trying to figure out how to get to happily ever after."

"Listen *mija*, the problem is you're trying to do this, life, alone. You need a partner. That's what you need." My mom legit glares at me, "What are you waiting for? I like her a lot better than the other one you brought home, Daniel. Grandchildren, I'm tired of waiting."

My mom has no chill.

"What do you need now?" My mom questions her, "What do you want next?"

Juliana looks at me, "You know what I want? I want a chocolate

milkshake."
 "*Ay dios mio*," my mom laughs, "Get her a milkshake."

JULIANA
December 14

It's so quiet out here. There are other people, but they're far away. There is a large funeral with a mariachi band and everything over in the distance. When I was younger, I had visions of having a funeral like that. Not that I even understand Mexican music, but I like the tradition. I wish I had learned *Folklorico* dancing in high school. That wasn't an option in private school.

I can hear traffic outside on Belmont Avenue and the wind moving through the trees. It's a little further out of town, here, this cemetery. When I was younger, me and Gabriel would come out and study headstones for fun. Look at the dates; make-up stories about the people here. Now, cemeteries are not my thing. I came too close to being in one of these for real.

I made a fool of myself. His mom must think I'm crazy. I talk too much and say weird things. She loves him. Her whole vibe is overprotective mom. She wants the best for him. I have no idea why he brought me with him, but it's nice.

"My dad died of cancer a few years ago. My mom, she's intense, but she's had so much go wrong for her."

Daniel's a good son. It's stupid, but it makes me happy that I've slept with him. No matter how badly this ends, he's worth it. It is worth it even if this is only for five minutes and totally pretending. My value increases because he's a good person.

"Life isn't fair, is it? I'm sorry."

He's quiet for a few minutes. "At least I have you to play Fortnite with."

"Is that what we're calling it? Fortnite?"

"That's a pretty G-rated thing to call it," he says, with a laugh, "Since it's nowhere near G-rated."

"Good for you, I love playing Fortnite." Sitting on the concrete benches, just the memories of how he made me feel last night make my heart thump. He was so good, my thighs are still quivering. I have to force the images of him naked out of my brain. "What was your dad like?"

Daniel sits with me, taking my pointer finger, my hand in his, and making circles on the tip of it. He likes holding my hand. He's always doing things like that. "Well, he was like most dads I guess. He was a cop too."

"Oh." My heart starts to thump harder in my chest. He's told me that before. I don't want to know. Just his tone, I know what he's going to say.

"They knew each other," he quietly says.

"Oh." It's there again, that empty feeling. This is not the shit I want to hear. How could my father just not want me? Why do I care so much about that? I shouldn't care like this anymore. Every time I think I'm over it, it comes back.

"I wish I could say something to you, I don't know, to make it better."

"It's not your responsibility to fix this. Everything is fine. I'm fine." I don't want to feel this right now. I can stuff these unwanted feelings into a box in the back of my mind, boxes on top of boxes. When I stay on top of my emotions, I can control them. "What was your dad like with you?"

"He was funny. A little bossy, kind of old-fashioned. He was a traditional Mexican American dad. He was strict and a total pushover. He danced with my mom in the kitchen, they had that kind of love."

"Helplessly in love? Is that what you want?"

"Not really. I don't know what I want. What do you want?"

"It doesn't matter what I want, Detective Fernandez. I have learned what I want is not what I'll get. I'm just here now. That's all that matters." I want this to be real, for him to want me, for him to pick me. "How did he handle your brother, Juan Carlos? That whole situation?"

"He was already sick and couldn't take up the energy to deal with that. It wasn't good."

"Why did he do it? Or are you not supposed to ask?"

Daniel thinks about it before giving me an answer, "He made a stupid mistake. That's all. That's what happened. He got caught up with the wrong people. He's not a bad person."

"People like to judge others."

"You don't."

"Because people like to judge me." Pulling my hand free, my body is electric right now, not a good electric. My heart is thumping too fast. Focus on not getting upset, and deep breaths. Please don't let it happen right now. Please don't, just breathe, and control. Just stay in control. "You're either judging or being judged."

"What am I?"

"You know, Detective Fernandez, I'm not sure." I'm positive he's a nice guy. Why is he with me, right at this moment? Why did he introduce me to his mom? "I've been trying to figure you out. I'm not sure what you are. Honestly, you're dangerous."

He smiles, that cute little dimple again, "Why do you say that? You keep telling me that. I won't purposely hurt you, you know."

"You're not dangerous because you're violent. You're dangerous because you…" And I stop talking. What I want to say is not what I should say. I want this to be real I'm not stupid enough to believe it is. This is just a hookup. He's a nice guy. He's not going to just walk away. Most likely, he'll move on in a few weeks. I'll be alone.

"I what?"

"You…" Then I jump onto the bench. Right at the edge of the grass, just next to the concrete, is a fat, moist, red earthworm. I hate worms with a freaking passion. I grab onto his arm and squeeze my eyes shut. A paranoid feeling of worms crawling in me takes over. Squishy, slimy bodies sticking to my skin. I know they're all over me. I can't make it stop, images of worms are all over me. "Oh my god, there is a freaking worm."

DANIEL
December 14

Juliana's afraid of worms? She is paranoid that something is crawling up on her Converse. She's fidgety, even though she's huddled next to me on the bench and grabbing into my arm. Her fingers are digging into me. She's scooting to me as close as possible.

Sensory input, she needs to feel safe. She's panicking.

"I'll protect you from the worms, baby girl." Nudging it with my toe, I knock it back into the grass. She's so afraid she's shaking. I've never seen anyone respond to a worm like this. Her reaction is inappropriately overboard, but it's one hundred percent real. She's terrified.

"There is nothing there," I say to her, double-checking her shoes. She's checking as if some random worm made its way onto her feet. She's panicked and swatting at invisible worms. "It's not on you."

Juliana looks as if she is about to cry. Tears flood her eyes, and she's turning a shade of red. That level of terror still has her.

"Listen to me, there is nothing there," I tell her, looking at her one more time. There is nothing on her shoes. "I'm looking, there is nothing there."

"Okay, okay, okay, okay, I'm okay, okay okay," she whispers to herself, pulling into a tight ball. "I'm fine, I'm fine."

She covers her head with her arms. I can't tell if she's crying or not.

"You're okay, there is nothing there. I'm double-checking." I rest my hand against her shoe. Then move my hand to her ankle, squeezing her. "There is nothing there."

She rocks slowly, calming down. She takes a breath, accepting that nothing is crawling on her. She needs a distraction.

"Tell me about your friend Gabriel. Who is he? Where is he now?"

"Gabriel? We grew up next to each other."

"Did you date him?" I hope I don't sound jealous. I'm totally jealous.

"No, he's gay." She gives a tired laugh, still glancing around for a worm, "I didn't tell you that? He has a partner. They have two kids."

"You only took the picture away. I didn't know he was gay."

Looking around the spot where she's sitting, she must be hunting for worms. "He lived a few houses down from my house. Our moms were friends. He is one of five brothers."

"When did he move? He lives in DC now right?"

She checks the floor again, no worms. "He moved about 6 years ago. He used to be my roommate. When he left, I just stayed there by myself. Aaron, AA-Ron, he owns it."

"AA-Ron, the guy from the coffee shop?"

"He's my protector, my dad. I'm always in his way. I get on his every last nerve."

Aaron Johnston? Roommate? I can't ask her a question I'm not even supposed to have. I really shouldn't know that information.

"Aaron and his partner live in the front of the duplex. They own the coffee shop. I'm a poser who pretends to be their daughter."

"He seems to care about you."

"He does. Gabe moved out of his house right after high school. As soon as I turned 18, I moved in with him. Aaron must have felt sorry for us. He never raised the rent. We were lousy tenants at first, noisy."

"Big parties?"

"Something like that. We were young and dumb, really dumb," she moves from me, checks the ground for a worm one more time, and sets her feet back down. "It's weird to say, but if it weren't for Gabriel, I'd be dead. If he hadn't left, I'd also be dead. We're better apart. I miss him, his kids."

"Do you want kids? In your grand life plan, do you want kids?" I kind of nudged her, "I know we joke around, but I am asking you for real."

"Well, like I said, what I want, Detective Fernandez, never happens. I have stopped wanting anything. I don't even have a life plan."

"If you could have anything, what would you wish for?"

"A different life," she says without hesitation, "That's what I would wish for. I'd be someone, anyone, just not me."

"But then I wouldn't get to play Fortnite with you." I notice my mom walking back so I kiss the top of her head.

She eyes me shyly. "Look at you all emo now, making out in a cemetery. Next thing you know, you'll be wearing a black suit and red tie, maybe eyeliner. That would be so hot."

JULIANA
December 14

Text from an unknown number: Fortnite?

I'm pretty sure it's Daniel, so I sent him my gamer tag, ChocolateJedi_anailuj.28. I'm not sure who gave him my number. I didn't but who else knows about my Fortnite obsession?

Fucking cops, or fucking sister-in-law. I'll bet it was her. Echo's playing matchmaker here.

I exit my game, returning to the starting point, the lobby. It gives me a chance to refill my bowl of potato chips. I'm starving. I have no energy to make food. I'd rather just eat junk food. Just a few minutes later, a yellow invite pops up on my screen, streamer_559.

Grabbing my wireless headphones, "Where we droppin'?"

I love this stupid game. It's fast-paced and challenging. There are multiple objectives and one goal. Keeps my ADHD brain entertained during some of my more challenging times. It's a good distraction for me. I can play all day and never get bored of it.

"What the hell is anailuj," Daniel questions me. "What kind of name is that?"

"Hey, that's my name backward." Grabbing the closest throw, I warm up on the couch. It's pouring rain outside. It's cold. It's nice to hear the sound of the rain against the roof. These old duplexes are drafty even with the heat on. I blame it on the old windows.

"Your name, oh now I see it."

"I thought you were a cop." I snort, "Really? You couldn't figure that out? My name is Ana-il-uj, pronounced like 'analyze you."

"Got it."

His game skin is of a bright pink bear with a heart on her chest. I hate that skin. I always have bad luck when I'm paired with someone in that skin. One of the fun parts of Fortnite is all the different types of skins you can choose from. Mine is a ninja with leggings. Nice.

"Listen, I don't know about you, but I take my gaming seriously. Change your skin, your character. I can't be in a duo team with that damn bunny, bear costume. I cannot, Detective Fernandez."

"You're not a newbie are you Juliana?" He teases, "I can't be saving you if you get shot."

"Dude, you have no idea how good I am at this game." I have to adjust myself on the couch and focus. I need my energy for this game. I really could use a cup of coffee but I don't feel like brewing one.

"I'll bet you have a lot of hidden talents."

"Not really, I'm a dork who bakes." Tipping my bowl, chips go everywhere, all over my coffee table, great. "I can sing every dirty rap song from the '80s and that's about it."

"That's talent."

"That's the extent of my talent." Picking up my phone, I saved his number under Detective Fernandez while waiting for the game to start. I have a silly rule of saving everyone's name under their legal name, like Esperanza Lopez or Gabriel Sanchez, not Echo or Gabe. It has to be their whole name, but Daniel Fernandez isn't as fun to say as Detective Fernandez. I like the way that sounds, *Detective Fernandez*. I'll save him under that.

Text to Esperanza: Did you give Daniel my number?

Esperanza: Yes, he asked.

Esperanza: Sooo…

Me: I'll text you later-talking to him.

Esperanza: Cool

"If you didn't become a cop, what do you think you would be doing instead?" Moving to the floor, I'm still going to eat these spilled chips, who cares? My coffee table is clean.

He starts laughing, "A teacher."

"Stop." Please tell me he's kidding.

"I'm serious. I thought about it, but I didn't want to get a credential. That's too much school. I'd rather be a cop."

"You're just messing with me, I know it."

"That's my story and I'm sticking to it. Before baking, what did you do? Or were you always working there?"

"I used to manage a shower gel store. I worked in the mall." I don't want to admit what a hot mess I used to be. I hate this part, the whole, get to know each other, part. I say stupid shit. "I used to buy Prada shoes and always had a Dooney & Bourke bag."

"Damn."

"I wasted a lot of money on clothing and shoes. I used to be high maintenance." I miss it and I don't. I lived a fake life, pretending to be an adult. "It's sad to think about it now. It's kind of embarrassing. I was all about the look. When I got to 30, 32, I decided I was done with all of that. I sold it all at some consignment shop. Now I look homeless."

"I never said you looked homeless. I just felt so defensive, you made me feel defensive. I just asked if you had a job. That doesn't mean homeless."

"I was a mess." Looking back, it's a good thing I did it. I called Matt and now we are friends. It's nice.

"No, you weren't. I would have gone home with you that day if you had asked me."

"Liar." Why does this man make my heart race? He gives me that warm feeling inside. I've got a goofy smile. I like this one.

"I should have ordered the Juliana Special. Someone is shooting at me."

"Oh my god, don't say that. I'm going to kill AA-Ron. Drop a pin. I can't see where your player is."

"Aaron means well. He says dumb stuff too. That's why we're friends." Locating his pin, the player shooting at him is now dead. Take that Anonymous_3310. "You seem to have a Jordan's obsession."

"You noticed that?"

"What's your guilty pleasure?" It's easier to talk to him like this, without having to sit near him. It's less like a date. I hate dates.

"Gaming. Lego."

"Give me a break. Gaming? Lego? Dude, are you a nerd?"

"Maybe, just a little bit. What do you do when you're not gaming? Not baking? Do you have a guilty pleasure?"

"You don't know anything about me, Detective Fernandez. Let's see, I watch every action movie at the movie theater. I read tons of books, but I don't order them online. I need to go to a real bookstore. I'm damn good at Fortnite." Glancing at the stats on the screen, we're in the top 10 players. "Focus, we could win."

"Action movies huh? Which is your favorite?"

I cannot say Star Wars. He has a freaking Star Wars tattoo, several of them, anything but Star Wars. Damn it, my gamer tag says Jedi. "Jurassic Park."

"That's not an action movie."

"Chris Pratt. Is that better?" I got shot. Damn it. He must get shot too because it's game over. The screen blinks to the waiting screen. New game, a new bus, new people. "Not those space movies he did. No, I cannot with space."

"So you don't like Star Wars? You have Jedi in your gamer tag."

"I do, just not other space movies. Anything that happens in space is a hard no. I got claustrophobic watching that one movie where that woman was stuck in space. No lost in the ocean movies either. No more space, no ocean movies. You seem to like Star Wars."

"Come on, Princess Leia, that's all you need to know. I have a framed poster of her in my room. It's one of those political poster types, not like a picture. It says 'REBEL.'"

He's a total child. I know what he's talking about. Maybe I'm not picturing the same one. There are tons of those. I've seen those on Pinterest and Etsy. I almost ordered one, now I'm glad I didn't.

"Is she your favorite?"

"Is Chris Pratt your favorite?"

"I asked you first. He's not. My favorite celebrity crush is not Chris Pratt, it's Stephen Curry."

"I thought you didn't like basketball."

"I don't but you can admit that Stephen Curry is a beautiful man."

"Stephen Curry is like 6'2". He's tall. Do you normally date tall men?"

I wonder if it bothers him. I'm maybe an inch, maybe two inches shorter than him. I'm not about to admit I normally go out with taller men. Shit, Christian is hella tall too. Hell no. I like this one. "Who's your ultimate celebrity crush?"

"Keira Knightly, Padme Amidala."

"Darth Vader's mom?" Oh my god, he's such a nerd. I love that. Between his tattoos, glasses, and nerdiness. He's perfect. That's scary.

"I might be a little bit of an obsessive Star Wars fan."

"Oh my god, are you one of those guys with all the Star Wars stuff in your house? Like a shrine?" I can totally picture it.

"Only the Lego sets. And the Funko Pop stuff. I have a hard limit."

"That's your limit? Lego and Funko Pop? They never stop making new stuff. Do you have a lightsaber? A Jedi cape?"

"Only three lightsabers and only one cape."

He's so nerdy it's cute. "For real?"

"Hey, someone is shooting at you."

I'm laughing so hard, I'm tearing up and I can't see where the bullets are coming from on the screen. I'm about to die but I don't care. I can picture him in a brown Jedi cape, with a lightsaber. And glasses, don't forget the glasses. "You're totally a nerd aren't you?"

"You're dying, do you need help?'

"I don't need your help." But he's right, my player is dead.

"Do you ever need anyone's help?"

"No. Well, maybe, I have the sex drive of a 19-year-old guy, so I need some help."

"Damn baby girl, are you sure you want to play Fortnite?"

"Fuck it, come over right now. And bring your Jedi cape."

DANIEL
December 15

Mom: I like her.
Mom: Ms. Too Many Boyfriends.
Me: Me too.
Mom: I know.
Mom: You should bring her to Lily's wedding.
Me: I'll think about it.

I don't know what to do with all of this. I spent my 20's like everyone else, meeting people, and dating. When my family fell apart, I turned my energy to that.

I don't know what is supposed to happen next. Normally I'd ask her out but she beat me to that. She asked me to go home with her. I did. I don't regret it, but what's next? I feel like I've missed a step.

******

"Put orange flowers in it," I say to the florist on the phone. Matt keeps walking to his desk with paper files. Of course, he picks today to catch up on paperwork. All morning he was off talking to everyone in the office. He picks the one time I'm trying to be sneaky to start hanging around.

The police department is nothing like the action TV shows. They're not real offices with windows. In reality, they're cramped cubicles with a ton of people wandering around. They're noisy, busy spaces.

Matt is rushing around trying to work. His excuse is that now that the baby is here, he needs to take time off next month. Echo's mom is helping at home for a while, but she leaves next month on a trip. He's touching things and starting one project, then abandoning it for another. I wonder if he has ADHD like Juliana. I never noticed it before. She's always moving around, touching things, and then stopping. Next level, stalker status, that's me alright.

We have to have a conversation. It's strange for sure. I'm his best friend, we're partners. I went home with his sister. It's not just a hookup. This might mean something more.

Zoey, dispatch chick, walks over with another stack of papers. She keeps stopping next to my cubicle to ask stupid questions, like where's the paper shredder? What the fuck? She has zero reasons to ask me for shit. I need to make sure I'm clear with her. She is not the one I want. I hold up a finger and gesture toward the phone.

Zoey leans against the cubicle, watching me while I'm on the phone. She's got that confused expression on her face. What the hell?

"What do you want the card to say?"

What would make her smile? "Just write Fortnite, question mark, and sign it streamer 559."

"Orange flowers, right?"

"Yes, orange flowers, lots of orange and yellow." Hanging up, Zoey gives me her helpless look, like she's lost. That would have caught my attention in the past, but not anymore. I want someone who will glare at me, give me a smart-ass comment, and then take me home and fuck the shit out of me. That's what I want, a woman who knows how to bake.

Juliana called Zoey a coupon. She was jealous of her. It's taken me this long to realize that. That's why she made Zoey look dumb and shallow.

Juliana's right. It's not a nice thing to think, but she's right. Zoey is all makeup and glitter. She's pretending.

"Are you sending someone flowers?" She uses her sing-song voice, batting her eyelashes. "Is she special?"

Matt stops, looking from Zoey to me. He gives her a "what the fuck," look. I'm sure he wants to know what is going on with Zoey. He doesn't give Zoey a nice look. He makes the same expression Juliana does, flat, unbothered, maybe a hint of "I'm better than you." While glaring at her, he asks, "Who are you sending flowers to?"

"My mom," I lied. This is too strange for me.

He shrugs and looks through his stack of files. He leaves with half of them. He's been avoiding conversations with me all morning. That I can understand. I don't have a sister. I can't imagine having to come to work and deal with that. It's awkward for me, so I can't imagine what it feels like on his end.

"That's so sweet, "she is all gushy, looking at her manicured fingernails, a flash of bright blue. Zoey has on a matching blue mini-dress. It's freaking 43 degrees outside, and she's wearing a summer dress. "You must be a good son."

Damn, I need to get rid of her. A few weeks ago, she was interesting to me. I was thinking of asking her out. All I can think of now is this beautiful woman who called me dangerous.

"Can you keep a secret?" Looking around, the office is busy today. No one wants to rush out and be in the cold.

"Yes," she leans closer. She's wearing some strong floral perfume. Juliana always smells like vanilla. She's always got a hint of vanilla clinging to her skin. She's perfect.

"It's Matt's sister." I don't want to lead Zoey on. I don't want her to think we might go out. I'm a lot of things, but I'm not purposely mean. We had a thing, and we did flirt a lot, but now I'm moving on. I found the one girl I want. "I'm sending flowers to his sister."

"Oh," her eyes grow wider, slowly figuring it out, "The girl from the party? The cake girl?"

I wink at her and she blushes. "She's beautiful. You know how Matt is."

"Yeah, cool, I won't tell him." She glances around the office, sighing, "That's so sweet of you, sending her flowers. I wish someone would send me flowers. Is it serious?"

"It's too soon to tell. You know? We just started going out." Damn right, it's serious. I know, I'm way ahead of myself, but it feels different for sure. Something about being with Juliana feels like forever.

"How long have you known her? You and Matt have been partners for a long time."

"I just met her. I didn't know her before. She kind of kept to herself, they have different moms."

"Oh, that makes sense. Well, she's really pretty."

"It's more than that though, she's funny. She's smart. Something is different."

"Well, good luck and invite me to your wedding." She swats me with her stack of paper and drifts off.

I am a total jerk, but I need to be honest with her. She's not what I want out of life anymore. There's a girl out there who wore a private school uniform that might need me. She called me dangerous.

DANIEL
December 15

    Watching the scene kid, I lean back in my seat. I'm the good cop. He needs a good cop. This one is mine. It's a weird cop thing, but you can get a feeling of who will talk to whom. His faded black hoodie is pulled over his head. His vivid purple hair hangs down, covering most of his face. He hasn't said much. He's humiliated. All those pictures are out there and shared among who knows how many kids. It only takes seconds for thousands of kids to get a text. Kids can be mean.

    If we get a call from any high school, it's always difficult, because teenage drama is raw and uncontrollable. All the rage, hormones, the social media shit, the moodiness. These are my least favorite calls. Now, the last person I want to see is Chris Garcia, the principal of Monte Vista High.

    That's how we know each other. I'm not his friend like Matt is. He calls us, we come here. Luckily, it's normally not this intense. Chris is not my concern right now. This is work. I have to force all the weird crap with Juliana back and do my job. Who violated this kid's trust?

    This kid is quiet. His black hoodie is his shield. He has his beat-up Converse up on his chair. His mom is bouncing her leg up and down and holding balled-up tissue in her hand. She is not making eye contact with anyone in the room. She's angry, disappointed, and hurt. She seems like she is lost too. Single parent? There is no dad here.

    In these situations, we try to stay on campus so the kids don't feel like we're hauling them off to jail. We all sit inside Chris's office. Just great, the principal's office, even now, sometimes, it's like I'm in trouble sitting here.

    I hate these kinds of cases, sexting, kids, and then the rumors. Then it turns out an adult is involved, and now the cops are involved.

"You know, my girlfriend likes all that emo crap. She wears all black and listens to strange music." Leaning forward, I got to get him to trust me. "She wears black, and carries a back umbrella."

Sometimes, a lot of the time, we make up stories that sound true to get people to open up. Sometimes people need quiet to talk. Sometimes they need stories that sound like their lives to talk about. He needs a story. "She makes black wedding cakes."

"She's your girlfriend now?" Matt huffs, "Shut up."

"Really? We're still doing that?"

The kid looks between us, his first glance up at us since we arrived.

"It's his sister," I gesture at Matt. The kid is watching me. "He's mad I'm dating his sister. Ignore him."

"His sister? Seriously?" He hasn't said much to any of us since we got here. He's scared, but he's interested in what I'm saying. I guess it takes his mind off his problems.

"Yeah, she drives me nuts with all that music," I keep talking. I have to get him to trust me. He needs to tell me who the adult in the pictures is. If it takes me telling a story that sounds like hers, fuck it. I'll sort that all out with Matt later. "It's nothing but yelling, or all this feeling sorry for me, shit. I have no idea how she can stand it."

"What's her favorite song?" He says it is like a challenge, like a dare to prove I'm not BS'ing him. Since he is all of 15, it sounds flat. But he is finally looking up at me. He's finally talking to us.

"Her song? I don't know the name of it. It's old though, let me think, how does it go, oh wait, I have it on my phone."

Looking through my history, there is. After the Halloween party, I had to Google Helen. I wasn't sure what she was talking about that night. I didn't get the relationship between the phrase and an umbrella. Then I found that song. The kid leans over and looks at my screen. A band with fire and outrage fills the screen. He looks back and forth between me, and the screen. He's making judgments about me. He's trying to figure me out. He's trying to figure out if I'm lying to him or not. The trust is building. He can see it's in my history, not a new search.

"She has a crush on the lead singer." I don't even know if that's true. I'm just making up shit.

"He's old, he's like 40," the kid sneers.

"How old do you think I am? I'm 35, she's the same age. We're old, dude." I need a Coke or something, something to offer this kid. "Mr. Garcia, go get me a Coke."

Chris must have a mini fridge in his office. He hands me one pretty quickly. He offers one to everyone else. Quit faking it, Chris. I know you're not this nice. I push mine to the kid. He takes it from me, returning to his huddle on the chair.

"You know, something like this happened to her. Her stupid ass ex-boyfriend took pictures and showed his friends. She was embarrassed about it too. She felt like shit." The kid glances up when I say stupid ass and shit to him because, you know, I'm an adult. I'm old.

Chris moves behind me. Fuck him. I know I'm being an insensitive jerk right now. I have to help this kid. I keep talking low, trying to get the kid to trust me. "It must feel like the end of the world that it's happened to you. It's not your fault. That person violated your trust. That's the asshole in this case, not you. This isn't your fault."

He pulls back into himself and hunches over, hidden again behind his hair. I turn sideways in my chair, looking at the wall so the kid doesn't feel stared at, watching him in my peripheral view.

"For a long time, she blamed herself. She felt stupid for trusting him. At the time, she loved him. It hurt. It broke her heart." That's what she said, he broke her heart. Fuck, this is wrong. I am using her private story to get something I need from this kid. Yeah, it's to help him, but at what cost to her privacy? I can't do this again. "It hurts when people do this. You feel tricked."

His mom, the first time she makes eye contact with me, asks, "Is she okay now? Like, she's an adult now, right?"

"She grew up to be the most interesting woman I've ever met. I can't stop thinking about her." Matt gives me a dirty look. I'm digging a hole here. "She's perfect."

The kid's mom gives a sad smile. She must be so worried for her kid. Mean kids suck. Adults suck. Kids, you love them so much and would do anything to protect them, and then someone does this shit? I don't know how parents do it.

I want kids with Juliana. Shit. Focus.

"She did go to therapy." Matt turns to the kid's mom, "We know a social worker who can help you with that. My sister said that helped."

Juliana wouldn't want Matt to know this. I have to reevaluate myself later. Right now, I have to push forward. I already came this far, I need to keep going.

"She's brave, you know. She told me this whole story. You know how strong a person has to be to share such a private story? She didn't want to tell me, but there was this one day it was bothering her. She felt better once we talked about it."

The kid is watching me. He's almost there, almost. He keeps blinking back tears. Being a teenager sucks, not an adult and not really a child.

"Sometimes I think it bothers her that he never said sorry to her."

"Does she want him to say sorry?"

"That's a good question." I lean back from the kid. I don't know if Chris ever apologized to her. I doubt it. "I honestly don't know."

"You're not mad? Are you mad at her?"

"Well kid, like I said, I wasn't there," I turn back to him, lean forward like I'm telling him secrets. "It was a long time ago. It's not my place to have an opinion on it. I am not upset with her. I don't blame her. That's for sure. I do not blame her for one second. It wasn't her fault. This is not your fault. Someone violated your trust. They promised to keep your secret safe and they didn't. The problem here is that the person is an adult. You can help me. We can make sure it doesn't happen to anyone else."

He sits up, just enough to let me know. He's going to tell me.

"Are you ready to tell me who that is?"

He leans forward and tells us the whole story.

******

"You know, if your girlfriend, his sister," he sneers towards Matt, in that teenage angst tone, like we're cool buddies now and Matt is not, "likes that band, they're going on tour next year. Not here in Fresno but in LA."

"Thanks, kid, but do you think I could handle 90 minutes of that?" I exhale, and roll my eyes, keeping that level of trust going. All he can see is an adult with glasses wearing a suit.

He smiles, "If you like her, you will." This kid will be okay.

"I'll tell you a secret kid, I'm going to marry his sister."

Matt's contempt is obvious. He's so pissed off. "Shut up, Fernandez. No, you're not."

******

"Tell me we did the right thing," Matt says, popping his Coke can open. He doesn't sip it. He just holds it. "That's her personal shit."

I don't have an answer. I just crossed a line. Honestly, I keep crossing lines I shouldn't. I'm a stalker, I watch Juliana when she doesn't know it. I told Matt about the 5150. I got involved with her Chris drama. I just shared her shit with some kid and his mom. I need to get it under control. I don't know what's wrong with me.

"Anyone going to tell me how much of that story is true?" Matt drops himself into the chair at the desk. He's exhausted. He has kids, his daughter is moving to high school next year. These cases are real. This is tough. "Is this what happened the other day?"

"It's not my story to tell," I glared at Chris, daring him to tell Matt, "It's not my story to tell is it, Chris."

Chris looks out the window that overlooks the quad area. There are thousands of kids moving from one class to another. He's not a bad person. It kills me to think that, but it's true. He's good at his job. He runs the school well. The kids trust him and come to him when they have problems. He's even won some educator of the year thing.

"Fuck off, Fernandez."

"That's your answer? Cool." I'm moving all my crap together, all the evidence I need back into the folder I carried in. This office is too small to stay in here pretending to be fine. "Just stay the fuck away from her."

"Are you going to legit fight over my sister?" Matt puts his feet up on Chris's desk. He's leaning back in his seat and stares at the ceiling. He looks tired. "This is fucking weird. All of this, the kid, Juliana, you, him, it's so weird. I didn't have a sister 6 months ago. Now you guys are fighting over her."

"We're not fighting over her. We're fighting because of her." Chris turns to me, "There is a difference. Fernandez can keep her."

"Hey," Matt sits up, banging on the desk, pissed off. It must be a Lopez thing, "She's my sister. You can't just give her to Daniel. She's a fucking person."

No one says a word for a few minutes. I have nothing to add to this. Chris Garcia made a pervy video of Juliana and showed his friends. What a bitch.

Matt leans forward and rests his head in his hands. He starts laughing. "This is fucking weird. Can we hit pause and pretend we didn't hear that? I don't want to be an asshole, really, but I don't know what happened and I don't want to know."

"It was a long time ago," Chris tells him, ignoring me. "Remember when we worked at the park, day camp at Holmes Playground?"

Matt has known Chris longer than I have. Chris used to be a recreation department director, managing a summer day camp. Matt was doing some high school volunteer crap with him. They crossed paths again later when Chris became the principal of Monte Vista High School. They are friends, him and Matt. I only know Chris through Matt.

"I was always sunburned," Matt laughs.

"I quit later and went to work at the Vons across the street. That's when I met her. I worked at Vons."

"That's crazy, huh? My missing sister was across the street?"

"She didn't work there," Chris corrected, "I met her there. She didn't work there. I met her in the checkout line."

"Dude, you picked up Fernandez's girlfriend in line?" Matt laughs at his own joke.

"Shut up Matt," I say.

"Something like that. I was still in college when I met her. It was a really long time ago."

"Well, whatever you did, she is still pissed about it. Did you cheat on her or something? Make me feel better about all this."

"She cheated on me." Chris crosses his arms against his chest. He leans against the bookcase next to the door. "She got mad about something, something stupid. She cheated on me. I don't know why she's still mad about that. She cheated."

I don't look up from my work. She told me that. She told me he was cheating too and that he would make her the bad guy. The least he could have done is kept it private.

"It was over 10, 15 years ago. I didn't know she was your sister."

"She wasn't my sister then. Now Fernandez is hooking up with her."

"You said you weren't hooking up," Chris says to me.

I don't have a chance to tell him to fuck off.

"It's your fault, Chris," Matt tells him, "If you hadn't pissed her off."

"Shut up Matt," I tell him, throwing a file folder at him. "She'd be furious if she knew we were talking about her like this."

Matt sits back up in his seat, studying the both of us. "This is weird, right? This is like Twilight Zone weird, like her meeting your mom, weird."

"Wait," Chris stops and looks at me, glaring at me, "What the fuck? Your mom? What's going on Fernandez?"

I'm instantly defensive, "None of your fucking business."

"Get out Lopez," Chris orders him, standing up.

"No, you're going to say some messed up shit about her, aren't you? Fuck that, she's my sister. Don't talk shit about her. I'll kick your ass."

Chris smacks Matt's foot off his desk, "Get out."

"Fuck off Chris, whatever you want to tell me, it was 12 years ago. It doesn't matter now. Leave her alone. She's," I stop. I don't want to have this conversation. Fuck this shit. I'm not even in a relationship with her, and I'm making a huge ass mess. "She's none of your business."

Chris looks from me to Matt, shaking his head.

"Where was your dad, Matt?" Chris questions him, "Where was he in her life?"

"He's an asshole. I get that," Matt tells him, with a mightier-than-you tone. Matt will always defend his dad. He's the only one who can criticize him, not even Adam. "He fucked up."

"You have no idea," Chris tells him.

He knows. What she can't tell me, Chris knows. She might have told him, she said something about that once. Did she trust the wrong person? This is messed up, this whole situation would make her agitated, and panicked for sure. She would be irate if she suspected we were talking about her like this.

Matt stands up, suddenly defensive. "Why did she cheat on you? Did you love her? Did you treat her right?"

"No." Chris drops himself into one of the chairs in his office. "I was an asshole too, I treated her like shit."

They both look at me. "What? I'm not an asshole. I'm not going to hurt her."

Matt studies me, then points at me, "You sent her flowers, didn't you? That was for her."

"Matt, shut up." The last thing I want to do is discuss Juliana in front of Chris.

Chris watches my reaction, "Take care of her, Fernandez. Don't fuck around with her."

"Knock that shit off, Chris. My relationship is none of your fucking business." He humiliated her. I know that. She told me. Bitch.

"Dude," Matt glares at Chris, "Fuck off, that's what I'm supposed to say. I'm her brother. Daniel, you better not hurt her."

"We sound like a bunch of bitches talking about her like this," I say to them. "What the fuck is happening here?"

"Look, this whole thing is weird as fuck. Can we be cool? You cool? I'm cool," Matt says, "Daniel, are we cool?"

I'm the weak link here. They both know it. I don't want to fake it. Matt doesn't know Chris was the trigger for her panic attack. That was because of Chris, too. What would Matt think about that? Matt made a judgment about what it was. He thinks it was a picture. Chris videoed Juliana. Then he showed his friends. It's more than a picture.

Matt doesn't want to know. He doesn't need to know. I shouldn't have told him about the 5150. He doesn't get it. Matt's just like his dad, just ignore it, and it will go away.

"I'm cool." It kills me to say it, but Matt's right. We work together.

"She's not your girlfriend, right?" Matt watches my response. "I mean, that was for the kid, right?"

"No, it's not like that." This is so much bigger than I'm ready to admit. When I'm with her, I don't need to fill up the quiet with useless nonsense. She's my future, I can see that already. I like the way she feels underneath me. "Don't tell her I said I was going to marry her."

I've betrayed her.

JULIANA
December 15

Daniel sent me flowers.

I was busy, trying to get the last pieces of fondant into shape for a cake I'd been working on when the florist popped in. I thought it was a mistake. I insisted she had the wrong address until she said, "Fortnite."

The fucking card says Fortnite, with a question mark? What the hell? I don't know what this means. What does this mean?

No one has ever sent me flowers. Hell, no one has ever brought me flowers. My heart is pounding and my palms are damp. I'm hot. It's a strange feeling, normally I'm so cold. I'm not there, but he thought about me. Does it mean anything? Or is he just being nice?

They're beautiful colors, orange and yellow tinted roses with a pop of lavender. They feel like sunshine. They are a nice contrast to the foggy day outside, gray, and cold. Totally colors that remind me of him. His Jordan's were orange. I can't stop thinking about him. My fucking heart hurts, not in its beating too fast, kind of way, like a cramp. It's squeezing hard in my chest. Does Detective Fernandez care about me?

Daniel might not understand it, but he is dangerous. He makes me feel wanted. Okay, maybe that's too far. Maybe he likes me as a person. Even with all my drama? I want to share my soul with him. I want to tell him my secrets.

But I can't. My shit is real. He doesn't need me.

I stuff the card into the register and leave the flowers on the counter. I don't have the bandwidth to deal with it. What he doesn't know is that orange is my favorite color. There is no way he knows that. I don't advertise it. It's my little secret. I have nothing orange. Okay, I have a pair of orange Converse. I haven't worn them when I've been around him. I never wear those.

Orange.

Orange is my favorite color.

Text to Detective Fernandez: Thank you.

I should have sent a picture of the flowers, so he knows what I'm talking about. How many people could he have sent flowers to today?

I don't understand Detective Fernandez, I really don't. He is a nice guy. He has his act together. He can't really want to send me flowers, right? Why? What's in it for him? I already gave him everything. I wouldn't say no to him if he asked me again. He knows that. He's not stupid. Echo said he wanted to be the hero. Is this what the hero does? In real life, is this what nice men do?

Detective Fernandez: I'm thinking about you.

Me: Are you having dirty thoughts about me?

Detective Fernandez: Damn right

Me: Oh yeah? Are you going to tell me?

Detective Fernandez: I'm going to show you.

Stop.

This is not what I thought was going to happen. I wanted to get to know Matt and Adam. Daniel is like dessert. He's not what I planned for. He confuses me. Or rather, I am confused about him. I don't know what the fuck is happening. He's nice. He's like cake. He's like chocolate cake. He makes me nervous.

Daniel is dangerous.

Me: Well Detective Fernandez, maybe you should stop over at my place.

Detective Fernandez: How about 7? Are you good with that baby girl?

My fingers are shaky. I'm squishy inside. Shit. This is not what I planned. Daniel calls me baby girl. He didn't laugh at me when I lost my shit over a freaking worm. He sat there, held me, and helped me get through it. Who does that shit? He took me to meet his mom. He sent me flowers.

Daniel felt my panic. He stopped. He made sure I was okay. Who does that? Who notices that? Damn, he's not a loser. What the hell am I doing? I've already managed to fuck this up. I suck. He sent me flowers.

What is happening?
    Me: I'll see you at 7. Spend the night with me?
    Detective Fernandez: Okay. See you later.
    I'm making the biggest mess of my life. I have cakes to think about. No more thinking about sex with a hot cop.

JULIANA
December 18

The life of a baker consists of waking up at dark o'clock. I need to be in the building at 5 or so to open at 7. It sucks. The only nice part is that it's quiet outside. I have time to relax and be still with my thoughts.

It's a good time to text Echo.

Esperanza: What the fuck? I've waited five whole days. What happened?

Me: What are you talking about, the baby?

Esperanza: Daniel

I want to laugh, but I might wake him up. He's sound asleep. Not my normal course of action. I don't usually have men sleepover, but he practically lives here since the weekend. He might as well move in.

He's beautiful. It's silly, but he is a gorgeous man decorated in dark ink. It is so nice, especially on freezing nights, to have someone to snuggle up with. It's easy to pretend this can be forever.

Me: What about him?

Esperanza: poop emoji, eggplant emoji, poop emoji

Me: That doesn't sound good. Is the baby sick?

I have to not giggle at my joke. I'm not funny, but I think I'm funny. She doesn't mean the baby. At least her texts force me to get my butt out of bed and ready for work. I try not to wake him up when I leave the room.

Esperanza: Knock that shit off. You know what I mean. Did you fuck him?

Me: No. I FFFUUUUCCKKKKEEDDDD him.

Esperanza: LOL! How did you like his mom?

Daniel's mom, I haven't given her too much thought. I'm always stuck in my doom and gloom. She was nice. I don't want to tell Echo about the conversations about his family. That is too private.

Me: He told you?

Esperanza: He told Matt, the same thing.

I have to keep that in mind as we move forward. If she's going to be my friend, I have to remember anything I tell her, she'll tell Matt. They're that kind of couple.

Esperanza: I won't tell him how many letters you used. LMFAO

Esperanza: It's not like I'm going to tell him "she said fffuuuccckkkeedd him," I'll translate that to, they hung out. She likes him. Matt doesn't want to know. He's freaked out about it. I want to know about Daniel.

Me: What? Want me to wake him up and let you talk to him?

Esperanza: Fuck, no. Is he really there?

Me: Don't tell Matt. Yes.

Esperanza: Damn. I like it.

I want to share all the details, the way he's just perfect, but I'm not ready to do that. When we're together, I am grounded. I am moving in the world. Besides, she wants the dirty details. So I won't tell her. I'll give her just a little to keep her dangling.

Me: He makes me cry, it's that good.

Esperanza: Shit. Cry?

Me: Cry. He's like cake. I'm making a huge mess, a fucking good mess, but a mess.

Esperanza: He's a nice guy. Just relax. Come see the baby again, bring me cake. Be ready to see my boobs.

Esperanza: Just breathe.

Me: Delete this text thread.

Esperanza: Of course! Don't want Matt to read it by accident. FFFFUUUUCCCCKKKK. You're bad.

Esperanza: Love you girl. Really, just breathe. You're good. He likes you.

I wish I could believe her.

DANIEL
December 28

When Chris's name flashes on my phone, I almost send it to voicemail. I have nothing to say to him. Maybe I need to hear what he has to say. Against better judgment, I take the call.

"Fuck off Chris," I don't give any more than that.

"Are you dating her?"

"That's none of your fucking business."

"I don't mean it like that," he sounds frustrated, "It seems like you like her? Like she trusts you?"

I don't give him an answer. He doesn't deserve an answer. "What?"

"Dude, I don't know what happened. I'm sorry. When I saw her, I don't know what happened. I didn't mean to be such an asshole to her."

"You said some fucked up shit to her."

"Dude, you know I'm not like that. I'm sorry."

"I'm the wrong person to apologize to."

"I can't talk to her," Chris sounds remorseful. "I didn't mean that."

"And?" I don't have any empathy for him. He showed people her private shit.

"Did she tell you about her stepfather?"

Holding my phone and listening, I have no words for him. My stomach flips. Fuck, I know what he's going to tell me. My fucking heart cramps up. I'm having heart palpitations. I'm done with this conversation. Don't tell me this shit.

"I didn't think she did. You need to know what she's fighting. She deserves someone to take care of her."

"And that wasn't you?"

"No, it wasn't me. It was never me. Don't fuck this up, Fernandez." He doesn't sound like such a bitch right now, but I haven't forgotten how he looked at her. He was going to kill her.

"Just tell me what you think I need to know."

"I shouldn't tell you this, but her stepfather sexually abused her. Her mom blamed Juliana for letting it happen."

My mother needed me to leave.

My blood runs icy. My throat is closing up. It's a fucking punch to my gut. I have to force a big breath. I don't want this to be true. I know it is. I've known all along. This is the guilt I watch her carry. This is the guilt she blames herself for. This is the reason why.

"Her mother made her believe it was her fault. When we were together, it was bad and dysfunctional. It wasn't her, it wasn't me. It was a fucking train wreck."

"Why not tell Matt this? Why are you telling me this?"

"Dude, come on, figure this out, Fernandez. I'm not stupid, dude. I can see it. Can't you?" Chris is quiet for a second, "She looked at you the way she used to look at me."

Shit. He misses her. He misses her so much I can feel it. That's why he went outside at Matt's house. I never really thought about that. She was outside; she didn't know he was there until he went out there to fight with her. Somewhere, deep in his subconscious, he still wants her.

Fuck that, she's mine. "And the video?"

"Give me a fucking break. I don't have that shit anymore."

"Look, you called me. Tell me the truth. Help me, help her. You owe her this."

Chris gives a big huff like he's annoyed with me. Bitch. He starts talking, so low. I have to turn the volume on my phone as high as possible. "For years I had some stupid techno-pop song downloaded on my phone. She used to like that techno crap back in the day. I didn't listen to it, but it was there."

I give him nothing. I do not want to hear this shit, but I know people need to talk to be heard. I need something from him, so I have to hear him out.

"She called me once. She ran out of gas or her car broke down. I was back with my girlfriend I had at the time, but I picked up anyway. She sounded all bubbly and fun. And then she wasn't. She was stranded by herself at 4 in the morning. I cheated with her. I destroyed my girlfriend. I broke her heart. We were supposed to get married. I threw it all away for Jules, and then I punished her for it every second forward."

She was 24 years old when she dated him. That was a lifetime ago.

"Sometimes years would go by, and I'd forget it was there and it would randomly pop up on a playlist. I'd think about her for the duration of the song, and that's all. I never knew what happened to her after we finally broke up for good."

He is still in love with her. It might not be that hopeless, lost-in-love feeling, but he definitely still has unresolved shit about her.

"Tell her I'm sorry. Really Daniel, tell her I'm sorry. Tell her that for me."

"I'm not going to make this right for you. If you see her, at Matt's house, out somewhere, don't talk to her. Just leave her alone."

After ending the call, I just sat at my desk. There is so much in that call I have to unpack. Things I didn't want to believe were true but are. Juliana has survived but continues to fight in her head. When I'm with her, I see her fighting these things. She's struggling with this battle she has not trusted me with. I have no idea how to help her.

Who the hell could do that to a kid? I've seen it up close. I don't need her to tell me anything. All my interest in her cutting, the 5150, no longer matters. I might be in love with her. I barely know her, but I know what I need to know. I need her.

I need to take care of her. I could easily spend the rest of my life with her.

I want her. I want her to have my baby.

JULIANA
December 30

    Text to Enrique Sanchez: Call me.
    Me: Call me when you can.
    Enrique: You okay? Gabe?
    Me: All good.
    Then he ignored my text for two days, asshole. If I did that to him, he'd text me a million times. Me, nothing, he ignores me.

    When the phone finally buzzes, I grab it as soon as I read his name, Enrique Sanchez. It's only 5 am, it's normal for people to call at 5 am, right? In the silence of the bakery, the metallic hum of the mixers running, my phone scares me for a second. I'm not totally awake yet.
    "It's about fucking time," I hiss at him, putting him on speaker mode. Ricky never changes. Everything is always his way, no matter what. "I never ask you for shit, and you ignore me when I do. I'm always there for you."
    "Jules knock that shit off," he sounds tired. Maybe he just woke up too? Ricky is not constrained by the conventions of society. He sleeps whenever he wants to and makes calls whenever he wants. Just does whatever he wants. Asshole. "I'm not in the mood for you and your needy ass shit. What the fuck do you want?"
    "Gabriel wants to know how you are," I say, hopping up on the counter, and reaching for my coffee. I have a few minutes to sit while everything runs on its own. "Where the fuck are you?"
    "Busy," he sneers, sounding annoyed. Rustling noises are coming through. Maybe he's in bed? Maybe he's on the street? Then he takes a deep breath, "I'm good though, tell him I'm good."

"Are you really? We don't lie to each other Ricky."

"I just got out of rehab." He's coughing and moving around, wind, noise, something in the background. "I'll stay clean for a little while. Why do you care?"

"I don't," I say to him, sipping my coffee, slipping my shoe off and keeping it on the tip of my big toe, balancing it there as I talk. Rehab, Ricky is always in and out of rehab. "I just don't want to have to claim your body one of these days."

"Shut the fuck up," he snickers, "I'm going to leave a note, don't call fucking Juliana Lopez. Call anyone but her. She will dance on my mother fucking grave."

"That's not very, ugh, maybe I would. I'll celebrate your death, but know this, I'm your only friend Ricky."

"I know, I know. You might be the only one who comes to my funeral," he laughs.

"I have a question for you." I know this is a bad idea, but I need to figure this out. Ricky knows everyone, at least he used to. "Do you know a guy named Juan Carlos Fernandez?"

"Not that I can remember," he's annoyed with me, cold and detached. "I haven't lived in Fresno for a long time, Jules."

"Well," I have to focus, I need information from him. "Maybe you didn't know him. He was in trouble a lot, and robbed a bank."

"That's what you think of me," he starts talking louder with each word, "I'm a bank robber? A fucking felon?"

"Shut up, I know you're just a drug addict. How about a guy named Eric Fernandez, did you know him?"

"Eric? No, I don't think so. What's all this about?

"I met a guy." Biting my nail, I push forward. This is a bad idea. "I like this guy. I'm so bad at this. You know how bad I am at this."

"Shouldn't you talk to Gabe about this?"

"Come on Ricky," I say to him, all the mixed-up emotions coming forward, "You know it's not the same anymore. Nothing's the same. I don't have anyone I can ask. Everyone is so afraid I'll do it again. No one will tell me the truth anymore. I'm not going to do it again."

"Well, they blame me for getting you that shit. If I had known you were going to do something that stupid, I wouldn't have given you that.

You fucked me over," he says, the sounds of traffic or a loud TV playing in the background. The noise of a phone moving around fabric comes through. Ricky breathes deeply, a sigh of disdain or pain. It's not clear.

"I'm sorry Ricky."

"I know you are. So who's this guy? Juan Carlos? Eric?"

"No, they have a little brother. He's a cop."

"Fuck me, Jules, what the fuck?"

"Ricky, I need your help. Shut up and listen to me. Please, help me."

"A fucking cop," Ricky sounds pissed off. "You sound like you're making a mistake already. You're going to get all fucked up. Don't trust him. Don't do this shit."

"Fuck off Ricky, thanks for nothing." I press the end call button. Shaking my foot, I flip my phone over, banging it against the countertop. I drum my nails on the back of the case, making loud sounds for no reason. This is the stupidest thing I've done this week. If Ricky thinks I'm making a mistake, I must be. My shoe falls off the tip of my toe with a bang.

Ricky calls me right back. "Alright, I'm sorry. Jules, you hear me? I'm sorry. What the fuck do you need from me? What's the cop's name?"

"His name is Daniel, Daniel Fernandez."

"Okay and he's my age?"

"No, he's my age. Maybe he arrested you?"

"Shut up. I'll hang up and delete your ass from my phone. I'll block you."

"Then how are you going to ask me for money? Asshole, think about that for a minute. Forget it, Ricky, block me. I don't give a shit." I end the call.

Hopping off the counter, I have to hunt for my missing shoe.

When Ricky calls again, I take the call. "Say, you're sorry."

He just sighs, "I'm sorry. What do you need? Who is this cop?"

"His name is Daniel. His brothers are older, closer to you. The older one, some people call him JC."

"That sounds familiar. JC Fernandez? I'm not placing him. Do you have a picture you can text me? I've done a lot of drugs, Jules. I need some help here. What's the other one's name? Eric? Eric Fernandez sounds really familiar too. I sure don't know a Daniel."

"I just want to know if he's crazy."

Ricky is quiet for a moment, "Like me?"

There was an accident. Aaron thinks Ricky broke into my apartment. Aaron was so pissed at both of us. He was mad at Ricky for doing it and me for defending him. It was an accident. Aaron just made it a big deal. It wasn't a big deal, a total misunderstanding. We had a huge fight. I moved out. I left. Gabriel had to talk me into coming back.

"You know that's not what I mean," I need his help. Ricky knows I need his help.

"Jules, I don't know this guy. I don't know if he's a nice guy or not. I've got to go," he says. "Wait, do you still have that debit card?"

"How much do you want me to deposit?"

"Just a hundred, no, two, just add two hundred dollars. No, don't add anything. Just throw the debit card away. Wait, send it to Gabriel. That will force me to call him, text him. Be good Jules. I'll text you later. I got to go."

"Ricky, don't die."

"You don't die either. I'll send you an E-40 picture later."

I might not have much, but Ricky loves me. In his weird, demented ass way, Ricky will always love me.

JULIANA
NYE

    I wasn't looking for condoms. I was looking for my hair-waving iron, I wanted to attempt to look like a normal human being, with makeup, and lipstick, maybe feel pretty on my own. I need to find my self-esteem. They just both are in the same place, under the sink. Yep, my self-esteem and condoms, are both linked in a way they shouldn't be.

    Holding the box of condoms, I want to throw them away. I'm running out of time. All I want is a baby, just like the one Echo has. It's time. I want to have a baby too. New Year's Eve is here. Soon another birthday will be here too. 37, tick tock Juliana, tick tock. Daniel said it. He said he would have a baby with me.

    What if he means it? What if he doesn't?

    I need to remember what this is. It's not a relationship. I can't be stupid and fool myself into believing this is more than a hookup. He is using me in a way that I've allowed him to. I set the boundaries. I taught him how to treat me. I cannot fool myself into believing that we have more than just a friends-with-benefits relationship. He is not looking at this as his forever. I cannot fool myself into thinking this is more.

    I put the box back under my sink.

    Tick tock… I have a party to go to.

    Text from Enrique Sanchez: Happy New Year. I miss you.

    Enrique: I miss you too Ricky.

    Of course, the second I don't answer him quickly, he's texting me again, typical Ricky.

    Me: You know I do. Be safe.

    Enrique: You too

Me: Don't die Ricky.
Enrique: You don't die either.

    A party with Quinn Johnston is over the top. His friends, Aaron and him, define what a party should be. His friends, their friends, they're a bunch of DINKs, double income, no kid, lots of disposable income. It's beautiful, a total 1970's disco party theme with strobe lights, and KC and the Sunshine Band blasting on the speakers. It's like Studio 54 here. It's 1976. Polyester leisure suits and disco bell bottoms are everywhere I look. I'm just waiting for John Travolta to pop out on the dance floor.
    I'm the child here. I'm a pretty pet. I'm here because my dad brought me. People say hi, and they stop and tell me Happy New Year, but for the most part, they are not my friends. They accept me, they just don't engage with me. Some judge me too like I'm just using Aaron and Quinn. Maybe that's just my insecurity talking, but I feel like an afterthought. This is the story of my life. I'm here, but no one cares. Nothing ever changes. I don't know why I expect it too.
    My friend Marquis is here. He's not a friend I talk to. He's a friend I know. He's more of an acquaintance than a friend. We know each other, we may hang out when we're in public, but we're not close. He would never call me and invite me somewhere, or vice versa. I guess we're more friends of convenience than anything else.
    "What's your deal?" Marquis uses his martini as a prop. He's scanning the room, looking, waiting for someone more interesting than me to hang out with. He's a shorter Filipino man with an orange plaid suit and purple velvet fedora. He's dressed like a 70's pimp, and even has a cane. "I never see you around anymore."
    "I'm a recycled virgin," I inform him, sipping some pink fruity drink Aaron brought me. It has zero alcohol. It makes me feel more adult to have something that looks like a real drink. "Global warming, just doing my part."
    Marquis laughs, shaking his drink at me, "You are full of shit."
    "Maybe so." I really could care less what he thinks of me. These are the kind of relationships I have, shallow, moody, not really friends, friends. He doesn't really care about me. I sure don't care about him.
    Matt and Adam, they're more of real friends. In the little time, I've

known them, I can honestly say they're my friends. Echo, even Kim, they're real friends. Even Daniel, who I barely understand, he's more of a friend than most of the people in this building. I can talk to them like real, normal people. I don't need to impress them. I don't have to play the part of pretty, but not girlfriend material. Marquis, he's a prop in my life, a character. It's not real.

I roll my eyes and sample my strawberry daiquiri. "What happened to your boyfriend?"

"I got bored."

My phone pings in my hand.

Text message from Enrique: Are you out? At a party?

Enrique: What are you wearing?

"Take a selfie with me." Marquise is gay and very good-looking. Those Asian boys are hot. It will make Ricky jealous. There's a strange sexual dynamic in our relationship. I know it, he does too, but we are not like that. We haven't seen each other in years, years. It's something we will never act on again.

Making sure my dress isn't revealing too much cleavage, I snap a picture. It's not my first choice. It's a totally 70's tube top-style dress I found at Goodwill. It's got bright pink flowers on a mustard yellow background. It looks like an old couch print. It's a long polyester nightmare. It's perfect for this party.

Me: image sent to Enrique Sanchez

Enrique: Is that the cop?

Me: Nope.

Enrique: Where's the cop?

Me: I'm with Aaron tonight. That's his friend Marquise.

Text message from Detective Fernandez: Happy New Year.

I'm sending him the picture too. Marquise and I look cute. Not like a cute couple. We look like we're having fun. I look pretty, not homeless. I'm a slob in real life. Daniel has never seen me dressed up. I used to be pretty. I should put a little more effort into my appearance. No. Maybe.

Detective Fernandez: You look amazing. Who's that guy?

He said I look amazing. Oh my god. That makes me all giddy inside, with butterflies and everything. What's my deal? He called me amazing. Now I feel like a little kid with a crush. Maybe I am. I'm totally crushing on him.

Enrique: Send me a picture of just you.

Me to Enrique: You wish. Knock that off.

Image from Enrique: It's a black and white picture of Ricky, with no shirt, covered in tattoos. I mean, from his neck, across his chest, his stomach, his arms. Ricky is covered in tattoos. My favorite one is of a skull with roses, it's right on his hip and has the phrase, "Mr. Serotonin Man, Lend me a Gram," but you can't see the words under his tight jeans in this picture. He's flipping me off. Nice. He's got some other girl's arms wrapped around his waist from behind. I can see her hair peeking over his shoulder. It was taken at a party. He didn't look like that as a kid. He looks like trouble. He is trouble, nothing but trouble.

Me to Enrique: Who's your girlfriend?

Me to Detective Fernandez: Thx! Where are you? He's Aaron's friend Marquis, gay, very gay.

Detective Fernandez: Adam's house. How is your party?

Me to Detective Fernandez: It's good. AA-Ron is glad I'm here.

Enrique: Jealous?

Enrique: Ditch the guy, send me one. Just you.

"Marquis, take my picture," I tell him, handing him my phone.

"Lean forward so I can get your boobs," he doubles over with laughter. He's probably drunk. Hell, it's New Year's Eve. He reaches forward like he's about to help me adjust them, so I slap his hand away.

"No," I say, resting my elbows on the table and striking a sexy pose, thinking about Daniel naked. All those damn tattoos are hot. That Death Star one he has on the side of his body, ugh. Just the thought of him makes me bite my lip. He makes me feel so good. I'm hot, it's so warm here. What does it say again? Mr. Serotonin?

Wait, no, I'm instantly burning, a fire just under my skin. I'm mixing them up, they are nothing alike, but I can't keep them straight right now. Panic creeps up, nothing makes sense.

Marquis still snaps pictures. I'm sending this to Ricky. I'm thinking about Daniel, but this is for Ricky. I'm getting them confused, about the tattoos. They both have a ton of tattoos. I need to be sane for a moment. What the hell am I doing? I hope Aaron is right, and there is no alcohol in that drink. I am so lightheaded.

Studying the images, it's not what I wanted it to look like. I'm at a party. I'm wearing a sexy dress. I'm wearing makeup. I have a flustered, flushed look like I'm drunk. You can see the people behind me. I look like that girl again. It's an act. I don't like it. Suddenly I'm deflated, everyone around me is pretending. I feel like I'm in a movie. It's all fake. I just want to go home. It's not right, something's off.

"You look fuckable," Marquis says, looking at the pictures too, "or just fucked."

"Shut up Marquis. Go play with someone else. Leave me alone." It depresses me to think that's all some people equate me to. It's not his fault really. For a long time, that's how I judged my worth. I don't want to be that anymore.

Everything is too loud. It's all too much. The disco lights, the fog machine, the music, I need a break. It's crushing against me, I'm worthless. I'm nothing. I'm drowning and there is no water. No one can tell I'm falling apart.

Enrique: I'm waiting.

Enrique: Send me one, come on. Just one.

Me to Enrique: No, are you drunk?

Enrique: Send me a fucking picture so I can lick it.

Image from Enrique: blurry close-up of something? Is that a ball stud? Ricky's tongue is pierced. Eww, he's licking his phone. He can be a gross asshole when he's drunk.

Detective Fernandez: Be careful.

Me: Don't say shit like that to me. What the fuck is wrong with you? Stop fucking with me. I'm going to seriously lose my shit right now. Leave me alone. Why can't you just help me? Fuck off and die.

Detective Fernandez: Juliana, are you okay?

Oh no, oh no, oh no, I sent that text to Daniel. My heartbeat is so hard, it's echoing. I can't form a clear thought. I only hear my blood rushing through my body. I'm sinking to the bottom of the ocean. My hand is trembling so badly, I can barely tap out a message. Oh my god, what did I just do? Great, just great. I told the wrong one to fuck off.

Me to Detective Fernandez: I'm good. Sorry. That was for someone else.

Me to Detective Fernandez: Come pick me up.

I send him a pin of where I am.

Me to Detective Fernandez: Text me when you get here.

Detective Fernandez: 30 minutes. Don't leave your party until I get there, wait inside.

Daniel is coming to get me. Is this what a hero feels like? I'm super nervous knowing he's on his way to pick me up. I even touch up the little make-up I am wearing. Marquis makes kissy faces at me. Daniel is stopping whatever he's doing in his life and coming to get me. Me?

Is this what a real boyfriend feels like? Someone who will come help when you need them? Someone who creates butterflies in your stomach when you least expect it? Daniel makes my heart race in a good way.

Ricky, I send him one of the stupid pictures.

Me to Enrique: I'm leaving the party. The cop is coming to pick me up. Happy New Year.

Enrique: Don't die.

Ricky isn't a bad guy. He's just an asshole. He likes to make me angry. And I fall for it, every time. It's my fault, I got myself mixed up.

Me to Enrique: You don't die either. Happy New Year.

******

Daniel takes me to Adam's party with him. It's still really early for NYE standards. I'm wearing a 1970's monstrosity, but I figure, what the hell? Why not? I might as well get my $17.98 out of this dress. It's New Year's Eve, a time for celebrations and promises no one will keep. I'll keep my promise. I'm going to have a baby. I'm doing that.

"What the hell are you wearing?" Echo laughs her ass off once we get to Adam's house.

Now that she's not pregnant, she's back to being all curvy. I hate her in her slinky-ass black dress. She's the freaking definition of an hourglass figure. She's got sexy ankle boots on. I wish I could wear that without tripping. "I mean, it's ugly, but it's pretty too. Only you could pull that off."

"I was at a costume party," I tell her, kicking my shoes off at the door. I'm sick of shoes, even if they're my old Converse. "I just got back from 1976."

"My parents got married in 1976," Daniel says to us.

"Dum dum de dum," Echo sings the wedding march song. She gets that damn smile again like she knows more than she does, "We need a good wedding."

"No, you need a disco party." I'm too light-headed to even pretend I'm not all up in Daniel's Kool Aide. I am dizzy. I must be sleepy or something.

Echo and I burst into giggles. I swear those drinks were not non-alcoholic. Everything is so weird. Everything is funny to me. Once I left the other party, I'm not exactly sure how I got here. I know Daniel picked me up and brought me here, but time is blurry. I'm not clear how we got here.

"Disco time," I sing, pulling Echo along with me. Adam, he's in charge of the music. I'm not in the mood for this EDM crap he's got on. No techno tonight.

There are too many people in his house. These Lopez people like to party. I'm totally related to them. This is no Quinn Johnston affair. It's more of a college house party vibe. At least what I think a college house party would feel like. I never went to one. No one's dressed up, it's like another weekend hang out, and just me and Echo have anything remotely party dress on. Mine is totally a costume.

Once I find Adam, I snap my fingers at him, "Playlist disco fever."

"Did I miss a memo?" He laughs, looking at my dress. "This isn't a costume party, Jules."

"This isn't a costume. Disco, now, I mean it, Donna Summers."

Adam only shakes his head and fumbles around with his phone. Catchy, rhythmic beats pour from the speakers.

Disco is my hidden talent, I know disco. Hell, I have gay dads, it's practically in the handbook, in capital letters, must know all the disco songs.

"Dance with me," I tell Echo, pulling her with me to the middle of the living room where no one is dancing. I don't care, this song, this is the song. Luckily for me, she doesn't ditch me.

There are at least 20, maybe 30 people wandering around, some now watching us make total fools of ourselves, most of them not. My dress is too long. I have to hold it with one hand, making it a challenge to dance. How did people dance in this crap in the 70s? It's freaking New Year's Eve. I need to have a good time.

"You," I point at Daniel, "Do you dance?"

"Not to this," Daniel laughs, crossing his arm against his chest.

"I know your mom has taught you how to dance. Don't act like that with me. Liar," I grab his hand and pull him, shimming up to him to the beat. "Besides, I don't need you to dance, I need you to stand."

Echo is laughing so hard, she stops dancing. I don't care, this is my song. I don't need either of them to dance. I can dance on my own. With my eyes closed, I lose myself for a second, music, light, fun, freedom. I used to love to dance. Maybe I should go dancing, and remember what it's like to be alive again. I used to have fun. I miss that. I miss being drunk, not falling on the ground drunk, but just slightly buzzed drunk. I need a drink.

As soon as the song is over, I'm instantly drained of all my energy. I'm so tired. The playlist switches to another great song. I don't have any desire to dance to that one. I'm exhausted and need a nap. I could curl up and fall asleep on the couch. I'm spinning in my own body. The world is spinning too fast.

Matt pops out of nowhere, startling me, "Are you drunk?"

"Me? I don't drink," I start giggling. I have to legit cover my mouth with my hand to stop. This is funny. He looks too much like my real father to question me about anything. "Rehab."

Matt looks at me, like a cop would, scowling and examining me for flaws, "Are you sure?"

Aaron gave me two, or three drinks. He said they didn't have alcohol. But honestly, I am drunk, drunk-ish. My brain is snapping two seconds too late. Everything is pretty. Everyone looks so shiny. Even when I blink, it's in slow motion.

Matt smacks Daniel's shoulder, ordering him, "Watch her. Don't let her out of your sight."

"Don't do that," I say, stamping my foot. "I am not a child. I'm fine."

"I didn't mean it like that," Matt's level of annoyance drops a level or two. "You're my sister. I just want to be sure you're okay."

"I'm fine."

"You know that's what siblings do right? I make sure you're okay, you'll do the same back. I didn't mean anything by that." Matt moves back a step, "Just stick with Daniel for the rest of the night. I want you safe.

That's all. No driving."

"I want to go home." Aaron must have made a mistake. I'll bet he handed me the wrong drink.

"I'll take you home," Daniel says. "Come on."

"I didn't mean it like that, Jules. You don't have to go home. Stay."

Standing still for a moment, the next song playing, it's another song that I love. Wigging in place, I want to dance. Bouncing slightly, I want to move to the music. I want to lose myself in the beat.

"Take me back to Aaron. Aaron will take care of me. I need Aaron."

"What did you drink?" Matt moves right in front of me again, studying me, "Jules, I swear, I think you're drunk."

"Nope, I'm bad when I'm drunk." I start giggling again, "I didn't mean that. I mean, I don't know what I mean."

Adam wanders over to us. Whispering to each other, the two of them looking at me like I'm the problem sends me into hysterics. I'm the oldest, I'm the most adult, and they're looking at me like I'm a child?

And this song? Someone turned the music back to hip-hop. I have to start dancing around. It's not my song, but that voice, I know it.

"Is this E-40?"

They ignore me. They're too busy trying to decide what to do with me, I guess.

"Yeah, it is," Daniel answers. It's only then I'm aware his hand and mine are intertwined. My stomach somersaults. Am I holding his hand or is he holding mine? Something is wrong. Everything isn't clear. Oh shit, I think I am drunk.

"Do you think someone might have put something into your drink?" Adam scrutinizes me, looking me over.

"No." Now I'm flushed. Maybe I am drunk? I'm warm and my face feels red. The music is speaking to me. It's E-40, I love E-40. I need to call Ricky. "No, not with Aaron, no one there is like that."

"I'm going to give her a ride home," Daniel tells them.

"No, I need to sit down." Walking away from the three of them, I need to be outside. It's too hot in here, too many people inside this house for me. I want to go outside, but I don't have a jacket with me. I planned to be inside for the night, not questioned by the fucking police if I was drunk. What a joke. Whatever, I'm going outside.

Outside it's foggy. Adam has a very small yard, but the open space behind his house makes it feel huge. The fog has already settled into the valley, making the night feel almost magical. It's freezing out here, but it's nice. No one else is out here in the dead of winter. I'm super-hot.

I'm not sure where I left my phone.

My socks are damp from the foggy mist on the ground. Great, I hate wet socks. I need a moment alone with my thoughts. I'm not sure what is happening. I don't like it.

"Here," Daniel hands me seltzer water. "You're not cold?"

"I'm hot. It's this dress. It's thick," I tell him as I slide off my wet socks. My feet are cold. That's a good thing. It's a normal thing. Sitting on the couch, I realize now that my brain has been spinning. Nothing is clear right now. I'm so confused. I'm not sure what is happening. I need to drink that water.

"Matt means well."

"I know. I can figure that out for myself." I misplaced my phone. I think I'm hungry too. I don't remember if I had dinner. I'm sleepy.

"Well, if you ever decide you don't want to bake cakes anymore, you have a promising career as a pole dancer ahead of you."

A wave of heat rushes through me. Humiliation creeps up my spine. Oh god, that's what it must have looked like. I'm such an idiot. No wonder, no wonder. "I didn't mean it like that."

"You just changed my reputation as the nice guy," he jokes, "I worked hard for that rep. It's all gone now. I'm never going to hear the end of that."

"You need to take me home now." I'm so embarrassed. I can't believe I did such a stupid thing. It's been a minute since I was so dumb. "I've lost my phone, I acted like an idiot, and my socks are wet."

"Your phone is in my pocket," he pulls it out and hands it to me. "You asked me to hold it."

"I did?" I don't have any memory of that. What is wrong with me? I have pictures on that phone that would be hard to explain away. Ricky likes to send half-naked pictures of himself. I need to delete those. I must have gotten the wrong drink. That's the only explanation. Whoever made those drinks for Aaron must have screwed up.

"Who were you fighting with? Earlier?"

"We weren't fighting." With my phone in my hand, I turn on a playlist, something calm, something nice and slow. My brain needs to stop spinning. "That's how we talk to each other. We pretend to fight. You don't argue like that with your friends?"

"I don't normally tell people to fuck off and die, not my friends."

"Some of my friends are straight-up assholes." Resting my head against his shoulder, I'm a little calmer. Things are not spinning as fast anymore. It's so nice and cold out here. "Honestly, I need better friends."

"And your drink?"

"That's an Aaron problem. He ordered the drinks. Someone just made a mistake. That wasn't on purpose. It was a busy party, lots of people."

"Are you going to be okay?"

"I'll be fine. I can stop." I wish I could see the stars. It's too foggy for that tonight. "I can stop. That's what you mean, right?"

"You're important to me." He leans closer, his dark eyes blazing behind his glasses, "No one should tell you to fuck off and die, no one."

Just the words give me the chills. Am I important to him? I want him to kiss me. Right now, right here. Oh man, I'm on fire deep in my core. I just want to fuck him. Shit, I hate this man sometimes. Fixing my gaze on him, leaning just slightly toward him, I lick along his bottom lip. He pulls me closer, kissing me against the seat. He gently sucks on my bottom lip, making my breath catch.

Oh my god, I'm making out with my brother's friend in his backyard. He presses against me, his tongue in my mouth. I wrap my arms around him, sinking back into the couch, letting him rest on top of me just enough that we're not visible anymore. If someone looked out the window, they wouldn't see us out here anymore.

He's so warm. My whole body is on freaking fire. My heart is pounding and my brain is spinning. Luckily, this dress is too tight to do anything regrettable. I'm so turned on, but I don't want to leave. I'm so mixed up.

"More office gossip," he teases, as he pulls back, upright into a sitting position.

Shivering, the cold finally hit, me, it was like a bucket of ice water poured over my head. From flaming hot to instantly cold, my skin breaks out into goose pimples. I have to run my hands over my arms to get warm.

"Here, give all these people something more to talk about," he says while taking off his sports coat. He's got a hoodie under that. I love that look, the whole jeans, hoodie, and sports coat. If he wore a baseball cap, it would be perfect, but he's got nice hair. It's okay. I've never seen him in a baseball cap. He takes off his hoodie, exposing his tight t-shirt. "Put my hoodie on. You look cold."

"That's a good look for you," I tell him, gesturing to his outfit. His hoodie smells like him, lime and shea butter. It's still warm from his body. This is my hoodie. He's not getting this back.

"Your dress is a good look for you. Color, you know, looks good on you. I kind of like the whole 1976 playboy stripper look you have tonight."

"I don't look like a stripper." I start laughing, that's the funniest thing ever. I look ridiculous. My hair is most likely all wild by now. I don't have a hair band with me to tie it up. Thrift store finds, a 1976 polyester dress, and a non-costume party. No shoes. Nice. Dork.

"You dance like one."

"I might be easy, but I'm not a stripper. You really know how to flatter a girl," I tell him, giggling. "You're not very good at this, are you?"

"No, I'm not. I'll send you flowers instead. I'm better at romantic gestures."

"You don't have to. You're not getting lucky tonight Detective Fernandez." I'm lying. He's getting lucky. Sipping the water, I'm calming down. Not completely, but my heart is starting to slow down. Maybe it's the cold. I'm calmer and cooler.

"Damn, I'm not? I'll still send you flowers."

"You're the only person who's ever sent me flowers. I normally get dick pics." I'm saying way too much, but I can't help it. I really should shut up. That's my problem a lot of the time. It's why I don't talk to people, I say too much crazy shit. "I need a nice guy who will send me flowers. He might have tattoos and wear glasses."

"I know a guy. He's nice, too nice. He wears glasses. He might like Star Wars, Fortnite. You might have met his mom."

"That's the type I want to take home. I might want to lick him."

"You know," he hugs me closer to him. "Everyone inside is

wondering what the hell, you're way too good for me."

"No, I'm not. I'm a dork wearing a dress from the thrift store. I'm a loser."

"No, you're not. You're the most beautiful woman here. Your brothers know it, that's why Matt was being so overprotective."

"Yeah, so overprotective, he put you in charge of me." Twisting the ends of his hair between my fingers, it's so silky, it's so relaxing. "You're the most dangerous one here. Detective Fernandez, you are dangerous."

"You're drunk, so I'm going to tell you the truth. You won't remember this tomorrow."

"Yes, I will. I'm not that drunk."

"You forgot you gave me your phone."

"Minor oversight, I would have remembered. Hey, take a selfie with me."

He leans toward me. With my phone ready, he gives me a quick peck on the cheek.

The picture is cute. That's who I want to be. I'm happy, totally covered up in his hoodie, smiling at him. He's kissing me, sweetly, not like a fucking pervert. It almost looks like we are a real couple. That's what I want, to be happy like that. I want this to be real.

Send image to Enrique Sanchez.

"Send me that." He takes my hand, holding it to heart again. He does that, it's so nice. Nice isn't the right word, it's finding home. "You command everyone's attention. You're stunning. And that dress? Come on, you look amazing. No one understands why you're sitting with me. I don't know why you're sitting out here with me."

"Stop it, that makes me anxious."

Homey, is a feeling of being comfortable, cozy, and inviting, not like homie, which means buddy. Daniel feels homey; Ricky is my homie.

Send image to Detective Fernandez.

"I know you don't like to hear it, but it's true. You're the most beautiful woman I've ever met."

"Liar," I'm blushing, and my stomach is turning. I am not pretty. I might have been pretty a long time ago. I'm a disaster. "You're just trying to convince me to take you home."

"Maybe that too," he moves closer to me. "It's like the night of the Halloween party. No one seems to know why you picked me. I don't even know why you picked me."

"I didn't take you home that night." That panic attack and that damn girl.

"But you would have."

"Too bad your girlfriend showed up," I remind him.

"She wasn't my girlfriend."

"You remember a lot for a drunk."

Message from Enrique: heart emoji

Enrique: That's the cop.

Enrique: You look happy. I'm happy you're happy.

"Tell me the truth." I lean over, resting my shoulder against his. He's so warm. It's cold out here now. I have to tuck my bare feet into my dress. I'm freezing now. "If you hadn't met me, would you be with her now?"

"Maybe. The problem is, I did meet you. Now, you're the only one I think of."

I can't help but giggle again, "Do you have a crush on me?"

"The biggest crush."

"Maybe you should take me to the prom." The idea of such a teenage tradition makes me laugh. I hate that kind of stuff, prom, graduations, even baby showers. They make me tense. I'm not sure how people even walk down the aisle to get married. I'm at weddings every weekend, and the idea of ever having one myself makes me nauseous.

"Did you go to prom in high school?"

"No one asked me. I wasn't nice in high school." Understatement of the year, in high school, I avoided people. I was a raging bitch. People were afraid of me. Even Celine, Senior's wife, avoided me.

"No one?"

"Nope, did you? Go to the prom?" The prom at private school was an event. No, thank you. I don't think I missed anything either. In one of my favorite movies, this girl talks about her friend who didn't go, and something stayed missing in her life. I'm not still thinking about prom like that.

"I went with my high school girlfriend, both junior and senior year."

"With the same girl?" Echo said something, what did she say? He likes to be in relationships. Hum.

"I had the same girlfriend for the last two years of high school."

"Why did you break up?"

"She went to UCLA. After her last summer home, we broke up."

"What happened to her? Do you know?" I like learning all these details about his life.

"She's up in Sacramento last I heard. She got married, and has a few kids."

"Do you want that, Detective Fernandez? Married and kids? A perfect wife who can bake you a cake?"

"You haven't baked me anything." He rests his hand against my knee again. He does that a lot. It's nice. "Doesn't everyone want someone? Someone to spend your life with?"

"Maybe," shut up, shut up, shut up. "There are things I want I can't say. I'm afraid to want them."

"What do you want?"

"One baby." FUCK, just shut up. I sit up, this needs to stop. What am I doing? I'm making a huge mess out of this. "No, five, ignore me. I'm being psycho again." Shut up, shut up, shut up.

"Five is excessive." He has that silly smile again, the one that shows off his dimples. Oh god, he's so cute. He has perfect hair, styled like a little boy. It's a look most adult men can't pull off, but he does and looks hot doing it.

"I'm all in, over the top. I need five husbands. I'll move to Utah, be in a polygamist relationship, but husbands, not wives."

He just laughs, "I hope you stay here."

"I'm lying. I'm never going anywhere. I can't leave Aaron."

"I'm glad you called me. If you ever need me, just call me. Something big, something little, doesn't matter. I want you to ask me. I'm kind of flattered you asked me to pick you up."

Tick tock. Would he? He couldn't. He doesn't mean that. He means something like, I need a ride, or I locked myself out of the house. Not, "Hey, help me have a baby," type of stuff. I just need an accident. What if I just say it?

"You're stuck with me now, I lied. I'm needy and psycho. I'm obsessed with you now. Fine, just this one time, you can come home with me."

He holds my hand. Who does that? He's like a real boyfriend. He's killing me. "You don't have to."

"Maybe I want to. Maybe I'm pretending to play hard to get. I'm not good at this either." Giggling, I pull his hand over to me and lick his finger, "I want a chocolate milkshake and tacos."

"You're an expensive date." He pulls me up to my feet. The concrete ground is freezing against my bare feet. "Where are your shoes?"

"I left them at the door. I know where I took them off. I left them at the door."

"Sure you did, emo girl. Let's go find your shoes and get out of here. Come on. Let's go get you tacos and a milkshake."

"Thank you."

"For what?"

"For this, giving me a few minutes to get my thoughts together. Thank you for just being nice, for being a nice guy. Now let me take you home with me."

Message to Enrique: 3 hearts emoji

JULIANA
January 2

Daniel sends me flowers, two days later. This time he sends them to my house. When I get home, they're sitting on the doormat, complicated peach orchids in a brushed gold pot.

What the hell am I doing?

"Girlfriend, who sent you flowers?"

I jump so fast, it's a wonder that I don't drop the plant. My heart is instantly pounding, Aaron scared the shit out of me.

"Flowers?" Aaron glances towards the vessel in my hands. He gives me a questioning look. He wants details.

I've avoided Aaron. I owe him something better than that. I've been superficial and fake with him.

"It's not serious." I love Aaron, but I can't talk about Daniel with him. Not yet. I don't know what we are, me and Daniel. What are we?

Aaron leans against the pillar on my porch. "More than one date?"

"Yes."

"Same guy who picked you up from the party?" He studied his nails. He knows more than he wants to tell me. He's giving me a chance to come clean with him.

"Sure." Not really an answer, but an explanation. He knows. He knows me well enough to know what I mean, even when I'm not ready to say it.

"It's not the cop, is it?" He pulls a cigarette out of his pocket and places it in his mouth. He seems to think better of it and puts it back into the box. He's always trying to quit. I swear, he and Ricky have too much in common. "He was looking at you, girlfriend. I'm telling you."

"AA-Ron, I love you," I put my palm out to him. The container is getting heavy standing here on my porch. "You know I love you, but I can't talk about this with you yet. Trust me."

He makes no effort to move. "And brother man? How's that going?"

"Dude, it's too cold to stand out here. Come inside." I tap my code into my doorknob. Luckily, my landlord is not an asshole. He upgraded my door so that I have a code and not a key. I can never find my keys.

After I've made a mug of tea for both of us, we sit on the couch. I don't even like tea. Aaron does. For him, sometimes, I make healthier choices or at least pretend to. It's just hot-flavored water, sort of like coffee. The heater is cycling on, so it's starting to warm up.

I love Aaron. I know he just wants to check-in. I'm complicated. I make messes. He just wants to be sure I'm okay. I'll fake it with the tea, just for Aaron, only for him.

"So it's going well?" He makes a sour face at me. It's not his favorite tea. It's chamomile. He prefers orange blossoms, but I ran out and haven't been to a store recently. Besides, he's the one who gave it to me. He thinks it will help me sleep. He might as well finish the box before I buy more.

"As good as I can expect. I think Matt has moments where he thinks he should be the older one of us. He's a little overprotective. His wife is cool. I like her a lot. She treats my brother like he's a freaking god though. I kind of want to get a restraining order against her."

"She has a baby." He says it as a statement, not a question. I know what he's fishing for.

"She has two. They have a five year old too."

"And the other brother, what is he like?" Aaron fumbles with the remote to my TV, turning on old 90's rap. That's his guilty pleasure. Aaron and Ricky have a lot in common. Too bad they hate each other.

"He's nice. He's way more laid back. He's definitely the baby of that family." Sipping my tea, I'm reminded why I don't drink tea. It's just hot water with a hint of dust. Yuck.

"Your family," he gives me a pointed look, right over the top of my Warriors mug.

"You are my family, you and Quinn," I reach over and hold his hand tightly. "They're related friends."

He gives me that look, "Who owns the white Jeep?"

Shit. That's my fault. Daniel is here all the time. I haven't said shit to Aaron about it. I know he'll be cool, but still. It's none of his business.

"Do we have to do this?" I am not ready to share Daniel. Daniel is mine to just hold in my heart. He's mine. I'm sure they've noticed him over a lot. He practically lives here. Hell, half of my laundry is now his laundry. I even took his shit to the dry cleaners for him. I don't want a lecture about how fast I'm rushing into this.

"Just tell me it's the cop," he says in his flat, indifferent tone, "Let me gloat that I was right."

"Fine, it's the cop."

"He sent you flowers?" Aaron moves the plant on my coffee table just a fraction, staging it better than I did.

"Twice, he's sent me flowers twice." My heart flutters. Just talking about Daniel makes me light up. I'm sure I have a stupid smile on my face. I'm so embarrassed.

"Is he treating you nice? Taking you on dates?"

"Yes, he's very nice." I can't tell him that all we do is game, hang out, and order tacos. That sounds pathetic, but it's perfect. That's what I want.

"Is it serious?" He returns his mug to the coffee table, actually using a coaster.

I set mine down, refusing to use a coaster. Gabe bought this coffee table when we lived together. He would be upset with me purely on principle for not using a coaster. "I don't have words for what it is yet. We hang out."

"Jules, men don't send women flowers for hanging out." He eyes me suspiciously.

"Stop that. I just told you. We hang out. He said he likes to be romantic. Let someone treat me nicely for once."

"Romantic huh," he smirks, "Are you interested in him, long term?"

"I don't know yet. If I say it, it won't happen." I cannot tell Aaron that I've toyed with asking Daniel to have a baby with me. Just thinking about it sounds so stupid. I can't do it. Tick, tock Juliana.

"You know I'm always here for you." He gives me "that" look again. He suspects I'm not telling him something. "Flowers huh?"

"Orange flowers."

"He's a cop. Quinn is going to lose his shit when he finds out."

"He doesn't really hate cops, does he?"

"Nope, he just hates your father."

"Me too." The sound of the heater starts again, a quiet rumble in my apartment.

"Has he asked for you, Jules?"

"No. That's okay, right? This was never about him. It was about my brothers." I am a little disappointed about that. I can't help but be childish about it. I went into this knowing this was going to happen. That doesn't mean that it doesn't hurt. I keep Matt Lopez Senior in a box in my mind where he belongs, like an afterthought. I can't even tell Aaron about the time I saw him. Aaron would lose his fucking mind.

"I know, but I hoped," he says, toying with the tea bag, "I was hoping he'd have a come to Jesus moment and apologize."

"I don't need that AA-Ron." Fuck this tea, I need a Diet Coke. I have Coke in my refrigerator. Moving to my kitchen, I dump my full mug and get myself a Coke. "You know what I want, AA-Ron?"

"What girlfriend?"

"I want to have a party for my birthday this year. I want Gabriel to come. Do you think he might come?"

"If you ask him, he just might. Tell him now so he can make arrangements. He said something about bringing the baby out to meet us, his mom. What kind of party are we talking about? You're not a party person anymore."

"I want a rave. I want a techno party." Dancing around, I change the music from old school rap to disco. "No, wait. I need it to be 1976."

"Jules, you weren't even born in 1976." Aaron starts laughing, "Like New Year's Eve? Quinn would love to plan a party like that. I'll tell him. Can we meet the cop before that?"

"Maybe, April isn't that far away."

"Jules, that's four months from now. If I catch you with him, you know it won't be good. I might be like a real dad asshole."

"Oh stop, I'm not five, AA-Ron." I keep dancing around. I love this disco crap, but I hate admitting it. I miss dancing.

"I'm just reminding you, despite the ridiculous moments in this relationship, I am still an old-fashioned man from the Bayou."

"Dude, you grew up in Sanger," I say, reminding him of the real truth. He's full of shit sometimes. I love him for that. He's just like me.

"I'm merely suggesting you introduce him to us before it gets weird. You know I can be an overprotective asshole too."

"I love you AA-Ron, soon."

JULIANA
January 5

    I hate my yearly visit to my gynecologist. Questions I don't have clear answers for, the date of my last period? I don't remember. I should monitor them, but they're not consistent. That stresses me out. Last period was 32 days, before that, there were only 21 days between.

    And, do I have to wear a stupid ass gown that doesn't cover enough of my body? Really, that doesn't matter because people, people, are looking into my freaking body. They're taking an instrument, ugh, even the word instrument gives me the creeps, and looking inside. It's not enough that it's an awkward position and difficult conversations, but it's also another reminder that I'm running out of time. Another reminder that time is moving and I can't stop it. Tick tock, Juliana, time is running out. I need a mistake. I just wish I could make a freaking mistake. A mistake that would totally not be a mistake.

    In the cold examination room, all the medical posters, images of what the cycle of life consists of, it's more than I want to see right now. I want to be one of those posters. I want to have a baby more than anything else, but I can't do that yet. I can't be like my stupid ass parents. I need a fucking healthy, eight-pound mistake.

    It makes no sense at all.

    "Okay, deep breath," she says to me, "It's going to pinch."

    Pinch? That's a fucking understatement. The last time she pulled something attached to my uterus and said it's going to pinch; it hurt for two freaking days. I was spotting for days after. It fucking hurt. It's awful. In the most vulnerable position, my gynecologist has to remove a freaking polyp from my uterus.

The cutting, searing sensation lasts only a few seconds. The burning pain lingers after, excruciating. The speculum prevents me from cringing. This hurts like hell. Deep breath, deep breath, my eyes tear up and I have to wipe them away. Breathe.

"Okay, send that to the lab. I'm sure it's benign," she says with authority to both of us, her assistant and me. But she's cool, I can tolerate her. "Periods still heavy?"

"They're bad. Not worse, but not better."

"Well," she's moving around, but I can't see her in this position. I just hear the clink of her medical tools. It gives me the chills to hear the metallic sound of her work tray. "I'd rather not try another hormone-based birth control."

"I don't want any birth control." I need a mistake. I desperately need a mistake to happen. "I'm fine, really. I just deal with it."

"I wish I had better options for you, but I don't," she moves the table tray at my feet. I can rest my feet there and no longer need to have them in the stirrups now that part of the exam is over. "Heavy periods are challenging, but I do not recommend that procedure we discussed last year. It will affect fertility."

"I don't want that either." My heartbeat starts racing. I'm running out of time. Tick tock, Juliana. Time is running out. Time is running out. I am lightheaded for a second. Calm down, just calm down. "This isn't changing my baby opportunities, is it?"

"Well, nothing is guaranteed, but I don't think so. Are you in a relationship?"

"No." Daniel is not a relationship. I am not stupid. Or maybe I am. I am pathetically stupid. I'm wasting my time with him, and I should be working on looking for what I need. I need a sperm donor, not a hot guy covered in tattoos who wears glasses. Shit.

"It's not uncommon for women to have their first child in their late 30's. However, the risk of complications increases after 35. I'm going to give you some pamphlets to read about your options."

"I should have frozen my eggs at 20. I wish there was a way to go back."

Daniel said he would help me. I wonder if he really means it? He doesn't. I need to be honest with myself about that. He's kidding. He's being a typical guy. We're having a fun time, but we are not in a relationship. Tick, tock. "I'm running out of time, aren't I?"

"It's hard to say, there are so many factors," she tells me, touching my knee. "Any other concerns for me?"

"No."

"See you next year."

Next year, tick tock, Juliana, tick tock.

*****

"I spoke to Doctor Cohen Juliana. How is the new medication dose working out for you?"

Susan pulls her long sweater around her, the chill in the office noticeable today. It's no more than 50 outside and super foggy. Fresno winters can be cold and damp, by California standards.

"I feel dizzy a lot," I answer, touching my forehead. It's been happening a lot lately, spinning, and vertigo. It's not lasting long, but it's happening more than I'd like it to. "Is that normal?"

"It can be."

"I'm running out of time." She knows, we've talked about this. I just never took the next steps. Now, I'm taking the next steps. Step one, lower medication dose. "I read stuff online. The lower doses won't hurt it. If it happens, the lower doses will be okay."

"Juliana, are you still planning to get pregnant?"

"I'm planning for a mistake."

"You're not that old Juliana."

"That's easy for you to say. You don't deal with what I do. My freaking periods are killing me. My body is turning against me." I sound crazy. If I want to avoid a meds increase, I need to sound sane. I need to prove that I am in control. I just want one baby. "Do you have children Susan?"

She gives a soft sigh, sometimes I think she doesn't want to the details she does with me. "I do. They live in Michigan. They live with my former partner, two girls. They spend their summers here, or at least they did until college. Now, they come out for the holidays."

"How old are they?"

"Oh, 19 and 21, now." She moves to her shelves. She has a ton of books, no pictures. She flips through one of the books and pulls out a well-worn picture she hands to me. Two happy, sun-kissed blond girls, no more than 12, maybe 13, stand hugging each other. They look happy. I would have been happy with Susan as my parent.

"They're beautiful, Susan."

"I understand what you're going through, Juliana," she sits next to me on the couch, taking the picture back. She takes her glasses off and studies me, "You want something, something so desperately, and even if it feels it's right there, it's not. You can almost touch it, but it's not there yet."

"It's never been there. I never had a mistake. I'm not that smart, I know something is wrong. I should have had at least one mistake by now, statistically speaking, I had a lot of unprotected sex. I wasn't careful before. I'm careful now because of the medications. I wasn't before. It never happened by itself. I'm grateful. Something is wrong. My people are supposed to be fertile."

"No stereotypes, Jules." She laughs, moving herself away from me and back to her green chair, taking her picture with her.

"Before, before my accident, I wasn't careful," I say to her honestly. Thinking back, it's a wonder I never did get pregnant. If there were condoms, yeah sure, I made him, whoever he was, use them. It wasn't like I was mindful about it. I always said I was on the pill when I wasn't. I wasn't consistent about taking them, no wonder I have so many problems now. "I pretend to be careful. Even then, I knew what I was doing. It never just happened."

"And now?"

"And now I am almost 40 years old. Tick tock, Susan. My time is running out."

"What are your options now?"

"I met someone, Susan. He's not a boyfriend, don't get me wrong. He's a nice guy, that's all. He might be the one." He's totally the one.

"Is this a romantic relationship?"

"No, I don't mean the romantic version of the one. I just mean, he might be willing to help me. I'm probably rushing into things here, but this is different. I can't put it into words, but he feels like orange. Not the fruit but the color. I know, this sounds crazy."

"It doesn't sound crazy."

"I'm getting way ahead of myself, aren't I?"

"I don't have an answer for that. What makes him different?"

It's not so easy to define what makes Daniel different, but he is. I can't even find the right words to make this clear to Susan. He's just, Daniel. He's sweet. He's nice. Daniel is more than I expected.

"He talks to me. He listens to what I say. He introduced me to his mom."

"His mom," Susan gives a genuine smile, "That sounds more serious than you described."

"No, it's not. He's just a good son, you know? He's a nice guy. I never knew someone so nice. It's almost scary. He's a cop."

"A cop?"

"No Susan, I am not doing that. It was just a weird coincidence. He's my brother's friend."

"So explain to me how you met him. I just want to be sure you are not…"

"I don't have daddy issues. They're cops. He's a cop too. Cops have cops friends. That's all. He's a nice guy, that's all. We went to see his mom. That's all. It's nothing. I'm reading way too much into all of this. Isn't that what I do? He was hanging out with me and she needed something. It was an introduction of convenience. But still, he didn't have to take me with him that day. He could have left me at home, but he didn't. He asked me to go with him. I'm reading into this, aren't I?"

"You know, some of the strongest relationships start with friendships. Those can be the healthiest."

"He sent me flowers, Susan. No one, no one, has ever sent me flowers before. Isn't that pathetic? He sent me flowers."

"Flowers?"

"They were orange. Susan, no one has ever sent me flowers before, orange flowers." I stop talking and look at her. I feel it. I never feel it here. This is my safe space, but I feel it. The thick grasp of panic starts at the base of my throat, squeezing me. Picture the boxes, everything is safe in a box. "I'm making a huge mess Susan."

"How?"

"I'm convincing myself I might have a future. I have no right to the future I want."

"You have every right to want these things."

"Susan, I like him. I really like him. I want," and I stop and look at her. "I don't know what I'm doing. I'm making a huge mess."

"Have you had an honest discussion of what your relationship is?"

"I promised him I wouldn't be clingy and psycho. I lied from the first moment. I'm both of those things."

"I want you to ask him what he wants from this."

"I know what he wants from me. That's working fine."

"Juliana, you need to stop equating your worth through sex. I recommend you have an honest discussion about your next steps in your relationship. That's a normal next thing to do. Ask him, where do you see this going?"

"And if he says it's just a hookup?"

"Then you can make a choice. You have choices."

I have choices? I don't think I have to make any choices here. I know what I want. I just need to ask him. He needs to make a choice.

JULIANA
January 8

"Don't play that emo shit in my car." Daniel pretends to be annoyed with my song choice.

He likes to argue with me about how different I am from him. We are nothing alike, but we're exactly the same. He's all bright colored hoodies, jeans and Jordan's. I'm all black, all the time.

But we get along. We talk. We joke about stupid shit. He doesn't pressure me about stuff, and I'm not expecting him to save me. We both have crap we can't talk about. We are something, but we're nothing. We're friends. That's what we are. We're friends with benefits.

Fixating on my iPhone, I ignore him and turn up my stupid emo shit songs, "Like you're so street. Give me a break. You're a fucking cop. You ain't gangsta. I'm more gangsta than you are."

"Where did you grow up?" He turns the music down from the steering wheel. "Private school girl, in Clovis?"

"I got stuck at my mother's house. We lived off Belmont and First Street, almost Millbrook."

"That's straight-up hood dude, what the hell?"

"I was a child, Daniel, I lived where she did. She was a child with a baby daddy who barely paid child support. Grant Street and Third Avenue, section 8 housing. I lived a glamorous life of being a hood rat. The other kids didn't like me with my stupid ass private school uniform."

"I like you in that uniform. You should wear that again. Were you a loner?"

"Nope, I had Gabriel. His family lived on the next block, a few houses from the corner. I had him. He has an older brother, Ricky. We used to be cool when we were young."

"Were they close? Ricky and Gabriel?"

"They were until Ricky went to high school. Then he changed. He didn't have any time for us anymore. Ricky is three years older than me. Aaron says he's homeless."

"Is he a criminal?"

"I mean, Ricky, he's difficult to explain. He was in trouble, a lot. The second he went to high school, something changed for him. He was kicked out, and had to go to alternative ed. He went to juvenile hall a few times for dumb crap. He's those things, I get that, but he's also a nice person." I have to sit up and focus. Ricky is not a bad person. I don't want him to think Ricky is a criminal. He's easy to peg as a waste, but he's not. "He remembers my birthday. He knows what my favorite candy is. He helps me. He lives in the Bay Area now."

"What does he help you with?"

"With life, that's all. He helps me." Fiddling with his radio, I focus on some sad, whiny music.

"Turn off that emo shit."

So I turn on NWA's Fuck the Police instead. "Happy now?"

"You're an ass."

Laughing, I can't remember the last time I felt this light.

*****

Tacos are my favorite food. Street tacos are even better, but I'm so embarrassed that I can't form Spanish syllables. I typically stay away from street vendors. Other people might not know, but there is a level of prejudice in Latino communities. I'm not Latino enough for people from Mexico, and I'm too Mexican for people from the US. It's this weird in-between place. I'm totally American, born and raised in Fresno. Always judged, not enough and too much, that's me. I don't even say my name right, not with a real /h/ sound for the J. I can't even say *champurrado* and I love that stuff; thick Mexican hot chocolate.

But Daniel can speak Spanish. It's sexy that he can. I haven't told him that, but it is. He doesn't speak it often. He orders my tacos for me and can pronounce the words perfectly. He remembers to order me *champurrado*. He's adorable.

"Why do you go to therapy?"

I wonder how long he's been thinking about that. It's not typical, that's for sure. Latino families, we hide our shit. That's a fact. I am not embarrassed about my own journey, maybe just a little. I'm glad I found my way to therapy. I would be dead without it.

"There are things that I haven't figured out. I need someone to help me figure out stuff and how to move past it. I'm tired of being, of feeling stuck." I think about that panic attack. I wonder what he thinks of that. We both pretend that didn't happen.

"Stuck," he questions, "Why are you stuck?"

There is so much he doesn't know. Sure, he knows some of the crap with Christian, but the piles of guilt, the pain, the horrible things that happened before Christian. No one wants to know those things. I don't even want to know. "I'm stuck in my head. It's not easy to explain. If I could explain it, I wouldn't need therapy."

DANIEL
January 8

Juliana sips her *champurrado*. I hate that shit, but I know she likes it. It's too thick for me. It's not hot cocoa. Whatever, she likes it. When we order crap, she just points at what she wants. I have to order for her. It's funny. She's so damn independent but struggles with ordering tacos.

"I was tired of the nightmares. Even when I'm awake, they haunt me. People don't let me free of what they think I am. If I was a guy, no one would judge me." She holds up her hand, ticking each statement off her fingers. "Because I'm a woman, I'm a whore, I'm crazy, I'm a drug addict, an alcoholic. I am useless. I cannot escape those labels. Even my own father writes me off as a mental health concern."

Chills run through me, even though it's warm inside of my car. People, especially Latino families, we judge based on a woman's ability to be a good wife and mother. She's not either of those things by outdated standards and stereotypes. Her father has completely written her off. I don't think he's ever asked Matt about her since that first day.

But she's perfect. "It doesn't matter to me."

"It will one day."

"It won't."

Chris said she doesn't believe she should be loved. She's definitely guarded. That's something I see every time I'm with her. She has a fortress around herself. "I don't want to be an insensitive jerk, but is it Chris? Is he the cause?"

"No." She's avoiding looking towards me. "He's a symptom. He's not the cause. It was a long time ago."

"It seemed you were pretty angry with him." I hate that it bothers me.

Chris was, damn, I hate to say my friend, but he was. Not a hang out on the weekend kind of friend, but definitely a hey, don't fuck with my ex-girlfriend kind of friend. I guess we're not friends now. I'm cool with that. I want to hear her say she doesn't care about him.

She's quiet for a few seconds. She's got that lost look again. "I thought I loved him, you know. I thought he was perfect. It was my fault for thinking he was perfect. I trusted him with stuff that I shouldn't have. And then it was just over."

"Because of the video?"

"No, it's not just that. I was never his girlfriend. I was just there."

"Do you still care about him?"

"I let him be a dick to me. I let him treat me like shit. I made a mistake. I thought, I don't know what I thought."

"You made a mistake?"

"I invited that shit right into my life. Ricky hated him. Gabriel knew it was wrong. But I didn't listen. I thought maybe he would change his mind. I'm glad he didn't. I could have been stuck with him."

"He built you a dog house." Sounds just like something Chris would do. He's been educator of the year. His staff, the students, the teachers he works with, they all love him. Everyone has something nice to say about him, everyone but her.

"I think that's the only nice thing he ever did for me."

"We're not friends, you know. We work together. Sometimes we see each other around." That's an oversimplification of the truth. That's what she needs to hear. We've been cool for a long time, but if I have to make a decision, she's the one I choose.

"I wouldn't want you to feel like I'm making your pick. You don't have to pick my side over his side."

"We're not friends," I interrupted her, resting my hand on her knee, giving her a slight shake. "I pick your side."

"It was a long time ago. He wasn't a teacher yet."

"He's not a teacher now."

"He's not?"

"He's the fucking principal now."

"That figures. He likes power, power over people. As long as they're doing what he wants, they'll be fine."

"Did he ever hurt you?" I have an idea of what transpired between them. "What happened?"

"He broke my heart, Daniel. I believed all the lies he told me. I believed he would leave her. He never did." Juliana stares out the window for a few minutes, watching the cars drive past. "I lied to you. I did cut because of him."

"You didn't owe me an explanation. I was being a bossy, overprotective asshole to you too."

"You made him leave me alone. I never told you thank you for that."

"Matt would have done it if I hadn't."

"Matt? I love Matt, don't get me wrong. I am so glad to have him, but Matt isn't sure what I am. He likes the idea of me until shit gets real. He would play that whole, 'let's look at both sides' crap. Sometimes, you need to just tell someone to fuck off and not know why. You did that."

Matt did say he didn't want to know. He told us that, both Chris and me. He didn't want to know, he just wanted to move on. Damn, Matt is just like his dad.

"Anytime you need me to tell someone to fuck off, you just tell me. If you need my help, just ask me."

"I do need your help," her voice sounds shaky. She's quiet all of a sudden. "I need something else from you, something really serious."

"You want me to build you a dog house too? Is that the standard?"

"Shut up. My car could use an oil change, but no, that's not what I need. I need something bigger, something really big, something really important. You can say no. You can even just think about it."

"What do you need?"

She's quiet for a moment. Sometimes I don't say anything, because I think she's trying to focus on what she wants to say next. She takes a big breath, and then looks at me, "I'm running out of time. I need a mistake. I need to have a mistake. Will you make love to me? Like for real?"

"What do you mean for real? What have we been doing?"

"I need to have an accident," she leans forward, and with a breath, she says, "I want to have a baby."

She's asking me to do this for her, with her. I told her I would. I want her too. If I could pick anyone, I'd pick her. I've known this since

Halloween. I want to have a baby with this woman too. "Are you sure?"

"I swear to god, you ask me if I'm sure, I'm going to beat the shit out of you. Yes, I'm sure. I wouldn't ask you if I wasn't sure. Just know this Daniel, seriously, I'll never ask you something like this without being 100% sure."

"You want to have a baby with me?" Please, don't let her change her mind.

She takes a deep breath, closing her eyes. "I do. I just, I didn't know what you'd say."

"Yeah, I say yes. Let's do this." Damn, I hope she gets pregnant the very first time. I need her to have my baby. "Right now, we're going to your house."

I just hope she doesn't change her mind. I don't think she will.

JULIANA
January 8

"So will you marry me when it happens? Take our fake relationship to the next level?"

"You sound pretty sure of yourself. What makes you think it's going to happen so easily?" Daniel has no idea of the level of noncooperation my body has with me. I doubt it will happen anytime soon.

"I'm a Fernandez, we're fertile people." He sounds so confident. It's scary. "My brothers might not have kids, but the rest of us, we're solid."

"This is scaring me." The butterflies in my stomach bounce around like it's rave night. What the fuck have I done now? Breathe, everything will be fine. It's not going to happen so quickly.

"Did you change your mind?"

"It's too late to change my mind. I'm probably already pregnant, you know since you're a Fernandez." The high school notions of swimming sperm fill my thoughts. What the fuck am I doing? Have I lost my fucking mind? I make exponential mistakes. One mistake makes so many more. They multiply into three, then nine. I'm so stupid. Just breathe. Oh my god, what am I doing?

"Ever done this before? Try to get pregnant?"

"Honestly, I didn't want kids until I was in rehab. After rehab, I realized how much I missed. I want just one kid."

"I thought you didn't like being an only child?"

"It's not for the reasons you might think. I didn't like being home alone. I was alone a lot."

"Did your mom work?"

"She worked nights. She was a waitress. She worked all night." Elizabeth Salazar is a lost soul. She's not my problem.

"You never talk about her. What was she like?"

"She was young. That's all. She made bad choices. She wasn't ready for a kid. Not at 16. She wasn't ready to be an adult so young. But I can't see her."

"You don't talk now?"

"Nope." I'm not in the mood to explain that Elizabeth Salazar doesn't know how to talk, she only screams. Her trauma isn't mine to heal. "It's cool though, I have Aaron, Quinn. They're my family."

"We can be a family too when it happens." He's messing with my hand again, touching my fingers. He likes to hold my hand. It's sweet.

"I don't understand you. I mean, I don't make much sense either, but I don't know how you're so damn calm all the time. This isn't strange to you?"

"There are things not worth getting worked up about, at least most of the time. With my family, things just work out or they don't. I can't give stuff like that energy." He snuggles next to me, pulling me closer to him. "Besides, you're a Lopez. You Lopez people make cute kids."

"This whole situation is a little wackadoodle don't you think? Me, asking you to have a baby?"

"Maybe I want to trap you into marrying me."

"Maybe it's me? Maybe I don't want you to leave."

"Well, then you wouldn't have asked. You would have just done it. What if it does happen? Would you marry me? What's the plan here?"

Married? Would he want to marry me? "If you really wanted to, I'd marry you."

"Can I ask you about your panic attack?"

"No. Yes. What?"

"Was talking about him the trigger, Chris?"

Daniel says he's not Christian's friend, but I think he was. I get it, it's weird. I don't have the energy for him anymore. I gave him way too much power. Just his name makes me exhausted. I'm embarrassed of the person I was with Christian. I am not her anymore.

"No. And yes. Sometimes I feel helpless like everything is happening so fast that I'm missing it. I'm stuck. I'm missing my life. So, when I thought about it, when I talked about him like that, I triggered myself. It's not him. It's everything I lost because I've wasted so much time. I've made a lot of bad choices. I don't care about him like that anymore. It was a long time ago. I don't have feelings like that for him."

"Does it bother you that I'm asking you questions about him?"

"Well, it's strange, I get it. I feel like you don't believe me. I just want you to believe me. No one believes me. That's how I feel sometimes."

"I'm jealous of him, that's all."

"You don't need to be. Why would you be jealous of him?"

"He met you first. You're right, I'm being needy. I promised you I wouldn't be all needy."

"No, I promised you that. Trust me, I don't want him. Not at all. You're here right? I'm not asking him, I'm asking you."

"And when it happens, I'll marry you."

"You're going to marry me, Daniel?" With him, I'm whole, not damaged. He makes me feel grounded and valuable.

"Yeah, when you're ready, I'm going to marry you."

Daniel Fernandez cannot mean that. Oh god, what am I doing?

JULIANA
January 11

I wanted a tattoo for a long time. It's a part of my journey. It's a fucked up part of it but it's no less real pretending it didn't happen. I used to cut. I used to cut a lot. I'm so glad to be alive. I'm not ashamed that I fell that far. If I hadn't, I'd still be a drunk, a drug addict, maybe dead, most likely dead.

So now I wear bracelets and stuff. I try to keep it hidden. People freak out when they realize what it is. I'm sure some want to ask questions. Most of the time, people get weird and try to pretend they don't notice, except Daniel. He doesn't feel sorry for me.

The guy inside seems like a typical homeboy, wearing khakis and a flannel shirt. He gives Daniel a hard glare, then puts on his sunglasses. Inside, it's dark. He might be just messing with me. He's the traditional Hollywood version of a Latino homeboy with tattoos and a bald head, Ray Bans and Converse. With the dark lighting and brick walls covered in tattoo art, it feels like a secret.

"Detective Fernandez, is this a friendly visit, or are you going to read me my rights?" He taunts him, giving him a mean sneer.

"Shut up," Daniel tells him. "Juliana, this is Santiago. He's Juan Carlos's friend. Ignore him if you can, he's not nice either."

"You're the emo umbrella girl," he questions me, crossing his arms and leaning back in his rolling chair. He's a big man. Since he hasn't stood up, I can't tell how tall he is. He is sizing me up. "Well little girl, what do you want?"

Santiago's purposely trying to intimate me. He might be glaring at me, but since he hasn't taken off his Ray Bans, I can't tell.

"Santiago, stop fucking with her," Daniel tells him. "Leave her alone."

"I'm just fucking with him," he says to me, gesturing to Daniel. "I know I can get to him by harassing you. Are you sure you want to be hanging out with Fernandez?"

"Do you know something I should know?" I will not show this man any fear. He can't scare me. I'm scared to death, but not of him. I'm going to get a tattoo.

"He's a cop. That makes him an asshole."

"I know he's a cop. That makes him adorable."

"Adorable," Daniel laughs, "That's not the word I would have picked baby girl."

"I don't work well under pressure," I say, covering my eyes with my hands. Shit, that is not what I meant to say. Sometimes I can't control what pops out of my mouth. "Give me a minute, I'll think of something better. I'm not used to being harassed by thugs."

Santiago snorts, and then starts laughing, "Where did you find this one? Daniel, she might be too smart for you."

Daniel laughs. "Shut up Santiago."

Santiago turns his attention back to me, "So, little girl, where do you want this umbrella?"

My blood pressure is slowly rising, "Can I tell you something first?"

Santiago just gestures, like, speak.

I have to rub my hands together. I have to explain this before I let him see my wrist. I don't know how to say it quickly. I don't want Daniel to hear me. I don't want Santiago to hear me. I don't want anyone to hear the words I have to say. I only lean forward and quietly tell him, "I used to cut. I want to cover the scars. I mean, I get it's not going to cover it. I just want to, I don't know, claim my body back."

Daniel stands behind me. He rests his hand on my shoulder, "No one will judge you."

I have to blink, fighting the tears back. "I don't want you to feel sorry for me."

"I don't feel sorry for you. Did you take care of the problem?" Santiago asks me, "Is the problem taken care of now?"

I can only nod yes.

Santiago points at Daniel, "Are you taking care of her?"

"Yeah, man," Daniel tells him, "Every day."

"Okay," he says, "Let me see."

I press my left hand against my lips and tap the fingers of my other hand against the table. I gesture with my right hand that I need a minute as I blink back tears. I want to do this. I'm fucking terrified, but I want to do this. Daniel does not judge me. Then I sit up, rub my hands together, and take off my black watch. Holding my breath, I stare out the front window. Then show him my left wrist. I refuse to cry. I don't want them to feel sorry for me.

Daniel takes the stool next to me. "I'm not going to judge you. I see you. Remember that, I see you, Juliana Lopez."

I can't look at him. I have to force myself to breathe. I have to keep blinking. Put it in a box, think of the ocean. It's just scarring, people cut. Lots of people have scars. My scars are just noticeable. Let the box wash away into the ocean. Do not cry. Do not cry.

Daniel takes my other hand, holding it close to his heart. He doesn't look at me. He must know I can't handle him looking at me right now. I hate how perfect he is. This will kill me. My emotions are all mixed up.

"A long time ago, in the 5th grade, I liked this girl with long braids," Daniel says, "Remember her Santiago, she was Eric's friend's sister. They lived next to you."

"Daniel had a lot of crushes on girls not interested in him," Santiago's tone is light, brotherly teasing. They have clearly known each other for a long time. "It's hard to tell with Daniel, he was always in love with someone."

"Shut up," he laughs. "Yolanda, her name was Yolanda."

"Oh, I remember her, quiet kid. You always liked the quiet girls."

My heart rate is slowing down. I glance at Daniel, "Did you write her a love letter?"

"Nope," he smiles. "I pulled her hair, just yanked on her braid. She never spoke to me again. All through middle school, and high school, she ignored me."

"Daniel isn't good with women," Santiago teases, "if he pulls some stupid shit, give him a chance. He's one of the nice guys. He might need two chances, but don't give him three."

Santiago shows me a sheet of white paper with purple ink. "Is this what you want?"

It's an image of a minimalist umbrella. It's nowhere near the size of my scars. It's not supposed to be. I just want something to remind me, that is not who I am. I am me. I am not defined by mistakes. I have fucked up. I will continue to fuck up but I am not fucked up. I am a person. I deserve to be alive.

"Can I change one thing?" I ask, "Can you add a semicolon? Right here, under the umbrella?"

He looks at me, then Daniel, "Eric?"

Daniel shakes his head no.

That's the closest confirmation I've had. I suspected. Eric must have died by suicide. I wonder if Eric felt the same way. Was he lost and made a mistake? I wish I could have met him. I want to ask questions about him, but I can wait. Daniel will tell me about Eric when he's ready. I wouldn't want anyone asking me a bunch of questions when I wasn't ready.

"Okay, let's get this started. Are you ready?"

"No. Is it going to hurt?"

They both say yes. Shit.

I just take a deep breath, "Okay."

The buzzing sound of the tool is more frightening than the actual needle. Not to say it doesn't hurt. It hurts like hell, but once I know what to expect, it gets better. The unknown part was scarier.

"How do you know Daniel?" The tattoo on the back of Santiago's hand is a rosary twisted around his wrists with beads running down his hand. I can't see where it ends because of the black medical gloves.

Santiago continues to work while he answers me, without looking up, "I used to be JC's best friend. I grew up down the street from them. I've known them my whole life, the whole *Familia* Fernandez. I grew up and got married. JC went his own way."

"Are you still friends now, with Juan Carlos?"

"As much as we can be, I'm more Daniel's friend now. Cops, he might be a cop, but I remember him as JC's pesky little brother. You know about JC?"

"I don't know how to answer that. What do you mean?"

He studies me and then turns to Daniel. "I like her. She's not stupid."

"Does he normally date stupid women?"

"No, helpless women," Santiago tells me, "You don't strike me as helpless. How did you end up with Daniel?"

"I asked him out." It's not quite the truth. It is close enough.

"Figures," he snickers again, shaking his head.

Daniel laughs. "She just knows what she wants."

"Are you sure about him? I've got a little brother the same age who's not a cop."

"You'd set her up with Orlando over me?" Daniel rolls his eyes at Santiago. Since Santiago is busy working, he doesn't see him. They do have a brotherly relationship. It's nice, just watching the two of them bicker. It's nice that Daniel lets me into his life like this.

"Does he have a tattoo? Does he wear glasses?" I have to keep talking, I'm slightly edgy. I'm getting a tattoo. Quinn is going to lose his shit. I know for him, that's a hard no. He's always been like that, kind of like Daniel's mom.

"No, Orlando is an investment banker. He lives a straight arrow life."

"Never mind, I need a guy with a tattoo and glasses, maybe a little drama. He might like gaming. He might even be a cop."

Daniel only smiles at me.

My heart flips. I'm lost in him. I hate this.

Stop, and relax. Everything is okay. Just believe that. Everything will be fine.

"After the first one, it's hard to stop," Santiago tells me. "What's going to be your next tattoo, rain?"

"Do you think you're funny? My dad is going to kill me."

Santiago glances at me, "I've met your brother, not your dad."

"My brothers and I don't have the same dad. We only share a father. Which one did you meet?"

"Matt," Santiago says, "He got an Aztec calendar on his back. Then he got his wife's name and their baby. And you're getting a minimalist umbrella, are you sure you're related?" He says minimalist with a disgusted tone.

"Are you judging me? I feel judged."

"You're damn right I am. You're getting an umbrella. If you weren't Daniel's girlfriend, I'd turn you away purely on principle."

Girlfriend? Did Santiago just assume that? Did Daniel call me his girlfriend? I don't know what I'm doing.

"What would you have picked? If I said do whatever, what would you have picked?"

"Well, talking to Daniel, before I met you, I would have said some vines and inspirational phrase shit," he says, still working, "But now that I've met you, I'd say a dandelion. You need a dandelion."

"Why a dandelion?"

"Because Daniel will make your dreams come true," he laughs, still not looking up from my wrist.

I walked right into that. "You guys think you're so smart. Did you plan that together or did you think of that on your own?"

"It was funny," Santiago says, "It was a good one."

I look over at Daniel, "Matt doesn't seem like a tattoo guy to me."

"Well, it's the only reason he has a wife." Daniel walks over and grabs a bottle of water and a straw for me. "That's the only reason Echo went out with him, at least, at first."

"Sounds like her. Were you friends when they met?"

"Yeah, I've known them for a long time, that whole family." Daniel's quiet. Maybe he doesn't want to discuss them? I don't know.

"This is weird right," I gesture to Daniel, asking Santiago, "This whole thing, it's strange, right?"

"Not really," Santiago says, "I hear people's stories all day. This is not that bad. The weird part is Daniel, why him?"

"He's got a tattoo. I've got a huge crush on him, but don't tell him," I say to Santiago while watching Daniel out of the corner of my eye. He knows I'm falling, right? He's got to suspect by now. This is not what I meant to do. I don't know how I ended up here. What am I going to do?

I watch the traffic outside the window for a few moments. The mist is dropping, so thick it looks like rain. One of the few things I love about Fresno is the winter nights like this one, cold, damp, and foggy. I love this weather.

I ask Daniel, "Why are you nice to me?"

"You're the most honest person I've ever met, Juliana."

"And you're pretty," Santiago laughs, "Dude. You tell her she's pretty. That's why you don't have any game, Fernandez. Come on now."

"And you're pretty," Daniel says with a smile, "No, you're beautiful."

"Stop, I'd rather be honest," I say, blushing. I don't like compliments like that. I don't feel pretty. "I'm not helpless. I can take care of my crap."

"You sure you know what you're doing, Fernandez," Santiago tells him, still snickering, "This one has attitude."

"This one," I question. "How many other women have you brought here?"

"None," Daniel answers. "I have never taken another woman to get a matching tattoo."

He shows me his arm, the Alice in Wonderland top hat. The band has a semicolon instead of a traditional hat pin. "Now we match."

"I think we matched before that." I think it's true. Not a look, but a feeling. We are a match. That thought is scary. I'm not sure where I fit in all this. He's a nice person. What am I doing?

"I think you're right."

"No kissing in my studio." Santiago laughs, "I think you might have found a good one, Daniel. Someone who can handle your needy ass shit. Have you met his mom? She's a little intense."

"My mom likes her."

"No shit? Your mom doesn't like anyone." Santiago goes on in a joking tone, "She didn't like my wife. She thought her dress was too short. Rosie is a hater."

"Santiago, it was. It was like this short." Daniel stands up, gesturing up on his thigh.

"His mom always told them not to bring any hookers or hoes home."

I flush, the sins of my past burning under my skin. I have to take a deep breath that causes Santiago to look up for a second.

"She's hardcore, but she likes you." Daniel rests his hand on the top of my free hand. "She likes his wife now too. He's full of shit, don't let him scare you."

"His mom likes my wife because we have three boys too. Our baby is named after JC. She loves my wife now," Santiago stops and changes positions, "We were young. She doesn't wear short skirts anymore. She didn't like that one girl JC dated for a while, what was her name? Fuck, Sally? Celia? Dude, she was like a nun. She didn't like your last girlfriend."

"Dude, really," Daniel huffs at him, "Really?"

"What was his girlfriend like?" Smirking at Daniel, I pressed on, "What was she like?"

"High fucking maintenance," Santiago teases, "All makeup and nails. What the fuck did she do again?"

"Santiago, fuck off," he tells him, although he's laughing. "It was a train wreck. It was a while ago, at least two, three years ago."

"Are you sure Daniel? I thought it was like a year ago, six months ago. It wasn't last Christmas?"

"Dude, it was at least two years ago."

"Well, she wasn't very smart," Santiago tells me, spilling all the tea. I like him. "She was needy as fuck. She was a secretary or some shit like that. Office assistant, that's what she was. She worked for the county or some shit like that, blond hair."

"No way," I say, imagining Zoey. Yep, she was totally his type. "Long fake nails or short?"

"Long."

"Fake blond or real?"

"Her name was Carmen, what do you think?"

"Okay, stop now," Daniel says, "No more."

"How did you meet her," I ask Santiago, ignoring Daniel.

"At his mom's. We still go to his mom's for the holidays. One day JC will come home and we're still family. Our moms are friends. I'm sure we'll see you at a family event soon too."

Family event? "Was she pretty?"

"She was, but it was makeup pretty. You're not make-up pretty. You're like my wife. You could wear a garbage bag and still be the prettiest girl in the room. My wife is too good for me. You could be my wife's sister."

"What's your wife's name?"

"Serena. She went on a date with JC first, then I stole her from him," he shares with me. "I crashed their date."

"That's why Rosie doesn't like her," I tease, "Now I know the truth. You stole his wife."

"Probably," Santiago shrugs. "She'll like you when you meet her, my wife."

"Hey, I need to take this call," Daniel tells me. "I'll be back in a few minutes."

Daniel walks outside. I can see him talking on his phone through the window. He's messing with his glasses. I'll bet they get all foggy from the temperature change. Must be a chore to wear glasses, but I'm glad he does. He'd be cute without them, but he's so much hotter with them on.

"Honestly, I think JC asked her out to force me to make a move. He knew I was too shy to talk to her. I'm the quiet one too. I have that in common with Daniel. It's most likely why I'm cool with the cop."

"You don't seem shy."

"You don't seem like you need to cut. I don't mean that like an asshole. I mean, you seem like you're a strong person. You seem to hold up okay with the Fernandez drama."

The Fernandez drama, Daniel hasn't told me everything. I know bad things happened to his family. They went from 5 people to two in a matter of years. Cancer, prison, and Eric, my heart hurts for him. That's a lot to keep inside. I remember how it feels to keep everything inside. It drowns you even if you're nowhere near water. It's an inescapable loop, dark thoughts, pain. It hurts my heart to think Daniel might be carrying that. I hope he can trust me.

"Strong people have limits. I know my limits. I've learned to honor them." I don't know what I'm doing. What am I doing with Daniel? Making an incredible mess I don't know how to fix. I'm falling hard for a boy who might not be mine. I don't know what to do. When this ends, my heart will be destroyed.

"I don't normally tell people what to do, but you can trust Daniel. He is a nice guy. You seem like you might need a nice guy. I didn't mean to insinuate that you were a hoe."

I say nothing for a few seconds. Only the buzzing of the tattoo machine makes a sound.

"If he gives you a problem, come see me and I'll kick his ass for you. I love him like my brother. He is my little brother. I promised JC I'd watch out for him. He cares about you."

"How do you know?"

"You're here, aren't you? You met his mom. He told you about JC, about Eric. He doesn't talk about Eric. His last girlfriend, he's right, it was three years ago, I'm just giving him shit. She didn't know about Eric."

I know Eric died by suicide. I want to take care of Daniel.

"Why are you telling me this?"

"I like you. You're smart. Honestly, he needs someone. He needs someone strong enough to be there for him."

"You think that could be me? You don't know me."

"I know enough. You could be what Daniel needs. He needs a strong woman who can handle his shit. He's a nice guy, but he's hurt. He needs someone to understand his hurt. You seem like someone who understands hurt."

"Maybe I'm not a nice person."

"Maybe you need to let go, stop thinking you're still hurt. You might have been hurt. You seem to have moved past it."

"I hope so."

"You should meet my wife. I think you'd like her. You might have some shit in common."

"Like what?"

"Hurt, moving past hurt." He looks at me, "Don't cry. Daniel will think I'm being a dick to you and want to get into a fight with me."

I blink, wiping the tears I have.

"You need to meet my wife. You will, soon. I bet you'll meet her soon."

When my tattoo is finally done, my wrist stings with a strange tingling, reminding me I did it. My body is mine.

As soon as I'm home, I fall right to sleep on the couch. I don't even dream. I finally got a full night of sleep.

DANIEL
January 15

"Hey, don't let your dick accidentally fall into her mouth." Adam is joking, but it's unnerving when he talks to me like that. Adam is something else.

Adam is the worst person ever. He's the most annoying, sarcastic person I know. He will go rounds with his dad, just to argue with him. The second he wins an argument, he'll switch sides and argue the opposite.

Juliana is curled up, asleep. She wanted us to watch The Blair Witch Project with her. Then she fell right to sleep on Adam's couch. The movie either didn't hold her interest, or she was just more tired than she let on. She struggles with staying asleep. I know that. She tosses and turns, and wakes up. It's never a full night of staying asleep.

"You want me to wake her up?" The top of her head rests against my thigh. I want to loosen her messy pigtails and run my fingers through her hair but now is not the time. It was an accident for her to fall asleep so close to me.

"Let her sleep, but don't feel her up while she's asleep."

Kim is used to him saying things like that. Hell, I should be used to it, but it's never really been directed toward me. He normally leaves me alone. I'm usually Uncle Dan, who might watch their kids once in a while.

"I don't give a shit what you do with her when she's awake. Don't mess with my sister when she's asleep. It's called consent, Daniel." He continues in his lecturing tone, "You make sure she wants you watching her all the time. I see you dude, quit looking at her, fucking stalker."

"Dude, I'm never going to stop looking at her. So fuck you and fuck Matt."

"Matt's full of shit. You know that. He's a perfectionist. He is trying to make my mom happy. He's a mama's boy." He points at me with his beer bottle and gestures towards Juliana, "Fuck Matt, just make her happy."

Juliana moves just slightly and presses her cold fingers into the side of my thigh. I hope she doesn't start talking in her sleep. I don't know if she suspects she talks in her sleep.

Kim brings over a throw from the other couch. "She needs a mom," she says, covering her with a thick blanket.

Adam shrugs, "She needs a dirty-minded guy with a big dick."

"You're a child," Kim tells him, laughing, falling into him on the couch. She presses against him.

"I'm your child Kim," Adam laughs, pulling her close and kissing the top of her head. "Daniel will take care of her for us. Right, Daniel, you'll give it to her."

"Oh god Adam," Kim hisses, trying to sound annoyed, but failing miserably, "What is your deal?"

"Daniel knows." Adam winks at me. "Just don't get her pregnant young man."

"She's going to have my baby," I tell them, reaching over to push a lock of hair out of her face. "I'm going to get your sister pregnant."

Adam looks at Kim, "I told you, you owe me five bucks." He points at me again, "You better give her romance and roses. I don't give a shit what kind of kinky ass shit you're into privately, but in public, you better love her like you mean it. Don't let Chris Garcia or anyone else treat her like shit. You treat her like a queen. You got that? She deserves a fucking king."

"It won't bother you? Seriously Adam, no fucking around, will it bother you if we did have a baby?" We're trying. Shit, that's like real adult stuff. Juliana and I are trying to have a baby. I need to marry her.

"No. Is she pregnant now?"

"Not yet."

"Not yet? Can you believe this shit?" he says to Kim. Then he turns to me, "I love my brother, I do. You make her happy, Daniel. Fuck Matt. He's going to be Matt, that's who he is. He can't help it. He's pretending to be mad. He's not mad. Don't treat her like she's some dirty secret. Just flat out be with her."

"I don't want to say I'm confused because I'm not, I'm solid. I know it's her. She needs space. She's not ready to say she's in a relationship with me."

Adam watches Juliana sleeping. "Dude, I can't pretend to know what happened to her. I don't know. I don't want to ask her either. She seems happy to be hanging out with you and your moody ass."

"Do you want to marry her, Daniel?" Kim sings softly, "She wants to have kids. You should marry her."

I forget how young these two are sometimes. With three kids, it's easy to forget they're so much younger. "You're not married."

"We are married," Kim says, "in the ways that count. We don't need a piece of paper to say we are."

"Fuck society and old-fashioned standards. Kim is my wife. My daughters have the last name, Lopez. My wife has that last name. We just didn't get married in some lame-ass ceremony. Not like what people expect."

"Juliana Fernandez," Kim sings, "I like it."

"We'll have to call her Mrs. Fernandez just to fuck with her."

"Your dad won't like me marrying her." I haven't even thought that far ahead. I've got to first get her to believe she is my girlfriend.

"Who's more important, him or her? There is only one right answer here, Daniel, who is more important?" Adam gives me that gaze like he can see my soul. He's scary. Sometimes, Juliana makes that same expression.

"She is."

"Then fuck Matt, fuck my dad, just love her."

Say what you want about Adam Lopez, but he's loyal as fuck when it comes to his family.

JULIANA
January 25

    Her questions are always so damn hard to answer. I can't just bullshit through them. I don't want to bullshit through them. I want to be better. I am overly defensive this time. Her questions seem to point out things that are easily explained away. I struggle with words to articulate what I mean. "I didn't see it like that. It's not like that."

    "I'm not judging you, Juliana," Susan declares as if a statement needs to be made. She knows I'm defensive right now. "I just wanted to point out a pattern. The only other adult relationships you had were hookups that evolved into relationships that skipped the whole dating situation. Have you noticed that?"

    "Does that make them less than?"

    "No, not at all, I just want you to see that pattern. What you're describing to me sounds like that pattern again."

    "So it's wrong?"

    "It's a pattern."

    "I don't like dates. I don't like the whole dating scene."

    "Why not? Millions of consumer dollars have been made on the idea of a perfect date."

    "I don't like all the small talk and stupid crap like that, that goes on in a date. Do I have to buy her a drink? Go out to dinner? No, I want the control to say, hey, you, do you want to go home with me? If we like each other we can hang out. Is that wrong?"

    "Do you think that is a lack of emotional availability? You are not investing in an adult relationship, so it's easy to leave when you perceive a threat?"

    "No." Thinking back, maybe she's right. I want things to be easy to move on from. I don't want drama.

"None were romantic?"

"Define romance. Is that code for having sex? I had a lot of sex with my friends," I want to play it off as funny, but it strikes me as incredibly sad and pathetic to say it out loud to Susan. I've never had a romantic relationship. The only romantic-ish things that have ever happened to me were one, someone built me a dog house, and two, someone sent me flowers.

Ricky. We have something different. It's not a romantic relationship. It's more than friendship. I never tell her about Ricky. Ricky keeps my secrets. My blood was on his skin. That connects us. Rick, we are always one soul.

"Did it meet the adult need for companionship? A mutual exchange of energy? A give and take of emotional support?"

"All those relationships were for getting drunk and not having to go home alone." I'm furious with Susan. This is not what is going on with Daniel. This is not what I want us to be. I hate that she pointed out holes in our relationship. Shit. "There was no cuteness, no let's wake up together."

Thinking back, it's embarrassing how awful waking up was. Vomit, blood, who knows what nasty shit I'd be covered in and hungover like hell, needing more alcohol just to work up the nerve to get up out of bed, or off the floor. Zero self-worth and zero self-respect. I was a pathetic mess. I know that. I am not that anymore.

Or maybe I am. What the fuck is Daniel? I'm doing it all over again.

"I got what I needed and left. There were no promises of, happily ever after, in those types of relationships. It's purely sexual."

"What about your other relationship?"

She means Christian.

"Susan, he doesn't matter. He was an asshole. I let him do bad things to me. I let him record private moments. Then he showed his fucking friends."

I haven't told her I saw him. I haven't told her that I've had two panic attacks about him in the last few months. She'll bring up my medication. I do not want to increase the dose again. I need to be sane right here.

My shame, my guilt of how I let Christian Garcia treat me, is my private information. He is still mine. I don't mean I want him back, but there is a part of me unable to move forward. I liked being loved by him. He made me feel loved. No one ever loved me like that. Hell, no man has ever loved me period. Well, maybe Ricky, but he's got issues too. Ricky isn't "in love" kind of love. Ricky is practically a cult leader. I'm his follower.

"How did you feel when you knew it wasn't an accident?" She scrunches up her face a little, all the while making some notes on a pad of paper. She knows this story. We've talked about it before.

"I guess, I felt like hurting him." I've told her in general terms about Nina, the one girl. I don't think of Nina. She wasn't really important. She was a means to an end. It was always about Christian. "I just wanted him to hurt as bad as I did."

"Did you reach your goal?"

"I made a mistake." I lean towards her, "What I need now, what I don't know how to do, is how to leave it behind. How do I move past this and just stop thinking about it? I need to learn to live with that. How do I move forward?"

"You cannot control another person. You can only control yourself. Think of it this way, why does it concern you so much that he might still have it? Do you think he's going to show someone else? It's been at least 10 years? Phones do not last that long."

"iCloud? Google Drive? What if he saved it?"

"What if he didn't? Again, what can you control? You can't control him. You can only control your reaction to it."

I sit back on her plush purple couch. I love this couch, overstuffed and crushed velvet. It's so Susan, kind of hippy.

There are parts of my life I leave out when I talk to Susan. I have never shared with her the stories about Christian's family. He told me stories about them. At the time, he told me he couldn't speak to anyone about it. His dad, and his mom, were violent. Their relationship was centered on domestic violence and making up after. He told me he never talked about it before. We were headed that way too. It's scary how close we got.

I should be grateful he pushed me away so hard. I couldn't forgive him after that. I got out of that. I haven't told anyone the truth, not about me and Christian. I don't want to. It's not about him. It's me.

"Do you want a relationship now?"

"I don't want to be alone. I don't want to die alone." I'm quiet for a few moments. I always appreciate that Susan knows when I need a moment to organize my thoughts. "I want someone to want to marry me. I know it's stupid and old-fashioned, but I want that one person. I want someone to pick me. I want someone to say 'You, you are the one I want.' But who will want my used-up shit?"

"Do you feel worthy of that?"

"My mother always said I was useless and a waste of her time. I ruined her life. I ruined my life."

"Is she still married, Juliana? Do you know?"

Picking at my nails for a few minutes, I hate the truth. "She has a nine-year-old she loves. She posts about her all the time on her social media. I have a fake account I used to troll her and my father. They forgot I'm alive."

"Social media isn't real. It's the perfect part of people's lives presented for instant consumption. Do you want to talk to them, to be a part of their lives now?"

"My mother is still married to that man. My father doesn't give a shit about me. Fuck both of them."

"I want you to think about something for the next two weeks," she says, resting back in her chair, "Why do you want to avoid an emotional connection before you have a sexual relationship with someone? What changes can you make to develop a relationship with someone, not just sex, a real relationship?"

Well, for starters, I can stop calling it playing Fortnite.

DANIEL
January 28

    Juliana's nervous. As soon as the door shuts, that loud metal clunk, and she starts to panic. Prison is not a fun place. It's not dark in the ways you expect; it's bright, filled with people who miss their loved ones, and families trying to make the best of an unusual circumstance. It's a strange place for sure. Her nervousness is there again, I don't mean it's noticeable, not like with the worm. It's much more than I expected.

    I invited her to come with us, to keep me company for the long drive to see my brother. Juliana is unlike anyone I've ever met. Something about her makes me feel at home like I am running headfirst into a relationship. She is the one I'm going to spend the rest of my life with. It's hard to believe, it's that easy. I haven't wanted to admit it to myself. Since she asked about having a baby, I know it's Juliana. I want to be with her forever. I want my brother to like her too.

    Juliana made my mom peanut butter cookies. My mom loves peanut butter. My mom enjoyed having her along. It's sweet in a strange way, the two most important women in my life getting along. I hate to admit it. I want them to get along.

    Inside the visiting area, Juliana can't stop moving, touching her hair, and moving her bracelets. When the second door slams, she jumps. She scoots as close as possible to me on the metal bench. She wraps her icy fingers around my hand. I can feel her trembling. Luckily, my mom already left for the restroom, giving me a moment to help Juliana through this.

    "You okay?"

    "Don't leave me," she whispers, holding my hand tighter. "I can't get out."

    "They'll let you out," I remind her, quietly, pressing her hand to my heart. I hate seeing her so nervous. She's only here for me. "I've got you."

How she manages to stay quiet is a wonder. She makes very little noise when she's under stress. She is extremely quiet. Even when she was having a panic attack, once she was in my arms, she was crying, but she did not make a sound. Is that a protective response? That old saying, "Don't cry or I'll give you something to cry about," pops into my head. Did someone tell her that? Has she learned to keep in because of that?

My brother is a solid 250 and at least 6'3". He has the typical homeboy prisoner look down. He stares at Juliana, who is extremely pale.

"You're Matt's sister." The way JC says it isn't even a question. He is an insensitive asshole. It's obvious Juliana's stressed out. Hell, who am I kidding, he's an asshole most of the time.

"Yes," she just answers and doesn't look at him. She's watching the door.

"Where's your mom?" He grumbles, taking a seat across from her and staring at her.

She only shrugs. She shifts her gaze to her shoes.

"Leave her alone JC, don't mess with her." I give him that, dude, look, but it's my oldest brother. It has no weight. JC has always been mean. He likes to intimidate people.

"You don't think that's strange," Juan Carlos says to me, ignoring Juliana. "She doesn't talk to her dad, her mom? What's wrong with her?"

"Dude, stop, leave her alone." He's heartless. I'm reminded of our age difference. It's not much, but he sure makes the most of it. I honestly forgot what he's like to other people, I'm so used to him. "There is nothing wrong with her."

Juliana watches between us, trying to figure out this new dynamic.

"Daniel, why," he questions me, with a scoff, flat out glaring at her. "Do you know why? Is it them or is it her? Maybe it's her."

"JC, don't." He wants to get her upset. I warned her. It is so much more intense now that we're here.

"We don't speak." Juliana leans to him, snapping her fingers at him, "That's all you need to know."

"Most people need their family."

"Stop it JC."

He ignores me, leaning closer to her, "You practically live with my brother without dating him. That's strange too."

"Is it?" She seems to have a way of being unafraid of mean men. She stands up from the bench. She isn't responding to him the way most people do. Most people move away, she moves closer. She glares at him, making the animosity apparent. "I don't need all that. Who are you to judge me?"

"He's my little brother and I need to watch out for him. I don't know about you, little girl. There's something not right about you."

She stands tall, crossing her arms in front of her, then tells him without being emotional, "If you call me a whore I swear I will beat the shit out of you. I am not afraid of you. Why did you rob a bank? Who does that shit?"

"You think you know everything, little girl?"

"I know you're full of shit. Don't talk to me like that. You might not like me. I don't like you either."

Juan Carlos looks at her. He crosses his arms against his chest and stares at her for a solid minute. It's a war of nothing. He starts laughing, "I like you."

"I don't need you to like me," she tells him flatly, gesturing to me, "I only need him to like me."

"He likes you too. We all like you. If anyone gives you any shit, you tell me. I'll take care of it. You tell him, you tell Santiago. We got you. Since you're not a Lopez, you can be a Fernandez now."

"I am a Lopez, fuck that, you can't take that from me. One day, I might be a Fernandez too," she blushes and glances at me. She bits her nail, then glares at Juan Carlos, "Fuck you."

Juan Carlos starts laughing, "You're just like him. You see that, don't you? All defensive, thinking everyone's out to get you. You guys are the same. Moody as shit, zero to 100 in five seconds flat. How did you manage to get this far? I'm surprised you haven't left him yet for stupid ass shit you think he did to you."

She is relaxing, figuring out he didn't mean it. He just fucking with her. She's quiet for a few moments, then looks at my brother. "You're an asshole, you know that?"

"I've been told that before. Why are you afraid of the door? Have you ever been arrested?" Juan Carlos asks her, giving her that cold stare he's mastered since he's been in prison. "Been put in jail?"

"That sound reminded me of being locked up in rehab," she says, gesturing towards the metal doors. She's relaxing, but still has some of that tension.

"Rehab?"

"I went to rehab. I needed to rest." Her eyes are glossy, filled with tears. I don't know what's affecting her more, the door or my stupid ass brother. "I drank too much because I wanted to matter."

"So, do you matter now?"

"I don't know. I hope I do. I don't really know. You think you fucked up? I fucked up too." Juliana looks calmer now, her fingers flat against the metal table, her forehead resting on her knees. "They gave me those cool hospital socks, so there's that."

My brother looks at me. His look is serious. He knows she is not talking about rehab. She's remembering being locked up somewhere, in jail, a hospital, or something, not rehab. They don't lock you up in rehab. We both know that.

Once my mom returns, she takes over the conversation entirely.

JULIANA
January 28

"Give me five minutes with her," Juan Carlos says. He points at me while he says, "I need to talk to her."

Their mom gets up and gathers stuff like it's no big deal. She hugs Juan Carlos and makes her way to the exit. Daniel doesn't want to give him that. He sighs and gestures like what the hell to JC.

"I'm cool." I want to know what he has to say to me. JC was a total bastard to me. The second his mom returned, he was the nicest person ever. It was almost scary how easily he switched from one version of himself to another. I wonder what version he'll be now. "I'll be fine."

"I'll see you at the door," Daniel holds my hand for a second and then lets me go. He points at his brother, "Don't be an ass to her."

Juan Carlos waits until they have both moved far enough away that they can't hear him. "He shouldn't be left taking care of my mom for the rest of his life. That's my fault. I know that. But you, little girl, can help him."

"What do you think I can do for him?"

"Just fucking be there for him. Make him happy. Shit, he's had to pick up all the pieces for the last eight years. You, you take care of him. You need something to take care of."

"He doesn't need a mom."

"No, he doesn't. He needs a girlfriend, a wife, something like that."

"What makes you think that's me?"

He studies me, "You haven't figured it out, have you? My brother worships the fucking ground you walk on. He's so fucking in love with you that he's lost his fucking mind. So what do you want? You want him to take care of you?"

"I don't need that." Does Juan Carlos think Daniel is in love with me? He's delusional. Being in prison must have made him insane. "I just want him. That's all."

"Then you do what I'm telling you to do. You help him take care of the shit he has to take care of."

I lean closer to him, "What if I'm crazy?"

He studies me, and then he taps the table. "You think I don't know who you are? I got nothing but time to figure out who you are. I know exactly who you are. I know where you grew up, I know the stories about you. I know all of it."

My breath catches, it's squeezed out of me, and I can't breathe in. "Does he know?"

"No. I won't say shit to him about it. He won't care, I guarantee you that. He won't care. But you do. You seem to want to keep it away from him. No one will tell him. The people who told me don't know him."

"I really do want, you know, I want to marry him. I do want to have kids with him."

"Then do it. Stop second-guessing him. Trust him. Do you trust him?"

I don't have an honest answer.

"Then do this. Just fucking do it."

"It's not as easy as you seem to think."

"Whatever shit Matt Lopez Senior put in your head about being a good girl didn't work. Why does it matter now?" Juan Carlos crosses his arms, watching my response.

"I don't want to be like him. I don't want to be like my parents." I want to give him an answer that makes sense, although he honestly doesn't deserve one.

"Look, I'm an asshole. I'm being a total dick to you. I'm going to trust you'll figure your shit out and see that I'm right. Do me a solid, you take care of him."

Does JC think Daniel is in love with me? I can't tell him there is no way I can let Daniel go now. I'm way too deep. I think I might love him too.

DANIEL
February 8

"Juliana Lopez," Aaron says as we pass him standing on his front stoop.

Juliana stops and looks caught, guilty. She blushes and seems embarrassed that he caught us leaving her place so early in the morning. "Hey AA-Ron, what's up?"

Aaron glares at me. There is weight behind that gaze. He wants to kill me. He's reacting as a dad should. He is making a judgment about me. It's not a good one.

"Hello sir, I hear you are Juliana's dad," I have to flip on the perfect boyfriend switch, this is what she needs right now. I need to prove to her that I'm for real. "I'm Daniel Fernandez." I reach out to shake his hand. "You're Aaron, right? We met at the coffee shop, with Matt."

He begrudgingly shakes my hand and then crosses his arms across his chest. He is not happy to see me at all.

"Be nice AA-Ron," she says.

"Come over for dinner tonight. You need to meet her other dad, Quinn. He's the one you should be worried about. Jules, we'll be expecting you at 7. You know Quinn. Do not show up in leggings and a t-shirt. Do not be late, Jules."

He turns and heads back into his apartment.

"Shit, I'm in big trouble. You'd think I was 12 the way he was treating me. I can't be mad. They really do love me. They're really my dad's." She leans to me and whispers, "Can you come over and pretend? Dude, I can't disappoint them again. Please."

"I don't have to pretend. I care about you. You're my girlfriend."

"Shut up Daniel, stop that," she says, pulling on my arm. "You can't wear a hoodie and jeans to meet Quinn. Let's go see what you own."

When we pull up to my house, I can tell she had no idea I lived in a house. She must have pictured me as some one-bedroom loser type. She seems guarded, almost upset. This is my fault. Somehow, this has sent her the message that I don't care. I can see how she would think that.

Honestly, it's not a big house. It's nothing special. It's what I could afford once I got myself hired as a permanent employee at the police department. No big deal. I haven't traded up for a new house or anything like that. It's only three bedrooms, nothing big. It's just an ordinary ranch style house near Fresno State University. Close enough to be in the vicinity. Not too close where I have to be concerned about loud college parties.

Juliana doesn't make a move. She just sits in my jeep, holding her hand against her forehead. She's really upset. She's not talking to me.

"Jules, are you okay?"

"Dude, you live here," she sounds disappointed. "What the fuck? I thought you lived with your mom?"

"Oh come on, it's no big deal."

"Do you own it? Like, is it yours?"

"Yeah," I have a weird shame that it's mine. I should say I'm only renting it but then I'd really be lying. I don't want to lie to her. I can see how this is so easily twisted in her head.

"Why do you hang out in my ratty old apartment when you have a house? Oh my god, Daniel. Are you ashamed of me?"

"Not at all, how the hell did you make that jump? Because I haven't brought you to my house, I'm ashamed of you? Juliana, you met my mom. I never take people home to meet my mom. And Juan Carlos? I don't even tell people about him. Come on, don't do that. You're really important to me. Don't make this a big deal."

"It's me? Is it my fault? What other secrets are you keeping from me?"

"Don't do that." Taking her hand, she won't even look at me. "Listen baby girl, it just never came up. We never came here. I'm sorry. I didn't know it was going to be such a big deal to you."

"This, this is what I mean Daniel, you say we're really in a relationship, but then, stuff like this, I didn't even know. I seriously thought you lived with your mom."

"You'd rather me live with my mom?"

"Sort of, I can't believe you live here."

"I don't. I kind of live with you." Taking her hand, I kiss it. I can't let her stay angry about this. It's not a big deal. "I live with you. I spend all my time with you."

"I don't know Daniel. This is just what I mean. What are we doing?"

"We're figuring this out. Whatever this is, we will figure it out. When you get pregnant, you'll live with me here. For now, I'll live with you. No matter what, we're together."

She smiles. "You do live with me. You might as well tell Quinn to put your name on the lease."

"So are we good? My intention was never to have a secret like this. I don't even see it as a secret. You live at your place. I want to be where you are."

She takes a big breath, "Fine, I won't overreact."

"Quinn wants to know if you have food allergies," Juliana calls to me while looking at her phone.

"No." I'm thinking that's a random question, unless she has allergies. Most people don't consider such a thing unless they have to. "Do you? Do you have food allergies?"

Juliana moves back to studying the shelves of Funko Pop figures in my kitchen. She doesn't mention how they're double boxed but she does smirk at me. "Dude, I have an epi-pen in my bag. I'm allergic to everything. I probably should have warned you before."

"What happens if you eat something you're allergic to?" She doesn't wear one of those medical alert bracelets. I've never noticed her hyper-focused on what she's ordering when we've gone out for take-out. She's not one of those girls who will order a salad with everything on the side.

"First, that won't happen," she says while running her finger across the top of the boxes, no dust. "I'm always checking. I'll break out in hives, then it escalates quickly. I got it. I'm always aware."

She moves to study all my shot glasses lined on the counter. "Are you an alcoholic, Detective Fernandez?"

"I have a friend who picks those up for me. I don't have it in me to tell him I don't collect those. He thinks I do." My stuff must seem so immature, hell, it is. It's a total bachelor pad vibe, gaming crap and action movies. There is no style, like her place. She's got adult furniture. My place is full of crap. "You know, it won't kill you to let me watch out for you. What are you allergic to?"

"Really, it might kill me. I'm allergic to shellfish and stone fruit, anything with a pit, like peaches. I normally have an epi-pen in my bag. Just stab me with it. Then call 911. But I've got it. I know what to do." She stops and studies me, "I don't know any of your friends. I mean, besides Matt and Adam."

"You met my mom, JC. You met Santiago. Those are the people in my life."

"I guess you're right."

Moving closer to her, I take her hand. "What else do I need to know about you? Baby girl, you know you're my girlfriend right?"

She doesn't say anything. She has that no trust expression again.

"You know that right? This is real."

She squeezes her eyes shut, "Is it? Aren't we just messing around? I didn't know you owned a house."

"Trust me. I care about you. This is real. You should move in with me."

"I can't do that," she doesn't pull, but she steps back from me. She's got a touch of that nervous energy. "No. I can't do that."

"Yes, you can. I need you here. I need you with me."

"You need to meet Quinn first. Let's see what he thinks of you."

"Do you think he'll approve of me?" I'm not worried, but I've only heard about Quinn. Aaron, at least him, I've met him. Hell, Aaron asked me if I wanted the Juliana Special. I think we'll be cool. Quinn, they both, Juliana and Aaron, seem to act like Quinn is the deciding factor.

"No, you think your brother is next level? Wait until you meet Quinn. Just know he had to take care of me when I was sick. He hasn't let that go. You can't wear jeans."

"I'll let you pick my whole outfit."

"Where's your closet?"

"Wait, I have a favor."

"What?"

"Do you remember our very first time on your couch? You let me make you feel pretty?"

She blushes and bites her nail. She won't look at me. She's skittish. I make her nervous.

"Let me make you feel pretty on my couch. Let me watch you."

"Watch me?" She blinks, like she's considering it. She bites her lip for a moment. "Like a freaking pervert? You're a stalker, I knew it."

"I want to hold you down Jules," I whisper to her, pulling her close, "I don't want you to get away from me this time. I want to hold you still."

"Hold me down?" Juliana glances at me. She's fighting it, whatever fears she has. She's clearly debating if she'll trust me. "Is that your kink Detective Fernandez? You want to control me?"

"Yeah, I do, but I won't hurt you. You know that. I like to watch you."

She starts talking to the space around me, and not to me. She seems to be talking to herself more than me, working through her anxiety. "Are you staying dressed like last time too? Do you want me all naked on your lap?"

"You're damn right."

Juliana takes a deep breath and closes her eyes. "Okay. Okay. But you can't talk. Just promise me you won't talk."

Juliana sits on my lap with nothing on, facing away from me. I can feel her heartbeat through her body. Caressing her arms, her skin puckers into goosebumps. She's got her eyes closed. She's resting against me, as I continue to run my fingertips over her arms.

"You're so pretty, beautiful."

"You can't talk to me right now. Seriously, don't talk. I mean it."

"Reach over and put your hands on the end of the coffee table."

The coffee table is a good three feet away from her. She has to reach for it and balance herself.

"Don't let me fall." Her voice sounds shaky.

Pushing her knees wider, she's totally off balance, but I'm holding her. I can feel her squirming on my lap, struggling to move, but not having much space to escape too. It gives me access to rubbing her butt.

"I've got you. Can I smack your ass?"

She says nervously, "Just don't let me fall."

With a firm slap, she makes a quiet gasp when my hand makes contact with her ass. It's not lost on me that she trusts me in this vulnerable position. Holding her down with one hand flat against the small of her back, she is trembling against me. I'm an ass for even asking her to do this, but she is incredibly sexy like this, quivering. Fuck.

Running my fingers along her inner thigh, she draws in her breath, small sighs. She presses slightly back to me. I push my fingers into her, and she audibly catches her breath. Shit. She's so heated and wet.

"Are you good? Tell me the truth."

"Yeah," she sounds all breathless. It's fucking hot.

"You look beautiful."

"Don't talk Daniel, I can't. Not like this."

I've noticed that. She doesn't want me to talk at all. So I don't, or try not to. Sometimes I can't help it.

Working my fingers into her, she can't rock against me without losing her balance. She has to stay still. She's making those soft moans, and her body is squeezing tight against my fingers. She's getting wetter with every movement. She's making those sexy little breaths again. She is so close, her body tensing up. She shifts slightly, resting her forehead against the coffee table.

"I can't."

"Yes you can, relax. I'm not going to let you fall. Come on baby girl, relax. You're almost there, I can feel it."

I slide my fingers down to her clit and press there, slightly. I want to say dirty shit to her, but I think she'd hate that. Slow circles, around and around, she starts making that "ugh" sound. Her body clenches up and she reaches her peak. She gives a big breath of air, and all her tension evaporates.

Juliana rests against me, still holding onto the table.

"Let me help you up," I reach around her waist and help her to her knees. She's all breathless and flushed. She looks exhausted in a good way. She stays on my lap and hugs me.

"This is my favorite memory of you."

"One day that's all I'll be."

"Don't say that. It's not like that. I want you. You need to trust me. It's you." Holding her close, I am not really sure how to make her understand this is real.

*****

Their apartment is an exact mirror of Juliana's apartment. They have white and light wood colors, and muted tones. There is old-school rap playing on the TV with images of the ocean scrolling through. Is she the reason they listen to this or vice versa? She had old rap playing at her bakery too. None of them strike me as hip-hop people, yet, here they are.

An oversized white sectional couch sits in the middle of the living room, with a formal set dining table pushed up behind it. Everything looks luxurious and deliberate. It's a Pinterest-perfect space.

There are touches of brushed gold everywhere, mirrors, frames, and a large oversized bowl filled with Starburst, but only the pink and yellow. Did someone purposely eat all the red ones first? Or do they only like the pink and yellow? There are black and white pictures crowded on one wall. Some pictures have Juliana in them, a lot don't. Barbeques, graduations, times at the beach, images of your typical family moments.

But there is one. It's just of Juliana, in a bikini top and long skirt. She looked like she was smiling at someone off to the left of her, relaxed, happy, and radiant. This is the girl I'm falling for. This is the girl who isn't carrying the weight of the world with her. She deserves to feel that light all the time.

There, painted in gold, underneath all the pictures, The Johnston Family, in fancy cursive. Aaron is the roommate mentioned in the 5150 report. Aaron Johnston. That must have been heartbreaking. He obviously loves her. He considers her his daughter. To have to find her like that? I remember Eric. My dad found him in his room with a single gunshot to the head. He died almost instantly. My mom held his lifeless body for over an hour, sobbing before they could remove him from the house. That's the thing, people think they happen fast, the coroner's office, investigations, but they don't. They're painfully slow. No parent should have to live through that.

"Is this the tattoo man?" Quinn towers over everyone else in the room. He's a husky build, wearing bright blue patterned slacks and a purple striped dress shirt with a green paisley vest. It's a lot of color for a man. His hair is silver and slicked up with style. He is the epitome of metrosexuals, if you can call a gay man that. Although he has a darker complexion, I don't think he's African American, maybe, Middle Eastern? He has a presence, manicured fingers and toes, painted dark blue.

"Yes," Juliana tells him, "This is Daniel. This is my dad, Quinn."

Quinn doesn't say anything to me right away, not a "Hi, nice to meet you," nothing. He just leans back in the chair he's sitting in and studies me. His gaze is heavy. He has intense, dark brown eyes that stare at me, sizing me up, with his hand resting against his chin. I can't get a good read, positive or negative, of how he feels about me. He has a flat affect.

"No more tattoos, Jules," he says to her, pointing right at her. He turns to me, "No more tattoos on my girl."

"Quinn, stop," she tells him, sitting nearer to him, on the couch. "Be nice to him, I like this one."

He continues his glare, cold, indifferent. He makes me uneasy.

"This is why I don't bring men home Quinn. You're mean and bossy." She pats the spot next to her for me to sit with her. Her attitude towards Quinn is also flat. It's a strange dynamic. There is a tension they seem to be skirting around.

She's waiting to see if he likes me. His opinion matters to her. She's trying to fake not being nervous.

"But you bring the cop home? Oomph."

"He pretends to not like cops, ignore him." She gives Quinn a look, "Be nice Quinn or he won't come back. Then you'll be stuck with me."

"A cop, Jules? A tattoo?"

She takes the candy dish and dumps the contents on the coffee table. Digging through the candy, she finds the final two orange Starbursts closer to the bottom. "Just be nice."

"I understand one, but no more," he points at her, then me, "Got that Mr. Policeman, no more tattoos on my girl."

"He's got a whole bunch, Quinn," she laughs. She unwraps the orange candy and pops it into her mouth. "It's hot."

"Ump," he makes that judging sound, like Aaron. "You do what you want, but you take care of mine."

"Got it, no more tattoos." I can't tell if he's serious or not, so I'll assume he is. He sure isn't acting like he's kidding around. He feels like a father.

"How did you meet her?" His question is definitely directed to me, not her. He crosses his arms across his chest.

"I went with Matt when they met up." Wow, that sounds so interesting huh? At least it wasn't on a dating app.

She scoots to the edge of the couch, picking up all the candy and putting them back into the dish. She seems skittish, as if she doesn't want to hear this part of the conversation. She keeps moving the candy around. Does she worry about what I'll say? Does she still believe I'm not serious?

"Her brother is my partner."

"And he's cool with," Quinn gestures, towards us, "This?"

"He's pretending he doesn't know," I answer truthfully. It's most likely what Quinn doesn't want to hear. I have to be honest. "He knows, but he'd rather not."

"AA-Ron, what the fuck is wrong with those Lopez men?" He calls over his shoulder, towards Aaron, who is pouring out several glasses of wine and one sparkling water. "Always pretending."

Juliana gets up and takes the glass of water, "I'll tell you, they're full of shit."

"Language," Quinn says to her, in that fatherly way. The tension is fading fast. I can see her soften, the stress leaving her.

"Jules, what men are not," Aaron says in that flat tone of his, handing Quinn a glass of wine. "Don't believe any of them. Do not take shit from any of them, even him." He gestures towards Quinn.

She just laughs, taking the extra glass of wine from Aaron and handing it to me. She pushes her water glass over to her as if she doesn't want it, but needs it closer.

"Well, without one Lopez man, we wouldn't have you, pretty girl," Aaron tells her, scooting into her spot so that he is now next to Quinn. Musical chairs, the people version.

"Daniel is nice. Be nice to him."

"Nice huh, what makes him nice?" Quinn talks over me, like if I'm not here. I notice both Aaron and Juliana don't look at him when they talk to him. They just talk around him. Quinn sits in his seat as if it's a throne.

"Well, he sent me flowers. He's nice to me. Um, he doesn't make me feel like crap."

Quinn looks at me, almost a glare, but not quite. "Jules, that's not a standard for dating. No one should make you feel like shit."

"Well, you know what I mean." She starts giggling, "He makes me feel, um."

"TMI. Stop it." Both Aaron and Juliana are laughing.

"You two are children." Quinn only shakes his head. "You, do you have kids? Siblings, is your family here in Fresno?"

"No kids. I've lived here my whole life."

"Never left?" Quinn sips his wine, still watching me. He's one of those people, you can feel the weight of his gaze.

"No, my family is here. We're close."

"Um hum," he runs his finger along the rim of his glass. "Do you know her father?"

"No Quinn, don't ask him that. Be cool. I don't want to talk about him." Juliana smacks his arm. "You be cool. You are my dad."

They feel like a family should. It's evident they care about her. She belongs here. I've never watched her be so comfortable with people before. Yeah, she's nervous, but it's not because of life. She's introducing me to her dads, that kind of nervous, expected nervousness.

"Aren't you guys too young to be her dad?" They can't be more than 10, 15 years older than her.

"She's a product of teenage pregnancy," Aaron answers, which sends them into hysterics. "We were 20, 23 when she was born. But since she's adopted, it doesn't matter."

"She's been ours since the day we met her and her boy," Quinn says, pointing at her as if reminding her of that.

"He means Gabriel," she clarifies for me. She rests back on the couch, sitting crisscrossed next to me, balling the extra fabric of her dress into her lap. "Gabriel is their boy, not mine."

"Gabriel is married and has two babies now," Aaron informs me, scrolling through his phone. He shares a picture of Gabriel and his partner, one baby and one toddler. He is an older version of the guy in the picture from her place. He's tall. She's got a lot of tall men in her life. "He moved to DC a few years ago."

"Yeah, he abandoned me here," she teases, "He left me here to deal with them on my own. Helicopter parenting, it's a thing, ask Susan."

"Does he know who Susan is?" Quinn asks her.

Juliana leans against me, "He knows I'm in therapy. I'm not ashamed of that. Susan is her name. She's my therapist and she helps me figure out what I'm really feeling. That's my problem. I can't organize my thoughts fast enough to figure out what I really feel. Sometimes I just say shit to be shocking."

"Jules, language," Quinn laughs. "And, no, you're not trying to be shocking. You are a mystery."

"Whatever you want to call it, Susan helps me figure out what I really mean. Sometimes I can't give my feelings a name. She helps me figure it out. That's all. Hey Siri," she calls, "Play You're So Vain by Marilyn Manson." It's nice to see her relaxed. I like her like this, happy. She glows when she's happy. She's fucking perfect.

"You know that story," Quinn asks. The way he moves towards me, his acceptance is building, slowly, "Did you know my girl was conceived to that song?"

"The Carly Simon version right, she told my mom."

"Your mom," he looks at Juliana, obviously shocked. He leans forward, turning all his attention to her. "You did not tell me you met his mom."

She blushes, sitting back up, removing herself from me. "I didn't? I could have sworn I told you."

"You introduced her to your mother," Quinn asks me. I've passed some test I didn't even know I was taking. He studies me again, "When?"

"After our first date," I say, not sure what to call that. What was that? A lucky hookup with an amazingly beautiful woman, with a girl who let me make her feel pretty on her couch, on my couch? Shit. I cannot think of her naked right now. I need to focus on this first. "My mom wanted to meet her."

Dead puppies, dead puppies, dead puppies.

I realize I've never taken her on a real date. It's just been hanging out, take out, gaming. No wonder she doesn't believe me. I'm screwing this all up. What the fuck have I done to make her feel special?

"We were hanging out. It's cool." Juliana blushes. She is staring at her fingers and is very quiet all of a sudden.

Is she embarrassed about that night? Does she regret how all that happened? She fought with Chris Garcia, told me things I don't think she meant to, and then took me home. She asked me to go home with her. She stole my line. I wonder if she feels like this is all some game, like I'm using her, like she's letting me use her. I don't blame her.

"I took her to meet my mom. My mom is pretty overprotective," I tell them, watching Juliana. She is still looking at her nails. "She likes her."

"Your mom likes my girl?"

"She does. She's never liked anyone before. She likes her. You know how moms can be. She told her she wants grandchildren."

Juliana finally looks up, just a hint of a smile, "I am not going to have your baby, Detective Fernandez."

"You'll have to tell my mom that. She said you would make beautiful babies."

"Oh course she will. My girl is beautiful."

"Knock that off, Quinn, you're making me nervous." She totally rolls her eyes.

"Juliana Lopez," Quinn looks from me to her, "Are you going to have babies with Mr. Policeman?"

She legit glares at him. "Do not ask me that, Quinn. You know better than that."

"Quinn," Aaron says, in that flat tone of his, "Don't fuck with my girl."

Quinn watches her for a moment, then gives me that heated look again, "And you sir, what are your future plans? What do you want with my girl?"

"I want to marry her one day."

Juliana stares at me. "Don't say that."

"It's true. You know that's true."

She looks away. I can see her have that look again, lost? Not worthy? Her eyes are glassy but she blinks it away. "We are not talking about that. Let's just be in this moment. It's a moment. We can't plan for things that are not here."

It's silent for a moment. The song playing earlier has already ended. The smart speaker didn't switch to a new song.

"Hey Siri," Juliana calls out. "Playlist slit your wrist and die."

The music starts again, this time a slow sad song. The title of her playlist has me slightly alarmed. No one else seems nervous about it. I shouldn't know these things about her. I need to tell her I know.

These men had to help her. Aaron is in the report. I'm sure Quinn was there too. Someone had to take over her life for her. She told my mom. Aaron had to have power of attorney for her. She was sick, and then she got better.

I think she's bipolar. That's what would make the most sense.

Eric was bipolar.

Juliana is likely bipolar. It doesn't matter. I want her.

"Why did you become a cop?" Quinn taps his foot against the coffee table in front of him.

"My dad was a cop. I wanted to help people."

"And you thought being a cop would help people? Umph."

"Stop, not all people hate cops Quinn. Daniel is a nice guy." She leans back against me. "Trust me."

"I don't hate cops," he huffs. "I just don't like them. And your dad, is he proud of you?"

"He was. My dad passed away."

"I'm sorry to hear that," he says, with a kinder tone, "I didn't mean to be an insensitive dick. Is your mom proud of you?"

"She is." For Juliana, I want Quinn to like me. It sounds so silly, but I can tell that his approval means something to her.

He leans forward, "Do you take care of your family? Is your mom able to depend on you?"

"She does. I try to be a good son for her. But that doesn't mean I can't take care of her too," I touch Juliana's knee, "My mom isn't helpless. She's very independent. She has a full life outside of me."

"So Mr. Policeman, did you go to college?"

"I went to Fresno State. I have a degree in criminology."

"You do," Juliana asks. Her surprise is evident on her face, "Seriously?"

"You didn't know that? I thought I told you that?"

"No, I would have remembered that." Juliana doesn't pull away from me, but her tone, she is upset, just like she was about the house. "You did not tell me that."

"Are you angry about it?" I told her about it, didn't I? I'm almost sure I told her I went to Fresno State. It's clearly making her uncomfortable. She seems agitated. I'm not sure what is wrong, the house, the degree? What is making her so upset? Why do those things bother her?

"No, it's fine. It's nothing. It's me," she tells me, fiddling with her glass. "It's always me."

I know when she says it's fine, it's not fine. I just don't want to have this conversation in front of Quinn and Aaron. Her anger, it's a much deeper conversation we need to have without an audience. I'm not sure why she's so upset about this.

"Where did you learn to make cakes?" I need to turn the conversation in a different direction. Anything to help her relax.

"Quinn taught me," she says, gesturing towards him. "Midnight Vanilla was his once upon a time."

"Oh no girl," he says, clearly watching her for emotional balance. I think he knows she's edgy too. He reaches for her glass and pushes it to her. "Do not blame that emo, goth shit on me."

He stands, moving to refill his glass of wine. "When I owned that place, it was not all dark like that. I made stunning cakes, wedding cakes for a queen. This girl could already bake. I just taught her how to decorate cakes."

"People like that emo shit," she tells him.

"People also liked the white stuff too, Jules," Quinn laughs. "You like that emo shit."

"What can I say, I have a dark soul."

Aaron laughs, "You're right about that."

"When it was time for me to retire from baking, I let her take over. She's the boss."

"Oh come on, you boss me around from the sidelines." She seems slighting calmer than a second ago, but it feels forced. She's pretending to relax. Her anxiety is right below the surface. I can see it. "I am not the boss really. He's the boss from the background."

"That I do, but look at you now, Jules," he says, returning to his spot with his wine bottle, refilling our glasses. "You are an amazing person. You are fire, Juliana Lopez."

"Stop."

Quinn looks to her, then gestures for Aaron to come sit near him, which he does. They seem like they've been together a long time.

"So, tell me, are you okay with the whole two dads thing?" Quinn and Aaron share a look, a connection. You can tell. They love each other. "The whole, we're her dads, but not really?"

"The weird shit we might say," Aaron clarifies, "We might be her dads, but we're still not. We say weird shit."

"What they mean is that AA-Ron can tell me you're hot, and none of us are going to trip out," Juliana says, "They will point out the hotness where a typical dad might show up with a shotgun instead."

Aaron snorts, "I did not say hot, girlfriend. I said he was looking at you."

"And I said," she starts, gesturing towards him.

"Don't you dare say that," AA-Ron says, giving her a warning look.

"I haven't. Just in case you wanted to know," she says to him, matter of factly, "I don't swallow."

Both Juliana and Aaron burst into uncontrollable laughter. And I figure out what they're talking about. Blow jobs. Oh damn, shit. I flush for a second.

Dead puppies, dead puppies, dead puppies.

"We're an odd collection of people," Quinn says, ignoring Juliana and Aaron. He gives them a look of disdain and pride, he loves them, in spite of their comments, maybe because of them. "We're the island of misfit toys. Ignore my inappropriate partner and his devil offspring. She gets that from his side of the family."

"I'm not evil," she says, "I don't know why you guys always say I'm the devil or evil."

"You're a charmer," Quinn says, pointing at her, "You charm men into shit. You cast evil spells on them and they can't escape you."

"If that was true," she responds, taking a sip of her water, "I'd be happily married by now. I'd have five kids."

"The problem is you charm the uncharm-table types, psychos."

"Thanks a lot," she says, laughing. She seems more relaxed again.

"Name one that wasn't psycho," Quinn glances at me, then looks at Aaron.

"Let's see, psycho brother, psycho teacher," Aaron names on his fingers. "All of them are psychos."

Psycho teacher? Psycho brother? I don't know much about either of those relationships, except they're both over now. They're not wrong about Chris. Something about his reaction towards her wasn't normal. I'm sure that's who they're talking about.

"Stop, you're making me sound awful," she says to them. She places her hand against my thigh and traces from there down to my knee, over and over. That simple gesture has me thinking about her on my couch again. Shit. I need to get her to stop that without being obvious.

"Are you psycho Mr. Policeman? Are you crazy too?"

"No, I don't think so. I think I'm pretty normal." Catching her hand, I link my fingers into hers, stopping her.

"That's what a crazy person would answer." She studies me for a moment, "Maybe you are crazy, Detective Fernandez, maybe that's why you're here."

"No," Aaron says, "He's here because he got caught, not charmed."

"That may be true, but he's here," Quinn states. "He didn't bail out. So, Mr. Policeman, if you're not crazy, not psycho, not charmed, maybe you really like her. And if you really like her, maybe, just maybe."

"Stop it, Quinn," Juliana says sharply. "Don't do that."

"Juliana, I was just making a logical connection."

"No you're not. Stop it. Don't do that. Ask him something else. Don't do that." Juliana is flushed, her cheeks are red. She lets go of my hand and holds the collar edge of her dress to her lip, biting the fabric.

If I'm not crazy, psycho, charmed, maybe I'm here because I could love her. I could easily love her. She doesn't want to hear that.

"Who was your first crush," I ask her, helping her refocus.

"I don't have crushes, but when I was a little girl, my neighbor told me he had a crush on me," she says, glancing at me.

"How old were you? Five? Ten?"

"Twelve. I was twelve. He told me on my front porch. Then he tried to kiss me and I hit him. I might have made him cry."

"You hit my boy," Quinn laughs, "I can see that. You are a violent woman."

"Gabriel, it was Gabe. He didn't really have a crush on me. He was a faker. He told me he liked boys. I asked him, why did you try to kiss me? And you know what he said?"

"What did he say?"

"Because he thought it would matter to me one day. He thought I needed someone to tell me they liked me. He thought it would be nice if we shared a first kiss," she starts to giggle, "But I never told him his brother kissed me. His brother beat him to it."

"Did you have a crush on his brother?"

"Nope, I did not have a thing for Enrique Sanchez."

"Enrique Sanchez," I tease, "I know an Enrique Sanchez."

"You do not," she laughs, "I already asked him, he doesn't know you."

"You talked to Ricky," Quinn asks, clearly not amused. He sits up in his seat, almost knocking over his glass, "When?"

"Gabe asked me to check in with him," she says to him, with a flippant attitude. She turns to me, explaining, "Ricky lives a nomadic life now. He's hard to pin down sometimes."

"Homeless is not a nomadic life, Jules," Quinn states.

"He's not homeless," she defends. She leans to me, "Ricky lives in the Bay Area now. He thinks he's in a band. He moves around a lot. Sometimes he sends me pictures of E-40."

E-40, she has said she's obsessed with E-40. Last week, she showed me a picture someone texted her of E-40. She said it was an old friend and moved on. It's Ricky, Ricky's texting her.

"Ricky should not be sending you texts," Aaron tells her, speaking to her in a tone that I haven't heard Aaron use before, sharp. "Block him."

"Give me a break," she tells Aaron.

She looks at me, "He's got all kinds of girl drama. I stay away from him for the most part. He's got kids all over the place. It's not what they're making it out to be."

"Umph," Quinn makes that sound again. "Ricky needs to stay gone. And don't you go looking for him, even if Gabe asks. You tell me, I'll find him."

"Yeah well, I asked him if he knew you," she says, ignoring Quinn, "He used to get arrested a lot. You might have arrested him. He just might not remember. He left a long time ago. Maybe he would have known your brothers. He didn't remember them."

"Juan Carlos went to an alternative high school."

There are two conversations happening, simultaneously. One, she is angry and having a mini argument with them, two, she's telling me Ricky is just a friend. Even the tone she uses with them is different than with me.

"So did Ricky. Maybe they did know each other and Ricky can't remember because he's a drug addict."

"Ricky is a waste of cells."

"Don't say that Quinn," she defends, moving to the floor. She cuddles up on the floor, leaning against me. She gives a deep sigh, "Ricky is lost."

"He's too old to be lost," Quinn says flatly, it's evident he has no love for Ricky, even if he is Gabriel's brother. "He needs to be found by now."

"I'm lost Quinn," she reminds him.

"Girlfriend, you're not as lost as you think," he says to her. "Ricky needs to grow up and take care of all those kids he's got all over the place."

On New Year's Eve, she texted me by accident. She was telling someone to fuck off and die. Was that Ricky? She said her friend was an asshole.

"Do I have to worry about Ricky? Is he my competition?"

"Nope. Ricky and I are not like that. We're not really friends, not really. We just have his brother in common. Him and your brother, they're closer in age. Ricky is not a nice person."

"Not a nice person is a fucking understatement. He won't call his brother, but he'll call you," Aaron huffs, "Don't call him anymore, Jules."

"Stop," she says, holding her hand against her forehead. "You're making it sound bad. It's not like that."

"You tell that boy not to do that again," Aaron says, pointing at Quinn, ignoring Juliana, "You know why he asked her to do it."

"Why," I ask, knowing what the answer is. Fuck Ricky.

Aaron points at her, glaring at me, but not angry with me, "Because Gabe knows Ricky will call her back."

"Wow, really? That's what you guys think? I've known him since I was five. I've known him longer than you guys."

"Aaron has a tendency to overreact when Ricky is involved," Quinn says to me. "Ricky is, how can I say this tactfully? Obsessive, is that a good way to describe him?"

"No."
"Infatuated?"
"No."
"Psycho?"
"Stop."

"Ricky had a restraining order put into place," Aaron explains. "The only time I would agree with her father, her real father. I don't know the details, but the cop had a restraining order issued against Ricky."

A restraining order did not come up when I searched for her. But, if she was a minor, and her real dad is a cop, someone could easily file that without her name. How did Aaron know?

I'm sure Ricky is still talking to her. E-40, she has all that E-40 shit at her place. She is hiding a relationship with Ricky from them.

Quinn described him as infatuated, obsessive, and psycho. I could be described like that about her too. Even Chris, he's weird around her too. Something about her triggers other people.

"I told you, my mother, my father, they thought something," she says, scrambling to her feet. "They were wrong. But Ricky was 19, and I was 16. So my asshole father threatened Ricky. That's all that happened."

"He was also a stalker, Juliana," Aaron reminds her. "Once you moved here, once you were away from home, you know I had to get involved with that situation. Do not call Ricky."

"Don't call him that. Stop that, stop saying that." Juliana stamps her foot against the floor and rushes out of the room.

Aaron and Quinn look at each other. Their glances are filled with a secret language.

"Give her five minutes," Aaron tells Quinn.

"Two, just two minutes," Quinn answers.

"You good, Mr. Policeman," Aaron leans closer to me, "Do you know what you're dealing with?"

I don't have a quick answer for him. "I don't know what I'm dealing with. I just know whatever it is, she's worth it."

Aaron and Quinn look at each other.

"It can't hurt to tell him," Quinn says. "He is the fucking police."

"She makes light of dangerous situations," Aaron says, "Even when she's in danger, she doesn't see it. She defends the bad guy. It's kind of fitting that you're a cop."

"Are you a good cop or a bad cop? Are you going to hurt my girl? My girl can't take any more hurt."

"I could never hurt her." Thinking back, she asked me that too. She asked me if I was the good cop. "I want to marry your daughter."

"Even if she's fighting?"

"I know she's fighting something. She's worth it to me."

"Mr. Policeman, I don't know if you understand how hard she is fighting," Quinn tells me. "But I like you. I think she likes you too. You introduced her to your mother, huh? Ump."

They're intense. They care about her. That's all this is. They want to be sure I am not like Christian Garcia or Enrique Sanchez. This is what a real father should feel like. Not like Senior, who pretends she doesn't exist. He's never once brought her up. I see her fucking father every day and he has never questioned me about her.

"When did she go to rehab? She told me she went to rehab."

Aaron moves his glass around. "Four years ago, she spent 30 days in treatment. It wasn't rehab. She says rehab because that's more socially acceptable. She had an accident, a moment. Then she went to treatment."

5150, an accident, a moment, is that what they call it?

"Mr. Policeman, bad things happened to my girl. She's trying. Know that she is trying to move past it."

"After Gabriel left, she realized she was not in control," Aaron says quietly, "She's in control now, but it's a fight. That's all there is to it. It's not drugs and alcohol, don't worry about those things. She fixated on those things, but it's not those things. There are things we can't tell you, Mr. Policeman. If you ever need us, we are here. Put our numbers in your phone and do it fast before she thinks we're plotting against her."

I hand Aaron my phone and let him enter both of their numbers. And I text him mine. Whatever it takes for her to believe me, to trust me, I will do it. I need her. I desperately need her. I need her to have my baby.

"Hey Jules," Aaron calls out to the bedroom behind us, "Come on back. It's dinner time. You know Quinn hates when dinner gets cold."

When she comes back into the room, it's obvious she was crying. Her eyes are red and puffy, but she pretends she wasn't and moves forward.

"You good girlfriend," Aaron asks her.

She nods yes.

"Well come help me in the kitchen," Aaron says to her.

Once they leave the space, I ask Quinn, "What can I do to convince her I won't leave? She thinks I'm going to leave."

"Mr. Policeman, don't leave," he says in a quiet whisper, "When she pushes you to leave, don't believe her. Just don't leave. There is no magic trick. She is not a project. She is who she is. You take care of my girl."

"I will." Fuck her father. I just met her real dad, dads.

DANIEL
February 8

"Why are you mad about that? Are you really mad because I went to college? And didn't tell you that?"

"No, it's more than that. This isn't real Daniel. Do you understand that? You deserve someone perfect, like Zoey."

"Zoey, give me a fucking break. Who's Ricky?"

"I told you, he's Gabe's brother, we text. We don't talk, we just text."

"He's the reason you like E-40?"

"He likes E-40, we text about E-40."

"Why doesn't Aaron like him? What did he do?"

"I don't want to talk about Ricky."

"We need to talk about Ricky. Aaron called him a stalker."

"Give me a minute," she says, sitting down, "It's hard to talk, to explain things when I'm upset. Let me organize my thoughts. Give me a minute."

I want to be an overzealous, jealous boyfriend but I know that will push her away from me. I need her to make me understand instead.

"You can't hear only one story to understand Ricky. One story doesn't explain to you who he is to me. Ricky has always been there. He doesn't judge me. He just is there. Aaron overreacted. Aaron convinced himself that Ricky was going to do something. He wasn't. He's Ricky, that's all. That's all."

"Why did Aaron think Ricky broke into your apartment?"

"Because he doesn't trust him, but I trust him. Do you know who once told Christian to fuck off for me? Ricky. He did. Without me having to explain it all to him, he told him to stop calling me. He just did what I needed him to do. He's that kind of friend."

"And Gabriel, why won't he call him?"

"Because Ricky is a drug addict and I am a drug addict. I might not take drugs or drink anymore, but we both have that same fight. I'm here. I can say I'm not going to do that again. Ricky can't, not yet."

"I don't like this."

"What? Ricky? I haven't seen him in years. We just text, that's all. I am not like that, Daniel. I don't have feelings like that for Ricky."

"Did you sleep with him?" I don't want to know the answer.

She presses her head against the edge of the coffee table. "It's not what you think. If I answer that, you have to believe me, it's not what you think."

"What is it then?"

"I was a kid. We were just kids. We didn't have a relationship. Who has a relationship at 16? It was an accident. That's all."

"I'm confused, an accident?"

"It was just two months. I think it was two months. Then he left. My mother lost her shit when she found out about him. His mom made him live with his dad. We didn't talk anymore. Then later, years later, we started talking again. Then he moved. He doesn't live here."

"So you never slept with him as an adult?"

"No, only a few times when we were younger. It sounds bad, I know it sounds bad. It's not bad."

I want to accept it. I want to leave it in the past. But I don't want her to text him anymore. I'm so jealous I don't know what to do with these feelings. I'm jealous about a high school relationship? I'm losing my freaking mind.

With her head still pressed against the coffee table, she starts talking. "I don't love Ricky. Bad things were happening, things I can't tell you. I needed to pretend it was true."

Sitting down, I have to strain to hear her. "What happened with Ricky?"

"I got into a fight. I had a huge fight with someone. It wasn't good. I called Ricky. He came and helped me clean up. Me, my room, it was all a mess. Ricky helped me. Aaron, Aaron thought Ricky hurt me. It wasn't Ricky. I couldn't tell Aaron the truth. Ricky knew, I was crying and Aaron was yelling at me. Ricky gave me his keys and said go."

She adjusted herself slightly, still keeping her head on the table. "I stayed with Ricky, with him and his girlfriend. Aaron sent him to jail. After a few days, he came home. He took care of me. But when he moved, he made me go back to Aaron. Ricky made me go back home. Then, every day, he texted me, don't die. If Ricky texted me, I knew I could get through one more day. Every day, same thing, don't die. One day, it switched, I texted him, don't die. He needed me to tell him that. That's what we are. We text each other, don't die."

Juliana seems so lost. This vulnerable side of her is what she normally hides from me.

"Ricky said he loved me. I wanted someone, anyone, to just say they loved me. Everything hurt, always, every day, everything hurt. I didn't want to be here. I didn't want to be hurt anymore. One night, he said he loved me. That's all that happened. He didn't love me. I knew it then. I know that now. I just wanted someone to say it." She sits up, wiping away the few tears she has. "I don't want anyone to tell me that now, no one. This isn't good, none of this. You should go. Maybe you should just go find someone like Zoey."

"Is that what you think I want? I want you. You know, I do…"

"Don't say it," she glares at me. "Don't tell me that. Please don't tell me that. I am not good enough for you." She covers her head with her arm. I think she might be crying. She's doing that quiet crying she does.

"You need to stop saying that." I hate that it's me making her cry. I need her to believe me. She just doesn't believe me. "You are important to me. I want you. I want to marry you, and you say no, we can't talk about that. So when can we talk about it?"

"Not now," she's wiping her tears.

"Then when? I asked you to move in with me. You never answered me. When are you going to believe that this is real?"

"You don't understand."

"Help me understand. Tell me what I need to know. What do I need to do for you, Juliana?"

"I want this to be real. I want you to know the words I can't speak out loud. I want to trust you. I want to have your baby. I don't know how to do that, Daniel. Are we an us? I don't know how to be an us. I need you and that scares me."

All the fight leaves me. She's not my enemy. She is the most important person in my life. She is everything I need and never knew. I need her. I don't want to fight with her. I want to protect her.

JULIANA
February 8

The words are there. I want to tell him everything. I just can't. Mine is a story that is not ready to be said out loud. I trusted someone once with it. He was the wrong one. I just wish there was a way for him to understand. I wish people could trust me and believe it's there, even when I can't say it.

"Bad things happened when I was younger. That's all I can say. Just please understand this. I needed Ricky. I needed him. My stupid ass father made him leave. He left me there."

"What was he then, a friend?"

"He was a typical teenage boy. We were friends. Then we weren't. Later, when we were a little older, more mature, we became friends again. Ricky and I are friends. That's all."

"Why did your dad have a restraining order against him?"

"He believed my mother over me. He never even bothered to ask me what happened." I move to the front window, looking out into the darkness. "It sounds so much worse than it was. No one believed me about anything. No one helped me. Ricky tried."

"Juliana, you can tell me anything."

"I can't talk about this anymore." I move to the window, resting my hand against the cold pane. "What are we doing? Are we pretending? What is this?"

"We are an us." Daniel comes to stand next to me at the window. "I understand the things you can't say. You don't need to say them. I know those feelings are there, even if you can't put them into words. You need to believe me when I say we are an us. Can you do that?"

Daniel is not like anyone I've ever known. He's perfect. He's fucking perfect. I need him. He understands the things I can't even sort out for myself. I want to trust him.

"Daniel, I have mental health concerns, for real. I'm not kidding." I can't say it out loud to him. I can't even admit to myself what's wrong with me. I fucking hate this. I just want to be normal like everyone else.

"You can say it. It won't change anything. I won't judge you. I see you, Juliana."

"Do you?" When Daniel says "I see you," it feels like love. Is this what love is? It can't be. It's not this easy, is it? Nothing is ever this easy for me. It can't be. But it feels like love. At least, what I think love should feel like. I feel seen. He can see me.

"I see you."

Susan thinks I should say it, at least say PTSD. I don't want to say those things. If I have to say it, they become real. I can't move past. Well, I can't move past them now. I hate struggling. Why do I have to be that person? Why do I have to have these problems?

"I have PTSD. I might have a mood disorder."

He's quiet for a minute. All we can hear is the faint sounds of cars passing by. "I know."

"You know?"

"Well, I didn't know for sure. I suspected. I knew it was something. I didn't know what exactly."

"I'm crazy." This will be it. He's not going to want to have a baby with me anymore. My heart is racing out of control, pounding in my chest. I'm going to have a heart attack. He's going to leave me now.

"You're not crazy. Don't say that."

"I don't want to be out of control. I should have told you."

"You don't owe me that. You don't owe that to anyone. That is your personal business. You don't have to tell me. It doesn't matter. We are still an us. You are the one I want to be with. Are we still going to have a baby?"

"You want to have babies with me? I'm crazy Daniel."

"You're not crazy. I never want to hear you say that again. I want you. I want five babies."

I have to laugh, "That's excessive."

"Ride or die, Juliana, go big or go home. We are excessive. It's you, baby girl. I want five babies that all look like you."

DANIEL
February 16

    Enrique Sanchez is an extremely common name. I have to figure out ages, 16 to 19, so there's a 3 year difference, and narrow down my search. I'm sure I have enough details to find the guy. I shouldn't want to do this, I can't help it. I need to see who he is. What does he look like? What kind of trouble did he get himself into?

    There it is. With enough clicking around, I find his records. Restraining order, unnamed minor, and statutory rape, Enrique was ordered to stay away from the unnamed minor. The officer assigned to the case, one Matthew Lopez Senior. The order expired and was not renewed.

    What does that do to a kid? I mean, I wouldn't want my daughter to have a relationship with an older kid from down the street. Who helped her heal from a broken heart? I'm sure at 16 she thought she loved him. Her father barged in and put a stop to this relationship. At the same time, he didn't. Twenty years later, she still considers Ricky her friend. She has nothing to do with her father, but Enrique Sanchez, she still talks to him. This feels like an overreaction.

    I don't like it. I'm not saying that. I can't judge her life and what she's done. I get that people have pasts. I'm not a saint. I've lived my life. I wouldn't want her to start asking me questions about that. She hasn't. She doesn't. She never asks me those types of questions. I shouldn't be looking at this.

    What about her stepfather? That was okay? What kind of message does that send a child? I'll run off your boyfriend, but I'll leave you at home with a pedophile? How do you even begin to process that as a child, as an adult? I'm an adult and I can't figure out why, who could just leave her there?

The list of other offenses starts shortly after that, petty shit, drugs, DUI, public intoxication. Then, years later, breaking and entering, a familiar address, unit B. Aaron Johnston made a complaint that Enriquez Sanchez broke into his unnamed tenant's unit. Then nothing, he's just gone. Juliana said he moved, he left Fresno a long time ago. I should have looked up Aaron Johnston. I knew he was the one I needed to shake down.

Ricky's mugshots aren't helpful, but I look at them anyway. I don't know what I expected him to look like. Maybe more like JC, who is clearly a thug. He doesn't. He looks like a kid, at least at first. He's angular and clearly has a flair for his hair, short, long, spiked up, flat out dirty.

Enrique Sanchez is lanky and tall. I'm sure many women would have found him attractive. He's got that bad boy look down pack. I didn't get a good look at the picture of Gabriel at Juliana's house, but this guy sure resembles what I remember. They must look alike, Gabriel and Enrique, Gabe and Ricky Sanchez.

He has a bunch of tattoos too. Some are documented. Most are things I wouldn't choose; he's got a gun, a pair of dice, even a shark, but one, one small one, it's her name backwards, curly cursive letters, ANAILUJ, her gamer tag right below an elaborate spider. It's her name backwards on his wrist. What the fuck?

Who the fuck is Ricky Sanchez, and why does he have a tattoo of her name?

"Who's that guy?"

I'm so wrapped up in my own world, I didn't hear Matt walk up. He scared the shit out of me. "That is Juliana's high school boyfriend. Your dad had a restraining order placed on."

"No shit? He did? What the fuck for?" Matt is genuinely interested in looking at her old boyfriend. I think it bothers him that he's not the oldest in that relationship.

I give him a look.

"Oh, I would have done the same thing," Matt says with authority. Matt has a smugness that comes from being the oldest. I may not like it but I understand it.

"You have sons, would you want that to happen if they made a mistake like that?"

"They won't. I'll make sure they understand how serious that is," he's full of shit. He knows it. "How old were they?"

"16 and 19. They were young."

"Fuck."

"I'm not saying I like it. Fuck that guy."

"So maybe he was trying to be a good dad to her, and not a total asshole."

"No, I think he was trying to control her life. Your dad is a control freak."

"You sound like her," he points out. The stress between us is instantly evident. "You sound like her when you say that shit."

"Fuck off." I don't want it to be true, but he's right. This whole situation has been tough. Matt used to be my best friend. Now, I can't tell him, talk to him about things I need to talk to him about.

"Look, we both know he wasn't a good dad to her. She has a right to feel that way. I won't fight you on that."

No matter how anyone else feels about it, I need his friendship. It's been weird, I know it has. I know the details of his life, he knows mine. At least, up until lately. I haven't tried enough. He hasn't either. One of us needs to extend an olive branch. If this is awkward for me, it must be the same for him, maybe more.

With a deep breath, I tell him, "He has a tattoo of her name."

"No shit? Your girlfriend's got a past, dude. Let me see it." Matt leans over, studying the images on the screen.

Gesturing to my screen, I give Matt space to see it. The fire burning in my veins is pure venom. No one should have her name on their body. No one but me.

"Is it backwards?"

"Yup." Fucking Ricky Sanchez couldn't even get her name right? Bitch. "What do you think that means?"

"That he made a mistake. Looks like an old tattoo. It was a long time ago, right? How old is this picture?" He's scanning the images for more information, a date stamp.

"They still text." I hate how this makes me feel. I'm jealous of an old, teenage boyfriend? It's burning through my fucking veins. I hate this guy.

"For real?"

"He lives in the Bay Area."

"Do they see each other? Wait? Is this the guy who broke into her apartment?" Matt sits in the extra chair at my work station. He's making himself comfortable, messing with all the crap on my desk. This is the longest conversation we've had in a while.

"Yeah, how do you know?"

"She told Echo. Echo told me about him. I guess he's another friend's brother. Echo said they don't talk."

"He's Gabriel's brother. They all grew up in the same neighborhood. They lived a few houses apart."

"But they don't talk? Are you jealous?" Matt gives me that Lopez look, flat and smirky, sarcastic. Who knew that was a thing? The three of them all make that same look.

"No." I am jealous.

"You are. I get it. I caught my girlfriend on a date with another person. It feels like shit. It sounds like this was a long time ago. You shouldn't worry about it. Are you worried?"

"Fuck no. I shouldn't even be looking at this."

"Look dude, I can't pretend to know what you're feeling. But whatever this is, you need to stop it. If you want to be with her, then do that. I'm always fucking with you about that and I always will. Don't go looking for problems. Enough problems are going to pop out of nowhere without you looking for them. Trust me on that."

"I just want to understand."

"Understand what? Look, I get it, you lost Eric."

"Don't make this about Eric."

"It's not? Come on man, I'm not stupid. She's got something going on, it might be anxiety, it might be depression, or she might be bipolar. Echo said it's PTSD but she's definitely…"

I interrupted him, a flush of defensiveness rising, "Don't call her crazy."

"I'm not saying she's crazy." Matt stops moving around, touching all the items on my desk, stapler, LEGO house pencil holder, bottle of hand sanitizer. "I'm saying she might need stability, that's what I'm saying. She might need someone who's calm. If you start messing with this shit, you won't be that for her anymore. It will start to eat at you too. I guess what I'm trying to say is, take care of her. But not like this."

"Dude."

"No, you think about it. Who are you? You're the good guy. You're the calm one. You're the quiet one. She was attracted to you in the first five minutes. You know that. I know that. Even AA-Ron knew it. This, obsessing over shit you can't fix, that's not going to help her. Just be you, be who she needs. Not this," he gestures to the monitor. His calmness about this situation actually makes me more relaxed about it too. It's nothing. It was a long time ago. I need to let this go.

I hate when he's right. Normally I can say he's full of shit, but today, he's right. I'm chasing ghosts that don't matter. What matters is her. I need to trust her. She said he's not important. I need to believe her.

"I think she's the one Matt. This is serious." I watch him as I say it. We haven't really had this talk yet. I know it's weird.

"I know. It's different for you for sure. I don't want to like it. You seem happy, she seems happy. I don't really know her, I know you. I know you will be good for her. You'll be good to her."

"This is strange for me too. It's one of the rules, you don't do this. I didn't plan to do this."

"Your dad and all his rules. He had some good rules." Matt gives a soft sigh. Again, I'm reminded that our friendship is deep. Things might have been strained lately. Our friendship is something I need.

"Carlos Fernandez was a rule follower." Senior and my dad had a lot in common, but were very different people. Carlos Fernandez was all about manners and traditions. He made sure everyone was included. Senior, although similar, he's more about how things look. What would other people say?

"Your dad would have liked her. He would have given you shit for dating my sister, but he would have liked her."

I can't give a response. Sometimes I think life has been so unfair to my own family. Life is too short to worry about stupid rules if I have truly found happiness. Juliana is the one, I know it.

"He might have asked her to dye her hair back to normal, but he would have liked her," Matt laughs at the thought. He's not wrong.

"Lopez, are you good with all this?"

"Dude, I'm not going to pretend that I was. I was pissed you took her home. I did want to kick your ass, but whose rules are those? Those are the rules our parents taught us. Fuck those rules, you both seem happy now. You're not a total asshole. I know you won't be a dick to her."

"I will take care of her. I'll do anything for her."

"I think that's what she likes about you. I mean, aside from the tattoos, she knows you believe her, believe in her. Honestly, I give you shit. I always will, but I couldn't have picked a better person for her. I know you wouldn't hurt her."

"I need to marry her." Glancing around the office, I'm glad there are so few people in here right now.

"Need, is she pregnant?"

"No, nothing like that, I need her."

"I get it. I need my wife." Matt leans back in the chair, "Are you asking me for permission to marry my sister?"

"Maybe."

"No," he sits up, tapping on my desk. "If you said yes, then I would have said yes. You can't be unsure."

"I am sure. I am 100% sure. I'm just not sure if I need your permission. You know how she is."

"Look dude, as your friend, as your brother, I'm telling you, I think you need her too. You marry her. As her brother, I'm going to kick your ass if you hurt her. Take care of her. You get a better tattoo of her name. Get her name reading forward, none of that backwards shit. Call Santiago, I need the baby's name."

"Her name and an umbrella."

"I can't believe she got an umbrella. How is she my sister, an umbrella?" Matt must be laughing at the thought of Juliana's tattoo, a minimalist umbrella. "But really, take care of her."

"I need to sell my house. I need to buy her a house."

"Dude, you can't just buy her a house."

"Why not, she likes the Tower District. I can get a house over in that area."

"You hate the Tower District, that's why."

"I need to be where she is. That's where she wants to live." I haven't admitted it to myself yet, the thought of moving isn't fun. It's what I want to do. She likes living over there. I need to be where she is.

"Daniel, what the fuck are you going to do? You're in love, for real. It's just too bad it's with my sister."

The irony of knowing this is the same talk we had when Matt decided to ask to marry Echo is not lost on me. We sat here, at work, having this same chat years ago.

Closing the window of Ricky's tattoo, is this important? Ricky Sanchez doesn't live here. He might have her name on his wrist, but she's not with him. She might text him, but what does that matter? She doesn't seem like she wants to go be with him. She's here. She's with me. We are trying to have a baby, she asked me.

Juliana Lopez is my fucking soulmate.

JULIANA
February 22

Nervous bubbles, sparks of electricity dancing through my veins. Daniel is taking me to his cousin's wedding. I don't know how to do this. I actually went out and bought a new dress. I can't remember the last time I went shopping for a real dress.

This means I'll have to meet his family, almost like we're on a real date. I know his mom will be there, but I'm nervous about the rest of them, cousins, aunts, uncles, and all his family. He's going to say, girlfriend. Our pretend relationship will be on display. People will make judgments. What if they don't like me?

Aaron helped me find a dress. I told him I was aiming for a 1976 playboy bunny look. After he laughed his ass off, he helped me find the perfect dress. Aaron found this emerald green halter top type asymmetrical cocktail dress that I could pair with black footless tights and Vans. Daniel said it would be outside. That means cold. I hate being so cold.

"You look, wow, Juliana, you look amazing." Daniel makes me feel pretty, the way he looks at me.

I wish I could believe him.

"I have a fairy godfather, two actually."

Aaron's friend fixed my hair so it rested in pretty waves, with midnight blue streaks. No ratty pigtails tonight. No makeup either, that's where I draw the line. I'm good with mascara and lipstick.

"You look beautiful."

"You're being too nice. Stop it. I don't do well with compliments Daniel, really. It makes me anxious, more than I already am."

"So, just to warn you, my mom has two sisters, my Tia Luiza and Tia Maria Elena," he says with the correct pronunciation. "When they're together, Lucy, Mary Ellen and Rosie, it's next level. They're the worst gossips, total *chismosas*. I'm warning you. They're inappropriate and nosy AF."

"What do you want, Daniel, the perfect Mexican girlfriend?"

"Just be you, the real you. That's all I want. I have something for you." He hands me a flat rose quartz stone. "It's a worry stone. When you get nervous, you're supposed to rub against the center of it. It's supposed to help you feel calm."

Taking it from him, it reminds me of the surface of the moon, a pale pink moon. It's a sweet gesture, really.

"I don't know if I believe it will work. It wouldn't hurt to try it. You haven't met my aunts yet."

"It's perfect. Thank you." Pushing it into my pocket, I am so glad he gets me.

******

The venue is stunning. Saying it is an outside wedding is an understatement. It's outside, but it's an outdoor barn with all the rustic charm and none of the animals. There are Edison lights hanging from all the beams, casting a warm yellow glow. All the tables have wood platters, like a slice of tree, sitting in the middle with jars of candles and wrapped with vines. It's beautiful.

The ceremony is very short, outside and simple. His cousin, Lilly, wearing a strapless cream dress paired with a thick bridal looking sweater, looks stunning. She has two bridesmaids and a flower girl who is only 18 months old. Daniel shares that the flower girl is her daughter.

"No way Detective Fernandez, I need to be married before, not after," I whisper to him.

"Can we talk about that now too? I mean it."

"Soon, not today, but soon," I tell him. I mean it too. Oh Lord, what is happening to me? Hearing the opening tones of "Here Comes the Bride," makes me tear up. I'm emotional at this wedding? That's not like me.

After the ceremony, we move towards a table. There are already people sitting there. One, his mom. The rest of them, I don't know any of them. The two women sitting with her resemble her enough for me to know they must be her sisters. My stomach does a queasy somersault.

"Ready," he asks, squeezing my hand.

"I guess so." My heart is ready to burst from my chest, his family. Now I have to talk to them? What the hell am I doing?

*****

"So who's your mom, Juliana?" His aunt Mary Ellen toys with her fruity drink. It looks so good, all slushy and salty. I miss drinks. "Maybe we know her."

"Most likely not, I was adopted." Sitting up in my seat, pulling my dark cranberry colored sweater tighter, it is hard to stay warm. It's chilly in this space. Outdoor weddings are beautiful, but it's cold even with the heater behind me.

"Adopted? I never met anyone who was adopted."

"Yup, the Johnston family adopted me." In my pocket, the worry stone keeps my fingers moving around and around the smooth cool stone, imperfections catching my nails.

"Where did you meet Daniel?"

"At a coffee shop, we met in the Tower District. I had to meet someone, and I met Daniel too. Then later, once I got to know him better, I asked him out."

The aunts' glance at each other. I'm being purposefully obnoxious, but this is all true. It's the truth that should have been, not the stupidity of Matt Lopez Senior. This is the only truth that should exist. It is shades of gray and little white lies. They don't need to know, the reality is that I was seeking someone who doesn't want me. This is just an upgraded story.

"Daniel, you didn't ask her out?"

"Well," I say, gesturing for him to stay quiet. I got this. "That's where it gets complicated. I'm sort of related to his partner, I was just born at the wrong time. The Johnston family adopted me. I'm Matt's sister, his partner's half-sister. It's weird, I get it. I'm sure Matt has unresolved feelings about me being his sort of sister. I'm sure that's what was taking Daniel so long to ask me out."

That answer seems to satisfy their curiosity.

"Do you have brothers and sisters?" His aunt Lucy asks,

"Adopted brothers and sisters?"

"I have a brother, Gabriel. He lives in DC. My dads were not happy he moved. They understood. Fresno was not for him. He is gay too. His partner is an attorney. They have two kids."

"Dads?"

"Oh, I didn't tell you? I have two dads." Forget trying to keep that worry stone in my pocket. This is harder than I planned. I openly twist the stone in my fingers, right at the edge of the table. "I have two dads and a brother."

"Two dads and a gay brother, but you're not," his aunt Mary Ellen gestures around.

Her reaction is calming, it's funny. I know this is a wild story, but it's based on reality. "No, I joke that they help me appreciate men. When you're surrounded by beautiful men, you know what beautiful men look like. I mean, no, no, I mean, that doesn't sound right."

Daniel starts laughing, "See *Tia*, she thinks I'm beautiful."

"No, you're dangerous," I correct.

"Well, maybe you can help me find some of these beautiful men," his aunt Lucy says giggling. "You can help me set up my app. I want a beautiful and dangerous man. I like the way you say that, Juliana."

"But Daniel isn't dangerous," his other aunt says, "He's the nice one."

"The nice ones are the most dangerous."

They make you fall in love.

DANIEL
February 22

"What are your plans? Do you want to get married and have kids?"

"Me? I want five kids. But, it's complicated." Juliana leans forward like she's about to share a secret with them, and then she points at me and makes a face. "I don't know. I'm waiting."

She just threw me under the bus. My two aunts look at me for an explanation. My mom giggles. Oh shit, I don't have an answer for them without saying hey, she won't even talk to me about it. I won't do that to her.

"So what's your plan, Daniel?"

"Well, my plan, my plan is that I need to figure out a plan."

Juliana starts laughing, "I'm kidding, Daniel. We don't need a plan. We need to stay friends. We're good this way."

"I don't want to be friends, Juliana."

"Oh, what do you want then?" Aunt Lucy leans closer, definitely too many drinks at this point, "If you're not friends Daniel, what are you?"

"He wants to play Fortnite," Juliana answers for me.

"The game," Aunt Lucy looks confused. "The game the kids play?"

"Men, just give them an Xbox," Juliana bites her lip as she answers, "Gay or straight, that's all they want, Xbox."

I never wanted to go play Fortnite so much in my fucking life.

*****

"Ms. Too Many Boyfriends needs better shoes," Lucy says to my mom once Juliana leaves the table for a moment. They purposely make sure I can hear them. They act as if I don't matter. They talk around me, treating me like a kid. It's who they are.

"Anna Nicole is a better name," Aunt Mary Ellen says. "That dress deserves better shoes."

"Hey, knock that off. Quit calling her that." It doesn't matter how old I am. They always treat us like kids. We are kids to them.

"Maria Ellen," my mom says, the three of them continue to ignore me. "Stop now. Do not speak of my future daughter-in-law like that. If she likes to wear Vans, so what?"

"I don't have faith in my Godson to ask her," Mary Ellen says. She is making sure I hear her. She even glares at me, "She will have to ask him."

"You know I can hear you right?"

My mom leans towards me, "She is my future daughter-in-law, right? You're going to marry that one right, Ms. Too Many Boyfriends?"

"Just give it time mom." If it was up to me, we'd go to Vegas right this second. I don't think Juliana believes this is real yet. She's almost there. "I can't pressure her. I can't rush her."

"See," Mary Ellen says, "She's going to end up asking him."

"She will too," Lucy says, "That girl isn't playing around. She knows Daniel is in love with her."

"No, no she doesn't. She seems like she is waiting for him to prove it," Mary Ellen says, pointing at me, "You need to prove it to her.

JULIANA
February 22

"You know, Daniel was the baby of that group, out of all the cousins," Mary Ellen shares with me. She is a *chismosa*. She's got all the tea. "Because of that, I think he was spoiled way more than the rest of them."

"Thanks," Daniel laughs, "Really?"

"Do you have pictures of him? When he was a kid?"

Mary Ellen pulls her phone close, searching for a picture. She leans close, "Here, that's an old one. That's him and his brothers."

I've never seen a picture of his brothers later, just the ones his mom showed before, when they were all so young, just kids. It's a picture of all three of them, in their 20's. Juan Carlos looks like the typical homeboy type, flannel and khakis, Eric, all black and long hair, studded belt, and beanie cap. He totally rocked the grunge look. And Daniel looks like a little kid, in jeans, a hoodie, and Jordan's.

"Oh Daniel, you were such a cute kid," I said to him. I hope we have a baby that looks like him.

Daniel just shakes his head. "That's not fair. Your dads didn't show me all your pictures."

"You didn't ask them."

"No, I was too busy being interrogated to ask them anything."

"Do they like him," Lucy asks me, "Your dads?"

"They like him," I say, "He's still alive right? I'm kidding. Yes, they like him."

"How did your brother have kids, if you don't mind me asking?"

"They used a surrogate. They were matched through an agency

with a surrogate, her egg, and their sperm. We don't know which one is the bio father."

"Is it weird? I'm sorry, I don't mean to be rude," Lucy says.

"No, it's not. I get it. They have a little boy named August and a baby girl named Delilah. They're biologically related, they have the same bio mom. My brother, Gabe, he's a stay home dad. Before that, he used to be a DJ."

"At weddings?"

"Weddings, night clubs, mostly clubs, I'd go with him. We spent a lot of time hanging out at the clubs."

"Were you a party girl?"

"Not really, I was just his sister, hanging out." Such an oversimplification of what it really was. It was a mess. I was a mess, Gabe was a mess. I am not that girl anymore.

"Was it hard as a kid to grow up with two dads?"

"No, I went to private school. It's a little different there. No one cared that I had two dads."

"Fancy," Lucy says.

"It's not as fancy as you might think."

"Did you go to college?"

"No. I did, and then I didn't. I just stopped going."

"Your parents weren't upset?"

"Well, what they were isn't easy to explain. They both had jobs that didn't require them to go to college, so it was easier for them to accept it."

"Who's older? You or your brother?"

"He is. He's a year older than me. What was Daniel like, as a kid?"

"Daniel was a brat," Mary Ellen laughs. "He still is."

"Hey, I'm right here," he tells her.

Mary Ellen just disregards his comment. She's had too much to drink too. "Everyone gave him everything he wanted, he's the baby but he's also the peacekeeper, the one who listens. He's everyone's favorite. He also tends to want the best of everything. It's fitting you're the one he brings home."

"What does that mean?" He gives her a heated look, like knock it off. I've never seen Daniel angry at anyone. Even with his brother, JC, he wasn't angry at him, just annoyed.

"Oh don't get like that, I mean, look at her. She's beautiful, Daniel. She looks just like Anna Nicole Smith."

Anna Nicole Smith. His mom said something about her to me too. The first time I met her. What did she say? I'm not sure what she said about her. I can't remember exactly.

"Anna Nicole Smith died of a drug overdose." Breathe slowly. Don't panic. Don't twist it in my head. Anna Nicole Smith was taking drugs. They don't think I'm a drug addict, alcoholic. Stop the thoughts, be calm. Anna Nicole Smith needed help. Breathe. No one helped Anna Nicole Smith in time. Anna Nicole Smith is dead. "Anna Nicole Smith killed herself."

Put it in the box. Don't do that right now. Think of the ocean, the beach, the feeling of sand between my toes. Everything is good. I'm okay. They must think I'm an idiot. I'm so stupid. Just breathe. Stop, think of the waves. The rocks, the rocks, keep my stone in my fingers, move it around, and think of that, smooth coolness in my fingers.

"She was very beautiful, though. His mom thinks you look like her."

"I don't look like Anna Nicole Smith." I drop my stone. It rests right next to my foot, right under my chair. I have to pick it up. Don't panic.

When I stand up, the biggest dizzy spell since my medication change hits, the world tilts and I stumble. Luckily, the table is close enough for me to press my hands against to catch myself.

Daniel stands up and rests his hand against the small of my back, "Are you okay?"

"I'm a dork. I'm fine. I just got dizzy. Maybe I am like Anna Nicole Smith," I say, sitting back down. The world is still spinning around me. Once I'm seated, nausea builds in the pit of my stomach. Blinking my eyes, I need it to stop. I'm so sick. I can't even take a deep breath. "I just need a Diet Coke."

"Daniel, go get her a ginger ale," his aunt says. "I'll go with you.

DANIEL
February 22

"Your girlfriend is pregnant," Mary Ellen says to me.

"No she isn't. How do you know that?" I turn and order Juliana a diet coke and water. "You don't know that."

"I have four kids and nine grandchildren, that's how I know. Look around, I knew when all these kids were coming," she swats at me. "She might not know it yet."

"You guys are messing with her too much. She's tired. She had a long day."

"Long day my ass, does she feel sick a lot?"

"She doesn't sleep well."

"Are her boobs bigger?" Mary Ellen tells the bartender to give me a ginger ale, taking the Diet Coke from me. "No, she can't have this. She doesn't drink? Why not?"

"I'm not talking about this with you," I take the ginger ale from the bar, "Do not tell my mom this either, you'll get her all worked up, and when you're wrong, then she'll be all heartbroken."

"You won't be upset if she is? When men don't want children, that's what they say, not now, not yet, don't jinx me," Mary Ellen says, leaning close so that all the other family around isn't listening. "Not, 'don't tell my mom.' You want that girl to be pregnant, don't you? Don't lie to me Daniel, I'm your Godmother."

"Look," I say, keeping my voice low. "I wouldn't be upset if she was, but you don't know her like I do. She needs space. Things need to be on her terms. I know that."

"Does Ms. Too Many Boyfriends want kids?"

"You guys are the worst. Don't call her that. Stop calling her

Anna Nicole Smith."

"She didn't like that, did she?"

"She's, she's very sensitive."

"It's because she's adopted. I read that when you're adopted, sometimes you can't figure out where you belong, even if you had a good family to adopt you."

"You're probably right." I hope she's right about all of it, even being pregnant. I hope she is. "Stop calling her Anna Nicole."

"I like her. Your mom seems to like her too," Mary Ellen stops right before we're about to get back to the table, "Just one question, what's up with her shoes, Vans and that dress?"

I can only laugh, "Leave her alone. She always wears Vans. I like that about her."

I give the ginger ale to Juliana, "My aunt seems to think this will help more than a Diet Coke."

"If you're not feeling well, that will help," Mary Ellen says to her, "It always works."

JULIANA
February 22

    I am such a dork. If I'm not focused, I'm going to lose my shit. My heart keeps racing. My brain hurts. This is hard. I knew it would be. I expected it to be. It's just more pressure than I realized it would be. His aunts keep calling me Anna Nicole. I know they don't mean anything by it, but Anna Nicole Smith killed herself. I tried to kill myself. I don't want to be Anna Nicole.

    "Hey little girl," Santiago moves to this table, pulling a seat out for his wife. "This is my wife Serena, your long lost sister."

    Little girl, that's what Juan Carlos called me. Santiago and JC are friends. Santiago told me they were still friends. Was it him? Did he tell Juan Carlos that shit about me? Stay in control, breathe.

    His wife is gorgeous. She's got big, innocent looking brown eyes framed by thick lashes. She's the type that doesn't need fake eyelashes. Her face is bright and welcoming, like you could lean into her and tell her secrets. She seems so sweet and innocent, there is no way we look alike.

    "You do," Lucy agrees, looking at Serena, then me. She gestures to Daniel and Santiago, "You guys are weirdos. They do look alike."

    "So you're the umbrella girl? Wait, the minimalist umbrella girl."

    "That's me," I say, that weird personality starting to push forward. Sip of my ginger ale. Don't lose my shit. I'm totally going to lose my fucking shit. Ocean, think of the ocean, breathe, I can do this. Let me be normal for one fucking second, one fucking night. Please, please, please, please.

    I gesture to Santiago, "That guy likes you."

    "He likes you too," she giggles, "Like a little sister. He thinks we would get along. Welcome to the family, Juliana."

Another cousin, carrying his own chair, plops himself right next to me, pushing himself right into the center of the action. His eyes are glued to the phone in his hand.

"I'm Tomás, nice to meet you," he didn't look at me, just watched something on his phone screen. He has a flat cadence that reminds me of Aaron, but I don't think his is purposeful like Aaron's. "Are you Daniel's girlfriend?"

"I'm Juliana."

"Hi Juliana, it's nice to meet you," he tells me, still looking at his phone, not making eye contact. "I brought you something."

He puts his phone down for a second, then digs through the oversized purple backpack he has. "I have my tools in here. My backpack clips in the front for sensory input when I need that. You can use it if you need that too. Here," he hands me a lap sized weighted blanket.

I take the blue blanket from him. It's much heavier than I anticipated, at least eight pounds. The silky fabric has a faint lavender scent. Holding it to my nose, I breathe that calming scent in. A deep breath helps me calm down. My brain needs a reset. "Thank you."

"You feel nervous. You feel like orange. Orange is not a good color."

"Orange, that's my favorite color," I place the blanket on my lap, pulling one corner up to my chin. The weight is calming. "What's your favorite color?"

"Blue. Blue is a good color." His blue phone is still in his hand, playing an action movie. "You put that on your lap. They make me nervous too. Do you have autism? I have autism. I don't like when they all look at me either."

I notice everyone at the table is looking somewhere else, anywhere else. No one is watching Tomás, so they're not watching me. I can take a moment to relax, visualize the ocean. Just catch my own breath.

I sip my ginger ale. I hate ginger ale. I'd rather have a Diet Coke, but I like the moment to myself, no one watching me. Because his aunt thinks this will help, I'm being polite. I want a fucking Coke. Once we leave, Daniel better get me a Coke, maybe some fries too. Maybe not, the thought of fries makes my stomach flip hard. I must be getting sick.

"No, I don't think I have autism."

"What's wrong with you? Do you have anxiety? Orange is not a good color. It's a worried color."

I lean closer to him, but not too close. He definitely has a tangible bubble around him. I'm sick of this shit. Susan says I should just tell people. People, most sane people, tend to respect the limits you give them. Susan says I should just say it. I whisper, "I have PTSD."

"That blanket will help." He glances over at me. That's how he looks at me, quick glances, then back to his phone. No eye contact. He uses his phone to point toward his aunts, "They ask too many questions. You can keep the blanket. Why do you have PTSD?"

"Tomás," Mary Ellen turns to him and snaps her fingers.

"It's okay." Turning my body towards Tomás without forcing eye contact, I look at his phone. He tilts it slightly to me, letting me see the movie. It's Star Wars.

"Why do you have PTSD?"

Daniel squeezes my hand.

"Bad things happened when I was younger," I say to Tomás, aware that although they're not looking at me, they're listening. Hard limit, do not ask. Susan says I can control the limits. "Things I can't talk about."

"Daniel is a cop. He can take care of you."

"I have to learn to take care of myself first."

"Me too, my mom, Mary Ellen, is my mom, she doesn't trust me. She thinks I'm a baby. I have a job."

"What do you do?"

"I work at a car wash. I go like this," and he pantomimes the drive forward gesture. "I signal people into the driveway. Do you like Star Wars?"

"I do. Do you?"

"I like Star Wars. My favorite one is New Hope, Episode 4. Daniel likes Star Wars too. He has a Star Wars tattoo. His favorite is Return of the Jedi, Episode 6. Which one is your favorite?"

"Rogue One."

"Rogue One doesn't count. I don't like that one. That's not a good one. There is no crawl. Everyone dies at the end. Pick a different one."

Watching his phone screen, I can see it is A New Hope. "It's a sad story, but they need to take that journey so everything good can happen next. They steal the Death Star plans. It's really a love story too. Diego Luna is in it."

"Diego Luna? Daniel looks like Diego Luna." He pulls up an image of Diego Luna and holds his phone toward Daniel.

"It's the hair. He has the same kind of hair," I say laughing, "I didn't notice that before."

"Diego Luna is not a Jedi. He is a rebel."

"He's conflicted in the movie. He struggles with trusting the girl."

"But he trusts her," Tomás reminds me, never taking his gaze off his phone, "Then they all die at the end."

"It's a good cry. I like the ending. It has to end that way."

"Yeah, I guess it's a good ending. I wanted to bring you that blanket. You should tell them you have PTSD. They'll stop asking questions. They don't ask me questions. Everyone knows I have autism. Do you cosplay?"

"No. Do you?"

"I'm a bad guy, an imperial officer. I like to be bossy. My mom says I'm too bossy. She says I'm pushy. What would you be?"

"I would be a Jedi."

"Daniel is a Jedi too. Jedi are always fighting their own internal battles, like they have PTSD. You can be a Jedi. You could have an orange lightsaber. You should just tell people you have PTSD. Then they'll leave you alone. I'm going to leave now. Goodbye. May the force be with you."

He collects his backpack, folds his chair, and leaves. Slowly, his aunts, his mom, return their focus towards the table. Maybe Tomás is right? I just need to tell people I have PTSD and just fucking deal with it.

"Are you good?" Daniel asks, quietly.

"I'm good. Are you good?"

"I'm golden."

"Is this song Candlebox?" I stop talking and listen. It's the familiar opening notes. I love this song. Before my accident, I used to tell Gabriel I wanted him to hold a boom box at my funeral with this song playing. It's not an original thought. I saw a video on YouTube once. After I had my accident, I deleted it from my phone. I haven't heard it in years.

"Sounds like emo shit to me," he laughs.

"Hey," his Aunt Lucy admonished him, teasing him, "Your mother doesn't like that language."

His mom glances back from the animated conversation she is having with another person from the table next to us, "What?"

"Nothing," his Aunt Lucy tells her.

"Maybe you're right," I say to him. Maybe he's right about everything. "I love this song. It's a sad song for a wedding, but I love it."

"Come dance with me."

Daniel is so warm, out on this cold night, he is so warm. I want to cry, so I just close my eyes instead. This is the most perfect moment of my life. Daniel's holding me. He feels like home. He accepts me. He introduced me to his mom, his family. Maybe he's for real? Oh my god, what if he's real? I don't deserve this to be real. I don't deserve a beautiful, dangerous man to hold me. Not me.

"Tomás must like you. He doesn't speak to anyone."

"I think he felt sorry for me."

"You can just say it, PTSD," Daniel says quietly to me, taking into my hair.

"I'm getting there." Let this feel real for the rest of the night. Just one freaking night, make my brain stop fighting me about this. "What are we Daniel?"

"This is real, baby girl. We're not pretending. I am not pretending."

I squeeze against him, pulling my arms against myself. He hugs me close, his embrace tight. I was never pretending. I can't say that to him. I hope he knows I was never pretending. Not one bit. "I'm sorry I keep asking you."

"Keep asking until you believe it. My answer is not going to change. I need you to know we have an audience, but I want to kiss you. Are you okay if I do that? My aunts can be next level with all their questions. They are totally watching. I don't care. I only care about what you want. Can I kiss you?"

I nod yes.

Daniel stops dancing with me. He reaches up and holds my face between his hands. With his soft lips pressed against mine, I cannot breathe. Warmth floods through my whole body. I'm dying. It's just a kiss, but no one has ever kissed me like this. No one, it is warm and soft.

It is home. It's better than sex. Okay, not better, but close, definitely close.

When he pulls back, I have to put my hand on him so I don't lose my balance. I'm so dizzy. My stomach is still churning. I feel sick.

Oh my god, I think he might love me.

He can't. He can't love me.

This is just pretending.

Oh my god, I love him.

Don't let me fuck this up and fall in love with him.

"I need to go home, I don't feel good."

"Let's get out of here," he says, taking my hand.

*****

It's so warm, in my bed, with this person who seems to understand me. I never want to leave the safety of this space. I want to stay at home with Daniel for the rest of my life. How did this happen? I just want to belong here, with him, forever.

I'm so tired. I want to sleep for two years, I am that tired. I want Daniel to stay with me, here, forever. I hate to admit it, I need him.

"When you get pregnant, we're getting married," Daniel says with authority.

Thinking about it, I have no fight left in me right now. Could he mean it? Who would it hurt? I should just marry him, "Okay."

He pulls the blanket over my head, and flicks it off super-fast, making it cold. "Okay? You're not going to fight me on this?"

"Not anymore. Today, yeah, okay. I promise."

DANIEL
March 10

Matt Senior's whole vibe is wrong. He's not looking at me, doing that anxiety provoking hand tapping thing he does. He never comes over to my cubicle to speak to me. He's a patrol guy, old school. It's a little late for this shit. He has no idea how important Juliana is to me. I guess that's his deal, he's always too late when it comes to his only daughter.

"What?"

"Matt says you're dating my daughter," he plops into the rolling chair adjacent to my desk. He doesn't sound happy about it. He crosses his arms and studies me.

"She's your daughter," I ask him, flipping the permanent marker in my hand onto my desk. It's strange, they look alike. At the same time, she is nothing like him. She is bigger than just him. She's real. "I've met her dad, her dads. I don't think they'll agree that she's your daughter."

Matt Senior shakes off my comment, lowering his voice and leaning forward, "Daniel, you're making a mistake."

"I think you made a mistake." Matt Senior was a good friend of my dad's. My dad would be so disappointed to know this side of him.

"You don't know her," he says, each word measured. "You think you do, but you don't"

"Why would you say that? When's the last time you spoke to her?" I lean forward on my chair, making eye contact with him. I'm not going to let him come here and tell me this shit. "You didn't even speak to her when you saw her at Adam's house. Who does that kind of shit to a person, your daughter?"

"She was not an easy teenager. She did things," he says to the floor, then to me, keeping his voice down. "She had an older boyfriend."

"She was a teenager, a kid."

"Her mom said she let him in the house, late at night, when she wasn't home."

"I know this already." Fuck him. I don't want everyone in the area to hear our conversation. He didn't even have the decency to pick a private place to have this conversation? I have to struggle to keep my voice down too. "I don't care, that's like 20 years ago, Senior. Give me a break. Can you honestly sit there and tell me you never did anything you regret? Wait, didn't you have a kid in high school?"

"Her mom said she lied a lot."

"You believe her mother because she was always honest with you?" I have to actively remind myself to keep my voice low. This man has the fucking nerve to come tell me shit?

"She made up stories about her stepfather. She was mad about her boyfriend. I ran the kid off. Juliana made up lies because of that."

"You think she lied about that?" He fucking knew what was happening to her. He's a bitch, he left her there. "Or was it easier to believe her over Juliana? You know what happened, don't you?"

"Did she tell you?"

"No," I lean back in my chair, making sure no one is hanging around, listening. People are walking around, and making loud jokes. It's a busy office. Juliana's life is not office gossip. "She can't say it. Whatever it was, she didn't tell me. I can see it in her. I know it's true."

"What are you doing with her?" He says, upset with me. Am I disappointment here? Somehow I've let him down? "You could have anyone, Daniel, why her?"

"I love her." I know that's true. I haven't even told her, but it's true. "She's fighting things that she can't tell me about. There is nothing I wouldn't give to help her. For her to see herself the way I see her. You don't know anything about her."

"Daniel," he says quietly, "She might not be well."

"Is that what you're calling it? She might not be well? Give me a fucking break," and I lose my temper, raising my voice just too much not to be heard. "Don't do that, 'let's call her crazy, shit with me.' She's not crazy."

Matt walks back over from the copy machine. He's clearly worried about this situation, glancing between us, fidgeting with the stack of appears in his hand. "What's going on?"

"Your dad is telling me Juliana is not worth my time," I say to him, gesturing to his dad. "Isn't that what you're saying?"

Matt leans against the cubicle, "Dad, stop. Leave it. It's none of your business."

"You are my business," he says, slightly louder than he needs to be. "You have no business talking to her, either of you."

"Are you honestly going to sit there and tell me you think she's lying? Why was she cutting in high school? Who would do that?"

"Her mom said it was for attention." Senior points at me. I want to break his fucking finger, "Celine agreed with her about that."

"Who gave her attention then? Who reinforced that behavior? Give me a reason that makes sense. Who gave her attention for that?"

"I don't know."

"She would not do that unless she was in pain. No one took her pain seriously, no one."

"Daniel, you're making excuses for her."

"You're making excuses for yourself." The picture of her at Aaron's house, she is dazzling in that picture. Happy, radiant, that's who she really is. "She told me she was hurting. Something at home was too much to deal with. Senior, you have no idea what happened. Or maybe you do, and you just didn't care."

"Her mom said she was lying."

It's easier to believe that whatever it was, it didn't happen. It's easier to not be culpable in this. She was a kid when her mother got married. Twelve years old. She's hinted to me what happened. Her stepfather touched her in ways he shouldn't have. Senior left her there, not believing her.

She told Chris Garcia. He told me. It's true.

I lower my voice, too many people in this space for me. My head is pounding. If this is anything like a panic attack, Juliana is the strongest fucking person on earth. This is painful, a freaking lightning bolt to the center of my brain. Leaning closer to him, I say, "Think about it, Senior, do you think she lied?"

He says nothing.

"Something awful happened to her," I said to him in a whisper,

"The people around her didn't take it seriously. They made her doubt her own experiences. They made her feel like she was crazy. She was gaslighted by the people who should have protected her. And now, all these years later, she still has to fight to be believed. You still don't want to believe her."

I have to stop. We're in our office. She wouldn't want all these people to know. She's so private about these things. I have to respect her privacy.

"That's her problem, you know. She doesn't know what's real because everyone convinced her it was all in her head. Who leaves their kid in that situation? You knew what her fucking stepfather was doing to her. It was just easier for you to leave her there."

"We don't know that Daniel," Matt Junior says, "You don't know that for sure. She's never said that to you."

"She doesn't have to say it for me to believe her." Matt is so much like his dad. "Give me a break Matt, you know I'm right about this. Even Adam knows it's true."

"You don't know what you're talking about." Senior is turning a deep shade of red. He's so angry I'm arguing with him.

I doubt he figured I'd argue with him. Or hint that it was his fault. Fuck this. Someone needs to tell him he's full of shit. "I see it in her every damn day. She doesn't trust anyone. You did that. That's your fault."

"Your dad would not approve of this Daniel," he says to me. "You know that."

"You don't know that. That's what you want to believe. I'll tell you what, my mom loves her. Juan Carlos, he loves her. They both love her."

He studies me, "Your mom met her? You took her to meet Juan Carlos?"

"I'm telling you, it's serious," I can't help but drum the pen against the desk. "I am going to marry her."

"I won't approve of that."

"I didn't ask you. She's not your fucking daughter, but she's going to be my wife. You decide how you want to move forward, but if you continue with this bullshit, I don't want you anywhere near her, anywhere near me. You can go to hell."

"Is this because of Eric?" He's reaching. He did not expect me to fight him this hard about it. "You couldn't save him, so you're convincing yourself you have to save her?"

"Eric has nothing to do with this."

"Are you sure Daniel?" He's getting louder with each statement, "You're not trying to save her because you couldn't save him?"

"Fuck off Senior. This has nothing to do with him." I cross my arms against my chest. He has no right to bring up Eric.

"Don't say that kind of shit, dad," Matt tells him. "Don't bring Eric into this conversation."

"Are you sure?" He looks at both of us, "You know what she did. Do you think you can save her because you couldn't save Eric?"

I don't have an easy answer. How does he know? I doubt he took the time to actually look her up. "Who told you? Matt? What the fuck would you tell him that for?"

"It doesn't matter. Think about it Daniel, is that what you want, to never know if it will happen again, to worry about her for the rest of your life? What if you had children and she hurt herself or them? How could you live with that?"

I bang the desk without realizing I would even do it. "Don't make her sound crazy. She is not crazy."

"Are you sure about that? Even if everything you said is true, I'm right too. You want that? You want to worry about this for the rest of your life?"

"You can go to hell," I lean towards him. "Don't talk to me about this shit ever again, you got that. You leave me and her alone. Fuck off. I promised her dad I would take care of her. That's exactly what I'm going to do. I picked her."

DANIEL
March 11

"I got into a fight with Senior yesterday."

Sunday morning, and I'm with my mom. This is my duty to her. She needs me to be a good son. It's cold today, no fog but cold. Yesterday it got up to 70 and clear. Today it's in the low 50's, got to love the Central Valley and it's mixed up weather.

My mom's busy cleaning her spotless kitchen and dancing around to 90's R&B, Eric's music. She's thinking about him. It's getting closer, the date. His birthday is easy, sometimes. His date, that day, that's a tough one. It's coming.

She glances at me, "Explain, fight."

"Argument," I say to her. Sitting at her kitchen table, I move the chair around, resting my feet on the next chair. She won't tell me to put my feet down. I know it annoys her. "He told me to leave Juliana alone."

"Well, he is her dad." She stops cleaning, tossing her kitchen towel onto the counter, and rinses her hands off.

"No," I interrupted her, "He's not. She has dads, they are not him."

"Mijo, I can't pretend to know what is going on with you and her." She leans against the counter, giving me her "mom look." That "you're my kid, I want to tell you what to do with your life, but I won't," look. "I know you care about her a lot. How serious is it? You're always so secretive with this kind of stuff with me."

"Mom, come on."

"I know, I'm your mom, I get it. You don't want to tell me

anything." She takes a new cup from the dishwasher and pours a cup of coffee. "Your aunt thinks she's pregnant."

"She told me." I knew Mary Ellen would tell her. So much for me being her favorite. That woman can't keep a secret for anything.

"You'll get married before, not after, right?"

"Juliana told me the same thing." It's funny how my mom accepts that as truth. There's no need for a test or a doctor with my Aunt Mary Ellen around. "I mean, at the wedding, I told her about Lily's daughter. She said the same thing. We have to get married before, not after."

"I like her," she says, sitting with me at the table, totally smacking my foot. "Get your feet off my chair. PTSD, what's that about?"

How long has she been thinking about that? She hasn't asked me about it. "You heard her, bad things happened when she was a kid."

"Aside from Senior leaving her?"

"Just trust me, trust her, it is bad. She can't talk about it." Juliana is very private about those things. I wish I hadn't mentioned it to Matt, to all of them, the 5150. If I knew her better then, I wouldn't have said anything. There is nothing I can do about it now. I need to tell her I know.

"Does she talk to anyone about it?" She touches my arm, "She should talk to someone."

"She does."

"Good, she's a nice girl. I really like her. She's very sensitive isn't she? Like an empath?"

"Empath," Chuckling, I move my coffee mug closer. My mom is zero to one hundred, she's all in, or she's not. I'm just like her. "Where did that come from?"

"I was reading some stuff online about PTSD. I guess it can make her sensitive to people. She's going to be my daughter in law, I need to know how to help her, support her. You should have told me before the wedding. You know we would have left her alone. Everyone is good with Tomás. You should have told me."

"I haven't figured out the balance, that's all. She's okay. She's got things in place."

"Therapy," my mom waits for an answer, watching my expressions.

"Mom, this is her personal stuff. Don't make it weird."

"I'm not making it weird. I want to help. Support her. I like her. After all, she'll be the mother of my grandchildren." My mom has a hopeful expression.

I hope Juliana is pregnant. I do want to be a dad. This is real adult shit. I know my future is with her. We need to get married. "Why do you think she's an empath?"

"Maybe she's not, but I've never shared so much. When I met her, I felt like I could tell her anything. Do you feel that too?"

I don't have a quick answer. I agree with my mom, but it's too personal to agree. Juliana is unlike anyone I've ever met. "She's very different from anyone I've ever dated."

"A good different," she moves her coffee mug around, "Do you think she wants a big wedding or just a small one? She gives me a small wedding vibe."

"She's a run-to-Vegas, type of wedding."

"Promise me you won't do that. I want just one wedding out of you kids. Have you asked her? I mean, really asked her? There is a difference between talking, joking about it, and really asking her about it. I mean, come on, Mary Ellen says she's pregnant. That woman is never wrong. Where is she? You guys are always together."

"Matt's wife wanted a spa weekend." It's funny how much I miss her already. She's only been gone since yesterday.

"Do they get along? Juliana and Matt's wife?"

"They do."

"Maybe it's her fault. You know, since she just had a baby. You know that pregnancy is contagious." She starts laughing. "I know it's not really, but tell me I'm wrong. It always happens like that. This is nice though, we can talk about this. I think you should ask her. If you really mean it, ask her right."

"I'll have to ask her dads."

"Ask them for permission, and then ask her. You know these rules, Daniel. Your father asked for permission before he asked me. You know how this works. We taught you boys how to be respectful men. That, your father did."

Messing with my coffee mug, I know she's right. I want to marry her. I haven't asked her. I'm making excuses, waiting for her to be ready, but what does that mean? Maybe my aunt is right. I'm waiting too long with everything, with Juliana. She's going to end up beating me to it.

Sounds stupid, I'm worried what my mom will say? Latino shit. It's real, but there is nothing I want more than to marry Juliana.

"Can I have your ring?"

"Oh Daniel, I've been saving that for you. It's her, it's really her. Are you in love with her?"

"I haven't told her, but yeah."

"She probably knows, you know, since she's an empath," she laughs, "You might want to tell her. Do you think she feels the same way?"

"I hope so."

Text to Aaron: I need to talk to you, in person. Nothing bad.
Aaron: When?
Me: Tonight? 6?
Aaron: 6 works. Where?
Me: My mom's house.
Aaron: Your mom, Mr. Policeman? Are you asking what I think you're asking?
Me: I want to marry her.
Aaron: We'll be there at 6, any food allergies?
Me: No.
Aaron: Does she know?
Me: No, I have to talk to you first.
Aaron: Good job Mr. Policeman. It will make a difference to her.

******

"Why here, Daniel?" My mom is totally over the top nervous. She's already straightened up the house, and made homemade enchiladas. It's funny. She has no one to impress. I guess being the mother of three boys didn't prepare her for this.

"Mom, you're fine. Everything is fine," I tell her, noticing their Lexus pull up. My mom is going to flip. I can feel the weight of her judgments. Juliana has two dads. My mom is going to flip out.

"So Mr. Policeman, why are we here?" Aaron asks with a knowing smile.

Aaron and Quinn made my mom feel at ease in five seconds flat. They can surely turn on the charm when they're not interrogating me. It's a different vibe now that I've passed their test. Their acceptance is evident. No twenty one questions from them anymore. No cop jokes. They engage with me like we go back years. I can see why Juliana loves them. They're good people.

"I need to ask your permission to marry Juliana." I'm sure I sound as nervous as I feel. "I want to ask her."

"Why, you tell me why," Quinn says, that gaze, flat and unreadable. It's interesting how fast he switches into that role of overprotective dad. "I know you do, it's been clear to me from the first moment you walked into our house. Why?"

"I can talk to her." I have to think, how do you articulate feelings? My world is incomplete without her. I didn't know she was missing until I found her. "She listens to me without judging me. She isn't expecting me to be perfect. She doesn't want me to save her."

"Humph," that sound, a judgment without words. Quinn sips his wine.

"I know, it sounds simplistic. That's the only way I can explain it. It doesn't hurt that she's the most beautiful woman in the world."

"My girl is fire," he says, using his glass to punctuate his comment.

"How did she become yours?" My mom is slightly buzzed; she's not much of a drinker.

"We've known her for a long time," Quinn is slow responding, seeming to protect her secrets, things she doesn't want others to know. "I think she was 18 when we met her. We watched over her as she grew up. She got sick a few years ago, very sick. She needed someone she could trust to look over things while she got better."

"What did she have?" My mom asks.

"She was exhausted. She needed to rest," Aaron says. "That's the easiest way to describe it. She's okay. She just needed rest."

"So we took over for her. Made sure things were taken care of, made sure she got the help she needed."

"What's Senior then?"

"Her bio father is an asshole," Aaron says, refilling her glass first, then his own. "I'm sorry, I understand you know him, but that is what it is. Whether she likes it or not, we've had her since she was 18 years old. Crazy teenager thought she knew everything. Then, we got to know her, the weight of what she carried. She needed a dad, we needed a daughter."

Quinn exchanges a look with Aaron, "I feel sorry for that Lopez man honestly. He doesn't know her like he should. He will never know her like he should."

"You know he told Daniel to leave her alone?" My mom has hit the talk too much stage of her wine glass.

"Umph. And what did you tell him, Mr. Policeman?"

"I told him to go to hell."

"He was friends with your father?" Quinn asks, looking at my mom but questioning me. He knows she's the weak link if he wants more information.

"He was," I say. Cop buddies, my dad and Senior were good friends. "We've known his family for a long time. They worked together."

"It was more than that," my mom sits up, working her memories through her brain. How did she miss a whole person? "They worked together, we knew their boys. We didn't know she was there. I had no idea he had another child. I don't understand that. Our boys knew each other growing up. They never said one thing about her. I don't understand who would do such a thing?"

"People hide what they are ashamed of," Aaron says, "We are not ashamed of her. She's our girl. She will always be our girl. You have to accept that if you ask her to marry you. We are her family."

"I love that girl," Quinn says, "I don't, we don't have our own children. We have her, her and her boy."

"What's up with them?" Maybe I've had too much to drink too. Juliana is very secretive about Gabriel too. "She's said it's better that he's gone."

"Your girl is jealous of him," Quinn says, watching my mom. He's talking to me, but doesn't want her to ask questions. He doesn't leave her out of the conversation. "I know she is. His fight with his demons was shorter than hers. For him, those demons were smaller. He had less healing to do. Society forgives boys faster than girls for certain behaviors. You know that. He found his happily ever after, faster. She doesn't need to be jealous of him, but she is. Don't judge her for that. She had to wait for you to find her."

"I think she found me."

"That may be true, but now that she found you," Aaron leans back, watching me again. "Now she has to learn what happiness feels like. Give her a chance to figure it out. She will figure it out."

"Do you have a ring?"

"He does," my mom tells them, holding up her hand and moving her rings around on her finger. "It's mine. Well, it's mine, but not mine. When my husband was first diagnosed with cancer, when we learned he was not going to win this fight, he bought me a new ring. It's beautiful. Three stones for three sons, past, present, future, all those things. It was more than I ever needed. I understood what it symbolized for my husband. He wasn't a flashy person. We have always lived a simple life. We didn't want to raise spoiled children."

"You did well, Rosie," Quinn tells her, glancing at me. "He's a good person."

She stops talking and digs around in her pocket. She pulls out a velvet box, opening it, showing them the sparking ring. She wipes her tears from her eyes. I hold her hand. I know this is hard for her. My mom doesn't like to talk about my dad being gone. She misses him.

Are you a good son, Detective Fernandez?

Juliana deserves a good man too. I just hope I'm good enough. I don't know how I got here. I was not looking for this. How the hell did I get here? I just went with Matt to meet his sister. A girl I never even knew existed. Now I can't live without her.

"After he passed, I put it back in the box. I wanted my old rings back. I didn't need this, like I said, he just wanted to remind me how much he cared about me. I figured one day Daniel could have it," she picks the box up, looking at it again, "Then one day he brought her home. I knew it was her. I don't think he knew it yet. I doubt she did, but I knew it. The way he watched her, the way she looked at him. My son fell in love with her right in front of me."

I'm an adult. I'm a grown man. I've witnessed horrific crime scenes and stayed stoic, but suddenly I can't look at any of them. They all could see it before I could admit it. I have always known it was her, from that first moment at the coffee shop. She called me dangerous. Even then, I just wanted to protect her, to take her home. To figure out what she was good for. Turns out, she's good for me.

"Do you think she wants to have kids?" My mom says with a

touch of hopefulness in her voice, "I want grandchildren."

"We're all waiting for grandchildren," Aaron laughs, "At least some that are not a whole country away. But the real question is, does my girl believe him? Does she trust you, Mr. Policeman?"

"I think so."

They exchange glances. Quinn leans towards me, "You have our blessing. We like you. You can ask her, but she has her own mind."

"Do you think she'll say yes?" my mom asks.

"She better say yes. She'd be a fool not to. My girl is not a fool."

DANIEL
March 16

"I need to tell you a story." I want to tell her about Eric. I need to trust her as much as she trusts me. "Come sit with me. I need to tell you something I have no words for. I need you to hear my story."

Juliana flutters around, turning the lights lower, grabbing a throw pillow. She moves to me, and then sits in the corner of her couch. She's able to hold me, hug me from behind, without looking at me.

"It's a story I can't tell. There is no unlearning this. Do you think you can hear it? Juliana, I have never told this story. People know the story, but I have never told this story."

"Don't rush." She's quietly whispering into my ear. She strokes my hair, soothing me. "There is no rush Daniel. You take the time you need. You can change your mind, but you know that I see you, right? I see you."

She squeezes me from behind. I don't think I could face her as I spoke anyway. If anyone can understand, it's her. Juliana understands me.

"My brother Eric was 32 when he passed away. He killed himself, Juliana."

She's trembling behind me. Sitting together on her couch, she makes no noise. I grab her hand and kiss it, then press it to my heart. When I'm with her, this lost feeling I didn't realize was there seems calm. She is my home. She wraps herself around me. She makes me centered. She's the only person I have wanted to share this story with. I don't know if I can do this. Juliana won't judge me if I cant. I know that. She is perfect. She sees me.

"I have so much guilt. I didn't see it. I should have seen it. We knew there was something wrong. We knew he wasn't able to live on his own anymore. He was spiraling out of control, but we didn't understand how bad it was."

Juliana presses against me. The warmth of her body calms me. I don't want to talk about this, but I need to. I'm drowning too. I don't know how to get out of this hole. How did she manage to move forward? I need her help.

"My parents knew he wasn't doing well. They convinced him to move back home. All he did was sleep, all day. He would be up all night talking about conspiracy theories and making wild speculations about people. He'd be on social media engaging with people, arguing with them about crazy shit."

She presses her leg around mine. She's tangled around me. She has me. I'm centered in this moment because she has me.

"When we talked, he would tell me he wanted to see heaven, but he was going to see hell first. He would tell me all about the afterlife and these ideas he had about purgatory. He was always the happy kid. Even though he was the middle kid, he was the happy one. But we didn't know that he was struggling so badly. We had no idea it was so bad."

Her tears drip against my neck, trickling down. She's not leaving me. She's with me right here.

"It was an awful day, Juliana, just awful. My dad was sick, my brother, Juan Carlos was in prison. My poor parents, they didn't deserve that. No one deserves that. Eric didn't deserve that either."

"I'm here Daniel."

"I have so much guilt now. I don't know how to move past it. I'm stuck too. I take care of my mom and try to help her, but it's an excuse. If I'm helping her, I don't need to focus on myself. I don't have to think of the things I should have done. I should have realized what was happening."

"You can't blame yourself for not knowing. People in pain usually can hide it pretty well until they just can't."

"He couldn't articulate what he was feeling. He just drowned in what he thought were his shortcomings. I wish I could go back."

"You need to talk about him, Daniel. Focus on the good times. You can tell me anything. You know that right?"

"You're the only person I can talk to." I hold her hand tighter than I need to. I can't let her go. I would go back for Eric. For her, if I could go back and find Juliana, I would. I'd go find her and get her away, away from all the pain she ever had to go through. She isn't alone.

"I wonder what Eric would have thought of you. I am pretty sure he would have loved you."

She catches her breath and squeezes me tighter. I can't say I love her right now. I want to. I want to ask her to marry me, but my grief is overpowering right now. I'm drowning in it. When she shares how she feels, hopeless, I know what she means. I am too. Sometimes there is no light, even though it's daytime. I hope she understands that. I can't tell her I love her. The words are right there. I hope she understands that actions are louder than words. I hope she knows that.

I want to say it but I can't. I hope she feels it. I fucking love her.

"I see you, Daniel," she whispers.

"I know you do. I think you might be the only person who has ever seen me."

JULIANA
March 27

Two blue lines.
Two blue lines.
Two blue lines.
It's really two blue lines.
Two blue lines mean positive.
Two blue lines mean it happened.
Two blue lines.

I can't keep my heartbeat in control. It's racing so fast I cannot breathe. I'm spinning, but I'm sitting still. I thought I would feel happy, excited. This is what I wanted.

I'm scared out of my fucking mind. My fingers are shaking holding the test in my hand. I tried two different tests. Both give the same answer. Both are positive.

I'm terrified. What am I going to do? I'm more afraid than I planned for. This is a deep, primal fear. I want to run. Where will I go? It's inside of me. I can hear my own heartbeat in my skull. I have a baby, half mine, half Daniel's, inside of me.

How can I get it back out? I can't do this. I am not ready to let something grow inside of me. No, no, no. Oh fuck, how do I make this stop? It's going to kill me. I can't do this. I am not ready to do this. No.

Think of the ocean. The ocean, the waves, it's okay. Take a moment and breathe. What would Susan say? She would say focus on what I can control. Take inventory of what is important. One, I wanted this. What changed from before to now? Nothing, it's just panic. I want this. It's okay to want this. Focus on pushing the negativity to the ocean waves.

I don't want it out. I want this baby. Keep breathing, everything will be okay. I'm going to be okay. It's what I wanted.

I just want to run.

What if I'm just like my mother? She would beat the fucking shit out of me when she was angry. She sided with my stepfather. She blames me for letting it happen. She hates me. I can't be her. I cannot do that to my own kid, Daniel's kid.

Oh my god, this is Daniel's baby. Oh my god, how can I tell him? How do I say it out loud? I don't deserve this. I am a failure. He can't want this. He will hate me.

What if I'm like my father? He ignored me, he still does. He pretends I don't exist. He didn't believe me. He thinks I lied about those things. He left me there. He didn't care.

I am not them. I am me. I will die trying to protect my own child. I will never do that to my kids. I will always believe them. I will believe in them.

I will not be my parents.

Holy hell, I'm terrified. I want this baby. I have waited a lifetime to have this baby. I need this baby to make it. My hand splayed on my lower belly. It's there. There is a baby there.

Oh god, no.

Fuck. I'm not married. I'm a loser. I am like my worthless mother, my father. I hate them.

Two blue lines.

There are two blue lines, and I'm not sure what to do. I have no idea how to say it out loud. The words are stuck inside. It's really going to happen.

I'm pregnant.

Fuck.

I need to call Susan.

"It's normal to feel this way, even when you want this," Susan says with such authority, I almost believe her. "This is especially common in women who have survived sexual trauma. Your body autonomy is being challenged. Like it or not, you have to work with your body to create a baby. You're bound to have feelings like this. This is normal."

"I'm not weird?"

"No, most people do not like change, even when it's something they want," She is happy for me.

"Do you think I'll be like my mother?" I ask her, biting my thumbnail. If I keep biting my nails, I'm going to make my thumb bleed. My skin is already raw and chapped.

"Do you think you'll be like your mother?"

"Absolutely not," Pulling my thumb from my lip, my voice sounds so flat, even to me. I'm lying to myself. I don't deserve this. "I will not be like my parents. They're both full of shit and didn't want me. I want this. I want this so bad."

She smiles, "Have you told the father?"

I'm not ready to admit I'm not ready to tell him. I don't know what he's going to say. "I need to be still with this for a little bit. I'll tell him but…"

"But?"

"What if I pushed him into this?" The truth is hard to say but I need her to hear me. He's not my boyfriend. We're friends who have a lot of sex. "We're not in a relationship. We're a hookup, that's all."

"That sounds like a conversation you should have with him, but tell me, what defines a relationship for you?"

"I don't know. I thought I had an idea. Now I'm not sure. We're friends for sure."

"What are your expectations of him? What do you think you want from him?"

I snort, tears flood my eyes again. "I got what I needed from him. I don't need him for anything more. I don't need child support. I don't need anyone. I don't need someone else telling me how to raise my child. I don't need him. I got this. I'm fine. I can do this on my own. Fuck him, I don't need him."

I sound like my mother. I'm ranting like she did. She did it all the time. She would go on and on about how she didn't need Matt Lopez and here I am; I'm doing the same thing. I am not my mother.

I need Daniel. I desperately need him. I need him to trust me. I need him to tell me this is not pretending. I need him.

"Juliana?"

"I need to give him a chance, don't I?"

"It might be nice to discuss the future plans with him." She moves closer to me, joining me on her couch. She really seems like she's excited for me. Maybe I deserve this? I don't deserve this.

She leans close, like we're friends, "You wanted this. He knew you wanted a baby. Juliana, don't forget you told him. He agreed. This can't be a total shock. You let him know what the plan was. You told him this was what you wanted from him."

"How long is reasonable?" I am so lost, so many confusing, contradictory emotions. Tell him, don't tell him. Do this on my own, let him help me. I don't know what to do. "I need time. I need space to think. I know I should tell him. I need to process this. This is real."

"Juliana, from what you have shared about him, he sounds like a reasonable person. You might want to think about talking to him soon. You should tell him as soon as you feel comfortable. Don't wait too long where it's a secret."

"Is it wrong to just hand him a baby?" Imagining the ridiculousness of that statement., I choke on a forced laugh. "Just say congratulations, it's a baby."

Susan reaches out and touches my knee, a nice firm grasp. It is centering, warm. This might be the first time she's ever touched me. "That might be just a tad too late. You might want to talk to him within the next week or so."

"Okay, I will. I can do this."

"Juliana, I have a team I work with that I think might be a good fit for you. It's an OBGYN and nurses who specialize in helping women through pregnancy after surviving childhood sexual trauma. They might be the team you chose to go with."

"I need my power back? Do you think I've lost my power?"

"You have your power. You have always held your own power. You need to let someone share your power. You are not the sole owner of power, Juliana. Power is not pie."

Damn that Susan.

JULIANA
April 9

It's my birthday. I hate birthdays, another year gone, and another reminder that I am a failure as a person. What do I have to show for myself? I am a loser who makes wedding cakes for other people. I've never even had a wedding. I suck.

I'm surprised I've made it this far honestly. I am still alive. I am still here. I should be dead. I'm glad I'm not. Really, I'm glad I have a chance to figure my shit out and push forward. I want a normal life too. I'm pregnant. It still feels weird to think about it. Is it a boy or a girl? Seven weeks. I'm not feeling that great, but I guess that's normal. I never feel great.

I need to tell Daniel. I have to tell him. I'm going to tell him. Tomorrow, I'll tell him.

I wasn't planning a night out. I normally just hang out and feel sorry for myself. This year is different. Aaron and Gabriel, they want to go out. Gabriel brought his new baby home to show off to his mom. They, him and his partner, Sam, are out here in sunny California to introduce his baby girl to his mom. It happens to be my birthday, so he wants to take me out for a party.

A party, what does that even mean anymore? I don't drink, now I can't drink, but I want to go out one time and feel beautiful. I want a pretty cake, a pretty dress, and a night to feel special. That's all. What's wrong with that? Isn't that a normal thing, to want to be celebrated?

I have to tell Daniel what's going on. I'm honestly being the biggest baby about it. It freaks me out to imagine saying it out loud. I can't say that to him. It sounds childish. This is real. I have to plan that conversation out. I'm doing that tomorrow. I'll tell him tomorrow.

Text message to Enrique Sanchez: Call me, I'm pregnant.
Message from Enrique Sanchez: WTF!
Me: I need your help.
Enrique: Go to Planned Parenthood.
Me: Fuck off Ricky.
Enrique: Jules, you can't do this.
Me: That's what you're going to say to me? You're an asshole.

I slam my phone against the countertop. I don't know why I give him the time of day. I should be getting ready for this party night. Instead I'm calling Ricky.

Missed call from Enrique Sanchez

I hear my phone buzzing. I'm not in the mood for Ricky anymore. I need to tell Daniel. I don't know how to tell him.

Missed call
Enrique: Answer your phone
Enrique: Happy birthday.
Missed call
Missed call
Enrique: Answer your phone. I'm sorry.
Enrique: image of E-40
Missed call
Missed call
Enrique: I'm going to tell Gabe if you don't call me right now. I fucking mean it. Pick up your fucking phone.

"What?" Furious with Ricky, I just yell, "I wanted you to be happy for me. You're not. Just forget it."

"I'm surprised, that's all," he doesn't sound as assholey as I figured he would. He sounds tired. "I am happy for you, happy birthday."

I know many people don't understand Ricky. Hell, I barely understand Ricky, but he's someone I can say anything to.

"I just needed to talk to you."

"How pregnant are you?"

"Almost two months. I saw my doctor yesterday. It must have happened in January."

"The cop?"

"I don't know how to tell him. Help me Ricky."

"Well, it's his fault." Ricky starts laughing, "Send him a text. Did your doctor do that picture thing?"

"An ultrasound?"

"Send him a text with that. Just say congratulations!"

"You're stupid. I need you to be serious. I need real help here."

"Jules," he sounds as if he's really struggling with being a sensitive friend, "Does he want kids? How shocked is he going to be?"

"Well, the truth is," I'm not sure how to say it. How do I confess we did this on purpose? I'm such a freaking failure. Even Ricky doesn't think I can do this. "We planned this. I promised to marry him when it really happened."

"Shit, Jules, what the fuck did you do to him?" Ricky starts laughing, which turns to coughing. I guess he hasn't quit smoking like he promised. "You're going to marry him? You're going to marry a cop? Daddy issues."

"That's a fucked up thing to say, Ricky."

"Do you want to marry him? Fuck promising him shit, I mean, do you want to really marry this guy?"

"I think I do. What does that even mean to marry someone?"

"You're asking the wrong person. I've been married 3 times, maybe 4, but the last one doesn't count because I wasn't divorced from number 3."

"Ricky, what are you doing with your life?"

"I plan on continuing my path of fucked up nothingness. What do you need from me? You want me to say marry him? Marry him Jules. You do that."

"You're not helping."

"Okay, give me a minute." The sounds of him moving around come through the phone speakers. "Let me pretend I'm Gabriel, do you like him? Not love, I mean, you won't kill him for leaving stupid shit on the floor?"

"I might, but I leave shit on the floor."

"Okay, check one. If we get three checks, marry him."

"Fine, this is a scientific test, right? Three checks?" Stupid ass conversations with Ricky always make me feel better.

"It's the Sanchez measure of nonscientific love. It worked for

Gabriel."

"Liar, I told Gabe to marry Sam."

"Maybe you should call him instead," he sneers.

"I'll see him tonight."

"He's there," he sounds genuinely surprised, "In Fresno?"

"He's at your mom's. He flew in last night."

"I miss him."

"Me too," I tell him in a whisper. I miss Ricky more, but he doesn't know that. I'm sure he remembers the past, those warm summer nights when we were all still so young, hanging out on the roof of their house.

"Back to our test, so what will you do when he pisses you off? I mean, next level, Juliana will fucking punch someone, give them a black eye, type of pissed off?"

"I don't think anyone but you ever made me that mad," I say to him.

Ricky called me a whore once, so I punched him. I may have punched him and given him a black eye. I'm lying. I totally punched him and gave him a black eye. He deserved it.

"So you'll be nice? Give him a chance to talk?"

"I'm going to try."

"That's two check marks. One more, here's a hard one for you, think about it before you give me an answer. When you need me, me, will he mind you calling me?"

"Ricky, we will always be friends. Whatever weird codependency shit we have, we'll always have this."

"He better take care of you. Jules, he better not hurt you."

"He wouldn't, he's really nice. If you weren't a criminal, you might like him."

"Shut up. Marry this guy, but make sure you answer me when I call you."

"Always Ricky, you're my boy. I love you." It's true. Ricky is my brother. "Now I have to tell him I'm pregnant."

"Fuck, we were supposed to get married and have kids."

"Dude, you have 16 different women who already have your baby. Fuck off. No."

He laughs, "We're better as friends."

"I think your brother told me the same shit, assholes. You Sanchez boys are both the same."

"Yeah, Gabe is gay and I'm a drug addict, we're the same," he says flatly.

"You know what I mean."

"Send me a picture of you when you're showing. That I need to see, Juliana Lopez is going to have a baby. It's about fucking time. When are you due?"

"October 29th. Don't tell Gabe. I'm not telling him until I see him later."

"Jules, I haven't called him," he confesses, "I'm sorry."

"You told me you would." Ricky needs Gabriel. I need Ricky. "Ricky, he misses you."

"He misses you more. Did you call him?"

I don't answer. I am just as guilty I have to fight tears. No one understands our relationship. I get it. Ricky is the only reason I'm alive. I'm the only reason he's alive. I need to make Daniel understand that. It's not what people think it is. I need him. He needs me. It's not a romantic relationship.

"You're going to need Uncle Gabe now."

"Hey, I need Uncle Ricky too."

"Your cop husband won't want Uncle Ricky anywhere near you once he runs a background check on me, your fucking father."

My heart hurts. My father was a bastard to Ricky. Aaron too, both of them, Ricky was just a kid. "I'm sorry Ricky. He's an asshole."

"I don't blame you. I never blamed you."

"Is all this fault, you know, the drugs?"

"Don't give yourself so much credit. I was a fuck up before, remember? Look, I got to go. Take care of yourself, seriously. Don't do all that, 'feel sorry for me,' shit you do. Marry the cop. He said he would?"

"He did. I told him I would once it happened."

"Then marry him. Don't be afraid. Just tell him and marry him. You can do this. And answer me when I call you."

"Don't die, Ricky."

"You don't die either, don't die. I need you to pick up the phone," he says, with authority, "Tell the cop, that's who we are. We pick up the phone for each other. You pick up the phone for me. I'll pick up for you. And don't die."

I love Ricky. I will always love Ricky. I'm not in love with Ricky.
I love Daniel.
Damn it.

******

I was surprised to find this black dress still in my closet. It's really from way back in my party days. It's got to be at least ten years old, maybe more. It's perfect for tonight, black, a line, and wrap around. Maybe too much cleavage, but the hell, it's my birthday. It's short. That's for sure. It's not obscene. You can't see my butt. At this point, I'm not going to attempt heels. I can't walk in them sober anymore. My vans are more suited to my clumsy walk anyway. Sobriety makes walking a challenge for me. I know it's normally the other way. Welcome to my reality. Walking is a challenge these days.

I hear Kim running into my apartment. I told her to bring me my keys when she was done adding some last touches to the cake she was decorating before I left the shop.

"Dude," she throws herself onto my bed, "Where are you going?"

"What?" Looking at myself in my mirror, "It's too much huh? I'm trying too hard, right?"

"Not at all." Sitting up and jumping off my bed, she sings, "Are you going on a date with Daniel?"

"No." I have to ignore her. She's a child. I focus on my hair. It's been forever since I tried to straighten it. The last thing I need to do is burn it.

"I like that lipstick," she says, digging through the makeup on my counter. "Oh, I love this color. You think I can wear that? It's too much for my skin tone, huh?"

"Orange might not be your color."

Kim pulls the edge of my dress straight. "You look really pretty. I've never seen you dressed up. Tell me you're not wearing those shoes."

"I can't wear heels anymore," I say to her, wiggling one foot at her. Yup, beat up Vans and my party dress. This is who I am. "When I was younger, dumber, I could. Now, I might fall down and kill myself."

She stops touching all my makeup, "Can I ask you something personal?"

"You can ask, but it doesn't mean I'll give you an answer," I say to her.

Flipping the off button on my straightening iron, hair done, make-up done, dress on, I'm done. I am a little self-conscious. This is still a part of me. I have to work past the shame. I am sick of living under guilt. I want to be free of it.

I'm tired of hiding everything. It's exhausting, all the pretending. There are hidden parts I've stuffed into boxes, so I don't have to deal with those emotions. I can be in a party dress and not drink myself to death. I can go out with my friends and not act like a total idiot. I have a reason not to be stupid tonight. I can do this.

"Why did you try to kill yourself?" She blurts out nervously, "Was it really that bad?"

"What?" All my breath leaves me. Does she know my secret? How does she know this? My blood is icy. "Who told you that?"

She turns a deep shade of red, embarrassed. She's not looking at me, her hands digging in her pocket for something, maybe her keys?

"Answer me Kim, who told you that?" I'm flushed with warmth. I was super cold, then instantly burning. It's literal fire in my soul. No one should know that. Only Aaron, only Quinn, Ricky, that's all. Not even Gabriel knows. Only they know. I have to sound like a fucking sane person to get my answers. "It's cool, I know, it's such a strange thing to talk about. Who told you?"

"Daniel did," she says. She's not making eye contact with me.

"He did? When? When did he tell you?" Trying to make light of this, I'm burning with shame. No one should know this. This is my secret to keep. My heart is racing, my body is trembling. No one is supposed to know this.

"You're not mad are you? I'm sorry. I didn't mean to make you mad."

"Kim," I say, struggling to sound calm. I have to convince her I'm not mad. I am fucking furious. I want to scream and throw things. I need answers from her. Deep breaths, big clearing breaths, fake it. "I'm not mad. When did Daniel tell you this? Who else did he tell?"

Kim picks at her nails, "Well, he told us the night we first met you."

"So," I'm going to be sick. Nausea burns up from my stomach, vile acid eating at me from inside. I'm such an idiot. I am not going to be sick right now. This is my fault. It's burning through me. "You have known this whole time? Does everyone know?"

"Yeah," she says quietly, "I'm so sorry, Juliana, we shouldn't know should we?"

"It's okay," I say, fighting back the sickness creeping up on me. If I start screaming, I might not stop. I am the stupidest person on Earth. I don't want to be locked up again. I cannot drown right now. I'm breathing, but there is no air left. Everyone must think they are so much better than me. Poor Juliana is fucking crazy. It was just a mistake. I made a mistake that no one is supposed to know about, no one. "Okay, okay, let me think."

"I'm sorry, I shouldn't have said anything."

"No, this is not your fault." Keep breathing, and stay calm. "Do me a favor and text Daniel. Find out where he is right now. I need to talk to him, right now."

******

I'm being irrational and immature. I do not care. I need to destroy it all. All of this, it's just so fucking stupid. I have been the biggest idiot on Earth. I am worthless. I cannot believe I have been such a fucking fool. I'm an idiot for trusting him. I am useless. I am the stupidest person. Daniel has known this whole time? He must think I'm pathetic. He must think I'm stupid. He must think I'm a charity case. What the fuck does he know about me and to tell everyone? Who the fuck does he think he is? He must feel sorry for me.

They didn't need to know this. This is my shit. It's mine. I hate him. How could he do this to me? All of this, all of it, it's just pretend. How could I be so stupid? I'm a fucking idiot. I made a mistake. It was just a mistake. I didn't mean it. I swear, I didn't mean it. It was an accident, a moment. I'm fine now.

Ricky, Aaron, Quinn, they know I'm okay now. They trust me. They know I'm fine. How could he tell people? That is so fucking perfect. In my pathetic life, that makes such fucking perfect sense. I hate him.

Echo lets me into her house. I don't even know how I managed to drive all the way over. I'm blinded by my own rage. I hate these people. What a pathetic mistake, all of this, even Echo, what her stupid ass good girl act, I know, she's got secrets too. Fuck her too. Fuck all these people.

"Wow, where are you going?"

"It doesn't matter." My anger is still bubbling. She is not my target right now but I will fuck her up if I need to. "Where is Daniel?"

"He's out with Matt, in the backyard. What's wrong? You look upset."

"Don't worry about it." I hate her. She thinks she knows everything with her fucking wannabe therapist shit. She doesn't know shit about me.

The two of them are sitting at the table. They make me sick. My stomach is filled with acid, eating at me. I do not know what I was thinking. We are not the same. We are not the same kind of people. I don't know why I convinced myself I needed to call Matt. I don't need him. I don't need any of these damn people. This will end now. I want my pathetic life back. I hate these damn fake ass people. I need to claim my power back. I don't need any of these people. I am fire. I can do this on my own. Everything will be fine. I don't need anyone. I can handle this on my own.

Slamming my hand down on the top of the table they're sitting at makes more noise than I realized. It causes them to jump simultaneously. They both give me that stupid look like I'm the one who's crazy. I am not crazy. Neither of them says one damn thing.

"Why did you tell them? Why did you look it up?" I'm furious but I'm not yelling. Yelling doesn't help me get my point across. I want to be sure he can hear everything I am saying. Daniel needs to hear me, really hear me. He owes me an explanation. "You need to stay out of my business."

Daniel's looking at me. I'm not even sure he knows what I'm talking about.

"You had no right to tell anyone that I had, had, an accident," Leaning forward, I'm fucking burning, but I'm not yelling. There is no need to yell, I need to be crystal clear. "That was not for you to tell. Why did you know? Did you go through the police report?"

"It's not what you think," he starts to say. "Let me explain it to you."

"No, do not make up excuses. You looked me up in your fucking police database and then you told everyone my shit. That was not for you to tell. No one knows. No one is supposed to know. I made a mistake. It was just a mistake. No one supposed was to know."

Daniel takes a breath, "I'm sorry."

"You're sorry? You don't get to be sorry." That familiar burning in my veins, the emotion I can't control. I need to fight it down. Blink, blink, blink, no crying. Do not cry. I am not allowed to cry about this. Panic is squeezing the back of my throat. Deep breaths, force air in and stay in control, I need my power back

"Juliana, stop and listen to me."

"Do not talk to me like I'm crazy. I am not crazy."

"I don't mean it like that."

"Do you feel sorry for me?" It's there, burning, killing me from the inside. No one can see it. I'm burning from the inside. I sound in-fucking-sane, I know it. I can't make myself stop. My heart is racing, I am literally dying. I'm an idiot, I'm useless. I can't breathe, air is coming in. I can't breathe. There is no oxygen in my breath. I have to finish this first. I need to stand up for myself for once. All of this shit is just a fucking mistake. "That's what all this is, isn't it? You feel sorry for me?"

He looks at me over, "Why are you dressed like that? Where are you going?"

"That's your concern right now?" It's there, all my anxiety. It's just at the corners of my soul, slowly burning through my veins. My head is spinning. I need control. "It's my fucking birthday."

Echo walks closer, but not too much. She must think I'm going to do something violent, maybe I am. Maybe I'm as crazy as they think. I should just knock her over, fucking bitch. Does she think she knows how to deal with crazy people? She doesn't know shit.

"Jules, I think we should go inside and calm down," she says in her patronizing tone. She's got that whole, non-threading stance down, palms open, 45-degree angle to me, at least four feet distance, fuck her.

"Fuck you, you are not my therapist. Do not talk to me like you know me." That's what all of this is. These people think they're so fucking perfect, and I'm crazy. I don't need shit from these fucking people. These people are not the same as me. "Fuck off, Esperanza."

"Jules, calm down. I know you're upset, let's go inside and talk."

This is all wrong. I need to leave. I don't belong here. "I don't need your help with this. I can handle my shit on my own. I've always dealt with this on my own."

Daniel takes another step toward me, "Can I explain this? Can we just talk about this? Let me explain everything to you. Juliana, I need you to listen to me."

"You leave me alone," I say, moving backward, don't fall, don't trip. My heartbeat is so loud, it's echoing through my brain. "I don't need your help. I don't need any of you. This was all a mistake."

I'm going to faint. My head is spinning. This cannot be happening. Even my words, everything I want to say, are swirled and confused. I can't form a clear thought. There was something I wanted to say, what was it? It's all pressing on me. The boxes in my brain are falling. They won't stay upright. It's too many boxes.

Imagine calm, focus on a calm color, green, focus on green. I squeeze myself into a ball. My whole world is tilting. I don't know where I am. "None of this is real, is it? It's just, not real. I don't know what is real."

Daniel touches my arm, "We are real."

"No, we're not," I can only whisper. Everything is spinning. I need to leave. This cannot be real. I'm such a waste, I'm useless. All of this is pretend. It's a fucking joke. "I need to go. "

"Stop and listen."

"Don't tell me what to do." I'm having a fucking heart attack. The whole world is whirling too fast. My blood is pounding from my heart to my brain. I'm so lightheaded. "No one tells me what to do. I have to go."

"Stop and listen, you need to stop and listen."

"I don't need to do shit. All of this is your fault. I can't believe you. I hate you, I just hate you. I'm pregnant and it's your fault." And I stop, full stop. All the boxes, rows and rows of boxes, are falling. I can't stop it. They're all falling. All of my emotions, everything is spilling out. The dizziness is back. Wave after wave of nausea washes through me, oh my god, I said it. "I'm pregnant. What do I do now?"

"Wait, what?" Daniel makes eye contact, "What did you say? Juliana, what did you just say?"

Everything is in slow motion. No one moves. I'm not worth being needed. I'm not worth his time. There is no way Daniel Fernandez wants this to be true. I'm just a mistake in his perfect life. He doesn't want this to be true.

My mother called me a whore. No one believed me.

No one ever believes me.

This is all a mistake. I stumble for a second and run back into the house, locking the door behind me. They're locked out of the house. They can't follow me. I have to get away. I don't even care. I need to leave. I need to get away. I hate these people.

I need to get away from all these fucking people.

Part II

1

Both boys have perfect teeth, dark hair, soft hands. The one in front will want to take you apart, and slowly. His deft and stubby fingers searching every shank and lock for weaknesses. You could love this boy with all your heart. The other brother only wants to stitch you back together.

Do not choose sides yet.

Richard Siken

Should I save her?

E-40

JULIANA
Twelve Years Before-December

"Don't be so shy. You're never shy about stuff like this, Juliana. Make it good. Tell me you love me."

"I love you, Christian. You're my fucking soul. I want to live inside of you."

"You look so pretty. Make it like cake."

"I can't."

"Come on, look at me. Think about chocolate cake."

"You tell me. Tell me in Spanish. Tell me you love me in Spanish."

"*Te amo.*"

It takes a full second to dawn on me. All the air in my lungs releases, and nothing, I mean nothing, will come back in. My heart is ripped from inside and exposed for everyone to see. It's absolutely silent. My brain is never silent. That video is not supposed to be playing, not on his fucking TV.

One of the most intimate moments of my life, something that is only supposed to be between us, is splashed across the screen in full color. I'm doing things and saying things nobody else is supposed to know about. He promised me, he swore he would never show anyone else. He swore he would never tell anyone else.

They stand there, his two stupid friends, not saying anything. Nobody moves for what seems like forever, but it can't be more than a breath or two.

"Juliana," Christian takes one hesitant step toward me. "It's not what you think."

"Oh my God," comes out of my mouth with a forced breath. My voice is choked off from me. I don't even know how I managed to say those three words. I can't move. I want to run from this room, to get away. I'm humiliated, but I'm not going to cry.

"It was an accident."

"Turn it off." It's one of those things, like an accident on the side of the freeway, you can't help but stare. With my eyes glassy and full of tears, I can't make myself not look.

Ray turns the power off. The image fades quickly. "We weren't watching it, Juliana, it was an accident."

"Listen, I didn't mean to show them." Christian takes a step towards me.

I take one away from him. "Fuck off Christian, what does it matter? I'm not your fucking girlfriend." It's easier to be angry than heartbroken.

Something about moving one foot in front of the other, that action makes me breathe. I'm hyperventilating, but I can't seem to get enough air in. This cannot be my reality, can it?

"You know what? You explain that shit to her, explain to your fucking girlfriend why you have that on your phone. Fuck off Christian."

I don't know why I'm so fucking pissed. I'm not even his fucking girlfriend.

JULIANA
July
Six Months Before

Wandering up and down several junk food aisles, I'm pathetic. It's like this all the time these days. I just exist from one moment to the next, waiting for someone, anyone else, to take charge and give me something more than what I have now. I have nothing now. Where is the patron saint of desperation? If there is one, I'll buy a religious candle and light it each day. Those candles from the dollar store with a picture of some saint on them? I don't even believe in that shit, but I'd try at least one. I'd make a *promesa,* and offer up a shot of tequila, the good stuff even. I'm bored out of my fucking mind.

So maybe it's my fault. I should try to get out, meet someone nice, but hookups are so much fun. Well, not fun, easier. I don't have time for talking and being cute. I'm not interested in going on a date. I just want it up against the wall. I want a beautiful man to tell me lies and buy me drinks. I have no interest in being anything to anyone.

I think of myself as a girl. Anyone over 21 shouldn't think about themselves as a girl anymore, but I'm a girl, a little too girly sometimes. The thing is, with my Mexican American background, I tend to seem younger than I really am. That keeps me developmentally arrested. It doesn't help that I pretend to be a Latina Barbie doll. I love sexy, tight clothes, short dresses and high heels. That is my style, tramp. With me, it's hooker or homeless, there is no in between. I have no interest in wearing jeans or leggings. I want to be sexy all the time.

Even my dress now, in the middle of the night, or is it technically morning? I don't know. Even this burgundy sundress is too short and hugs my boobs, making them look bigger. Even drunk, or maybe half drunk, I managed to make sure I looked hot. That's the only thing I'm good for.

With my thick brown hair and way too tight clothes, I'm cute. I'm not valuable. I'm invisible too. People don't know I'm here. For some reason, it's like the Mexican American guys don't see me, or for that matter, neither do the girls. I don't fit in.

I blame it on private school. I had to go from kindergarten through high school. Stupid ass private school. I sound, all white girl-ish, makes me seem pretentious, full of myself, and conceited. Maybe I am? My dad, the stupid ass, thought private school would make me a better person. What he didn't know is there is so much more trouble there. I got myself into way too much trouble. Who cares, he doesn't care about me anyway. He was the one weekend a month dad who never asked about me since the day I turned 18.

I'm not sure why I'm at Vons right now. I remember driving here and coming for something specific. What that was, I'm not sure now. I might be slightly buzzed. I only had one shot, or was it two? I just needed some help to get my ass out of the house. I feel fuzzy, floaty and strange. I'm not sure I ate any food today, so maybe that paired with my shot of tequila has me all dizzy. It doesn't help that it's like 4 or 5 in the morning.

This Vons is not near my house. I don't live over here, over near Roosevelt High School. It's close to my mom's house. Maybe that's why I initially drove here? I'm not really sure. I hate Roosevelt. I don't really like my mom either. I am a waste of cells, according to Elizabeth Salazar, or whatever the fuck her last name is now. I think it's Smith? I don't give a shit. She's always Elizabeth Salazar in my mind.

I would have gone to Roosevelt if I were allowed to go to public school, but no, I had to go to private school. I don't even know if this part of town has a name? Low income, that's what this neighborhood might be called. I grew up here and was forced to go to private school? My dad is a total asshole and made me. I hate that. Life sucks.

Luckily, I have my iPod. I have my earbuds in and I'm wandering around Vons. There is literally no one in this place. Maybe it's too early in the morning for most people. I don't even remember why I got up this early. I need to stop drinking so much. Wait, did I go to bed? Maybe I never went to sleep. Maybe that's what this is. I need to stop drinking so damn much. I needed something. What was it?

I focus on the song playing through my earbuds. What I love about an iPod is that I can listen to this stupid ass song over and over and over. ADD much? I want to breathe this song in and make it part of my fucking DNA.

E-40, I love E-40. My guilty pleasure is old rap music. This song, I love this song. I lost my virginity to this stupid ass song. At least the virginity that counted. Warm summer night on his roof, he didn't know what to do. I did. I knew how. He was playing this song on his radio. Then like a typical male, he acted like a total dick to me once it was over, asshole.

I need some stuff for the house. Gabriel doesn't believe in food. Gabriel is my best friend, he always has been. Now he's my roommate. We actually grew up near each other. His stupid brother is the virginity dick, literally. I never really told him. We don't talk about his brother.

Gabe's got the perfect body, so I don't blame him too much. I need sustenance. Bacardi, tequila, and chocolate cake, that's what keeps me alive. That and Diet Coke. That's why I'm here, of course, damn Diet Coke. It's like 5 am and I'm here in this damn store? I need to get out of here.

At the checkout lane, there is no one here to help. All the lanes are empty even though this one has the light on. Everyone must have disappeared, it's spooky and quiet here. I swear I'm the only person in the store right now.

Waiting, patiently, I take out my earbuds, but don't stop the song. I can still hear it playing while I pick up a mindless soap opera magazine and flip through it. There was a time when I was totally obsessed with General Hospital. I loved watching way back in the day. I think Gabriel might have even bought me the *Ultimate General Hospital Fan Handbook* or some shit like that. I wonder if Sonny is still there. He's just the cutest guy. I have a kink for dark, tormented men with issues. I've got issues myself.

"You need some help?"

"Yup," I announce, without looking up from the magazine. While tucking a lock of dark curly hair behind my ear, I'm drawn into the article about color. It seems like the new black is going to be pink. I can live with pink. Mexican American girls tend to look good in pink.

"So you want me to go over there and get your stuff too?"

I begin to roll my eyes at him, getting ready to cuss him out or something. It's not like he was here a minute ago, and now he's trying to rush me? I look up and see him. My heart just stops beating. It's silent for one moment, before continuing as if amplified up on caffeine. Not that I ever believed in it or nothing, but it's love at first sight. He's so freaking hot.

Standing behind the register, he is nothing like my type. First off, he's Mexican American. I may be Latino too, but I've always been into white boys. Come on now, private school equals white pretty boys with Adderall. He's not a pretty boy either. But don't get me wrong, he's fucking flawless.

He is muscular and thick. Maybe he played football in high school or something. He's way taller than me. I'm taller for a girl. His skin is so golden, he seems luminescent. He has really short hair that looks good on Mexican men. My heart just freaking stops, I forget to even breathe.

He could build a doghouse. My mom told me that a man has to know how to do three things. One, change oil, two, I forgot what two was supposed to be, but I remember three. Three, he should be able to build a doghouse. This one could build me a doghouse.

"Well, hi." Like a dork, I can't move. My heart's beating so fast, like I've only had coffee for breakfast and mocha for lunch, which might be better than the truth of just alcohol. I'm almost afraid he can hear it. I just set everything in my cart onto the conveyor belt, glad to have something else to do. I'd rather just stare at him. So I fixate on his name tag, Christian. Why does his name have to be cute too?

"Nice night huh," he efficiently waves the items over the scanner, totally not impressed with my boy toy charms. Damn Latino boys, they never are. "It's been so hot during the day. It's nice that it's finally cooled down."

"I like the heat." I'm an idiot. I just can't find the words to talk to him. It's my tongue, thick and graceless, I can't figure out how to form one coherent word. Maybe I'm drunk more than I realize. I'm not such a dork normally. Totally ADD, but not a dork. "Could you put that in a paper bag? No plastic, save the environment."

He stops and looks at me. I mean, not a glance, he checks me out. My skin breaks out in goose pimples, it's that obvious. He might know I'm nowhere near sober. It's kind of funny, really, being checked out by the check-out guy? I know when I'm being checked out.

"Hot flashes, I'm pre-menopausal," I blurt out, embarrassed by my own behavior. So maybe I'm not too graceful. I'm sure my warmth is apparent on my face. My cheeks are definitely flushed by now. He's got to know it's him. I'm so into him. It's fire just under my flesh. I just want to take this one home.

He smiles at me. He totally breaks eye contact, he knows I'm not sober, "Why are you at Vons at 5 in the morning? Are you drunk?"

Already my brain's lost in some perverted fantasy where we're rolling around on his bed and he makes me cry. Watching him pull out the paper bags from under the counter, quickly switching my Diet Coke from plastic to paper, I can already feel his rough fingers scraping along my skin. "Something like that."

"*Livin' mi vida loca y todo?*"

I have this thing for guys who speak Spanish with the right accent. I wonder if he would pronounce my name right. "You speak Spanish?"

"*Si. ¿Y tu? No habla español?*"

"Nope, I know what you're saying, but I can't speak it." I realize I'm staring at him . I can't believe I'm acting so stupid. I know how to flirt, don't I? "I never learned."

He stops ringing up my stuff and rests his palms against the counter between us. "Why don't you get your boyfriend to teach you?"

"What boyfriend?"

"You mean to tell me that a pretty girl like you doesn't have a boyfriend?"

"Not today," I blush. It's not the cute, pink in the cheek kind of blush, but the whole moist palms and burning up inside. He's not the kind I'm supposed to like, but I'm so attracted to him. "Not lately."

"*Pobrecita.* That's too bad. What are you doing?" He picks up my extra-large bottle of tequila, "Having a party or something?"

"I'm just an alcoholic."

He laughs at me. It's not one of those, ha ha, you're kind of cute and I just want to humor you, but a real laugh. "Well, at least you're not in here with your slippers on and rollers in your hair. Then I would be worried about you."

I want to see him naked. I want to know what he feels like. I want to take this one home. I want him to make me forget my name. I want him to make me cry.

"I need to see your ID."

"You're kidding right?" I don't even move. Finally, my fantasy reaches its orgasm and my blood pressure drops. I'm able to breathe again. "You don't really think I'm not 21 yet, do you?"

He's fixed in his spot, the conveyor belt still turning, even though my crap is already at the end of the counter. He makes it stop somehow, then crosses his arms like he's the fucking check out king. "I've got to see it."

I exhale, trying to seem so very put out about having to find my ID. So I dig through my tan Coach Hobo bag, with all the C's all over it. I love this bag. It was one of those spur of the moment splurges. I sure hope I can find it, ADD is real.

Damn, he's hella fine. I want to just take him home and have pervy sex with him. Oh, maybe he'll spank me and call me a bad girl.

Shit, I hate when I'm so ADD. What was I looking for again? Oh, yeah, the wallet. Once located, I flash my driver's license at him like a cop would. "There. You made my day. I haven't been carded in a long time."

"Juliana, huh? Ms. Lopez?" He takes it from me, and reads the damn thing. "So you're a regular J-Lo huh?"

"Juliana is fine." I wonder how many girls a day this boy picks up on.

"So Juliana," he puts my stuff back into the cart, before leaning on it, "What do you do for fun?"

I just don't know what to say. Nothing I can think of sounds good. I like to dance? I like to drink? I like having hot wild sex with boys from the grocery store? "Not much."

He glances at me like he's not sure if I'm flirting with him. Or maybe it's against store rules or something like that. He seems to need an extra push.

I want this one. I lean against the little stand where the credit card thing sits, "What time do you get off work? I need help getting my groceries inside."

He stops, leaning toward me. "What kind of help do you need?"

"I think you know what I mean. I need your help. I think you can help me out."

"I think you're drunk. I don't think you really mean it."

"You don't know anything about me, Christian," I say, over enunciating the syllables of his name, while gesturing to his name tag. "I'm telling you, I need your help."

He is totally thinking about it. He might think I'm crazy and drunk, but I can tell he's imagining what I'm offering.

"Tick, tock, Christian, your time might be up. Is it a yes or it's a no?"

"Maybe," he says, waiting for my credit card to do something to his register. The familiar metallic sound releases the cash drawer that he instantly slams shut.

"Maybe isn't a yes or no. I don't have time to be fucking around with you. Yes or no? I need a sure thing. I'm not looking for it to be all gentle and stuff. I just want a guy to say 'hey, I can make you cry.' I just want it to be so good, I could cry."

He blushes. Should I even be having this conversation with some man that I don't even know at five o'clock in the morning? "Cry huh?"

"Yes, I just want to cry." It gushes out in a rush. "I don't need it to be all soft and sentimental. I want it up against the wall. I don't even want to know your name, Christian."

The world just stops. Standing there, neither one of us says anything for the longest second of my life.

Then he leans forward. "I can make you cry."

Oh lord. What? Shit.

He presses a button at the register, running extra tape at the bottom of my receipt. "I get off at 6. Give me your number and I'll text you."

I try to hide that my hands are trembling. Biting my lip, I've blanked out on my own number. What's my number again?

"Don't try to give me a fake number. I'll remember you the next time you come in. There is no way I could forget you."

I am so embarrassed that I am attracted to some random check out guy. I scribble my phone number and tear it off. When I hand it to him, my fingers brush against his, sending chills down my spine. His fingers are warm. I glance up at him, my eyes locking on his for just a second too long. I'm totally going to have sex with this guy.

"I'll see you later." I let go of the slip of paper.

At the entrance of the store, I glance back. He's just standing there, watching me leave. He's just so pretty.

*****

He texted me right at 6. I gave him my address, stupid, but I'm too tired to drive. I let him in and just led him to my room, avoiding Gabriel. I'm not in the mood for a lecture. It's not like he doesn't do the same kind of shit. He acts like he's perfect.

"I need you to make me scream," I tell him, turning my speaker hooked up to my iPod. In my room, I double check the door is locked. "I need it so good it hurts. Can you do that for me?"

"Damn girl, where have you been all my life?" He removes his hoodie and tosses it onto the chair in the corner. Jeans and a tight royal blue t-shirt, he's killing me already. His jeans are just a little snug, so that the spot where his t-shirt is supposed to meet his jeans leaves his waist barely exposed. That is my fucking favorite part of men. Right there, that little pinch of exposed skin. I want to lick him right there.

"I'm not playing with you. I need this good," I say, closing my eyes and waiting for him to join me in my bed. Fresh out of my shower, I'm in a t-shirt. I don't have time for playing games. I need it badly right now. I need him to make me forget my own name.

He yanks off his shirt and jeans and climbs onto the bed with me. He kisses me hard, tasting of mint. His tongue is in my mouth, and his hands are up my shirt, squeezing my breasts. My nipples get hard under his rough touch. It's almost painful how hard he's pinching me, but it is so right. The wave of pleasure waves through me. This is what I want.

He takes my breast into his mouth and bites me, causing me to jump. He hurts me just enough to make it good. There is a very thin line between pleasure and pain. I lean over that line just a little too much. I don't give a shit. I'm so wet I have to reach down and touch myself. I'm going to fucking explode. Taking my fingers, he licks them while his other hand, fingers scraping along my thigh.

"Shit, I need to fuck you right now."

"I need it hard."

He rests on top of me, his weight pining me to the bed. I love that, being under a man, pushing into me, filling me. My body is tight against his. I swear he presses all the way up against my cervix. I lost all my breath, "Oh, oh, oh, shit."

My whole body is clenching against him. With my hair wrapped around his hand, he's thrusting into me so hard I have to grab him by the shoulders to gain leverage to meet his thrusts. I can barely catch my breath. It hurts, but it's so good. It's just how I need it.

"Christian, fuck." He's so deep in me I can't think. I hope that was his name. The pressure in my core is building. I'm going to explode. I'm totally going to pass out after this. I reach down and touch him, wrapping my fingers around the base of his penis.

He takes his hand and wraps it around my throat, but he doesn't squeeze. He holds me. Panic floods through me. I don't know this guy. He could totally kill me. What the fuck is wrong with me? This is such a bad idea.

"Just don't kill me." I'm almost there again. I'm literally on fire.

"I'm not going to kill you." Then he starts sucking on my bottom lip, "I need you alive for a few days, but no more than a week."

Well, he's an asshole for sure. That's just my type. He can kill me next week. Today, I need to get off.

He does squeeze my throat, just enough to make me know he's got a hold of me. Fuck, I'm going to have another fucking orgasm. I lean forward, right to where he'll hit me perfectly. There, all the heat burns from my core to my fingertips. I'm dying under him.

GABRIEL
July

    Juliana keeps secrets. I keep her secrets too. I wonder where she found this one. She thinks she's so sneaky. I can hear her talking to someone. I just turn the music up on my radio. I don't want to know what she's doing.

    I wish she would look for a real boyfriend. I worry about her. We are not the same. I am looking for love. I don't know what she's looking for.

    She's always been like this. I hate to admit it. Ever since, well, ever since she started having sex, she's always been looking for something. She measures her value through sex.

    I don't know what's going to happen to her. I wish I could help her. If I lived with her demons, maybe I'd be the same way. She has nothing, no one. She only has me. I'm not strong enough for her.

    I won't say shit to her. I'll just help her pick up the pieces.

    I'll keep her secrets.

JULIANA
July

    It's beautiful tonight, crystal clear sky and a warm breeze. I have no idea when Christian finally left this morning. I was able to sleep right after. I struggle with sleep.

    Spotting an empty table in one of the corners, I make my way over. It's nights like this when I like living in Fresno. There is something spiritual about this place, warm breezes. It's the land of hopelessness lost in the San Joaquin Valley. This is where I belong, in a land of despair. Fitting really, I am stuck in the middle of nowhere with no place to go.

    Pretending to read my book I've been carrying around in my bag, I can't relax. It's this gothic dark vampire story that someone suggested I might like. Tonight, I can't find the energy to concentrate on the words. I keep thinking about how good he made me feel. Why can't I find that every night? Little bruises all along my shoulder, I need a man like that.

    Filled with coffee shops, restaurants, and unusual gift shops, the Tower District is one of the few places to get out and walk around without having to be inside a mall. It's my favorite part of town. A lot of people like the new construction past Shaw Avenue. I prefer this part of town. Number one, I can walk everywhere here. I live about a mile off the main part, only a few blocks from Fresno City College.

    The opposite way, off Olive Avenue, there are cute little shops and restaurants. Gabriel, my roommate, found an affordable duplex when he moved out of his house. I moved in with him once I was old enough. That was always our plan, grow up, move out, and have sex with all the boys.

    It's a busy place, but it's safe, here in the Tower District. The only drawback is that sometimes it's hard to find parking. We're so close to the local community college that students take up all the parking. Usually I walk everywhere so I don't lose my spot. Besides, I hate driving. My car is a piece of shit.

Several couples lingered about, making their way from one place to another. One couple catches my eye, the gentle way he touches her hair, the way she seems so content with him. I wonder if they're married or just dating. I mean, they seem too happy to be married, but then again, it's too cozy to be only dating. He must love her, the way he looks at her, like she's beautiful. Even from here, I can tell he thinks she's beautiful.

I don't believe in love. I've seen what deep levels of desperation people have been pushed too in the name of love. My stepmom, she hates me, so my dad is okay with pretending I don't exist. Fuck off. I don't need him. My mom ignores me to make my stepdad happy. I'm nothing but drama as far as she's concerned. She even turned my dad against me. If that's what love is, fuck it, I don't need that. I'm cool with sex. Sex is great.

Using an extra chair as an ottoman, I can make out the soft music playing. It's the Romeo and Juliet soundtrack. Two star crossed lovers in Verona. I love all those old contrite notions of romance, where everyone dies at the end. I want to die at the end too.

"Hey, sorry I'm late," Christian's arrival pulls me back to this reality.

"It's okay." Getting stood up after a fantastic morning of sex would have been appropriate. That's the way my life usually works out.

"So, what should I order? Do you want anything?"

He has short hair, kind of too short. I want a guy like Christian, hot, dangerous, kind of rough.

"I'll order you something. I need to run inside anyway. What do you want?"

He looks at me, "I'll take one of you."

It's a stupid pick up line, but it makes me blush anyway. I like this one. He's at least trying to be charming, sort of. He's sort of an asshole. I like that.

"So Juliana, what do you do for fun? I don't know shit about you except that you hang out in Vons at 5 am, drunk off your ass."

Christian says my name like poetry. He's chocolate cake.

"Nothing much, I'm a loser, you know."

"I might have some suspicions about that. It's not every day I hook up with girls from the grocery store."

"Just on Fridays? Or is it coupon day?"

"You come home with me and it will be coupon day."

"I'm not cheap. I like Prada." Wiggling my left foot at him, I show off my cute shoes. I spent way too much on them, but I will wear them every day. I have a connection and get a discount. Still, a huge waste of money. I get that. Just one pair, maybe two, it won't kill me. You can't take money with you when you die anyway. I don't think I'll make it past thirty five.

"Prada huh, I don't think I could afford Prada."

"Maybe you can't afford me? Maybe this is your lucky day." I shake my cup at him.

He only smiles, toying with his paper coffee cup.

"What are we doing? Is this a date or an excuse? I think this is an excuse. I don't need all this really. I'd rather be under you."

"Come to my house," he says, pulling me up to my feet. "Leave your car here. I'll bring you back later."

"As long as you don't kill me, just to be clear, my dad is a cop."

He stops and looks at me, "No shit?"

"Yup, he's a cop, Fresno PD baby. Don't kill me okay."

Christian has no idea I haven't seen my dad in at least five years. He doesn't need to know that. Besides, my dad wouldn't even care if I did end up dead.

Christian turns off on one of the streets, thick with trees. I've always liked this area, near the airport. No sidewalks, not too many streetlights, and large yards with thick, green lawns decorate this area. One day I hope I can afford my own house. He pulls up in front of a simple blue house, with light blue trim. Big windows open out to the front yard. I followed him.

Inside, only a well-worn cinnamon leather couch and a large screen television sit in his living room. There are a few things here and there, but not like Gabriel's house. I'm used to having everything look like a Pinterest perfect space. This is just a little pre-rummage sale. Okay, maybe not that bad. It's not an Aaron approved space for sure. It's a little post college, not quite adult, style. There are a group of pictures with some preppy looking girls all wearing stuff from the Gap. Didn't he say he has a sister? I think he mentioned he had a sister.

Flopping onto his couch, I should have some grace, right? Oh well, he's already seen me naked. Images flash through my brain of his bronzed skin pressed against my own.

"Where do you want it?" I sing, "Over here or over there?"

I could love him. How does anyone love anyone in 24 hours? Less than 24 hours? It's me, I'm getting too far ahead of myself. It's scary. I shouldn't be this into him, but there is no denying the excitement building in the pit of my soul. I want him to kiss me again, his hands to hold me down again. I am here for one thing. This is not about love.

"How about my room," he gestures down the hall. He makes me fluttery, nervous. I'm not like that, nervous about sex. Christian makes me nervous.

Leaning against the door frame, I study him. He seems guarded all of a sudden. His room is not what I expected. It's actually nice. It's decorated much nicer than the rest of the place with its muted green colors and touches of lavender. It smells like lavender. It feels like a girl.

"What's your fantasy, mister? What are we going to do here?"

He blushes bright red while staring at the lavender candle in his hand like he's never noticed it before. He places it back on top of his oversized distressed dresser.

"Come on, tell me. What's your porn star fantasy?"

Picking up the lotion on his dresser, I notice it's one of the lines from my store. We sell tons of this raspberry cream crap. I hate raspberries. It's a strange scent for a man to pick out. Usually it's vanilla. Men love vanilla for some reason. I wonder if he bought this himself, or if someone else gave it to him? There is only one of the stores I manage in Fresno. Was there when he came in? I would have noticed him, right? Setting the lotion down, I need one more time. I don't want to think about his lotion, I want to have sex.

"Porn star fantasy, I can turn on porn if you want."

I can't even pretend to be embarrassed. "Porn, porn is good."

With several kisses, we're on his bed. He stops for a second, fumbling with the remote, and there it is. Just what I thought it was going to be. The funny thing is that I've seen porn. Trust me, I've seen a lot of porn, never straight porn. This is straight porn splashed across his TV.

It's this stupid hip-hop looking girl with a bunch of tattoos and some not cute, thick boy. She cusses at him in Spanish. I guess it's supposed to be hot or something. It's not. It's different. It's just different somehow. I've never watched real Latino people porn.

I maneuver away from him and just flop over at the end of the bed, lying on my stomach. It's a window into some world I'm usually left out of. It's interesting. I guess there is no other word for it. It's interesting.

"What are you doing?" He sounds bewildered or embarrassed.

"Nothing," I don't want him to think he disgusts me. I have a high pervy hot boy threshold. "I haven't seen this one."

"You're not going to say anything?" When he sits on the bed, his weight shifts the blanket gently. He's afraid of what I might say? I picked him up in Vons.

"What do you want me to say? Oh you're such a bad boy? Oh you're such a naughty boy? I'm so disgusted with you."

"Yeah," he's just so at ease and dumbfounded. He's fun. "Call me a pervert or something."

"You're a bad boy." It's porn, I know that. We're taught not to like it, but we do. How did they maneuver into that position? She seems to enjoy it. She's not talking anymore, and just making this animalistic grunting sound. But that's not what gets me. It's the glazed look. I live for that look. It's that, "Now, I can die," look.

Glancing back at him, I know what I want. Already wiggling out of my shirt, I just tell him, "Do that to me and leave it on."

*****

"Are you going to get dressed or what?" He's sitting up on the counter, tossing grapes from the bowl next to him into the sink. With the lights still off, he's missed more often than not. It doesn't seem to bother him.

"You're not into a naked girl in your kitchen?" I'm not really naked. I have his t-shirt on, but the way he looks at me, I might as well be.

"I'll never be here without thinking about it."

Dancing around, the radio is playing some hip-hop music I don't like. The same type of thing is playing in his bedroom. "Don't you like anything but hip-hop?"

"That's a good song."

"No it's not." I'm in search of something else. I love dance, and alternative music. Hearing something worth dancing to, I leave it there. It's an old song, reminding me of summer nights. And tonight is a hot summer night? It's perfect. "That's my song buddy, deal with it."

He puts the grapes down, admiring his mess all over the floor. He starts picking them back up and tosses them into the sink, this time making it. "I haven't had sex to porn in a minute."

"I thought I was special." Feigning shock, I exclaim, "How many girls have you shown your porn collection too?"

"I don't have a porn collection." Christian starts cracking up. As if he's never heard such a stupid comment. I'm a dope, so it's most likely true.

Looking through his refrigerator, I can't locate one thing worth eating. He's got beer and string cheese. Nice. I'm starving. I'm so tired that it's turned to extreme hunger. "You work at a grocery store and have nothing here. That's sad."

"What do you want?"

Closing the refrigerator door, I touch the floral note paper with an aqua message about a plane's arrival. What am I in the mood for? Something sweet, something with chocolate, I want cake. "Who's in Virginia?"

"A friend," Christian moves in front of me, reminding me of how tall he is. He's built like a football player. He could totally kill me. "What are you in the mood for?"

"Chocolate cake."

"Let's go out. I haven't taken you anywhere. You must think I'm a cheap bastard."

"Are you feeling guilty about that?" Standing there with one hand on my hip, I'm surprised. Doesn't everyone want someone else to take care of them? Could he take care of me? "Why does it matter?"

"It doesn't. Come on, let's get out of here."

Closing my eyes, the flavor of the cake hits me. I love chocolate. There is nothing that chocolate cake can't fix. It's so velvety and rich. Cake is the most perfect food on earth. Mashing the next mouthful against the back of my fork, I notice he's watching me. "What?"

"Nothing," he chuckles through a smile.

"What?" Maybe I have cake smudged on my face? Moving around in the booth and touching my hair, I hope I don't seem so dopey. "Just tell me."

He scoots closer to me, whispering, "You make the same face during sex. It's cute."

Instantly, I'm burning red. There are times when maybe I don't have so much shame, but right now, in this second, I'm burning alive. "You're not supposed to notice things like that."

He has the nerve to give me a dismissive look, "You think you're so hella hardcore, but you're not."

My eyes grow large for a second. This damn Mexican boy thinks he knows everything. "What does that mean?"

He moves back from me, fumbling with the empty straw wrapper. "Where did you come from? How come I never noticed you around before?"

"I usually don't shop at Vons. I got to Costco instead." Finishing off my cake, I push the plate away. "Actually, what we do is go to Costco and eat all the samples for dinner."

He raises his perfectly shaped eyebrows, "Who's we?"

"Gabriel, my roommate."

Christian sounds offended, "You live with another guy?"

With my hand, I dismiss him, while rolling my eyes, "He's gay."

"Are you sure about that?"

"He's really gay." Pointing my fork at him for emphasis, "I've seen him kiss guys. How many guys have you kissed for a girl?"

"None." Christian touches his Fresno State baseball cap and then gives me a sideways look, "You need to be careful."

I really don't want to burst out laughing at him, but he sounds so concerned. It's cute. "Are you serious?"

"Yeah," he sounds like someone's older brother, "Be careful."

"Dude, I picked you up in Vons. I don't even have my car. You could totally be a serial killer."

"You can call your dad the cop. He can come out here and shake me down."

"My dad is an asshole. He's a cop, but he's also an asshole. He honestly wouldn't care." It's a sad truth I have to face. Some days I can easily accept he's not my dad. Others, it kills me.

"How about your mom? She can come pick you up."

"You're going to leave me here?" I push my coffee mug around. I need to keep myself in check. I am not all needy and clingy. I know a hookup when I see one. "You can leave if you want. I can call people. I'm not helpless, you know."

"I'm not going to leave you here. We need to go back to my place at least one more time tonight. I should have asked before, but are you on anything?"

Anything? Idiot, just say it. "No Adderall but I could use some if you have it."

"Don't be dumb."

"Are you asking me if I'm on birth control? I know how to take care of myself. I'm not looking to trap you or any other man into a relationship. I'm not stupid. This is not a relationship by the way."

"Are you a party girl, Ms. Adderall?"

"Not today. Do you party a lot?"

"I do and I don't." Christian takes his time, thinking about what he's going to say before he says it. "I hang out a lot, but not like going out at a nightclub or anything. We sort of all hang out at each other's houses. It's cool and all. It's nothing major."

Maybe he sees me as a real person? Sometimes I hookup with men and that's all. There are no conversations. I haven't been on a date in a long time. Gabriel says I should date, but I'd rather not. It's so hard talking, waiting, it's not for me. I want the power. Everything about Christian is confusing. Is this a date? I just want to pack him into a box and never let him go. "Do you like working at Vons?"

"No." Christian laughs again. Maybe I'm a little bit of a dork. "I hate it."

"What do you want instead?"

"Well, really," he looks at me with his dark eyes for a second, before returning his gaze back to the retro printed pattern on the table. He seems to measure his words suddenly. Maybe he doesn't trust me? "I'm almost done at Fresno State. I'm going to be done by the end of summer."

"Really?" I wish I was smart. College, it's an idea I've toyed with myself. I never had the courage to do it. I love reading, but what does that mean in terms of a job? Besides, I barely made it out of high school. I'm too ADD to focus on work. "What are you getting a degree in?"

"I'm getting my teaching credential. I was going to teach high school history. Later, I changed my mind. I decided to go with the younger kids. I'm glad I did that."

"You're going to be a teacher?" I thought he was this pervy hip-hop boy. It's the sweetest thing I ever heard. Isn't that just perfection? A mature Mexican American man who speaks Spanish, has real dreams, and a porn collection? I can't believe he's real. I poke him to check if he's real.

"What?" He's self-conscious now, touching his baseball cap.

"I think it's great."

"It's something I have always wanted to do. Most of my friends don't even know what I'm doing in school really. They think I'm wasting my time. It's not that they don't care, they just don't understand."

"People suck."

He gives me this look, like maybe he's saying too much. Christian doesn't say anything more until the waitress is done refilling my coffee cup. "I don't know why I'm telling you all this."

"I like hearing about it. Are you scared? I would be afraid of all those kids depending on me. Kids scare me."

"It's not the kids. I worked at the recreation department before. It's the rules, the standards, and all the testing they want to do to the kids. It's too much for them. The kids are the best part. They keep me young."

"You want your own kids one day?" Sometimes, I wish I could just be married and be a stay home mom. If I'm really honest, I am never honest, I really just want to have a kid and be a mom. That's never going to happen.

"Yeah, one day," He stops, it's like he has this wall around him instantly. "What about you? I know you work at a store, which one?"

"I work in the mall." I hope I sound bored. My job is nothing. I'm a waste of cells. "I do make-up for a living."

"You work at those makeup counters?"

"No, I manage one of those bath and shower gel types of stores. I sell people crap they don't need." It's sad really. Then I remember it, "Actually, your lotion, the raspberry one? We sell that."

"I have raspberry lotion?"

"You do. Maybe one of your random girlfriends left it there. We sell tons of that stuff. It's crap really. All our stuff is a waste of money."

Adding more sugar to my refilled coffee, I'm sure I sound immature. Who cares about lotion and hand cream when you're about to embark on a real career of helping others? "I think it's great that you want to teach. I mean, I'm totally surprised."

"Did you think I was a loser who only watched porn?"

"Maybe." Christian has a bruise on his arm, the leftover remnants of a fight? I can see the outline of fingers, a closed fist. Slowly, as I trace the edge, he locks his gaze on me.

"How did you know you wanted to be a teacher?" I ask him, still tracing the outline of his fading bruise. I wonder where it came from.

"It's more of a calling. I just felt it, you know? I always knew it was something I wanted to do." Again, he starts talking to the table before looking at me. He presses my hand flat against his arm, stopping me from tracing his bruise. "Nothing else seemed right for me. I tried a lot of things. Nothing seemed to fit. When I finished school the first time, with my BA, I was working in this office. It was so boring. I went back to school. This feels right."

Why I didn't notice it before, I don't know? He's got honey colored skin. It's just so smooth and golden. He looks like glitter, I want to lick him. "That's beautiful."

The smile he gives me, it's just sweet. "Now you're making fun of me."

"No, really, it's beautiful. You are a beautiful soul."

"A beautiful soul, huh? No one has ever said that to me," he blushes. He actually nudges me like I'm some guy pal of his. "You sound all girlie all of a sudden."

"But you are. You have this light. You're cake."

"Cake huh? Chocolate cake?"

And with my eyes closed again, I add, "Chocolate cake with fudge frosting."

JULIANA
July

    No one ever told me the zoo could be romantic. Okay, so maybe I'm getting ahead of myself. It's been years, I mean years, since I last traveled to the Chaffee Zoological Gardens, but here I am.

    Even though it is hot outside, Christian takes my hand and tells me about the different exhibits. It strikes a chord inside. Maybe I missed something? It's one of those things I don't allow myself to think about. My life is what it is. I don't normally date. This scares me. He's taken me on two dates now.

    Something about him holding my hand, the way he kisses me, I am perfect with him. I don't mean that in a conceited way. He makes it all wonderful. It's sweet. He even knows his way around. He sounds like a teacher, pointing out the important details that I would have missed without him. I didn't know that certain monkeys are very social and have to be with other animals to keep their sanity. No one has ever taken the time to teach me anything.

    "You come here often," I asked him once we walked into the rainforest exhibit. It is shaded with a canopy. It's warmer here, thick with lush trees and coves to wander through. The air here is thicker, moist and heavy. The sound of a waterfall is twinkling, somewhere close.

    "Not really."

    "You seem to know your way around." A fragile bird floats towards the nearby benches, and I'm captivated by it. With its delicate wings flapping so fiercely, its beauty is spellbinding. Here, the birds are free. I can't believe this, we're on a date, at the zoo?

    "It's a zoo, Juliana. They don't change much over the years. When's the last time you've been here?"

"I don't know. I can't remember." It's an honest answer. I think I came here once on a field trip, in the 4th grade.

"Where do your loser boyfriends take you then?"

"Not here," I tell him. Plopping onto the bench, the tiny blue bird is startled and flies away. I have zero grace. "I don't date."

Christian sits next to me, "What do you do for fun?"

"Nothing special," I shrug. My last date, I don't have a last date. I picked up some guy at the club. We went to his house. I don't remember much. "Where do you take your girlfriends?"

"Here," he laughs when he answers me.

"Very smooth, you can get a girl all hot at the zoo." Giggling, I notice how cute he is again. He is the type I insist is not my type. I tell myself so many lies; I'm not honestly sure what's true anymore. It's startling really, how intense I burn in his presence. I think, hell, I think I love him.

"I don't know anything about you," Christian tells me.

"What do you want to know?"

"Where did you come from? What do you do with yourself most days?"

"I work at a store selling overpriced crap people don't need. I like to read. I like music, just not all that hip-hop crap you like. That's all you need to know."

My secrets are sinful. Maybe I wear them on my sleeve, but I'll deny them to the grave. Moving from him, I channel my mom, Elizabeth Salazar, attitude and everything, "I ain't nobody's mama, and I ain't looking to be saved."

"What are you looking for then?"

The weight of his question hangs in the air. I don't know what I want. I don't want to be alone anymore. My clock isn't ticking, but I sure don't want to be alone anymore. I want a man who can build me a dog house. "I don't know."

"What do you want out of life? Come on Juliana, what the hell are you doing with your life?"

Standing in the warm afternoon, I can't move. For some reason, I want to cry. My damned tears are pressing against the back of my eyes, and if I blink, which I desperately need to do, they'll fall from my eyes. I refuse to cry in front of this boy. I won't do it. No one wants me. My parents, they don't want me. I am here, I am alive, but no one ever wanted me in the first place.

"I want a margarita."

All my energy is focused on one concentrated point right, at the tip of my finger. Squeezing it, I'm able to control everything outside of myself. Pressure building, I'm amazed at the intensity of my own heartbeat, right in my own finger. With several cleansing breaths, I'm reminded of who I am. I am fire. I can't be cornered by other people. I might be nothing to most people, but someone, somewhere, one day someone special will love me.

"I want to go dancing and have sex with guys who work at the grocery store. What do you want Christian? What's your life plan?"

"I don't want to be like my parents." He rubs his face, "I didn't mean that."

"What are they like, your parents?"

"All they do is fight." He absently rubs at the bruise on his upper arm, just covered by his shirt.

I know this. I know who gave him that bruise. Reaching to him, I rest my palm against him, covering the bruise with my hand. "You don't have to say anything."

His gaze locks on mine, we just sit. Neither of us says anything for a moment. In the middle of the zoo, we are connected. I know his pain. He knows, I know.

"One day I'd like to have my own kids and stuff," he quietly says. "I guess I want to get married one day, be a dad, I want to be a little league coach."

The power of his words just hit my soul like a drug. It's like something I didn't even know I needed and craved. Normality, the state of being normal. I want to be normal too. He's made it to the other side. I can see it. Where I am still drowning in my pain, he has made it. I want to live inside him. "You're cake Christian. You're just like cake."

He laughs, "Do you even know how to cook Juliana? Can you even bake a cake?"

"Little boy, you don't know who you're messing with. Can I make cake? Damn Christian, you have never had cake like I can make. I am not talking about cake from a box. I can make the best chocolate cake you ever had."

"I don't believe you. I doubt you can bake a cake."

"Okay, I admit it, I can't cook, but I can bake. You want cake? I'll make you a cake."

I'm going to make this boy the best cake he's ever had.

*****

Chopping the chocolate, Christian watches me like I've lost my mind. Ignoring him, I'm careful to pour the fine crumbs into the batter. Mixing everything, balancing my art, I double check the temperature of the oven. I take this crap seriously.

"Why don't you make me a drink or something?" It's funny how he seems so lost in his own kitchen. He doesn't seem to know where anything useful is. I had to dig through countless drawers seeking out the simplest tools.

"What do you want?" He's rummaging through his refrigerator, "Beer, beer or beer?"

"Put salt and lemon on it for me, and a dash of Tapatio." Again, I check the texture of the mixture. It's got to be just right before I pour it into my waiting pans. I think the name of this recipe was something like Decadent Chocolate Cake. It was on some Pinterest board I like.

Picking up my beer now that my pans are in the heated oven, I hop up on the countertop. "Have you ever done it here? I mean right here, right here up on this counter."

"No."

"What a shame," in my mind, I'm already wondering how it would go down. He's the right height. He could do it. "I'm sure it would be good."

Christian blushes bright red, "Damn Juliana, you need to stop saying shit like that."

Leaning back on my hands and dangling my legs, I just smile at him, before whispering, "What's wrong Christian, too hot in here for you?"

He steps up to me, resting his now empty beer bottle next to me. "Don't start anything you can't handle."

"Oh I can handle it. Can you?"

And he leans over and kisses me. Before I can even breathe, we're yanking off everything. He does me right there, right on the counter.

*****

"Well?" I'm biting my bottom lip, waiting for his answer. Why his opinion of matters so much is evident. I have an uber-crush on him, I think I'm ten steps away from being in love with him. With my heart pounding, I can't get my breathing back to normal. "What do you think?"

Christian rests his fork next to his place before saying anything. He puts his finger in the air, requesting more time, while lifting his coffee mug with the other.

"Stop that."

He sets his coffee mug back down. "This is the best damn cake I've ever had. Where did you learn how to make this?"

"Do you think it's good?" It's such a sweet compliment. I want to be good at this. I know how to bake. This is my superpower, as dumb as it might be, it's my superpower.

"This is great. Don't eat any more of my cake," he teases, moving the rest of the cake platter towards him.

"I'm glad you like it."

"I owe you an apology." He is sheepish. "I didn't believe you. After your performance on my counter, I thought you couldn't make a cake. I thought that was supposed to distract me from the truth."

"I hope it distracted you, but not from my cake."

JULIANA
July

    Resting against him, our bodies twisted up in the sheets, everything is flawless. How have things gotten so intense so fast, I'm not sure? Somehow, the air has this flavor when I'm around him. He's perfect.

    Listening to his heart beating, I love that sound, that thump, thump, thump sound. How soothing, how comforting to know that under my hand, the muscle that keeps him alive, that keeps blood pumping from one vein to another, is under my fingertips. It's a miracle, how the body knows to keep blood moving. If it didn't, would we drown? Would we simply close our eyes and smother ourselves from inside? Wouldn't that be a wonderful way to die?

    "There is something I have to tell you."

    "What?" I want to kiss him, but everything is so perfect right in this instant that I don't want to move. I don't want to do anything that will make it stop. I just can't have fallen in love with this boy so fast. I just can't. I don't believe in love.

    "It's really important."

    "What?" Looking up at him, it's true. I am in love. He's everything I ever wanted and would never confess. I only trace the faint remnants of the bruise on his arm. I see his secret.

    "I have a girlfriend."

    "Oh." I've just spent the last few nights in this man's bed, and now he tells me this? Damn, he used me. Damn, I let him. Isn't this the stupid story of my life? I let boys use me. I use boys.

    "She lives with me."

"Oh." I'm confused. I've been to his house. There wasn't any sign of her around. Then it's crystal clear, yes there are, I just didn't want to see them. She's there, little things, pictures and make-up, tucked in corners that didn't quite make sense, but were easier to ignore. She's there.

It sneaks up on me. I know what I've done. I know what I am to him. I'm nothing more than some random girl who picked him up and used him. At most, I'll be a memory stored in some long forgotten file in his brain. He will play house with some other girl, some other girl he loves and will one day marry. He will never belong to me the way he must belong to her.

"Oh."

Christian is picking his words one at a time. "She's been out of town. She's coming home tomorrow. She went to see her parent's in Virginia."

"Oh." The post-it, I saw it. I knew it. I knew it this whole time. I'm not going to cry over some stupid boy. "Oh."

"Say something." Christian seems guilty, "Say anything."

"What? So you fucked me. So it was fun. Go home, just go home Christian. Leave me alone." I hold it in until I make it into the bathroom. Of course, he has a real girlfriend. This is my punishment.
Turning on the water, I don't want him to hear me cry. Stupid boys, I swear they are not worth it. They are not worth it. How could a boy I barely know break my heart?

JULIANA
July

"Do you remember that night, on the roof of my house?" Gabriel whispers into my hair. He loves to mess with my hair.

We're on our couch, some overpriced thing he insisted we buy. It's a beautiful dark gray, nothing I would ever pick myself. Thick chenille fabric and a few matching throw pillows. Gabriel snuggles with me in a thick blanket under us. I'm cold. He isn't. We compromised with a blanket under us. I'm the one on the losing deal of that compromise, I'm freaking cold.

I know what he's talking about. We never talked about that before. The one time we tried to hookup. Stupid really, I was 16, Gabriel must have been 17. It didn't quite happen. We were so young and stupid. We're still young and stupid. Maybe I'll stay stupid my whole life.

"You're mom beat the fuck out of you that night," he goes on, lighting a cigarette. I wish I liked smoking. I wish it gave me the same satisfaction it gives him. "You ran away. You came to my house."

My mom was furious with me. She was always furious with me. I never did anything right. That was nothing special. My memory of Gabriel is stuck deep inside me where it belongs. I keep that one, not because of the beating, but because of Gabriel. I remember him. Gabriel is beautiful and light. He has always been light for me.

"We went up to the roof of my house, where she wouldn't be able to find you. We were up there forever. We watched her leave the house. Where did she go?"

"Work." He forgets her days were opposite of mine. "She worked nights."

"I wanted to give you romance, Jules. I wanted you to feel loved."

Hot tears press against my eyes. I have to keep my eyes closed to prevent myself from crying. I hate these feelings. I hate remembering how awful it was at home. "I know Gabe, we don't have to talk about that."

"I tried," he says, lacing his fingers in mine. He rolls over to me, pressing his body along mine. "I just wanted to take care of you. I loved you, Jules. I love you."

"I know you did, I know you do," thinking back, the memories of that night fresh in my brain. I don't want to remember this. Gabriel, my best friend, we tried. It didn't really last. He's not attracted to me like that. He tried. I love him for trying.

I never told him that I slept with his older brother a few days after, up on the roof. Gabriel didn't need to know that. Ricky was in an old school rap phase. It was just me and him listening to music and watching the stars. I think Gabriel went to see his dad.

They don't have the same dad, him and Ricky. His mom just gave all her kids the same last name, her last name. Connie Sanchez, mom to Enrique, Gabriel, Isaiah, Edward, and Michael Sanchez. Five boys, what kind of luck is that? I don't believe any of them have the same dad.

Ricky was playing Captain Save A Hoe by the Click, featuring E-40. Ricky told me he loved me. He swore he loved me. Ricky said he wanted to be with me.

Later, when Ricky's friends were hanging around, he said the most fucked up things to me. He'd called me names in front of his friends. They laughed, thinking it was funny. Gabriel's fucking brother was 19 years old. I was 16. He called me a whore.

That's what my mom called me. She called me a whore.

I lost my shit on him one night. I screamed and punched him. Ricky didn't even get mad. He just held me when I was done yelling. He let me cry. He said he was sorry. He told me he was sorry. No one ever said sorry before.

A few days later, Ricky knocked on my window at 3, 4 in the morning. I let him in. I guess we made too much noise because my stepfather walked in. I wasn't allowed to have a door that locked. Who does that shit? I couldn't have a door that locked? He caught us. Once he realized what we were doing, he didn't say anything and left, slamming my bedroom door behind him. He left me alone for two months after that. For two months, he left me alone.

But Ricky didn't.

Suddenly, he was an invisible boyfriend. When we watched movies at Gabe's house, he would sit next to me and hold my hand. If Gabe noticed, he never said one damn thing. Ricky was my first boyfriend. I liked how he looked at me. He made me feel pretty.

I don't know what happened. One night he stopped coming over. I think he moved in with his girlfriend or some shit like that.

But for two months, my stepfather left me alone.

GABRIEL
July

    Juliana doesn't know her parents threatened Ricky.
    My brother Ricky fell in love with her. She was messing around with Ricky. She doesn't know that I know that. She was too good for him, and he knew it. He had a huge ass crush on her. When it happened, he freaked the fuck out. She was his first. He really didn't know what to do with her. I don't mean sexually, I mean emotionally. He didn't know how to be a boyfriend yet.
    Ricky was stupid and immature. He was a kid too. He called her names, but he liked her. I don't think he knew what to do with all those feelings. He knew her since she was just a kid. It was weird to suddenly hook up with her. But for once in her fucking life, she seemed happier. It's sad. My brother isn't the greatest guy ever, actually he's a loser, but he treated her nicely. At least, after she told him to fuck off and stop calling her names.
    One night she marched into our house, and she asked for me. Ricky lied. He said I wasn't home. She had no idea I heard the whole fight.
    She called him a punk ass pussy in front of his friends. She told him he couldn't handle a real woman and stop trying to fuck around with her. She shoved him and called him a fucking loser. She legit knocked him to the ground. His friends, these two guys he always hung out with, seemed a little nervous when she threatened them too, called them faggots.
    Then she started crying. It broke my heart to hear her crying. Ricky took care of her. He held her tight. Ricky held her, telling her he was sorry, over and over. His stupid ass friends had no idea what was happening.
    She scared the shit out of all of them. She scared me. She was

over the top angry. I've never seen anything like that. She gave Ricky a black eye, but he told her he was sorry.

Her mom told Ricky it was statutory rape. She reminded him that Juliana's dad was a cop and would believe her. She said she would press charges. She said, no one would ever need to talk to Juliana since she was a minor.

One night he did come by, her dad, wearing his cop uniform and everything. He parked his stupid patrol car in front of our house. Interestingly, Juliana was at his house that weekend. She hadn't been over there in months. He insisted she go stay the weekend with his family. He talked to my mom and made her cry. She was so worried about Ricky. My mom told me not to hang out with Juliana anymore.

I fought with her about it, reminding her of all the bruises Juliana had to cover. My mom said she wasn't our problem. We had to take care of our family first. She made Ricky go live with his dad. My mom told me if I invited Juliana over, she would send me to live with my dad too.

Her mother was a fucking bitch.

Her father was a punk ass pussy.

They did this to her.

I think it broke her heart that Ricky left. She thought he moved in with some hood rat we knew. I never corrected her on that. I let her believe it.

Ricky is the only reason she likes E-40. He likes E-40.

I did this to her too.

JULIANA
Late July

Text message from Christian: How are you?

How am I? I am fucking heartbroken. Fuck you Christian.

I ignored his text for three days. I want to delete it, but I can't. What does he have me saved under, Pizza Hut? Stupid ass, I should value myself more than this. I can't stop thinking about him. I've had other hookups in the meantime. I'm not waiting for him, but they're not the same. They're not him.

The strange thing is with Christian, it wasn't just sex. He took me on real dates. We talked and had real conversations. Even though it was just a short amount of time, the level of connection was high. I liked hanging out with him. He made me feel special.

Text to Christian: I'm good. How are you?

Christian: Want to hang out?

Do I want to hang out? I know what this means. Do I want this? I don't want this. Not like this. Don't I deserve better? Maybe I don't. Who would it hurt?

Text to Christian: Still have a girlfriend?

He doesn't answer me for a few hours.

That's my answer. Gabriel always says stupid shit, like believe people when they show you who they really are. Christian has a girlfriend. I should never be second, but who else makes me feel like he does? Even contemplating this non-relationship makes the butterflies in my stomach flutter. My heart races when I imagine being with him again. I miss him.

Please say you broke up. Lie to me, please. Just lie.

Christian: Upside-down emoji

Text to Christian: I have a date.

My heart hurts. I'm either stupid or super smart. I'm not sure which one. I can't make up my mind right now. One time wouldn't hurt.

Christian: Where is he taking you? Tell me about this date.

Text to Christian: I haven't met him yet. I'll find him tonight.

Christian: I can make you cry.

Text to Christian: Go fuck your girlfriend.

And I turn off my phone. I can't. I will and I shouldn't. I want to be with him, just one more time.

"I'm not giving you anything girly," Gabriel's laughing. Everything is ridiculous. His slender fingers are resting against my shoulder. He leans to me like he's going to lick me, but then he doesn't. "You don't have what I want, chick."

If Gabriel wasn't my best friend, I'd hate him. Gabriel is perfect, tall, and has beautiful wavy hair. He wears mascara and sometimes bronzer. Those touches make him stunning. He's approachable and conceited. He's pretty.

"Shut up, you're stupid!" Everywhere I look, beautiful men dance like glitter floating in the air. None of them ever notice me enough to make me feel pretty. All of this feels plastic. I just drink the rest of my beer.

My cell phone is vibrating. It startles me each time. Something's not right about having your phone start moving around when you don't expect it.

Again, it's Christian's number. Again I remember why I'm here. He has a girlfriend. He already has someone to share his life with. He needs to leave me alone. Damn, in the past month, I haven't even answered his calls. I only respond to his texts. Who the hell is he to be messing with me? Fuck that, who am I to be afraid of my own fucking phone?

So even though he can't see me, I'm huffing and rolling my eyes and being dramatic. My internal temperature is so high I could pop. I don't want to be this person, but guess what? I am. "What do you want?"

"I need to talk to you."

"I have nothing to say to you." I'm making faces at Gabriel, who's too amused by the situation for me. He's not supposed to enjoy my suffering. In light of my desperation, Gabriel makes me laugh. "I'm not a whore, Christian. You have a girlfriend, talk to her."

"Talk to me," he pleaded. It breaks my fragile heart. "You understand me, Juliana. No one understands me like you do."

"What do you want from me? You want me to tell you that I want you? You want me to say you're the best I ever had and I can't stop picturing it?" I'm off on some pervy tangent. It's easier to be oversexed than distressed and deranged. "I want you to make me cry, Christian, is that what you want to hear? You want me to beg you for it? Do you want me to say please? What the hell do you want from me?"

"Give me that fucking phone." Gabriel takes my phone with a forceful yank. He's taking a hold of my hair and twists it around his finger. "You need some therapy."

I'm kissing his ear for no real reason except that he loves it. Gabriel might be gay, but he loves it when I lavish all my attention on him. He's fun to kiss.

What Gabriel says to Christian, I can't follow. Gabriel starts laughing, letting the strands of my hair fall from his fingers. He pushes me off him. "She's got a boyfriend, a lot of them."

I'm so buzzed. It's not funny. I can't keep in the giggles. Every time I go home with a random stranger, I know I have something. I've lost count of all the men I've used to replace Christian.

Sometimes I imagine it's Christian. I'm obsessed with him. I know it. I can't break free of him. I don't want to break free of him. I want to live under him. I love him.

The reality of understanding that I love Christian isn't the soap opera scene I've always envisioned. I won't be waiting in an overpriced dress as he swoops in through the double doors, always some strange shade of mauve. This hurts. My heart's got nothing but stick pins in it. I'm drowning in my blood. I can't breathe. Each breath is forced and strained against the glass that lives in my chest. Where is the patron saint of denial when I need his skinny ass?

Gabriel gave me a knowing look and a kiss on my forehead, before continuing his conversation, "Leave her alone."

His newest boyfriend takes a handkerchief out of his pocket. Who the fuck actually carries a handkerchief? He fixes my make-up. It calms me instantly. I am tethered to Earth, I will live. Right now, at this moment, I will live one more minute without Christian.

Gabriel hands the phone back to me, "He wants to talk to you. Lie, tell him you're dating someone else."

Taking the phone back, I start hiccupping with weeping mixed in. I'm in an airless vacuum. I can't breathe, or maybe I can breathe. The air doesn't satisfy me. I don't know what's wrong with me. "What?"

"Let me come get you. I just want to talk to you. I miss you, Juliana." Again, the way he speaks to me, it's just like serenity. He could save my soul. I want him to be the one. For once in my life, let me have what I want. I just want him. "Just for fifteen minutes."

Looking around the club, I have a choice to make. Yes, I could easily find a new guy, but who's to say that he won't have a girlfriend too? What would it matter if I went with Christian? I'm not the one who's cheating? I am not a cheater. I am not the one making a bad choice, am I?

"Come pick me up. I'm at DV8. Do you know where that is? Text me when you get here."

Gabriel gives me a pointed look. "No."

"Shut up. This is none of your business."

"You can do better."

"Show me," I yell, looking around the club. "Point out one that is better. Where? There is no knight in shining armor coming to rescue me. Christian is the best I can do."

Gabe can't give me a better option, he knows that. Christian is the one I want to fall into. I kiss Gabriel and leave. There is no way I could ever find what I have with him, with anyone else. It has to be Christian. I need to be loved.

*****

Outside, it's clear. My brain can breathe. It brings me down to a level where I remember that I am a person, not just a wild girl, out on a mission to destroy her own life.

Christian is cake. It doesn't make sense to say that. I'm not supposed to lust after someone like him. No, it's not lust. It's so much more than that. I can't put my finger on it. My blood boils for him. My soul craves him.

"I can't stop thinking about you." Christian leads me over to his car. He even opens the door for me. Isn't that love? He opens the fucking car door for me. "You're all I think about."

"I can't do this." I have to stand up. I can't just fall for him. As much as I want to, I can't be that kind of girl. I have to draw the line somewhere. I don't know if I'm talking to myself or him. "I can't."

"I'll leave her."

"No, you won't."

Without looking at him, I can't imagine where this ride might take me. It's already gone in a direction I can't understand. I wanted him to be mine. He isn't. He loves someone else. I don't want to be second.

"I will. I promise." He kisses me like I want to be kissed. E pushes me against the wall, holding his rough hand against my throat. He doesn't squeeze, just holds me tightly. "Look at me. I need you."

"You don't need me."

"You're the only person who understands me, Juliana," Christian tells me, never taking his dark eyes off me. He leans forward, sucking on my bottom lip then pressing his lips against my throat. "I need you. I need you."

My body is reaching in ways I can't control. His breath is hot against my skin. My heart is pulsing in my chest, my skin breaks out in a light sweat. I want it against the fucking wall. I love him so much, but I hate him. It's just so intense, hot, wet, and complete. He's destroying me.

"Just give me a week, one week. I'll tell her."

It hurts to have this sort of heartache. I don't ask men to leave their girlfriends. That's not who I am. I don't care if he's lying to me. I just want to take him home with me. I just want to be with him.

It's so quiet in his car. I thought he was going to my place, but he didn't. It's almost easier that way. My brain doesn't work too well in the heat of passion.

Instead, he drove us out to Lost Lake. Outside of Fresno is a lot of beautiful space, including Yosemite National Park. Closer, there is a popular lake. It's called Lost Lake, and for a long time, I didn't even know there was a lake here. I knew where the river was. I always thought the river was called Lost Lake.

He's so quiet I can't touch him even if I want to. We're talking about his life. We're talking about her life too, and she doesn't know it. I wonder where she thinks he is right now. Should I even be here?

"Everywhere in my house, all I do, all I think about is you. You're everywhere."

"It was just sex, Christian." It pains my heart to say it. He's not mine. I wish with my whole soul he was, but he isn't. It hurts that I want to be with him. That's how badly I want to be with him. There are only so many guys I can kiss. It's just not the same anymore. Not after being with Christian. He's tangible. He's real. "Maybe that's all it was supposed to be."

"You don't believe that, do you?"

"I don't know what I believe. I used to think I was cool. I used to think I was in control, but then there was this one boy. He's just a boy and I'm not supposed to love him, but I think I do. He's someone else's. He can't be with me."

"But I can. Tell me what you want, Juliana." He sounds like he's trying to convince himself to do it. He sounds strained. He makes me valuable. Maybe I'm worth it? "What am I going to do?"

"Do you love her?"

"I'm not going to lie to you and say no." He looks right at me and doesn't even blink. "I do. I love her."

"Maybe I'm just a mistake. Maybe you should forget about me." When I blink, the tears I didn't want him to know about fall from my eyes. I don't want to use the crying card, I can't cry over this. I barely know this boy. He makes me cry, both in good ways and in bad. "Maybe it's just one of those things."

"You're not a mistake." He touches me. He traces his finger along the path the tears created. "I can't stop thinking about you. I can't. This past month, you're all I can think about."

"Does that make it right?" There is so much bubbling in my own head that I can't sort through it. I want him to be mine, but at the same time, isn't he already someone else's? I don't pressure him. He has to choose. He has to choose me.

When his phone rings, we both sort of jump. The metallic tone against the silence is disruptive.

"Shit, it's her. Don't say anything, don't make one sound." He holds the phone to his ear. "What?"

Why did this have to happen to me? Am I heartless enough to ask him to leave another woman for me? But then again, if he's thinking about it, is it my fault? I haven't called him. I haven't tried to go see him or anything this past month. I let him go. Even if it broke my heart, I just let him go.

"No, I didn't say I was going with Ray. No. I just have some thinking to do. It's not that. I don't want to talk about it again. Come on, don't start with me. I'll be home later. I'll call her."

Hanging up the call, he scrolls through his phone list. "My sister, she called. She needs something. Hold on. Did you call? What? Where are you? I can't right now. Don't. Fine, I'm on my way. You better mean it this time."

"Is everything okay?"

"Don't worry about it. It's nothing. My sister, she's always got drama."

"She must need you?"

"She always needs something." Again, I'm reminded that he has too many adult responsibilities. We are the same. Christian and I carry the shit no one wants to deal with. "She's in a relationship she doesn't belong in. He's an abusive asshole."

"Will she be okay?"

"She's like my mom." He's quiet. There is definitely a wall he's working through. He's not sure how much he can trust me.

"Your mom?"

"My parents were abusive," he says quietly. "I've never told anyone. Even my sister, we don't talk about it."

Watching him, this huge man, share something so private makes me crave him more. We both know pain. He carries his deep. I carry mine on my sleeve. He seems so young, lost, afraid, right now.

"You can tell me anything Christian."

Christian doesn't turn to me. Instead, he watches the river in front of us. He takes my forearm in his hand, hot, wrapped around me. His fingers dig in, just slightly.

"All they ever did was fight. Huge physical fights. Then, they'd make-up. I didn't understand what was happening when we were younger. My sister and I hid in the closet."

"How old is your sister?"

"She's three years younger than me. I thought for sure one day they'd kill each other. At least, until I got older and realized it was what they did. That was their relationship, fighting, and then making up."

I have no comment for him. I know this. It's the way my mom and her husband were. Fighting, sex, it was all so twisted. I get it. I just ended up getting caught in the middle of it. My stomach does a hard flip, I am so nauseous. My heart hurts knowing Christian and his sister went through the same things. Maybe Christian is my soulmate?

"I couldn't leave once I was old enough. I had to stay for my sister. That's the hardest for me. I was old enough to leave. My dad turned on me. He wanted to fight with me, and kicked me out of the house. We'd fight too. It's just, I don't know. I just rather live without them, but they're my parents."

"I'm sorry Christian, that shouldn't have happened."

"I need you. You understand me." He stares at me like I'm his salvation, like whatever I say he'll do it. He takes a lock of my hair and twists it around his finger. "What do you want from me, Juliana? Tell me what to do."

From some random folder in my brain, the simplest question springs forward, "Can you build a dog house, Christian?"

"What?" He's so confused by my question, he lets go of my hair. "What are you talking about?"

"I just need to know. Can you build a dog house?" I hold my breath, waiting for the answer. Nothing will ever compare to him. I know it. I can't love anyone else after this. I just can't. He has captivated my soul in a way that I never thought possible. If he can build a dog house, he's the one. That's what my mom always said, right?

"Yeah, why?"

It's the answer I've waited for. I can breathe. As wrong as it may be, I want him to want me. I want him to leave her. Without him, I will never have my sanity. "You can?"

"I can."

"Then be with me." I'm sobbing. Tears and crying, I'm clinging to him. He is the only thing that matters. I've never wanted anything in my pathetic life. I want him. I want Christian Garcia to belong to me. "Just be with me. Please. I will do anything for you, anything."

"You want me to do it? I'll do it for you. Give me a week then.

Just one week."

"Take me home. Don't call me until you leave her."

*****

17 days… That's more than one week, more than two, asshole.

To forget, that's all. Using my razor blade, I drag it slowly along my wrist. Not enough, not deep enough to hurt myself, just enough to make it bleed. Just enough to remind me that I'm alive inside this fucking despair. He's one stupid boy. Why does it hurt so much? I'm used to people leaving. I'm used to being hurt. I just need a long line across, beads of blood, faded scars, decorating my wrist like bracelets of shame.

I'm worthless.

I'm nothing.

I'm useless.

I have no right to be here.

I just want to go to sleep and never wake up. I hate my life. I hate myself. I just want to sleep forever.

GABRIEL
Late July

    Juliana is cutting again. I can see the traces of it on her wrist. It's not just Christian. I know that. She's depressed. She could use some therapy, but she would lose her mind if I suggested that to her. She needs to talk to someone. I know we talk. I don't have the answers she needs. I'm not a therapist.

    I know who loves her, my brother Ricky. He always asks how she is. He has a tattoo of her name. She doesn't know that, because she avoids him. That makes me wonder, does she still care about him? If she saw him, would she have a relationship with him? Sure, he has two kids with two different moms. He isn't with either of those girls. He's honest about it. We come from those kinds of girls. Our moms have kids. Right now, he doesn't have a girlfriend. She needs a real boyfriend.

    Ricky is in a band. They're awful. They play dives, but they have a small fan base. Ricky, he's got that whole bad boy thing. She likes the bad boy types. Ricky is downright bad. He would never hurt her. What Ricky feels for her is hard to explain. It's this weird idolization. Ricky thinks she's perfect.

    If she was with Ricky, maybe, just maybe she could be happy. She needs to be happy. She needs therapy. She's depressed. She needs help.

JULIANA
August

Christian stares at me for a moment, before realizing that I'm looking at him. There's a spark of connection, then a sudden evaporation of everything. It didn't matter to him. I don't matter to him. I'm just a girl who picked him up. He ignores me.

This is what we are, nothing.

He stayed with her. My only consolation is that I didn't go home with him last time. I stood my ground. I didn't do it. I would have, hell, I still want to, but I didn't.

I wonder what he's thinking. He acts like I'm just another random person in the theater lobby waiting for the movie to start. He sure knows her, the girl he's with. That must be her. He's talking so sweetly to her and holding her hand. She's cute. She seems quiet. She even wears glasses. In her denim skirt and matchy, matchy lavender cardigan, she looks smart. I'm a fucking idiot for letting him use me. I invited that shit into my life.

She's a fucking white girl. I knew it. I'll bet her name is Madison or Kimberly, or some stupid shit like that. I don't even know her fucking name. I hate her. She is my enemy. Fuck her. How in the fucking world can he pick her over me? Fuck that shit. I can handle my shit. I can take his shit. I can make it pretty.

She looks like a wife. She's the type who can be a mom. She hasn't had fucked 33.3% of the men living in Fresno. She probably can name all of them off one hand. She is a good girl. Christian loves her. He has never looked at me like that. He cares about her. It fucking kills me to watch them. I can't stop staring at them.

Grateful for my water bottle, I squeeze it only slightly. It's funny how an emotion can be controlled by a physical distraction. He wants to pretend he doesn't know me, fine. There is nothing left, is there? I had sex with him. I gave it to him. Hell, I fucking threw it at him. While my heart is still broken, he's moved on. Fuck it, he didn't move on, he just went on. It's me. I made a fool of myself. I invited that shit right into my life. Add him to my long list of mistakes.

"So you want butter on the popcorn or not?" Gabriel rolls his eyes because of my distraction. He has not noticed him. "Ms. ADD, pay attention to the conversation. Can you focus for five minutes?"

I just huff, trying to dismiss his attitude with me, "No butter. Put pepper on it."

"Yuck, no pepper, let's do butter." He's already adding butter to the popcorn.

"Fine, why do you even ask me?" I know I'm displacing my anger onto him right now. My voice is rising too loud for this simplistic disagreement. "Fuck you Gabriel, you're going to do whatever you want anyway."

"Whatever, butter and pepper, are you happy? I swear girlie girl, you're getting on my nerves. You must have PMS or something." He's adding just a tiny, almost not even there, amount of pepper.

Gabriel notices Christian. He huffs, and obviously sizes up the two of them. He turns to me and fixes my hair, pushing my long locks back. He uses his thumb to fix my lipstick.

"You are beautiful. She's cute, but you are beautiful. Do not forget your worth," Gabriel's leaning close, kissing my cheek, "Shall I make a scene? Want me to ask him why he fucked my girl?"

"Please don't," my eyes hurt. I don't want to cry. "I've had my fill of drama for this year."

"Let's dance like we're in one of those crazy-ass Indian music videos on Channel 9!" Gabriel hands me the popcorn bag, then hops around the lobby. He relishes everyone's attention. "I'll be the handsome, yet gay leading man, and you'll be the damsel in distress. I can save a hoe."

I know he's right. I can't let another person make me feel ashamed. I am not the only guilty person in our relationship, hookup, whatever the fuck he wants to call it. She has no idea I fucked her boyfriend. She doesn't have power over me. I have the power. I just wiggle around, pretending to dance with Gabriel, trying not to spill the popcorn. "Shut up! I am not a hoe, maybe just a little bit."

"Come on girlie. Let's go see this damn chick flick you insist we watch." Gabriel walks way too close to Christian, ignoring him. As far as anyone else can tell, we're just strangers passing. Gabriel pauses just for a moment, waiting for me to catch up to him. "Juliana Lopez, you are the most beautiful woman on Earth. Seriously, any man would be lucky to have you."

I love Gabriel. He makes me feel pretty, even if it's just pretend. I don't even look at Christian as I pass him. Fuck Christian Garcia.

GABRIEL
August

    I almost want to tell his girlfriend. Just walk up to her and tell her, "Hey, your boyfriend is cheating on you."

    The thing is, Juliana doesn't realize he's not worth her time. He's beneath her. She is letting him use her. She has convinced herself she loves him, but that's only because he hasn't beaten the holy shit out of her.

    That's why she thinks it is love.

    That's what her mother has taught her.

    I don't know how to save her.

    She loves me. I know that. But she needs to be in love. She needs to be loved. I can't love her the way she needs to be loved. She deserves more than some asshole that will use her and make her think she needs him.

    Juliana needs someone to love her. I love her. I am not what she needs.

JULIANA
September

I have a fucking flat tire? I don't have one fucking idea of what to do. I don't even know where the tools are in the car to fix it. I'm wearing a dress and heels for fucksake.

At four in the morning, I'm stuck on the side of the road. I should call a tow truck, but something about those guys always seems so creepy. I've seen too many spooky movies.

I could call 911. Is this really an emergency? Maybe some cute cop will come out here and help me out. Do cops even do that? Is that just something you see in the movies? I never called the police before. I could call my dad, but then I'd have to talk to him. I haven't done that in several years. We don't talk. We are not close. We are not family. Fuck Matthew Lopez.

Scrolling through my phone list, it dawns on me that there is no one on my list that can help me. Not one. I have no friends. Not real friends anyway.

I can't call Christian. Seeing his cell phone number, I can't help but press the green button that may connect me to him again. I shouldn't involve him in my stupidity. I hang up before he even answers. I can figure something out.

Sitting on the side of the road, feeling sorry for myself, I watch the cars passing by. There are not many out here this late. I have a knack for getting myself into situations that are not safe.

My phone buzzes almost instantly. I knew he'd call back. I knew he would. He calls me all the time. I never answer. Usually, I just look at my screen when his number pops up. I want him, I desperately do, but I don't want to be his second choice. I am not a second choice.

Picking up the call, my heart is jangling in my chest. I have to remind myself to breathe, to not get caught up in all my unresolved feelings for Christian Garcia. "Well, hi."

"Hey *chica bonita*." His voice, even after weeks, still melts me down instantaneously. "What's up?"

"I have a flat tire."

He's laughing at me. The sound of his voice makes my heart race for no reason. He makes me feel alive again. Why does he have to have a girlfriend? "Where are you?"

"Near Blackstone and Olive." There is humor in my situation, I'm not an adult. I'm an overgrown child pretending to be an adult. I have zero life skills.

"Do you need some help, Juliana? Do you want to cry?" Again, it's that teasing tone that drives me crazy. It's like I talked to him yesterday. It's like no time has passed at all.

"Something like that." Flirting with him is so easy, it's comfortable. I whisper, "I'm near that adult book store, the one on Olive."

"Are you starting your own porn collection?" He sounds just a little buzzed, like maybe he's been hanging with his friends and drinking all night long.

It's not right. He has a girlfriend. I have ethics, I do. I have values. I am not a whore, or at least, not one who messes with boys with girlfriends. My ego deflates.

The reality of my situation presses on me, "I shouldn't have called you. I shouldn't say things like that to you. I don't know who else to call and I really need to get out of here. I need your help."

"Listen." It's a wound on my heart. Even my best friend is out having a good time, not even concerned that I didn't even make it home. Christian cares. "Lock the doors and stay there. I'll be there in a little bit. Don't get out of the car. Just wait for me."

"Christian?"

"What?"

"Thanks."

*****

Not taking my eyes from Christian, and sitting up on the hood of his car, he fixes my tire. I love the way he moves. I love the color of his skin. He's still so golden. He seems like he's been outside a lot lately. He's always had this golden tone to him, but now it's almost bronze. He's got a hint of sunburn, right under his eyes. Maybe he had on sunglasses when it happened. Nothing else about him has changed. I'm still in love with him.

It's warm and balmy, even late at night. Sometimes, I hate the heat of summer. No one should live in 104 degree weather, but there is something about a warm night. It's like a techno pop song. It's magical. It's like my fairy god mother could actually appear out of nowhere and make him mine. I can make him mine, even if it's only for tonight.

"I like your dress," Christian says, only stealing glances at me.

"Thanks." My dress isn't special. It's an old black wrap around thing I found on the bottom of my closet. It's the shoes that make the dress. These stilettos have thin satin ribbons that wrap around my ankle. I love shoes.

Christian can build a dog house. He told me he can. I need a man who can build me a dog house, a man who can fix a flat tire, a man who can make me cry.

Once he's done, Christian leans against his car, allowing himself to study me. There is no denying that I still want him, even if I pretend to be silly. He still gets my blood going. "Did you finish school?"

"Yeah," he smiles. "I started teaching in August. I teach 5th grade."

"I'm proud of you." I'm sure it sounds so stupid. Someone else my own age has dreams and goals? I wish I could fit in with him. Why did he have to have a girlfriend already? "I knew you could do it."

"You're proud of me?" He seems unsure instantly, and he gives me one of his lost little boy looks. "I'm worried about it. What if I do everything wrong?"

"You won't. You're too nice for that. You'll make those kids learn if it kills you."

"You think I'm nice?"

"You are." Sitting forward, using my shoe to keep me from sliding off the hood, I lean to him, just looking at him for a minute. There's a tangible intensity radiating from him. "You're really, I don't know, you're energy. You draw beautiful things to you."

He looks right at me. Maybe he's having dirty thoughts and he's struggling not to? "Like you?"

"Maybe."

He remembers her, I guess. He's got an instant wall between us. The static charge just dissipates. "Well, start the car. Let's make sure nothing else is wrong."

So climbing back in, sure enough, the damn car starts. Why couldn't it just completely break down? I'm not ready to let him slip through my fingers again.

"Well, looks like you can make it home now."

Resting my arm against the window frame, maybe I'm looking at him too hard, but it's like a dream. He's perfect, and it breaks my heart that he's not mine. "Thank you, Christian, really."

Leaning against my car door, he's talking to the street. He begins so quietly, it's a strain to hear him. Each of his words is measured as if he's not sure what he's trying to say. "I saw this movie once where there was this beautiful girl who was stranded on the side of the road. Then this guy came over and helped her out."

Twisting a lock of hair around my finger, I don't want to look at him. It's kind of sinful the way he's proposing it. "Then what happened?"

"You know what happened." He moves slowly, tracing his finger along my shoulder and up my neck. Chills burn up at his touch. At this moment, I realize I haven't been living, I merely exist. I'm sick of this. I want to burn. "So in this movie, he's not that nice to her."

"He's not?" I don't know why we're whispering? My body is craving him. My eyes are glassy with teardrops. It's the perfect fantasy. It's so hot.

"No. He doesn't hurt her, but he's not nice either." He sounds self-conscious saying these things to me. He pauses for a moment. I'm not going to pressure him to say anything. If he wants it, he's got to say it. "I guess you could say he's sort of rough with her."

He's mine. In this second, I know he's mine. "So what happens? I mean, in this movie you saw?"

"Well, the thing is, in this movie, he goes to her house and stays with her for a little while. He makes her cry."

"She cries?"

"Oh yeah, she cries." He leans over so that he's even with me, even though I can't look at him. His voice is decadent. "But the thing is she doesn't know that she makes him cry too. He thinks she's chocolate cake."

He remembered. My stupid little things, he remembered them. I only glance at him, too shy to destroy the delicate balance hanging in the air. "So this movie, how does it end?"

"He has to go." He shoves one of his hands into his pants pocket. "He can't stay with the girl because, well, just because. He thinks about her a lot. He thinks about her all the time. Sometimes he calls her phone just to hear her voice."

So that's the deal. Is it a reality I can live with? I don't know, maybe. "And what happens to the girl?"

"She stays in his memory forever. She's always perfect in his memory. You know that? When he thinks about her, she's perfect. No one can ever compare to her. *Nadie, por vida.*" Christian looks at me with that suffering look, like I'm air. "You think you might want to watch this movie with me?"

I can't find my voice. I just nodded my head. I want to be perfect, even if it's in his memory. That's what I want. I want someone to think I'm perfect.

"I'll meet you at your house."

I'm dying. I'm just dying. Nothing else matters in this one moment. It's so right. At this moment, I'm under his skin and there is nothing more beautiful. All the built up pressure is finally released in a way no one could do it before. He said I'm chocolate cake. He said I'm perfect. He said I made him cry. I love him. Christian can build me a dog house.

*****

"I'm a little nervous about it." He's sitting on my bed, only glancing at me in intervals. I assume it's his Catholic guilt. I have no idea if he's Catholic. "It's way more work than I expected. I was ready for it to be hard, but it's really hard."

He is already dressed and ready to leave me again. I'm not getting out of bed. I'm staying naked and enjoying my afterglow moment. It's supposed to be like this.

"Mr. Garcia, doesn't that sound funny?" Christian's messing with the books piled on my nightstand. Settling on one, he flips through my well-worn copy of House on Mango Street. "I don't feel like Mr. Garcia."

"Don't overthink it. Come on, to them, you're hella old anyway."

"Thanks a lot," he says, but sounds amused. He's reading my highlighted pages and comments. I have a habit of writing all over my books. "You're right. What have you been up to?"

Staring up at the fan, watching it spin, there really isn't much to say. I'm obsessed with him. I can't tell him that. I shouldn't mention the nights of drinking until I'm incoherent, so I won't think about him. Nothing I have to say sounds interesting. My life is a pretty nonexistent drift through space and time.

"Still work in the mall?"

"Um hum." He doesn't want to leave. I get that vibe from him. He's stalling. "What else can I do? Make cakes? I'm helpless, you know. I barely made it out of high school."

He checks the cover of the book again. "You've read this book. You understand all this magical realism crap. I never could understand this. I almost failed one of my English classes because of that."

"I like to read."

"You're smart, though." He's scanning the titles again, "Some of these books, I couldn't read them without falling asleep."

"Whatever," I say, rolling my eyes. It would kill me if he were just making fun of me. I always wanted to be smart. I'm an idiot who barely made it through high school.

"I wouldn't have guessed you liked this kind of stuff." He's reading the titles slowly until he gets to the Spanish-English dictionary, "Are you trying to teach yourself Spanish?"

"Sure." Another reminder of how un-smart I am. I have to look up so many words when I'm reading. "In high school, my Spanish teacher told me I should drop her class and take something else. I was advised to drop. Isn't that a riot? The Mexican girl was told to drop."

"You let people convince you you're dumb." He sets the last of my books on the table. He looks right at me, "You're not dumb. You have a smart ass comment for everything."

It's my turn to be so embarrassed. I am not smart. I'm an idiot who let a boy with a girlfriend in her bed, into her heart. "So smart that I pick up on boys who already have girlfriends?"

"It's late huh?" He tries not to laugh, resting against my headboard watching me. He checks his watch. "I need to go home, don't I?"

"Where does she think you are?" I can't help wondering how one person would trust like that. It's already morning. Doesn't she care? I would care.

"She thinks I'm with my friends." He touches my hair, coiling the lock around his fingers before letting it go. "We hang out a lot, sometimes she doesn't want to go."

Well, that explains the flirting on the phone. She wasn't there.

"You know," he gives me a sideways look. "I could call you."

"Don't. It's perfect right now. I shouldn't have done this. You shouldn't be here."

Just the swish of the fan makes any sound for several long minutes. It's time to digest what we are really doing. There is no way around how wrong this is. This is sin. I might actually have to go to church and confess one of these days.

"I got to go, but listen, if you ever need anything, call me. I don't care what time it is. Call me, Juliana."

"Okay." In the back of my mind, I know I'm not going to purposely put myself in situations that may require his assistance. I can't do that. I shouldn't have done this. This is going to hurt. Tomorrow, next week, this will hurt again. Christian Garcia has a girlfriend. I am not her. He loves her. He doesn't love me.

"Go home Christian."

GABRIEL
September

    She invited Christian over or something. They rolled in overnight, super late. It's going to kill her when he disappears on her. He's not looking for a long-term relationship with her. He has a girlfriend. She knows this. She was doing a good job keeping him out. Then, last night, I don't know what happened. She invited him over? He called her at the wrong moment? I'm not sure, but somehow he ended up here. I'll be left to pick up the pieces. He's breaking her heart.

    We used to be best friends. I could tell her anything. She was the first person I came out to, but over the years, most recently, something's different. Yeah, we both had shit to deal with when we were young, but we left that neighborhood. I still go to see my mom, but she doesn't. I wouldn't either, but the problem is she's ignoring the problem now.

    That's what Juliana does. She ignores things until she can't take it anymore, and then does something along the self-harm route. Sometimes she cuts, sometimes it's reckless men, sometimes I'm not sure what she does, but I know she isn't okay.

    It wasn't always like this. When she first moved in with me, everything was good. Things were good finally. We had fun, normal good fun, then she turned 21 and something really changed. She got weird again on me, like when she was 17. When she was 17, she stopped talking. She stopped talking for a month. She refused to come out of her house. I always thought it was because I was about to move out, but now, I'm not so sure that's what it was. I promised to let her move in on the day she turned 18. I was too young to realize that wasn't normal. I never asked her why she stopped talking.

    I think she's bipolar. She would kill me if I ever suggested that to her, so I don't. I can't let her take off either. Where would she go? She has nowhere to go. Somehow, I've turned into her parent. This is not what I planned for. She needs help I can't give her.

    I hate admitting that something is wrong. She won't hear it from me. Aaron tried to talk to her about it. She told him to fuck off too. I trust Aaron. Aaron isn't really the bad guy, but she's good at fighting with him, like a parent. Sometimes I wonder if it's because she wasn't allowed to talk back to her own mom. Maybe she missed a developmental milestone? Isn't that a stage? Be an asshole to your parents? I don't know. Somehow I've become a faker parent. It's not the relationship I want to have with her. I just want to be friends again.

    I miss her. She's not herself anymore.

JULIANA
Late September

    I have nothing to do and nowhere to be. I have a sad, pathetic life. Day drinking has become my reality. I'm even tired of picking up boys. I'm tired of all of it. I just want to sleep for a week. My life is not supposed to be like this. My heart, my fucking heart keeps racing. I'm having a heart attack, and then it just stops. Then, when I'm not expecting it, it starts again, racing out of control. I think I'm dying. I'm so scared. Everything is pressing against me, even air has weight. I just want to stop. I just want everything to be black. I don't want to be here anymore. I want to stop breathing. I want to fall asleep and never wake up.

    I need a break from life.

    "Come with me to see Ricky." Gabriel saunters into my room, plopping himself right onto my bed.

    "No thanks." Ricky left me. He called me a whore. Yeah, maybe I punched him and he said sorry, but still. I don't want to see Enrique Sanchez. I love him. Not like I love Christian. There is a hole where Ricky used to be.

    "Oh come on. He's in a band. He's performing. He thinks he plays the guitar now."

    Rolling my eyes, I'm slightly amused. Gabe's brother Ricky has always played the guitar. He's not even my brother, and I know that. I remember him sitting outside, up on their porch, strumming it and singing dirty rap lyrics. Charming that one, Ricky is nothing but trouble. "He always played the guitar, Gabe. Do you know nothing? A grunge band? What hole in the wall club are you going to?"

"Red Raid, over downtown. Like a block from the jail. We'll be safe." He's up off the bed and searching through my closet.

"Punk rock isn't my thing." I'm lying, I totally want to go. I want to watch Ricky perform. In a band, that's kind of cool.

"I would go with you." He pulls out a black dress I forgot I owned. It still has tags on it. It's too short and frilly for a dive bar.

"Fine, but I'm wearing a bright orange dress," I say to him, getting up off my bed. I find the dress I mean and show him, tangerine satin, a line dress. "I'm blaming you if I get Tetanus."

*****

Without Gabriel, I would already be on the floor. I keep touching him and licking his ear. He keeps pushing me away. His new boy toy, and that's exactly what he is, a boy toy, is just a little too into it. Gay guys are a bunch of perverts. He seems to like the attention I lavish all over Gabriel. He just watches and giggles.

Gabriel's skin is the perfect golden tone. His beautifully shaped face, high cheekbones, and full pink lips make him impressive. He's so pretty. Gabriel is glass. He's just so precious. Gabriel's showering me with butterfly kisses. His long dark lashes tickle me.

We look ridiculous. We're so out of place, even the bouncer asked us if we were sure we wanted to come inside. Gabriel is in a pair of tight blue jeans and thin white tank top with a bright pink dress shirt that matches his shoes. I'm wearing a coda mini dress in satin tangerine. We look ridiculous among the punk rock scene. Nothing but black and silver studs around us. The bartender sneered at us when we ordered blended margaritas.

I haven't seen Ricky. I don't know why this is making me nervous. When they were young, people always figured he and Gabe were twins, not two years apart. They used to look alike, but as they grew older, Gabe became the fashionable one, the hipster one. Ricky, he went dark, first into old rap, then punk rock. His fashion journey took a hard 180 when he went to high school. Black, black, black. I haven't seen him in years.

"Hey," some older looking guy moves towards us, "Ricky wants to see you guys backstage."

"You have backstage?" I stumble forward, using the guy as a brace, my stupid heels are too high and the floor is sticky. What the hell are we doing here? "Lead the way, dear sir."

The bouncer just shakes his head, "Come on, and follow me."

Backstage, Ricky sits with no shirt on. He's got some tramp on his lap. His bleached hair is trimmed close to his head, and he has a few tattoos on his chest. I can't make them out, because the girl is in the way. He gazes at us, like we should be honored to be in his presence. Then he pushes the girl off his lap.

Ricky Sanchez is still an asshole, great.

"Get out," he orders her. "Juliana Lopez? What the fuck are you wearing?"

"She looks like a pumpkin," the girl says to me as she makes her way out.

I step right up to her. She doesn't scare me in her black skinny jeans and band t-shirt. I give her a shove, don't come at me bitch. "I will fuck you up if you talk like that to me again."

She just rolls her eyes and keeps walking. She probably can feel my need to fight. I want to chase her down and rip her hair out. I need violent actions.

Ricky starts laughing, "You never change."

"You just don't want me to kill your girlfriend," I tell him, slipping off my stilettos. They're high and my feet hurt. I'd rather be barefoot here. It's dark, the lights are lowered, but it's relatively clean.

"She's not my girlfriend."

"Lies," I say to him, giving him a sassy glare. "When is your band going to perform? I'm tired of waiting around here. It's like a bad Halloween party here."

"Okay pumpkin," he says, "Come here, I need to show you something."

"I don't want to see it, Ricky." Making faces at him, I know I'm being totally immature. I don't want to get close to him. His energy is wild. He still looks like Gabriel, but with all the tattoos, the tight jeans, and the no shirt. It's a look I'm not ready to admit that makes him flaming hot. It's nothing like Christian, but it's all bad. Very, very bad. I love a bad boy.

Christian has a girlfriend. Christian used me. Christian broke my heart.

That dark feeling, unneeded, unwanted creeps up my spine,

reminding me, I'm not wanted. I hold my own wrist, knowing that the cutting is there, hidden under my watch.

Ricky holds his wrist to me, black letters decorating his skin. I glance at him. His deep brown eyes study me. The curly cue letters read, ANAILUJ. Oh damn, it's my name. JULIANA. This crazy fool has my name tattooed on his wrist. I'm suddenly sober. Ricky requires my full focus.

"What the hell did you do that for? Ricky, that's kind of creepy, you stalker." Why does he have my name tattooed on him? It's clearly not new. How long? Why hasn't Gabriel ever told me?

"Gabe told me you broke up with your boyfriend," he says, pulling me onto his lap. His long legs are splayed, as he forces me to sit on one thigh with his arms around me. Pinning me to his body, he's holding me tight against him, not feeling like the boy he used to be. Ricky is a grown ass man. Oh shit, this isn't good.

I'm totally embarrassed that he's got me all turned on. I have to force myself to breathe. It's not an involuntary action anymore. The more I fight against him, the higher my satin dress rides up. I have to stop and stay still. "Let me go, Ricky."

"Leave her alone," Gabriel kicks Ricky's foot, hard, "You said you wanted to talk to her, I brought her with me, be nice to her."

"Don't you push me off your lap," I tell him, teetering on falling. Ricky is a total asshole, I know that. I've always known that. I wish I had my shoes on, now I have to tippy toe to keep my balance. My heart is racing. I'm going to have a heart attack.

Ricky doesn't move. "No. Sit with me. We have to talk. Everyone else get the fuck out."

Everyone but Gabe and his date scrambled out of the room. Just one harsh order from Ricky and all his minions make themselves scarce. It's crazy how they all listen. In another life, I am positive Ricky was a cult leader. He has that kind of power, that kind of energy. As much as I fight him, I like it too.

"Don't leave me here with him, Gabe." Panic is setting in. Ricky won't let me go and it's making me nervous. He smells nice. In light of this weird situation, Ricky smells like coconut and vanilla. He's got a strong grip on me. It is so nice to have him hold me. Shit, no. Stop that, do not think of Ricky like that. Damnit. This cannot be happening. Ricky

Sanchez has me all turned on, and I'm humiliated. Shit.

"Get out Gabe."

My heart is racing out of control. It's Ricky. I've known him since I was five. This doesn't feel like the boy I knew. He's an adult now, this is different. He's scaring me.

Gabriel looks conflicted. It's his fault I'm here. "Ricky, let her go."

"Get out Gabe." Ricky's been drinking, the scent of Bacardi is on his hot breath, "I just want to ask her a question."

"Don't leave me Gabe." Locking eyes with him, I tell him again, "Don't go."

"Shit Jules, I won't hurt you. Get out Gabe." He holds my face and presses me to his cheek, so we're both cheek to cheek. "I would never hurt you. You know that."

"Let me go first. Let me go, and then Gabe can leave." My brain is mixed up, no, don't stay here. This is dangerous. He's Ricky, he's not Ricky anymore.

"You promise you won't run away?"

"I'm not scared of you. I don't like this." I am totally scared of him. I'm scared of myself. "Let me go, I'll stay. Then Gabe can leave."

He releases me and I almost fall, but he catches me. It's nice to have his hot hands press against me. Shit. Oh shit. No.

"Stay right outside the door." I push Gabe and squeeze his hand. I don't trust myself. I can tell. I can feel it. I'm so desperate to be in love, to be loved. I might do something stupid.

As soon as Gabe is out of the room, when we're alone, he tells me, "Give me your underwear."

"Fuck off, no," my heart is in my throat. My blood is rushing through my veins. "You're crazy. You're acting crazy. What's wrong with you?"

He walks to me, each step he takes to me. I take one away until we're against the door.

"You owe me this."

"I don't owe you shit."

"Your dad threatened to have me arrested." He presses his hands against the wall, pinning me against it. His voice is rough, quiet. He knows

Gabriel is right on the other side of the door. "I want you to give me one thing. Give me your underwear."

"What are you talking about?"

"Ask Gabriel, now do it. Give them to me."

I'm shaking, my whole body is trembling. This is sheer insanity. I haven't seen him in years, and he's demanding my underwear? Holding my breath, I work them off, one foot, then the other.

He takes them from my hand, leaning forward. He catches my wrist, clearly aware that I'm hiding cutting under my watch band. He presses his thumb against my wrist. "Stop that shit Jules."

"I'm trying." I can't lie to him if I tried. I don't want to lie to him.

"Try harder. No more boyfriends with a girlfriend, do you understand? Don't let him use you like that. Knock that shit off."

Ricky has a strange power. He didn't have this before. Something about the way he talks, the way he moves, you just want to listen. I want to belong to the cult of Ricky. No I don't, I did not just think that. Not Ricky. What the fuck is wrong with me?

Then he licks me, right across my cheek. Yuck. He's a pig.

"Now be a good girl. Go watch the show. I'll see you after, Pumpkin."

He gives me that damn dismissive attitude.

"Fuck you too Ricky."

GABRIEL
Late September

    Ricky is over the top. He purposely scares the shit out of her. He's dangerous. He's mean. He's an asshole. But I guarantee you, Ricky would never hurt her. Never. He's got a weird obsession with her. He watches her. She hasn't realized it. He's like a safe stalker. It's hard to explain. I don't understand it myself, but I know he wouldn't hurt her. He sometimes follows her around. He knows where she works, what clubs she likes, things like that, but he also remembers her birthday, her favorite candy, even her favorite coffee shop.

    As his brother, I can't tell him to stop it. He won't listen to me. I'm his little brother. Honestly, he's not hurting her. He just watches her from a distance. As her friend, I know he won't hurt her. It's a strange situation, believe me, I wrestle with this a lot.

    She needs him, or at least someone like him, someone who will love her unconditionally. If she gave him a chance, he would quit all the other girls. Ricky has a lot of girlfriends. But he wouldn't have a girlfriend and lead her on. He wouldn't do that. Not to her.

    Ricky loves her.

JULIANA
October

"Come on Juliana, you can dance better than these girls." Gabriel is wiggling to the beat. "I used to like this song."

We're at the Big Fresno Fair. After spending the hottest parts of the day wandering through the exhibit halls and listening to presentations of knife sets we'll never buy, the sun has set. It's finally cooling off on a warm October evening.

We're here to see Ricky. He's got a gig playing at one of the smaller stages. Gabriel asked me to come with him. I picked a coral sundress just to mess with Ricky. Since the first time I saw him, he's been calling me pumpkin.

Ricky left me alone. He was just messing with me. I can see it now. At the time, I was scared out of my mind. After they finished their set, Ricky told Gabe to take me home. He's been nothing but nice to me since.

Gabriel will always be his little brother. Gabe might be 25 now, but he's still just a little kid when he's around Ricky. Ricky commands that type of power from most people. People want to do what he says. Gabe, Ricky's bandmates, all do what he says. I'm not immune. I follow him around. He could totally be a cult leader.

The stage is small and tucked in the corner. It's not time for Ricky's band to perform, so there is a DJ playing old freestyle music. I guess he doesn't know that the 80's were a long time ago. Did no one tell him he's being followed by a punk rock rap band?

"Come dance with me. You can dance better than these girls," Gabriel says, already walking backwards to the minuscule dance floor.

"No one else is dancing." We used to dance to this song at Gabriel's house when we were kids. His mom loved this song and danced with us in the kitchen.

"Dance, now," he orders, pulling me with him.

Before I can argue with Gabriel, we're in the middle of the empty dance floor. Bouncing around, it's too fun to pretend to be embarrassed. I'm here to have fun. Gabriel sometimes seems to know me better than I know myself. Dancing is freeing for me.

"Damn perm chick Mexican girls, they're just so fabulous with their breasts all on display. You'd think they'd at least let me touch them." Gabriel's funny this way. He is totally into women's breasts, he's not into women. It's more of an appreciation, really. If a woman did come on to him, he would just stare at their breasts and get away with it, because he is so damn handsome.

"You're just mad, they aren't into you."

"These damn Mexican girls never gave me the time of day." Gabriel is purposely behaving over dramatic and still moving around on the dance floor. "Fuck them and their big breasts."

"Damn Mexican boys never gave me the time of day, and I'm not gay."

Gabriel stops dead in his tracks and points at me, "You have gay tendencies."

I don't even bother arguing with him.

Afterward, I'm alone at a table, waiting for Ricky's band. Gabriel has left me here while he gets me bottled water.

"How are you doing?"

Christian Garcia is here too? He's so perfect. It hurts to look at him. He's everything I'll never have. My heart misses him so much. He sits with me.

"How's teaching going?" I'm cold. The air has a slight chill, even if it's warm in the sun. The more it sets, the cooler the air becomes.

"I feel like I'm doing everything wrong, and they're never going to learn anything. I don't know what I'm doing sometimes."

"All that matters is that they know you care about them. No one remembers what they learned in the 5th grade. All you remember is how the teacher made you feel." It's one of those situations where being together is worth the pain. It's sand in my eyes, but at least he's right here. "How are things at home?"

He gives me this look like he was waiting for that question, like he wants to tell me something. "Honestly?"

"No, lie to me." It's comical. I shouldn't be all up on him so fast. He shouldn't make my heart beat the way it does. "Tell me you're miserable."

He smiles, and messes with his stupid Fresno State baseball cap. His whole tone changes, "Nothing's the way it used to be."

My heart sinks. It's nothing I want to wish on him, on anyone. I can't let my hope rise. It's not like he's left her or anything. He's not mine. "I'm sorry to hear that."

"Well, I deserve it." He has a guilty look.

This mess is not my fault. I have to get away from Christian. He drives me positively crazy. "I need to go."

"Wait, can I text you?" He takes my hand, rubbing my fingers gently.

Rolling my eyes, I pull away from him. It's my full circle moment. I have to make a decision. Right now, I can become his dirty little secret or I can let him go. What's that stupid ass saying, "If you let something go and it comes back to you, it's yours?" Well, he hasn't come back to me. He's still with her.

He doesn't want me the way I need him. That knowledge is heartbreaking. Unless I let him go, I mean texting and everything else, I will never have peace. My sanity will eventually evaporate. He will go on with his happy little life while I end up alone.

"Don't go. Sit down for a little while. Please, sit down."

"I can't." Before I know it, I'm biting my lip. Gabriel will kill me if he sees me doing that. In his world, it's all about presentation. A girl should never be without lipstick. I can't move from my spot. There is an undeniable connection to him. Something about him keeps me wrapped up in his madness. Even being right here is better than living without him. I want this boy to love me the way I love him.

"Hang out with me."

Crossing my arms against my chest, I need some sort of barrier to protect myself. "Why?"

"I like talking to you." He's talking above my head, or to the air, but not to me.

"Don't you have a girlfriend?" In the pit of my stomach, it's nails, scratching and churning. "Aren't you supposed to talk to her?"

"It's different. You know me." His own confusion is evident. He seems troubled by the whole situation too. It's almost like he's curled up in his seat, but yet, he hasn't even moved. The stress is indisputable. "You understand the things I can't talk with her about, Jules."

His parents, she doesn't know. Christian takes my hand, presses it to his chest. I can see the faint edge of purple, just right at the collar of his shirt. "My sister, she's finally left her boyfriend."

"Is she okay?"

"She's pregnant. She's staying with us until the baby comes. Then she'll figure out what she's going to do next."

"You're going to be an uncle?" He said "us." She's still there.

"Yeah, that's crazy huh?" He's so distant and measured. "It was a big fight. I think she's done with him. I can't anymore. I told her that. I can't."

He's her protector. I wish he'd protect me. "And your girlfriend?"

"She doesn't understand. She thinks it should be easy to just walk away. She doesn't understand me the way you do." He smiles at me again, taking my hand in his. "I tell her I need to watch porn, and she tells me I'm a pervert."

My bubble pops. The bubble guarding my heart just dissipates into nothing. I'm laughing harder than I should be. It's funny. He might be with her, but this boy is mine. I sit back down. "You're so stupid."

Christian leans over and says it so quietly, but he's looking right at me, "Yeah, but I can make you cry."

I want to cry.

"Hey man, where have you been?" Two slightly drunken boys I don't know drop themselves into the other chairs. "You've been gone awhile."

Christian seems caught. He releases my hand and looks from me to them. "Oh Juliana, meet Ray and Alex."

Ray, the one with the baseball cap, looks around nervously, "What are you guys talking about?"

"My kid's in his class." In my mind, I'm doing the math. I could be the mother of a ten-year-old, couldn't I? Yeah, I would have had to have him at 14 but hell, it happens. So I channel her, Elizabeth Salazar, useless mom, the whole ghetto girl attitude and everything. "My baby can't read too good."

Christian is trying not to laugh. He's managing to keep his cool and seem like a concerned teacher.

"He's one of those little mofo's who's always in the office." It's not that I like to lie, but I love making up wild stories. "I ain't got no control over him. What do I do with him, Mr. Garcia? I need your help."

"He's a good kid. Give him one more chance." He struggles with some lie that will mesh with the story, "Just give him some time."

"No." I slam my hand on the table for emphasis. "My mama ain't much help, you know? She's all, come get your son, I need to go dancing. Ain't a grandma supposed to want to watch her grandkid? She's all, don't be calling me grandma in public, I'm Eliza, got it? What kind of crap is that?"

The band comes out, Ricky and his band mates take the stage. They're gesturing and setting up their spots. Ricky's recently dyed his hair bright red, has no shirt on, and is wearing low slung jeans that show off all his tattoos. I'm not stupid, Ricky is fucking hot. Women stop and stare at Ricky. That's the type of guy he is. I stop and stare.

"Your boyfriend is ready," Gabriel says in his sing-song voice, dropping himself on one of the open chairs. He studies Christian and his two friends. "Well, hi."

"Which one is your boyfriend?" Christian asks me, a hint of jealousy in his tone.

"Ricky," Gabe leans over to him, answering for me, pointing Ricky out to him, "The guitar player."

"He's not my boyfriend. I'm just a fan."

Ricky's band rolls into a cover of The Red Jumpsuit Apparatus's song, Face Down. Ricky is so focused on his music; he doesn't even glance over at us. As the set moves forward, his band moves towards more grunge and punk types of music. The crowd gets a little bigger. They're not great, but they're fun.

Christian and his friends don't leave. They stay with us, watching the show. Well, Christian's two friends watch, Christian watches me. He places his hand next to mine, drumming his fingers with the side of his palm in contact with mine. I'm not sure what his friends think is happening. I'm not moving my hand away from him.

Ricky looks great up onstage. He looks like a rock star. He performs shirtless. His loyal groupies scream at the foot of the stage. After about four songs, Ricky pulls a black t-shirt on and moves towards the mic. He looks around the crowd while adjusting his guitar.

Looking out to the crowd, he shades his eyes as he searches. Then spying us, Ricky points at me, "This is what it should have been."

Ricky plays one of my favorite songs, Nothing Compares 2 U but not the version by Sinead O'Conner, the original, the version by Prince. It has a different vibe, not to say Sinead O'Conner can't sing, she sang the shit out of that song. This version is more Ricky, more low key and more vulnerable. Ricky is not a singer, he doesn't sing in public much, but he can sing. He knows I love this song. My heart is in my throat. Ricky loves me in a way I don't deserve. I know what he's talking about, our first time. Oh my god, I'm fucked.

This is insanity. Christian, this stupid ass boy I love, is sitting here with me. Ricky, this other stupid ass boy, is singing a beautiful song to me. What the hell is happening? It's a freaking horror movie. My heart starts to pound in my chest. It's so hard. Everyone is looking at me. They all know what I'm doing. I'm making a huge fucking mistake with my life. I want to go home. With heavy heart palpitations, I'm going to die of a heart attack.

Christian leans over, "Who's that guy?"

"Ricky. That's Ricky."

"Is he your boyfriend?" He has the nerve to sound angry with me.

"He's Gabe's brother." I'm trying to sound indifferent. I'm sure I'm failing. Finally, he knows what this feels like. Hurts, doesn't it? It's glass against your soul.

"That doesn't answer my question."

I just glare at him, who is he to judge me? "You don't get to ask me that Christian. Where's your girlfriend?"

When he's done, Ricky points at our table, "Love you, Jules."

Some of his groupies scream like he just said that to him. My heart leaps in my chest. This is too much for me. The familiar burning pain of a migraine is building right behind my left eye.

Gabriel starts laughing, "I think Ricky just hit stalker status. I thought the tattoo was bad. Damn, what did you do to him?"

I want to die. I'm so humiliated. I'm so flattered. I'm mixed up. It doesn't make sense. It's all twisted and confused. My heart is about to pound right out of my chest. I'm drowning from the inside. Christian is sitting right here. I want him. Ricky is over there, he wants me. What the hell is happening?

Christian looks at Gabe, "What tattoo?"

"Ricky has her name tattooed on his wrist," Gabe gestures to his wrist, "He has her name right here."

Christian looks at me, then at Ricky, "What the hell? Who is he?"

"Stop it, Christian, we are nothing."

One of Christian's friends asks, "What's your son's name?"

"Son," Gabriel wrinkles his nose. He looks over Christian's two friends, "She doesn't have any kids. When did you start telling people you have kids?"

"I was just kidding." Knowing the corner I must have put Christian in, I'll only admit to being partly sorry. So maybe they have some doubts now. Whatever, that's his problem.

"Oh so you can lie and I can't?" Gabriel leans over and fixes my fallen strap for me. "Ricky is her boyfriend, sort of."

"No he's not." There's this thick lump already forming in the back of my throat. It's just so concentrated and heated.

"What?" Gabriel looks at me, with his huge chocolate eyes, letting the words fall from his mouth, "He has a tattoo of your name. That's the kind of loyalty you need. He's not ashamed to say he loves you."

"Ricky only loves what he can control." It's true. I know that. If we were a couple, Ricky would get all weird and stalker-ish on me. As friends, he's cool, as a couple, he would be next level.

I'm sinking into a black hole. Maybe I've been sinking longer than I realize, but right now, in this instant, it's reality. I have nothing. I have to focus on my breathing to stay in control.

Gabriel, he's got this look, like he knows what he's done. He seems so remorseful, he quietly asks, "You want a drink?"

"I think I need one now."

"I'll be back, my love," he blows kisses at me.

"You're kidding yourself if you think that guy doesn't want you somehow," Christian tells me once Gabriel's made it out of earshot, sounding envious. "He's all over you."

I remain flippant with him. "It's not like that."

"Don't be so naive." Christian sounds angry. "Come on Juliana, you're smarter than that."

"But he is." How dare he be mad at me, while he plays house with some girl? "Trust me."

"You let him touch you a lot." It sounds dirty when he whispers it to me, "I think you like it."

"You need to stop." I'm sure I'm a shade redder than I planned to be. It's just so insane. How dare he suggest that we're anything more than friends? "Knock it off Christian. Leave me alone."

"Exactly what is going on with those two?"

"Do not try to make it sound dirty. They're brothers for fucksake." Sounding like I'm having a temper tantrum isn't helping. It's escalating into a full-blown hissy fit, "You don't know them like I do."

"Why do you sound like a jealous boyfriend, Christian?" Ray says then laughs it off. I guess he catches himself. Maybe he doesn't want to put the pieces together.

A weighted silence permeates us. No one says anything for a minute. The sins of my past are so tangible, I can almost see them. He really thinks I'm a whore?

So then the other guy asks, "So how do you know each other?"

It's the look that Christian gives me that does it. He's got this distraught and pleading look. He doesn't want me to say anything. It's instant mortification. I know what I am to him. I am nothing more than some girl who he'll fuck when there is no one else around, not a girl he could love. My heart literally breaks. It just breaks. With each breath, it's glass scratching against me. Why do I let him treat me like this?

Struggling for an answer, I can't find one. "His sister, I need to go." With that I stood up, wondering which way Gabriel wandered off in.

"Juliana?" Christian won't look at me. "You want me to tell my sister anything?"

I'm sick of this. I'm not some tramp, I'm not. With my bruised heart on the floor, there is nothing I can say. "Tell her that her brother, can fuck off. Fuck you Christian."

Stomping off, I'm the most immature person within ten feet of me. I'm pushing through people and maybe I'm overreacting. I just can't stand being anywhere near him. My skin's ablaze from the inside. I'm burning from inside with remorse and regret. I shouldn't have ever spoken to him in the first place. It's too much pressure. There is no way I will heal from this. I can't escape the mess I've made with Christian Garcia.

Gabriel catches up to me somehow. "What the hell happened?"

"I hate him." Against him, I'm crying like a lost little kid. I'm sure I'm making a scene. I don't give a shit anymore. "Gabriel, I love him."

"Oh honey," Gabriel holds me close to him.

Christian is here instantly, yanking hard on my arm, forcing me to take a step towards him. "That's not what I meant. I swear."

"Get away from me, Christian. Leave me alone." Trying to pull free, I have to escape. His grip is so hard, my blood pooling under my skin. Right now, he is nothing but poison burning through my veins.

"Listen, I'm going to leave her. I swear, I'm going to leave her."

"Just stay away from me." I can't move from this spot. I can't even look at him anymore. It's not supposed to be like this. It's not supposed to hurt so badly so fast. I can't be in love with this boy.

All my energy is concentrated, and I shove him. I'm ready to knock him out. His friends are standing here, surprised.

Christian grabs me again, fingers digging into my arm.

"Let her go." Ricky pops out of nowhere, shoving Christian back. "Fuck off and leave her alone. You got a girlfriend."

Christian releases me. My arm is throbbing.

Ricky points at his two friends, "Tell her the truth. Tell her he has a girlfriend."

One of his friends, I think he's Alex, nods, "Yeah, he does. They live together."

"Did you hear that?" Ricky stepped up to me, his eyes locked on mine. "You need to believe people when they show you who they are. He's fucking with you. You got that? Take her home Gabe, now."

"Come Juliana, we're going home," Gabriel's pulling me. There is no energy left in me to fight the tug. I stumble after him.

Christian has a girlfriend. I am not his girlfriend.

"Give me five minutes." Christian isn't even looking at me anymore. It's more like he's talking to Ricky. "Let her talk to me for five minutes."

"Fuck you," Ricky tells him. "You're just going to lie to her. I can't have that. Leave her alone. Stop calling her."

"What the fuck is going on, Christian," Alex finally says something. He still seems like he's in shock. "What the fuck are you doing to Shelly?"

"Look at me," Ricky orders, while snapping his fingers at me, "He's fucking with you. He's lying to you."

"Give me five minutes. Talk to me for five minutes."

"No." I'm a shameful secret. I want to be loved in the open. That's the thing, I want to be loved. I want someone to cherish me. "I'm not waiting for you."

Gabriel is still talking to me, but I can't hear him. The sounds of my blood, the sounds of the merriment of the carnival, it's all surreal and distorted. Nothing makes sense. I just want to go home.

GABRIEL
October

    She cries so much, I almost want to call Aaron. I'm not sure this is a normal response anymore. I don't know how or why Juliana cares so much about that asshole. He is not worth her time. I got her drunk. At least now she's in bed and asleep. I can watch over her and make sure she stays away from Christian.

    Let his friends figure out what he's doing. Of course, he's a guy. Men can do shit like that and be cool, and they'll call her names. They'll call her a whore and laugh about her behind her back. They have no idea he made her fall in love with him. Yeah, she hooked up with him first, but that asshole has led her on from the first minute. He won't leave his girlfriend. He won't do that.

    Instead, he will break her heart over and over. He will call her, give her enough attention, and make her think he wants her. He'll use her and go home. He'll move on. I will have to take care of her. I love her, and I'll do it. I'm tired of this shit.

    Ricky is my fault too. He's crazy. I know that. Now I've gotten her into a situation I don't think she knows how to handle. I know, I knew, he was crazy about her. He has a fucking tattoo of her name. When he sang that song to her, she looked like she would follow him into hell.

    But I am glad he was there. He barged right in and told Christian to fuck himself. Ricky might never have her either. He will fight for her. He's scary, you know, Ricky? He's unhinged when it comes to her. Ricky's feelings for her are hard to explain. He has her on some pedestal in his head. She's like a sister, like a lover, I don't know what it is. I know he will protect her at any cost. I'm guilty of getting her involved with him. I need him to protect her.

If we were one person, Ricky and me, we could love her the way she deserves. I love her. He's in love with her.

This is all wrong.

I did this. I made this mess for her.

She doesn't deserve this.

JULIANA
October

The pounding house beat makes my heart race. Computer-synthesized music blares from every direction, right into my soul. All the different people, all the heated bodies, push at me from every direction until we find a place to dance. All the lights, flashing red, purple, blue, and orange, it's almost what I imagine a convulsion would feel like. I want to die just like this.

"You're leaving right now."

Opening my eyes, it's absurd. Did I call him? I don't even remember anymore. I need Xannie, more Xannie. Ricky can get me more. Ricky doesn't like when I ask him for that shit, but he won't tell me no.

Why this boy insists on coming into the Express, it's beyond me? My intoxicated brain only seems to understand bubbles. I just want to enjoy bubbles of insanity and euphoria, not hurt and despair. Don't kill my Adderall vibe. "What are you doing here?"

Christian ignores my question. "Leave with me. Come home with me."

With the industrialized music still pounding, it's light and golden. It's like living inside a water globe where everything is swirling glitters. I can't stop laughing. My world is spinning too fast. It's a struggle to stay upright.

"You have a girlfriend."

Wandering, I'm not clear where I'm going. It can't be anywhere near him. Leaning against the wall, I know I'm going to be so sick in the morning. I don't care. I can't live with a hole in my heart. I just need to be numb.

Christian keeps me from sliding down the wall. "Let me take you home."

"You have a girlfriend."

"Tell me to leave her. I will. Tell me."

"You already said that. You didn't leave her." He's blurry, but yet, he's just the most ravishing man in my life. He's everything I never wanted, and everything I can't live without. Aren't I worth it? Can't he just want me? "You picked her over me."

"Just tell me, Juliana."

Moving from his grasp, I can't deal with him anymore. What does he want from me? Why does he need me to be the bad guy? Why does it have to be my fault? Why can't he love me on his own?

"Leave her. Do it for me."

"I will, as soon as she comes back. I'll tell her. But you're coming home right now."

Taking his hand, his skin rough against my own moisturized one, I know there is nowhere else I want to be. With him, I am whole. I want to live under his skin.

"Don't do this Juliana, come on, I'll take you home." With his voice low, yet firm, Gabriel talks to me like I'm lost. "Don't let him do this to you."

It's too much pressure. We are not supposed to have an audience. We're standing in the parking lot and having a tug of war over morality.

"Listen, I'll take you home okay?" Gabriel says it like it's the simplest thing in the world. What he fails to understand is that I have become obsessed with this boy. I want so much from him. I want to burn for him. "You're going home with me now. Say bye, Juliana."

He will not let go of my hand. That's why he's my best friend. In my moment of greatest need, he's here and making sense to me. He repeats himself with greater authority, "Say bye."

Gabe's right. I have to demand a little more respect from this boy. I've already given him too much. He has seen my soul. "I have to go home."

"Go." Christian lets go of my hand after a moment, "But go home. I'll call you."

"Don't call me. You need to leave her. You need to leave her for me. Don't call me until you leave her."

"I swear I'm going to do it."

"I'm done with this shit, you leave her or that's it." With my open palm against his chest, his heartbeat is under my fingers. As much as it kills me, I have to go home. "I'm not waiting anymore."

GABRIEL
October

    He will make her the enemy. He will hate her. In his mind, he will make her the bad guy. She pushed him into leaving his girlfriend.

    But she is standing up for herself. Finally, she's demanding more than just crumbs of love.

    This will end badly.

JULIANA
October

"She's gone." His voice is so thick and raw. The pain of what has happened has hit him. "I hurt her Juliana. I broke her fucking heart."

It hurts me to see him like this. A few days ago, I was out of control. Now it's my turn to hear him out.

I didn't want it to be like this. I didn't know he had a girlfriend. I didn't want him to leave her or anything like that, not at first. I want him to love me. I can't explain it. I should have said no, stay with her, but I want him. I want to belong to him.

"She cried. You understand that?" He reaches like he's going to touch me, then he doesn't. He just glares at me, reminding me that I am the reason we're in this situation. "I hurt her. I never hurt anyone like that."

Standing here, I want to cry too. The guilt of what has taken place is harsh. It's flattening. It's my fault. I've shattered him. I've made him do things he didn't want to.

"She cried and she…" He just lies back on my bed. He's haunted. "I hurt her. Tell me I did the right thing."

"I'm sorry Christian." I can't find words to soothe him. There are no words that can defend my actions. I really didn't mean for this to happen. He never told me he had a girlfriend. I wouldn't have messed with him if he had told me.

"No, you're not." He watches me for a moment. He's so angry with me at this moment. I physically feel it. "You're not sorry."

"Yes, I am," shame and resentment burn in my soul. This isn't a pretty moment. It's not the homecoming I envisioned.

He grabs me hard and kisses me, making it hard to breathe. He kisses me hard. It fills me with a throbbing passion. I want him to make me belong to him.

Clenching my fingernails against his arms, I ask quietly, "You want to hurt me, Christian?"

For a second, he doesn't say anything. He stares at me. Maybe I have passed some imaginary line. I've crossed over to insanity. It's me. We will be his parents. I'm afraid, but I want it too. Chills are running through me, I hate myself.

Just the sound of his breathing is all I can think of. I can't make sense of this situation, and honestly don't want to either. I'm one step away from it. I'm one step away from damnation, but if that's what it takes, so be it. I'd give him anything. I can't say why, but I know it's him. I love him.

And then he traces my bottom lip with his finger. "I want to hurt you."

"Hurt me then."

Leaning back, I just close my eyes, still gasping for breath. He continues to kiss me, leaving a sloppy trail of kisses down my neck. Without much care, he's in me. Clothing just pushed to the side.

Christian pins me, pushing into me without a moment to prepare for him. It's like home all over again. It's wrong, it's all wrong. But it's all right. I love Christian. I want to be everything to him. I want to be It's what he needs.

I need him.

******

Christian did what I needed. I needed him to just take it. He just took it. I hate needing that. It's too much like before. I needed it like that then too. Or did I? Who needs that when they're just sixteen, or seventeen years old? I hate my stepfather. I don't know what I'm doing. How can I tell if it's real?

Christian is real, isn't he? I want to be everything to him. I want to be everything to him.

"I love you but you don't need to say it back. It's not like that."

He brushes a few strands of hair from my face. "You know me, Jules. No one, not even my girlfriend, knows me like you do."

He said, girlfriend, not *ex*-girlfriend.

"We won't be like my parents. I won't do that."

I curl up with him. She's still there. I can feel her. I'm not sure if he's lying to me or lying to himself, but she is still there. I don't give a shit. It's the start of this. We'll fight, and we'll hate each other. We will be his parents. We already are.

JULIANA
November

"What high school did you graduate from again?" Christian's pushing around the stacks of papers. I can tell he's just not up to doing this tonight. He's trying to talk about anything to avoid the reports and math sheets. "You went to a private school, right?"

"Saint Paschal's."

Christian's correcting papers and I'm trying to help him. Everything is so difficult to read. How do teachers correct spelling tests? After the first five, the words start to look correct.

"Why did you go there?"

"My dad's wife works there. My dad wanted me too." Shoving the stack of papers aside and stretching, this whole correcting worksheets crap is giving me a headache. "We're not close. I have brothers. I wouldn't know them if I saw them on the street."

"You have brothers?" Christian seems so dumbfounded it's cute. He forgets his papers and moves next to me onto the couch.

"I never saw them much. It's not like I grew up with them. My mom was 16 when she had me. It was one of those high school things. Then he grew up. He just moved on."

"Your dad sent you to Catholic school and then just never saw you?" Christian's studying me sort of sideways. "That's kind of crazy, huh?"

"It was my payoff. His guilt got me a better education, that's all. With him, it was always, 'next weekend.' He didn't get along with my mom. They always fought about everything."

Christian's quiet for a long time. When he does that, again I'm reminded why I love him so much. With him, it's never this contest to be talking all the time. He's comfortable with silence.

"I could never do that to my kid."

"Don't be so dramatic." I have to remind myself that I'm over it, whatever it was. It's not like I haven't spent the better half of my life searching for something missing. It's over. "It's nothing. I know he tried and he must feel guilty about everything, but he's got a real family now. I can't hate on that."

"So why don't you see your mom anymore?"

He takes my fingers and kisses them lightly. When he does stuff like that, he makes me believe I am worthy of this. I can't explain it. I believe in the patron saint of denial. This isn't denial. It's something more. It's like real, honest-to-God love.

"I just don't. I don't fit there either. She's married. She's got three other daughters."

Christian sits up. "You have brothers and sisters?"

"It's nothing. They're not my family." The thought of those people being my family, it's pathetic. I am not related to any of them.

He nudges me, teasing, "Are you jealous?"

"No, it's not that. It's not like that." The heat is rising in me. It's just the worst sensation, acid burning up my spine. What I did, what I allowed to fester, it's repulsive. I sold my soul to the devil.

"I never thought you had brothers or sisters."

"I don't." I'm on my feet and stomping around. If I keep moving, I won't have a panic attack. I will never be saved from it. I can never escape it. Blackness will always linger in the corners for me, waiting for its chance to squash me again. As much as I struggle, air cannot reach my lungs. "I can't talk about these people. They're nothing to me."

"Juliana, what's wrong?"

"I can't breathe." I am reminded of what he did. What we did. Struggling for breath, I have to remain in control, even if everything within my DNA is screaming the memories throughout my brain. I struggle for breath, trying to force air into my tightened lungs. I'm dying. I'm having a heart attack.

"What's the matter?"

"Nothing," I whisper. Standing still, I measure myself. I cannot do this. I can breathe and make it through this moment. Clenching my fingernails into my palms, the physical pain releases something in me, calming me. I bite the inside of my cheek until it bleeds. I'm drowning. I just want to sink to the bottom of the ocean. "Just let it go."

"What's the matter?"

"It's nothing. They are not my family. None of them are."

Then I'm crying. I'm crying so hard, I'm shaking. It's such an ending to such dramatics. Tears, blistering and intense, fall from my eyes. Everything is so raw and fresh in my brain. No matter how much time has gone by, the smell, the way he touched me, the things we did, it's like yesterday. "I hate him Christian. Please. Just don't."

He's holding me and in his arms, is exactly where I need to be. "Juliana, are you okay?"

"I'm fine." I have to focus, keep focusing until I force those feelings down. Push them back of my mind. Why did I even tell him? What's he going to think of me now? I can't just go around telling people. "It's nothing."

"You're okay. You hear me?" He traces a figure eight on my back, reminding me that he loves me. I have value with him.

"I don't want to talk about this." For the moment, I know I'm safe within his arms. And even though I'm safe, I have this urge to release. I have to just get it out. I just allow myself to cry. I can't tell anyone, ever.

If I give it energy, it makes it real. If I refuse it, don't give it power, I can make it go away. I don't want to feel this. Not now, not ever. The memories, swirling in excruciating vividness-there are some things I haven't gotten over, no matter how much I pretend I have. I have no words for him.

"No one cared."

"But your dad, he's a cop, right? Didn't he ever ask?"

"I never saw him. His wife didn't like knowing that I existed, you know? You know how you can tell someone only tolerates you? She just tolerated me. She told me she didn't know what to do with a girl. She was a princess. Her house only had room for one princess."

He holds me close.

"No one really wanted me. You know? I don't think either of them wanted me. I just am."

"I want you."

"No you don't. Not really." I want him to insist, to swear he does, but he doesn't. Maybe he doesn't want me. I forced him into this.

"You understand me, Juliana," he says to me, "No one knows me like you do. Too bad you're only good for one thing."

Asshole. Christian Garcia is an asshole.

I have no right to be here. I shouldn't be here.

We're just like his parents.

JULIANA
November

"I have something for you. Come on." He helps me to my feet, leading me through the house and into his uber-organized garage. Typical man, his house is always disorganized, but his garage, it's perfect. It would be like him to have everything so impeccable here. "You wanted a dog house, right?"

It's the nicest thing anyone has ever done for me. It's large and he painted it white, with real roof tiles and everything. I don't even have a dog, but if I did, I know my dog would love this house. It's unreal. I can't believe he did this. No one has ever done anything like this for me. He did this for me? Maybe he loves me?

"What kind of dog are you going to get?"

"I don't know." It's a sweet thought. I'm not getting a dog. I don't like dogs. I just needed him to do this for me. "Thanks for the dog house."

He built me a dog house, a real dog house. Maybe I'm wrong, maybe he loves me. Who else would build me a dog house? Maybe he could love me the way I love him. I love him.

GABRIEL
November

    Christian built Juliana a fucking dog house. Now she thinks it's true love. It's not love. He's keeping her on a fucking string because he doesn't want to let her go yet. He still has a girlfriend. She doesn't want to hear that. Yeah, he said he broke up with her. I doubt it. I'm sure she's around somewhere. Juliana doesn't ask enough questions and does not demand more. She just wants to believe him.

JULIANA
December

"Don't touch me like that!" Pushing away from him, it's a wonder why I haven't tripped over any of the random leftover toys everywhere all over the floor. We're supposed to be looking for a toy truck for his sister's unborn baby. It's going to be a boy. Christian had this wild idea of buying him a Tonka truck, just like he used to have until he pushed it under his dad's truck.

"What?" Christian cozies up to me, putting his hand into my back pocket again and pressing against my ass. "I'm not doing anything to you."

The static from that movement, usually nothing worth noticing, is intensified while he's got a hold of me and refuses to let me go. He's much stronger than me. He can catch me and keep me still. It's so scary and a turn-on.

"Mr. Garcia," leaning close to him, I continue, speaking softly, "Am I in trouble? Are you going to keep me after school?"

The stupidity of my statement sends us into hysterics. He picks up a hand puppet and kisses me with it. The acrylic fur tickles my skin, causing me to giggle even more.

"Juliana?"

Turning slowly, my laughter just dissolves. Looking at the man I resemble so much, I don't know what to say. We have the same skin tone, *café con leche*, the same almond shaped eyes. I haven't seen him in who knows how many years, but here he is, inside the same store. Every time, it surprises me how young he is. I can't hate on him. In all honesty, I don't even know him. "Well, hi."

"How have you been doing?"

"I'm okay." There is never much to say between us. All we share is our DNA. He's just my sperm donor. I look like him. My mom never let me forget that. Somehow, it's my fault that he left her. It's not that they were both so young and only in puppy love, it's me. She still blames me on some level for robbing her of her youth.

He looks at me, never taking another step closer. For some reason, it disgraces me to know I wasn't wanted by him. I just motion towards Christian. "This is Christian, my boyfriend."

"Hi," he leans over and shakes Christian's hand. "I'm her dad."

I want to say "no you're not, you're full of shit." My words have escaped me. I want to hate him. I want him to be my dad. He has never been my dad.

"You're a cop right?" The sarcasm is so evident in Christian's voice.

"Christian's a teacher. He teaches 5th grade." I'm gesturing wildly, seeming totally ADD. I'm struggling to breathe. "His wife, she teaches Spanish." Why that seems important right now, I don't understand.

"That's great. My wife loves it." My dad nervously glances around. "So, are you still working at the mall?"

I just nodded my head.

"She's going to school, tell him Juliana." Christian is proud of me, it's strange. I should have solace in that fact, but it makes me unworthy of him.

My dad looks at me, seeking clarification. "Do you need anything?"

"No. It's just Fresno City." What I needed, I don't need from him anymore. He can't fix what's already been broken. "I'm okay, really."

"Your brothers, they're in here somewhere. You know those boys."

I don't know those boys. They're not my brothers, but I'm not about to tell him that. I haven't seen them since, well, I don't even know. "That's cool."

For a moment, the PA system is the only thing making any sound. "And your mom? How is she doing?"

"I guess she's okay. I haven't heard from her lately." For some reason, I'm gesturing like she's nearby.

"Shouldn't you check in on her? She's your mom."

"Wait a minute, what did you just say?" Christian forcefulness takes me by surprise, understated strength. "Who are you to tell her what to do?"

"Christian." I can't stand here pretending everything is okay. It's hurt that cannot be contained by mere words. This man is not my dad. He never was. "Don't."

"She's your daughter."

"I don't pretend that I'm the perfect dad, not at all." My dad, he seems so troubled. I'm not supposed to exist.

"Do you know anything about her? How old is she? Do you know? Do you even remember what day she was born?"

My dad seems to ponder, letting me know that yeah, he didn't remember. "Where did the time go? You've got to be, what, 24 now?"

"Don't worry about me. I'm cool." I take a step back, it's just too much. I can't stand here pretending that I'm good. Maybe I'm not good. Maybe my heart's been broken for so long that I never even noticed it. Maybe people are not supposed to have this hole in their soul that they try to fill with sex and chocolate cake. "We got to go."

"Listen, I made mistakes, I know that, but I am still your dad. You have my number."

"She shouldn't have to call you. You're a cop, protecting everyone else except the one person who needed you the most. You have no idea what happened to her, do you?"

My lungs squeeze every last bit of air out. Stunned, I stare at him. Oh Saint Jude, patron saint of hopelessness, don't let him say it. I pray to you, please, don't let him say it. "Christian, don't do this."

"You need to tell him." He thinks if I tell him, I'll be free of my sin. My sins, he doesn't know how deeply they cut my soul. "Tell him."

My dad is looking at me. "What is he talking about?"

"Nothing, it's nothing." Taking another step back, with them both looking at me, I need to get out. I can't breathe. I just can't find air and my lungs burn.

"Do you have any idea of what that man did to her?"

"Christian, don't do this." Struggling with breath, I wipe my tears away, damning their very existence. I just wish he'd shut up. He's not supposed to do this to me. He can't do this to me. I wouldn't tell his secrets, who is he to tell mine?

"Her mom made a choice. She didn't have a choice."

My dad looks at me. He wants me to tell him it's not true. He knows what Christian is hinting at, he's a fucking cop. He knows. "Juliana?"

"Christian, how could you tell him?" Looking back at my dad, this practical stranger, I'm pleading with him, "You can't tell her you know. She hates me already. You can't tell her you know."

Matt Lopez doesn't say anything. He looks at me like it's this strange moment he doesn't belong in. He's repulsed by me, I know it. He never wanted me. "What am I supposed to do with that information now?"

"You're full of shit. I just want you to know that. She doesn't need shit from you."

With that, I'm gone. I'm not running, but I'm moving faster than I need to. My heart is racing. I'm having a fucking heart attack. Bugs, worms, something is crawling on me. My skin is alive with crawling. I'm 24, but I'm dying of a heart attack. I have to get away from this moment. It's not pretty. I never thought this moment would ever happen. It's the past. I'm not a prisoner of my past. I can live in denial. I believe in the patron saint of denial. He's my friend. His name is Jose Cuervo.

Christian catches up to me, yanking me to a stop, his hand on my arm. "I'm sorry. I don't know what came over me. I just had to tell him Juliana. I'm sick of seeing you punish yourself for something that isn't your fault."

Glaring at him, my heart's suffering in a way that goes beyond torture. Shoving him away, I don't care if people are watching us. Fuck them, fuck Christian and fuck Matt Lopez. Blood pounds through my brain, nothing's real. I'm floating, but I'm right here. I don't know how I'm supposed to feel in this second. I am so confused.

"I don't want to talk about it."

"You never want to talk about it." He talks to me like I'm one of the kids in his fucking class. He's careful to structure his words. The harshness of his demeanor is evident. He's scolding me. "You need some help. You need to learn to let it go."

"You need to let it go. I don't worry about it anymore. It's you."

I see this for what it is. I'm the problem. He can pretend he's innocent if it's me. I made him like this.

"It's you." He's not touching me. He must sense I can't handle physical stimulation right now. "You need some help."

"Shut up. Just shut up." Everything he's saying, it's too true for words. I can't, I just can't make myself listen to him, not as we're standing here in front of the crowded store. People glance at us, arguing at the entrance. "I'm not crazy, Christian. Don't talk to me like I am."

"I'm not saying that."

"Don't do this to me." My heart is broken. It's always been true, no matter how much I already know, it's always true. My dad, my dad doesn't care about me. He doesn't want me. No one wants me. "Take me home. Please, just take me home."

*****

Watching my cell phone glowing, vibrating roughly against the table, its existence is a reminder of my own faults. I can't move to pick it up. It's been, I don't know, it's been a long time since her phone number flashed across my screen. I just sent her call to my voicemail.

Christian thinks he knows me. He doesn't. He wants to be my savior. My soul is already damned. There's supposed to be freedom in truth, right? My truth will sentence me to hell. I want him to say that nothing before him matters. Let him tell me that he loves me.

"Listen, I'm sorry."

Hearing the familiar beep, I can't even imagine what she may have said. I'm sure she's cussed me out and called me a whore. She's got this wonderful way with words. Elizabeth Salazar is really motherly. "My mom called. It's never good when she calls. He called her. I know he called her."

"I'm really sorry."

"Maybe, maybe you should leave me alone for a little while. I need to go home."

"What do you mean, go home? You are home."

Shaking my head, I restate my meaning, "I need to go see her. She's got to be so mad at me right now."

"You're not going over there to let her yell at you."

The memory of how it happened, I am not innocent of this crime. I am not. "It was my fault. It was my fault."

"Juliana, what the hell are you talking about? It wasn't your fault."

"You don't know, Christian. You don't know."

"Then tell me. Tell me what happened."

It sounds so easy. I can't form words to explain it. I don't want to say what it was. I'm guilty too.

"She picked him over me. She didn't believe me. She said it was my fault."

"It's not your fault."

"I couldn't cry." I have nothing left to say. I can't breathe, the air trapped in my lungs doesn't give me oxygen. The memories, those haunted memories, have to be pushed into a box. That box is full now. My head is pounding, my brain on fire. I have no right to be here. Nobody wanted me. No one ever loved me. I'm worthless. I'm useless. I want to just sleep.

I am so tired.

Christian doesn't say anything. At this moment, when I need him to say everything is okay, he's silent. This, me, I am not what he wants. I'm a burden.

"Go away Christian, I want you to leave. I need you to go."

"After everything I have given up for you, you want me to leave? This is bullshit, Juliana."

"I don't want to fight with you about this. I just need a few hours to myself. I just want to be alone." I'm exhausted. I need someone to fight for me. I don't know what I need. Just say you love me. I need a fucking break.

"I'll go. You just remember why I left. You told me to leave."

His girlfriend, that's what he's thinking about. He's going to go see her. I'm about to fall off the fucking cliff, and he's thinking about his girlfriend? He doesn't care either. I don't have the energy for this. I just want to sleep. I made this mess.

"Don't call me Christian." I'm not sure if he hears me. He slams the door before I finish talking. I don't know what I'm doing. I just want to sleep.

We have become his parents.

JULIANA
December

    Juliana told him to get out. It's about time. I don't know what happened to cause the fight. It's the first time she kicked him out of the house. Good.

    Later, she tells me the whole story, how she saw her dad. He's really good at being a total jerk. He always does the wrong things. He always says the wrong things. Matthew Lopez has never been a dad to her. He always causes more trouble. And his wife, who hates Juliana, what is wrong with that woman anyway? Who could hate a child? Yeah, now she's an adult, but let's be real here. Celine Lopez has hated Juliana since she was a kid. What a bitch.

    And her mom called her? Left her messages? Her mom is, I don't know how to explain her. She still lives down the street from my mom. Over the years, my mom has forgotten all the crap Juliana went through. Eliza has other kids, younger, more the age of my younger brothers. My mom has boys. Eliza has girls, three younger girls. The youngest is just a baby. According to my mom, everything is fine now. I don't know.

    Juliana sleeps all day. She makes it to work when she needs to, then comes home and back to sleep. She doesn't go out, she doesn't answer her phone. She just sleeps.

    She doesn't even answer Ricky.

JULIANA
January

    Text message to Christian: Are you back with her?
    Christian doesn't answer me. I get it. I totally get it. I might be slow but I'm not stupid. I can't pretend I don't care about him. It's consuming, falling into the rabbit hole, kind of love. I love him, I do. I think about him all day and all night. I just want him to love me the way I love him. Why can't he just want me instead of her? Christian built me a dog house.
    Text message from Christian: I miss you.
    Drumming my fingers against the counter, I busy myself at work. I see it, his text. I shouldn't be doing this. It's taken me a while to get my act back together, but I finally did it. And what do I do? I go and text that fucking jerk. I deserve this shit.
    I really don't understand why my soul craves him so much. When he calls me, I want to be with him, to burn in his presence. I don't have an answer to why. Gabe keeps asking why? He built me a dog house, that's why.
    Maybe it's because I love him? Do I really love him? I think I love him. Honestly, without him, I'm just drifting in space. I don't belong anywhere. Why does he go back to her? Why does she take him back? Why am I not good enough?
    Me: I miss you too.
    I do. I miss him so much. My heart hurts under the weight of loving him.
    Message from Christian: Friday night? Want to hang out? It's my birthday.
    Do I want to hang out? No, I don't want to hang out. I want to

have sex with him. I want to belong to him.

    Me: Is this a date? Are you going back to her? Where is she?

    Message from Christian: She's going to a party. Yes, we are back together. I'm not going to lie to you.

    I have to rub my eyes, "Hey, I need to go wash my eyes. I think I rubbed some lotion into them." One of the bored girls who work here with me can manage the store while I take a five minute break.

    He's using me and I let him. Yes, he built me a dog house. He's not the one. What if I go out with him one time, just one last time and then that's it? I can do it. I can go out with him one last time and then I'll find a real boyfriend. Who gives a shit if he can build a dog house? No more guys who can build a dog house. I want a guy who's nice, someone who's a good person. I need someone who's romantic without me telling him to be.

    Who am I fooling? I am not a good person. I'm gonna fuck Christian, and I'll wait again. I'll wait for him to call me again. I suck. I'm pathetic. I totally deserve this shit.

    Me: Okay.

    Christian to me: I have a favor to ask you. I want something from you for my birthday.

    Me: What?

    Christian to me: I'll tell you when I see you.

JULIANA
January

It's dark and I feel stupid. It's all me. I'm so self-conscious. I can't relax enough to make it good. I can't get into it. He wants to record it. Fine, I can do that. Maybe his girlfriend will find it on his phone and leave him for good.

Then he'll be mine.

"Don't be so shy. You're never shy about stuff like this Juliana. Make it good," he says to me quietly. "Tell me you love me."

Fixating on his voice is easier. It's so low, it's sexy. It scrapes right against my soul. If I concentrate on him, I don't feel stupid. Struggling to relax, I try to imagine that it's not really happening, that he doesn't have his phone in his hand and is recording this. "I love you."

"You look so pretty. *Te miras hermosa. Mirame a mi*, Juliana." He's teasing me in that tone, that "you're the perfect girl" tone. He told me he loved me. He said I'm perfect. "Make it like cake."

Squeezing my eyes shut, I giggle slightly, even though I'm already so heated. Such a private joke and Spanish; he knows I love it when he talks to me in Spanish. "I can't."

"Come on, look at me. Think about chocolate cake."

"You tell me," looking past the phone and seeing him, the man I love and would do anything for. "Tell me in Spanish. Tell me you love me in Spanish."

"*Te amo.*"

JULIANA
January
After

    What I don't understand, what I may never understand is why? I don't like women like that. I don't. But Nina, something's different about her. She's this slow burn rising from some long forgotten memory in my DNA. I look at her and want to kiss her. Maybe it's because she knows heartbreak? She's just so, I don't know, I guess it's her skin. She's got skin like Christian and he broke my heart.

    Fuck Christian. I'm going to fuck with his life. He thinks he can destroy me? I can destroy so much more. I will burn this shit down. I don't give a shit what people think about me. I will destroy him. He doesn't know who he's fucking with. If I have to drag Nina to hell with me, so be it. Fuck her too. Let them all know how fucking hard this hurts. Let them bleed for me.

    Sitting on the edge of her couch, watching her wander around, I made my decision. She's got lipstick on. She's got glassy tears in her eyes, and when one falls, I lean over and kiss it away. I'm too afraid to move.

    Nina doesn't move either. My lipstick print is like a bruise under her eye. She stares at me like I've hit her or something. A lock of her hair sticks to her glossy lipstick. With my hand trembling, I reach out to her and brush it away. She still does not move. She just looks at me. She stands there.

    I lean into her and kiss her. Slowly, pressing against the sensitive spot on her neck. Nina gave a slight gasp, then ran her fingers in my hair. Then it's a blur of who we are and who we want to be. Her skin is flawless.

The differences between us are striking. It's this surreal strange out of body type of experience. It's just so real and not real. It's one of the truest things I ever had. It's just so pretty.

    I am fire.

******

    She's crying, over and over again she's asking me why we did this. I have no answer for her. I don't care. All I can think of is Christian. He's going to hate me. I want him to hate me. Right now, right at this moment, I am done with Christian.

GABRIEL
January

    She's destroying herself. Now that she knows the truth, she's on a path of self-destruction. Every night, she goes out. I don't know what my role is supposed to be here. I am not her parent. She's an adult. She's behaving like a child.

    I don't have the heart to tell her Ricky's leaving. He hasn't told her either. We had several long conversations about how to tell her. I've proposed having Aaron help, but Ricky and Aaron don't really get along. Aaron and Juliana don't get along.

    Christian is still texting her all the time. She's not answering him, but I see the texts pop up on her screen. He needs to fuck off.

JULIANA
January

    Standing in the bathroom, there is no escape from this. It's horrible. Everything I know is wrong. It hurts like nothing else. It's this severe ache scraping against my essence. Scorching and feverish, I'm on fire from inside. And yet, though I've prayed, I begged, I am alive. I don't want to be. I just want to go to sleep. I want to sleep forever. I have to make this stop. I don't want to feel like this anymore. I'm so tired.

    Christian stopped calling me. I'm heartbroken that he stopped. I want to call him, but I can't. I know I shouldn't. Why has it taken so long to realize that? I don't know?

    I don't remember going to get the knife or the bottle, but they are both here on the cold tilted floor of the bathroom. Me and the bottle, my patron saint of denial, we're empty. Maybe we've been empty for so much longer than we even knew. I'm so tired. There is nothing I can do to make it better. I've tried. I've really tried. I'm so sleepy now. I never rest anymore. That's the thing, I'm exhausted. There has to be a better place, right? I'm already living in hell. My escape will send me to purgatory with *La Llorona*. I too can be the crying woman with no soul left to sell.

    There is nothing left to do. I am alone. I don't have a family. I don't have parents. They never wanted me. That's the truth, isn't it? I am not supposed to exist.

    My mom sided with my stepdad. I did it. I made him come into my room at night. I didn't do that. I didn't want that. No one believed me.

    My dad has always been too busy with his perfect wife to care about me. I am not his daughter, who am I trying to fool? I'm never going to be good enough for him or his fucking wife, who probably can't wait for my funeral anyway. I can just see her there, walking around in some fucking red dress. She'll go on about Matthew Lopez's dysfunctional daughter. I never fit in in her fucking perfect world.

Christian doesn't want me anymore. He left me. If he had just stayed and said sorry, I would have loved him. He didn't. He never said sorry.

I don't have anything. I live in a void. There is nothing left on this Earth for me. There is no redemption from this pain. I tried, I really tried. I am so tired now.

It's not one of those things I want to rush. I want to suffer when my flesh is ripped by the serrated edge of the knife. I want to hurt when my brain realizes it's dying. I want to lose myself in the anguish. I scrape it against my flesh, barely tearing the skin. Thin white lines decorate my wrist.

The knife is finally scratching deep enough, the blood welling up right under my skin. The pain, it's not what I expected. I thought it was going to hurt, and it does, but there is also pleasure in it. It's redemption. It's releasing. My soul is free from this body I hate. I hate myself. I just hate myself.

I'm a waste. I'm useless. I am worthless.

I just want to go to sleep. I am so tired. I'm so tired.

*****

Oh my god, what did I do? I don't know why I did that. I didn't mean it. I am so sorry, I am so sorry. I didn't mean to do that. I just made a mistake. All of this is a big mistake. Gabriel is going to lose his shit. He's going to tell Aaron. They're going to make me sound crazy. They're going to think I'm crazy.

I can't make the bleeding stop. There is blood everywhere. I need help.

Text message to Enrique: I need you. Come help me. Please. I made a mistake.

*****

"What the fuck happened?" Ricky looks at the blood dripping from my wrist to the floor splatters. "Shit."

He takes my wrist and cleans it up in the sink, making a bigger mess. Blood splatters in our otherwise immaculate bathroom. Luckily, the cut is deep, not dangerous. He's able to stop the bleeding and wraps a bandage around it.

He doesn't ask why, he just holds me, sitting on the cold tile floor of the bathroom. He lets me sob, thick, body wrenching sobs rack my body. Ricky just rocks with me, letting me get it all out. I just made a mistake. It's just an accident. I don't mean this. I am so sorry. This is all a horrible mistake.

Once I can breathe a little easier, feel a little calmer, he helps me run a bath and sets me in, then he cleans up the mess on the floor. I don't have the energy to make words. Ricky doesn't need me to explain anything. When it's all cleaned up, he helps me get dressed and into bed.

"We're one person now. Your blood, my blood. We're always linked. Go to sleep," he says, tucking me into my bed. "Don't die. Got that Jules, don't fucking die on me."

He just climbed into my bed with me and passed out. With Ricky in bed with me, curled up next to him, I can finally close my eyes and sleep.

*****

I can't sleep anymore. I'm still exhausted. I just can't pretend to be asleep anymore.

All day, Gabe, Aaron and Ricky have been arguing. I can hear them. Ricky won't let them into my room. Aaron thinks Ricky hurt me. I'm not clear why he thinks that. Everything is foggy. My brain is on fire, nothing makes sense. It's the worst migraine I've had in a minute. I won't come out of my room. I won't tell Aaron the truth, I won't even tell Gabe. Only Ricky knows what happened. Me and Ricky, we're the same. We both know when to keep our mouths shut.

Aaron calls the cops. What the hell Aaron? He calls the police. I hate the police. Aaron, he thinks he's my dad. I don't need shit from Aaron. Aaron needs to stay out of my fucking business.

"Get up, put on jeans and a long shirt. Put on a baggy hoodie. Keep the hoodie over your head." Ricky tosses an old hoodie at me. He seems to be rushing but watching him, it feels so incredibly slow. "Quick."

I am so groggy. Nothing is clear. My world is fuzzy at the edges. I feel drunk, hungover. I haven't had a drink. I keep blinking my dry eyes, hoping something will be clearer, make more sense. I didn't mean it. I made a mistake. It was an accident. They can't know, nobody can know what I did. My heart is thumping. I have to scramble around. Aaron is knocking on my door.

"Jules, answer me," it's Aaron. "Tell me you're okay."

"I'm fine, Aaron. I told you already, I'm fine."

"I need you to come out here and talk to me."

Ricky grabs my hand, pressing his keys into my palm. "Listen to me. When I opened the door, run to my car, do not stop and talk to Aaron. I'm parked about two blocks over, and one up, over near the yellow house you like on San Pablo. Run, don't talk to Aaron."

"I'll tell Aaron you didn't hurt me."

He touches my wrist. "If the cops see this, they'll lock you up. Don't say anything, Jules. They'll take you to crisis intervention. It's like jail. Don't let anyone see your wrist. I won't let them take you."

"I don't want to be locked up."

"If they take me to jail, fuck it, I'll be fine. I've been in jail before. You go to my house. It was just a mistake. You promise me you'll never do that again?"

"I promise." I will never do this again. It was just an accident. I didn't mean it.

"The cops are coming. You run to my car and go to my house. Don't come back. No matter what happens, do not come back. Go to my house and stay there."

Before the police made it to the house, I made it out the door. Aaron and Gabe want me to stop. Ricky blocks them from getting out after me. I run. I need to find his car. I'm 24 years old and I'm running from the police?

I made a mistake. If people would listen to me, they would know I made a mistake. I didn't mean it.

It's cold out here, scrambling around, looking for Ricky's car. I need to get out of here. Find Ricky's car and go to his place. I got to move. Even if I'm running, everything's in slow motion. This can't be my life. I've royally fucked up this time. I don't want to go to jail. I don't want to explain to people what I did. I'm so sorry.

All the college kids took up all the parking. I have to hunt for Ricky's car, two blocks away. He said near the yellow house, I know where the yellow house is.

As soon as I'm in the car, a fucking patrol car pulls up with the lights on and blocks me into the parking spot. Ricky said don't talk. I don't want to get locked into crisis intervention. I just made a mistake. It was just an accident. He's got a blanket in the car. I cover my head and hide. Don't let them lock me up. It was just a mistake.

Just don't be my dad, please, just don't be my dad.

DANIEL
January

"Good evening ma'am," I say to the college students walking by me. The two women smile and keep walking towards their car as they wave. Women like men in a uniform right?

With my cruiser lights on, I'm babysitting a girl in a car. I'm a real cop but I'm always delegated the easy stuff. I'm surprised I haven't climbed a tree to rescue a cat yet.

"Excuse me ma'am," I say to her, knocking on the rolled up window. I might as well try again, she might start talking. There's not much else to do out here. I've got nothing but time. "Can you tell me your name?"

"Am I under arrest? I don't have to tell you my name unless I'm under arrest."

It's not quite dark yet, but the sun is setting fast. It's fucking cold out here. It's making my glasses get all foggy. Damn it. The sky is dark, but doesn't quite block out the setting sun, the brightness like an evil smile against the horizon, reminds me of the cat from Alice in Wonderland. The storm of the century is supposed to arrive in about 45 minutes. It's supposed to pour all night long. Only an idiot would be out here, standing in the freezing cold.

It must be a bummer to live in this neighborhood, all the young, broke college students taking up the street parking. I guess that's why the boyfriend parked so far from her house.

The Tower District, not my kind of place, it's too historic, too Art Deco, too retro. It's this weird space between Roding Park, City College and the Tower Theater, covered with neon lights and coffee shops. People love it here, not me, but other people. Sure, it's walkable, tons of restaurants and interesting gift shops surround the area, but it's also very trendy. I wouldn't live here. I never come over here. I'm not into this revitalization of the historic space movement here. I'm moving into the brand new construction area, a master planned community. None of this retro shit for me.

"Ma'am, it's my job to make sure you're okay."

"I'm fine. Can I go now? Are you detaining me?"

There is a girl locked in the car. She's hiding under a blanket. She ran from the apartment she lives in and locked herself into an old, beat up Mustang. She tossed a towel, a small blanket, over her head and curled up into the front passenger seat. She won't open the windows.

To talk to her, I have to yell. Instead of doing that, I'm just leaning against the car door. The neighbors peek out their windows. This must be embarrassing. She has to live here. Later, nosy neighbors will wonder why she had a cop car staged behind her car, her boyfriend's car. They'll make judgments. That's going to suck.

The rest of the team is at the apartment. I was ordered to go a block away and watch the girl. They deal with domestic incidents. I'm babysitting a girl in the car, great, just fucking great.

"Well, ma'am, there seems to be an issue at your home. Your landlord seems to think there was an altercation."

"He's wrong. Can I refuse your help? I don't need your help."

This is bullshit. This is definitely a Carlos Fernandez issue. My dad is being overprotective. He's a cop. I'm a cop too, but he's my superior. He's the one who ordered me to come babysit. In reality, he's babysitting me. He's keeping me away from the commotion. The rest of his team already treats me like a kid, this is just adding to the problem. I can't escape who he is, and he can't keep protecting me. I need to get out of this job, anything else in the department.

I always wanted to be a cop, just not like this. Growing up, I always wanted to be like him. I want to help people, serve the community's needs. I wanted to be a real cop. Instead, I'm lost behind my dad's shadow. I've got to figure out a way to make my own path. I can't keep following behind him.

"Well, ma'am, I just want to be sure you're okay."

"I'm fine. He's overreacting. I refuse your help. I'm good. Can I go now?"

These situations can be emotional. People call the police and everything goes well, until it doesn't. We don't arrest the right person. We do arrest the right person. People are always over emotional in a domestic incident. They can be dangerous, and here I am, babysitting a girl in the car. I hate this. It's getting darker, and it might start raining any moment. How much longer do I have to stand out here in the freezing cold watching her?

As the first drops of rain start to fall, my dad's cruiser rolls up. He too leaves his lights on, blue and red flashing. He parks right in front of the car and strolls towards me, towards her car. He's got the whole FPD look down, tall, older, distinguished in his police uniform. He commands respect. He makes me feel like a little kid. I hate to admit it, he is my hero. He's a good person. I want to be like him.

"Did she say anything?"

"No, she refuses to talk to me." My dad studies me, like maybe this is not what he wants me to do, police work. He is so tired right now. I'm sure his mind is on my oldest brother, JC. He's always getting into trouble. This feels like a JC problem-domestic incident. "She wants to leave."

He taps on the window with his flashlight. "Ms. Lopez, I'm Officer Fernandez, can I talk to you?"

"No, leave me alone. I need to go. I refuse your help." She doesn't come out from under her blanket, and I'm slightly vindicated. It's not just me.

"Ms. Lopez, your landlord seems to think Mr. Sanchez hurt you," he says to her window.

"I'm fine. He doesn't know what happened. He needs to mind his own business. He's not my dad. I don't need to speak to you. I want a lawyer."

"You're not under arrest," my dad tells her, "You don't need a lawyer."

"If I'm not under arrest, you need to let me go. I want to leave."

Glad that happened to him and not me. She's right. I have to fight laughing. My dad would be so pissed if I started laughing. It's nice to see he's not perfect either.

She reaches out her hand, placing her phone on the dash, still keeping the towel or blanket, whatever it is, over her head. All I can see are traces of a bright blue hoodie and her orange fingernails. With her finger, she taps the screen, causing music to play loudly.

It's that grunge shit my brother Eric plays, Rage Against the Machine, or some shit like that. Definitely an "I hate cops," song. Smart move. Whoever she is, she is definitely done with cop shit. She wants us to leave her alone.

Eric set me up on a blind date tonight, fucking great. I love my brother. He picks the wrong type to try to set me up with every time. I don't know why I agree. He always picks the girls who talk too much and giggle at everything. I'm not actually sure what my type is. It's not that. I'm treated like a child at work and at home.

I need to move out of my parents' house. The realtor I'm using sent me a list of houses he thought I'd like. I need to move out as soon as possible. I don't need a forever home, just a place to get away from my family. Latino families, there is always so much drama.

"I'm refusing your help. If I am not under arrest, you need to let me leave. I know my rights," she has to yell to be heard.

She must watch those YouTube videos of how to annoy the cops. The good news for me is she didn't pull out her phone and start recording everything. I may not be a rookie, but I'm not 100% confident in my policing skills. Not yet at least. I'm still so new to this.

"Lopez," he says, only loud enough for me to hear. "Wonder if she's related to Matt?"

"Dad, there are millions of people with that last name." Carlos Fernandez thinks everyone must be related to everyone else with the same last name. It's a joke in the family, with his friends. "Stop that, not everyone in Fresno is related. Besides, he doesn't have a daughter."

"Maybe a cousin or something," my dad shrugs, resting against her car. He keeps a normal conversation volume. "Make sure you don't forget your mom's birthday next week."

"I won't." Carlos Fernandez is the perfect husband. He adores my mother. I should be grateful they created such a happy home to be raised in, but I'm the baby of three boys, and there is no escaping that. Everyone in that house tells me what to do all the time. "I have it set in my phone.

I'll send her flowers."

"Always send women flowers," he says, fiddling with the equipment on his belt. "If you care, send flowers. None of that,' let me just text her shit.' You kids these days don't do shit right. You do things right."

"Yeah, sure." He's always saying shit like that to me; send flowers, be respectful to her father, don't say I love unless you mean it. He hasn't realized I'm a total failure with women yet. I doubt my soulmate is even out there. I'll never have what my parents have.

My dad studies me for a minute. To him, I'm a little kid who doesn't know what he's doing. I am. I'm totally lost right now. I need to figure out what I want out of life, but first, I need to move out of his house. I need to grow up. I need some space. I'm tired of being delegated to babysitting a girl in a car. This sucks.

"You can go. I'll take care of this. We're letting her go. Her boyfriend will spend the night in jail for breaking and entering."

Now I'm being dismissed by him? Great, babysitting a girl in a car? I'm never going to live this down. I need another job.

JULIANA
January

Ricky is in jail for a few days.

At his place, his girlfriend takes care of me. She doesn't blame me in front of me. She doesn't ask me questions. I can hear her talking to him on the phone in the other room. She's yelling at him and crying. I can hear him telling her everything is fine. He's coming home soon, just a few days in jail.

She makes me a cup of tea then leaves me alone. We don't talk. We have an uneasy relationship. I don't think she likes me much. She doesn't come out and say it. She just tolerates me. I've dealt with worse.

I refuse to go home. Aaron called the cops. He sent Ricky to jail. I hate him. He is not my dad. Ricky says I can stay here until it's time for him to go. He's moving with his girlfriend to Oakland. He's going to the Bay Area with his band. Three of his bandmates are going. Only their lead singer refuses to go. He's got a wife and two kids.

I have nothing left to say to people. I don't speak to anyone. Not even Ricky. Ricky isn't freaked out when I stop talking. He seems to understand it. We've done this before. He knows me well enough to trust that I will speak when I'm ready. I have nothing left to say.

Christian doesn't call.

I changed my number. I leave them all behind, my mom, my dad, and Christian. No one gets this new number, just Ricky and Gabe. Not even Aaron. I just want to be alone.

I really was nothing to Christian.

I let Christian Garcia use me. I'm done with him. I'm finally done with him.

JULIANA
February

It takes a few days, almost a week, before I start talking again. Ricky tells me that when I'm ready, I need to go home, go back to Aaron and Gabriel. I don't want to go back. Aaron wants to be my dad. I don't need a dad. Aaron shows up at Ricky's house and demands to speak to me. Ricky doesn't let him in. Gabriel begs me to come home. He's the only person Ricky lets into the house to talk to me.

Ricky tells me he's moving. I promise to go home. I'll go home when Ricky leaves, not until then. I'll stay with Ricky. I need to be close to someone who loves me. Ricky loves me without any questions, not demands for why. We don't even have to talk about it.

On our last night at his place, his girlfriend leaves early to finish packing. She leaves us after pizza and one spooky movie. Tomorrow they're leaving. I promise Ricky I will go home tomorrow. I don't want to go home. I almost want to go with him. I don't want to go either. I just want to, well, I don't know what I want.

"Tell me the truth, who was first, me or Gabe?" Ricky already cleared up the remnants from our mini pizza party.

"Don't you have a girlfriend Ricky?" It's nice next to him. He's so warm. He lets me curl up against him.

"I didn't ask you to sleep with me. I just want to know, who was first?"

We're sitting in his house, on the floor of his room. He has what feels like ten different roommates. His bedroom is only his. He had it set up like an elaborate man cave, music equipment, bed, huge ass TV, but now there's just his bed and a TV. Everything else is in boxes in the rental truck outside.

"Ricky, what do you think? Nothing ever happened with Gabe." I pretend to watch The Shining. Watching this helps the dull ache in my soul. I don't want Ricky to leave. I'm not ready to let him go again. Once he goes, I'll be alone again. I don't want to be alone.

"You know you were my first." He leans close to me.

"I don't want to have this conversion with you." I really don't have the energy to say no to him. Honestly, I don't want to say no. "Look, blood, focus."

"Just tell me the truth." He toys with the ends of my hair, sending chills down my spine.

I have to stop and think. How do I want to phrase this? Yes, we tried. Once, just once we tried. It never worked. I am not what Gabe wants. It just didn't work out. "It was only you. Is that what you want to know?"

He laughs with that flat affected tone. He loves to mess with me. "I already knew. I just wanted to hear you say it. That's why I got your name. You were my first."

Glaring at him, I give him a hard shove. I'm flattered he has my name on his body, even if it's backwards. No one has a tattoo of my name on their body, just Ricky. He loves me. Not like in love, just love.

Ricky and I, it's an odd grouping for sure. We didn't see each other for years. Now we've fallen into this easy friendship. He knows what I did. He didn't tell anyone, he didn't ask me any more questions about it. It's just our secret. Ricky went to jail to protect me. I need that.

"In jail, I told them it was ANAILUJ, like analyze you. Stupid cops didn't question me about it. Was I your first?"

Virginity, it's such a big deal to some people. I want it to be a big deal to me. It's not. I was too young to even have an idea of what I wanted to be like. Then it was gone. Does that count? I've honestly thought about that, does that count? If you don't consent, can that count?

"You know he doesn't count, right?" He knows what I was thinking. "He doesn't."

Ricky massages my fingers. He notices that I'm trembling. I don't talk about these things with anyone. I want to pretend they didn't happen.

"I'm sorry Jules," he says, kissing me gently on my forehead, "I didn't mean to make you upset."

"If he doesn't count, yes, you were the first," I whisper. I want Ricky to be the first. If he is, if Ricky counts as the first, it makes things better. I love Ricky. Not like a boyfriend, more like a brother, a protector. He is my protector. Ricky is the keeper of my secrets.

"Say it, my first."

"Yeah, you were my first, Enrique Sanchez." My blood pressure is rising. It is burning through me. That need, that pressure, I can't fight it sometimes. It's already building, deep in my core. I know where this is going. I might be a lot of things, but I'm not stupid. I haven't gone out looking for easy men. I have an easy man right here.

"Will you ever want to do it again, with me?"

My heart is thumping in my chest. There is an undeniable ache in my soul without Christian. It's over. I won't ever take him back. I won't let him back into my life like that again. I made that mess.

Ricky's leaving tomorrow. His girlfriend is pregnant and going with him. Will one time hurt? Will one time count if we already did it before? S it cheating if we already did it?

He starts singing into my ear, into my hair. He keeps singing, moving closer. Isn't this what little girls' dream of, a handsome man singing to them, willing to be with them? A handsome man who has a tattoo of their name on their body? He wants me. I want to be wanted, to be number one. I want to be loved like this, but not by Ricky. I'm so mixed up.

"I'm going to give you a better first time."

"I want to be saved," I sing, quietly.

"Shut up."

Ricky pulls me up onto his bed with him. He helps me get my dress over my head and my bra off. There is no need for sublet foreplay with Ricky, he's got something most men don't have, Ricky can sing. It scraps a knife against my fucking heart.

Ricky lives in my soul. I know that. We might not be in love, and we'll never be in love, but Ricky and I; are each other's souls. He is part of my DNA. My blood was on his skin. We are connected. We are the same.

With my nipple in his mouth, he sucks hard and causes my breath to catch. My nipples peak, tight under his forceful touch. He uses the tip of his tongue to trace the outline. Working his way down, Ricky leaves a trail of heated kisses on my stomach.

It's not hard to work off my panties. He takes a long, flat lick around my core. I'm fucking melting. I can't help the gasping, it's an electric shock. My whole body is on freaking fire. My vaginal muscles are cramping in anticipation. His tongue is wet and hot, and he's got a piercing on his tongue that just sends me over the edge. I don't expect to come so fast. I can't stop making loud gasping sounds.

"Shh, they're going to hear you," he says, laughing. His words are hot breaths against my thigh.

I can't catch my breath as he does it again, painfully slow stokes against my clit. I'm fucking burning against him. My whole body is tensing up, but he doesn't stop. The pressure is building. From deep in my core, chills burn through me. I'm covered in goose pimples. I'm finally dying.

He pressed me against his bed with a flat, hot palm against my lower belly, nudging my knees farther apart. He's got me spread out on his bed. I'm so wet, I'm dripping down my leg. He sinks his fingers into me. My body tenses up, my next orgasm building. I can't catch my breath. Watching this sexy ass man, covered in tattoos, Ricky is downright bad. I'm throbbing with need, I need Ricky.

"Tell me you love me," he says, his fingers pushing in and out of me, in a beautiful rhythmic pattern, "Lie to me. Just for tonight, lie to me."

"I love you, Enrique Sanchez," I say, breathlessly. All the pleasure is radiating from my core. If he wants me to lie, I can do that for him.

"Enrique, huh, I like it." He drags his tongue up and down, one more time, triggering all the nerve endings in my body. I come so hard I'm going to have a headache after this.

All the feels, between his fingers, his tongue, makes me come again. My heart is about to explode.

"Jesus, Enrique, you're killing me."

"I love you, Juliana," he says, pulling his fingers out and moving. He positions himself to enter me. With a sharp thrust, Ricky fills me. Blood rushes to my fucking brain. I swear, I'm going to pass out. It's so good. I finally got to make love to Ricky again. And this time it's perfect.

"No one can know," I tell him. "Not even Gabe."

"No one, this is between us, Jules. My girlfriend would flip out. I promised her I wouldn't do this shit."

His girlfriend, great, what the hell am I doing? I seem to have a knack for finding myself in positions where my heart is the one always broken. I'm not stupid. I know he has a girlfriend. I didn't forget. I knew this was a one and done. I just don't want to talk about her right now. I don't want to get twisted.

"I didn't mean it like you're a dirty secret. I mean, you're my best friend. That can't change." Ricky runs his hand along my back, his fingers scratching me lightly and sending chills down my spine. "I need you. You need me too. We're the same fucking person. Do you understand me? We are connected."

Tracing all his tattoos along his chest, I am home. "Why did you get my name?"

"Right after my mom made me go live with my dad, I wanted to send a fuck you to your dad. A reminder to him, to me, that he can't change what happened. I got arrested for some shit, I forgot what now. I demanded to speak to him."

It's a childish thing, demanding to speak to my dad. Ricky at 19, must have been funny.

"He came into the interrogation room, looked at me, he knew who I was. It was just a few months after. He didn't say shit to me. I just held out my arm to him and stared at him. I might have said what the fuck are you going to do about that? I think even told him I fucked his daughter."

I'm embarrassed he did that, but then, why? My dad doesn't care. I need to face that reality. My parents don't give a shit about me.

Curling up against Ricky, it's surprising that he still smells like coconut. He's so warm. Too bad his girlfriend is having a baby. Too bad he's leaving me tomorrow. No, honestly, this is nice, but it's not what I need. This isn't real. We're pretending right now. I get that. This is just pretending.

"He didn't say shit Jules, he just scowled at me."

"Sounds like my dad."

"He's full of shit. I need you to know that. Promise me you're going to get some help. Stop fucking around with men who don't deserve you."

Ricky thinks I'm crazy? Wow. That hurts. I mean, I can see how

Gabe would say something like that to me, even Aaron, but Ricky? I need some help. Maybe he's right though? The thought hurts my heart. I need to do something for sure. I can't make a mistake like that again.

"I promise you, Enrique. I'll get some help, soon."

He touches the small bandage on my arm. It's healing. Now it looks like a normal accident. It's just an accident. I made a mistake. I need him to believe me.

"You know, I will always keep you in my heart. You are my first love, my first girlfriend, you, you are my first everything. That's why I keep your name. I'll always have your name."

"Enrique Sanchez, you are my first too." I can hear his heartbeat through his chest. "I'm going to miss you."

"Me too, I'm going to miss you and all your drama. Just promise me you won't die."

"You don't die either."

It's comforting to be held by him. As I drift off to sleep, he starts to sing that song to me again. I wish I could be in love with Enrique.

******

When I get home, I lock myself into my room for days. I refuse to talk. I lost my job. I don't care. I only have time to sleep. I don't eat. I don't want to be alive anymore. I want to die. That's all I can think of. Just end it. I'm tired, just so tired. Christian never loved me. My fucking heart hurts.

Still, after everything that happened, I love him.

I am worthless.

I am nothing.

I hate myself.

Text message from Enrique: don't die

Enrique: don't die

Enrique: don't die

If he doesn't text, that will be the day. Every day, I look at my phone. Every day, same text, different times. Once I have to wait until 11:57 for that text, don't die. Every day, I live. I live for my text from Ricky. I live for them until one day, I don't. I forgot to check. I make it a whole day, then a whole week, then a whole month. Then, it doesn't matter as much as it did. I can move. I can leave the house, I can be outside. I can breathe again.

It's a new path, not better, not darker, just different. I have to figure out what I want. I don't know what I want. I still want Christian. I don't call him.

Then, one day, Gabriel tells me Ricky needs me. He's in rehab, the first time he's in rehab, I need to tell him. He's so far away, I can't help him. He needs my help.

Text message to Enrique: Don't die.

Me: Don't die.

Me: Image of E-40

Me: Don't die.

Message from Enrique: You don't die either.

It's not always better. It's sometimes way worse. I need Ricky.

Part III

24.

You're in a car with a beautiful boy, and he won't tell you that he loves you, but he loves you.

Richard Siken

I wanna be saved.

E-40

JULIANA
Juliana
After
April 9

"Quinn, I said awful things." Quinn is sitting with me on his bed. I'm curled up in a ball. He's stroking my hair. I need him right now. I need my dad. "I was mean to everyone. I said, I wasn't, I had no control. I said horrible things. I said mean things to Daniel."

"Jules, you need to breathe. You have to explain this to him, girlfriend."

"I said it out loud, Quinn, I said I was pregnant out loud." I'm so angry with myself. That's not how I planned to say it. I wanted it to be special. I wanted a beautiful moment, and I ruined it. The sad, pathetic story of my life, I ruined everything.

"What did Mr. Policeman say?"

"I ran away, Quinn." Tears won't stop streaming. My heart hurts because of my immaturity. I am simply exhausted. I have nothing left. I'm just a shell of a person. "I didn't give him a chance to say anything."

"You need to be an adult, Juliana Lopez," Quinn starts, his voice is nowhere near quiet. "You have to talk to him. This is an adult situation. You have adult decisions to make."

"I'm a loser Quinn. I don't deserve this. No, I deserve all of this. This is me, I'm trash. I'm just like my mother, my father. I suck."

"You don't suck," he rubs my head. "You just panicked. You need to give Mr. Policeman a chance to hear you out. You need to explain this to him."

"Do you think Daniel is a mistake?" I'm almost afraid to hear his answer. Quinn will tell me the truth.

"No pretty girl, I have faith in Mr. Policeman. I hate to admit it, Mr. Policeman might be the one," he laughs, "I like him. Maybe he'll get a new job."

"You think I'm being immature?"

"No. It's not that. I know you girl, you react before thinking. You need to stop and think now. What is real?"

"What if Daniel hates me now?"

"Why would he hate you, Jules? He'll give you a chance to explain. He's a decent person. Tell him you panicked. He knew you were trying to get pregnant. That's not a surprise. Give the man a chance, Jules. Don't do this. Let him back in. Tell him the truth, you just panicked."

"I don't know if I can do this. What if he doesn't really love me?"

"Girlfriend, I shouldn't tell you this, but that man wants to marry you. He asked us, me and Aaron. We met his mom."

"No shit?" Did he ask them? What the hell?

"You need to talk to him. You need to calm down. You'll see I'm telling you the truth."

"I have a migraine, Quinn."

"Well, now that is a problem. You need to go to sleep. You look tired. You'll feel better after a nap. It's been a long day."

"Will you stay with me?"

"Always, rest your head, pretty girl. Go to sleep. Jules?"

"Hum?"

"Happy birthday."

"Some fucking birthday."

DANIEL
After
April 9

It wasn't easy to break back into the house. Matt's a cop, he has that damn house on lockdown. Juliana locked the door and we couldn't get it. Matt's alarm automatically resets.

Thankfully, Echo called to Matt III and he came down the stairs. His little five year old fingers had a hard time working the lock. He got it open after a few tries. It felt like forever, but couldn't have been more than twenty minutes.

"Where is she?" I know she's go to Aaron. He's where she would run to. Aaron, he's the one who helps her, he will know where she went.

"She's asleep inside," Aaron is sitting on the step of his duplex, holding an unlit cigarette. "She's going to be okay. Let her sleep. You need to go home."

"I have to talk to her. She needs to know I'm here. You know she's panicking."

"I know, Mr. Policeman, but we need to give her a few minutes. She's exhausted. She's confused. She needs to figure it out herself. Give her a minute. She's going to figure it out. Give her two minutes. In the morning, she will figure it out."

Another man comes out of the duplex. He's familiar, but I've never met him. He gives me a once over. "This is him? Well, she always had good taste in men. They might be trouble, but they're always handsome."

"Gabriel?" The man from the pictures, this is him. He's much taller in real life. Of course he is. Shit.

"The one and only," he grabs the cigarette from Aaron, smashing and tossing it into the shrubs. "I heard you got our girl pregnant."

Oh shit, it's true. She said it. When she said it, I knew it was true. Echo thinks the hormones are making her feel out of control, not to take anything she said personally. She needs to be reassured everything is okay. I need to convince her that everything is still okay. Echo thinks she's bipolar. I don't care what it is. I need her.

Quinn appears at the door, holding the screen door open, "Hey, baby daddy, we've been waiting for you."

"Is it true?" It must be true. I know, it's got to be true. I've known since my aunt told me. I knew it then. Juliana and I are having a baby. Fuck. A good fuck, but, fuck, damn. I'm going to have to be a better man for her, for our kid. Fuck, kid. We're having a kid.

"She is," Gabriel says, "She's going to be pissed, we all know, but we all know."

Quinn playfully swats Gabriel's head, "Boy, let her tell him. She's asleep right now. Tomorrow, she'll be okay. She needs rest."

"Let me do one thing. Let me put her ring on her finger," I'm talking and digging in my pocket, I have the box. I should have asked her the other night. I should have just asked her. "That might help her. Stop all those thoughts before she has them. When she wakes up, she will know I'm still here. She'll know I need her. She's bipolar right? That's what all this is, right? I need to know what to do to help her."

Quinn looks at Aaron, "He's the fucking police right?"

Gabriel huffs, "Yes, she is. But it's trauma related. When she's calm, she's fine."

"Gabriel," Quinn hushes, "Stop."

"No, this is the problem. You guys are trying to protect her and it's not helping her. You need to just tell him the truth. You guys are too overprotective. You need to let her fuck up a little so she can see she's okay. She's fine, she's just fine. She got mixed up. Whatever she said, Daniel, just know she was terrified. She didn't mean it. She panicked. She's not always like that."

Juliana was angry. Kim told her about the 5150. I should have told her the truth. I knew that was going to blow up. I knew it. I'm at fault too. "I get it. Trust me, I get it. It doesn't matter. She matters."

"That's what you have to do, when she panics, tell her she's okay. You have to convince her she's fine. Don't do what they do, they don't ever let her live. Don't overdo it," Gabriel says, gesturing towards Aaron and Quinn, "We all love her, but let her live."

"Everything is perfect. Juliana is having our baby. We need to get married." My fucking aunt was right. My mom will lose her shit. We're having a baby. I'm going to have a baby with Juliana. Shit, I have to tell Matt it's true. "I need to tell her I want to marry her."

"I knew I liked you," Aaron says, "Come on in."

Juliana's sound asleep, curled into a fetal position. She looks so young when she's asleep. What is our baby like now? Cells splitting or some dot on a monitor, where is she on that timeline? Is there even a heartbeat yet? It can't be that far along yet, maybe two months? I want babies that look like her. She's perfect.

I want to shake her awake, tell her everything is okay. I want to marry her. She doesn't move when I uncurl her fingers. She's so deep in her sleep state. Her body is making a baby, our baby. I slide the ring onto her finger. Let her wake up and know I'm still here. She's mine.

I love her.

JULIANA
April 9

    It's dark inside Quinn's room. It takes me a few seconds to realize where I am. I almost think I've started to fuck up again, went home with some nameless man, and then realized I'm in Quinn's house. Then I remember that, yes, I have fucked up. Not the old-fashioned kind, but a whole new level of crap-filled life. I told Daniel to fuck off. Nice. I told Echo she was a fraud. I make a mess out of shit, sometimes. Nice.

    There's a ring on my finger? Where did it come from? Quinn held me until I fell asleep. He did not put a ring on my finger. It's an engagement ring, three stones. It's perfect.

    Slide it off, inside, inscribed, Fernandez 1976. Oh my god, Daniel. When did Daniel put this on my finger? What does this mean?

    Daniel. Shit. He must hate me. I don't blame him for hating me. Why did he give me a ring? Quinn said, what did Quinn say?

    Outside, I can hear techno music playing. Gabriel must be here. Gabriel loves techno and EDM. Quinn and Aaron hate techno purely on principle.

    Gabriel almost lost his shit when I barged into the house crying. He came to see me for my birthday. Aaron told him I was pregnant and needed him. I scared his baby. His son, August, was napping and stayed napping. The baby, Delilah, woke up and started crying. Samuel, his partner, had to calm us both down at first before Quinn got me into his room. It's silly, I'm glad he's here. I've missed him so much. I wish he wasn't so far away.

    Wiping my eyes, I'm reminded that I've got a ring on that I'm not sure where it came from. Fernandez 1976. When was Daniel here?

    My head hurts. I need Advil. Shit. Can I take Advil? I need some water. I definitely need some water. These duplexes are so old they don't have en suite bathrooms. I will have to leave the safety of this room to get to the single bathroom. I'm not ready to do that. I can't see people yet.

I'm a fucking loser, hiding in Quinn's bedroom. I don't have to face the consequences of my actions. I have destroyed my life. I have done bad things. My sins have been shared out loud.

I got to pee, I need some water.

I made a mistake.

I ran like a coward.

Fernandez 1976, does he love me? I love him.

Shit. I love him.

That's why this matters. I love him.

I have to apologize.

I need to let him apologize.

I need to pick the right path.

There is only one right path.

I am fire.

    I AM FIRE.

I need Daniel. I don't. I do. I don't.

I don't need shit.

I don't need Aaron.

I don't need Quinn.

I don't need Gabriel.

I don't need Daniel.

I need to go home. I want to go home.

I've made a mess of everything. All this, I deserve this shit. I don't get to have a baby or a family. I just want to go home.

I don't deserve someone like Daniel to be with. There is no way I deserve that. I need to go home.

I am so confused. Someone help me. Oh god, please, someone help me.

I need Susan.

I need Ricky.

I need Daniel.

DANIEL
April 9

Quinn sent me home. He let me put an engagement ring on her finger, and then sent me home. They, Aaron and Quinn, seem to think she'll figure it all out in the morning.

Gabriel told me she is bipolar. I've known since the beginning. She reminded me of Eric. My brother Eric was bipolar. She admitted to having a mood disorder. When he was in high school, Eric was diagnosed with a mood disorder. She tried to kill herself. Eric is gone. He died by suicide. I knew all these things about her and never told her the truth. I've lived with this before. I'm at fault too.

As far as she's concerned, I lied to her. I did lie. Omission of the truth is a lie. It's a pretty serious lie. I knew she tried to hurt herself. I knew she was bipolar. I told other people her private shit. She has every right to hate me right now. I'm as bad as Christian Garcia. I didn't video her and show people, but I told her private shit to people.

I need her to know that I love her. I want this baby. I need her.

Text message from Matt: Did you find her?

Message to Matt: She's with Aaron.

Matt: Is she okay? Are you having a baby? You better marry my sister.

How do I explain this? Of course, I want to marry his sister. She's just not talking to me yet. As soon as she forgives me, I'm going to marry her.

Me: Everything will be fine. She's still upset.

Matt: She'll get over it. She's a Lopez, you know how we are. We get angry, then we get over it.

Will she? I sure hope she will.

JULIANA
April 9

    Opening the door, I peek out like a childish brat. Gabriel, Samuel, and Aaron are all sitting on the couch. Quinn is leaning against the counter, prepping some fancy snacks. The door clicks behind me.

    Aaron notices me, "Feeling okay? Did you get some rest?"

    I can't make a move forward, just gesture to the bathroom and rush that way. Everything is so mixed up. Nothing is making sense. I need just a few moments in the bathroom to reset myself.

    Everything is okay, right? Nothing is wrong. Everything is wrong. I need to breathe, to figure out what is happening. My brain is hurting. Luckily, it's not the intense pressure of a migraine, just a dull thump, like I need water. I need to face the world. I need to go out there. I can do this. I'm hiding in the bathroom like a baby.

    I can't live like this anymore. I'm sick of this. I know they know. Everyone knows. I know they know, and yet, I'm still a child. It's not a secret. It's not shameful. What would Susan say? Susan would say that I'm reverting to past feelings because I'm not sure what will happen next. I have an unnatural fear of the unknown. I create an image of what I think will happen, and then sabotage until it happens. What does she say, self-fulfilling prophecy, maybe so? I'm a fucking failure. Daniel gave me a ring? He asked Quinn if he could marry me.

    Who does that?

    What the fuck is wrong with him?

I know who does that, Daniel Fernandez, that's who. I need to be an adult. I can do this. I have to do this. I don't want to be this kind of parent. I can do this. I can face it, right?

I don't want to do this. I want to be a child and cry. I want to drop myself on the floor. I want to go home.

I want Daniel.

Back in the living room, everyone is normal. It's so normal, it's scary. I linger back, afraid to move forward. My eyes are burning, and dry, there cannot be another tear left in my body to cry.

"Girlfriend, you need anything," Aaron calls one hand on the back of the couch and the other on the pack-and-play next to him where Gabriel's son is sound asleep. "You might need a snack."

"Don't treat me like I'm helpless." I sound angry. I'm not. I'm worried. I'm exhausted. My head hurts. What the hell is happening?

"No one said you were helpless," Aaron doesn't respond to my tone. He just continues in his flat cadence, "Girlfriend, you're making a baby, you need to eat."

"That's where we are," I say, stamping my foot down. Breathe. What would Susan say? Susan would say to breathe, to imagine the ocean. To let it all go. Do not get upset. Breathe. "We all know?"

"Jules, we can't un-know," Gabriel sings, up on his knees and watching me from the couch. "Let's just be honest. Come sit, come hold your niece."

"I have a headache." The adrenaline levels start to fall. Ocean, keep thinking of the ocean, I want to be on the ocean. The waves, the waves take my worries. Let it go to the ocean. What would Susan say? She would say to enjoy it. "I want to go home."

"You need to eat, Jules. You've had a long night."

I'm super lightheaded. Maybe Quinn is right. I need some water and a snack. I am nauseous. Quinn moves, pulling me towards the table and handing me a snack of fancy cheese and crackers. Aaron hands me a glass of sparkling water. That I do drink. That I need. I feel dehydrated.

"Are you okay?"

"I have to talk to Daniel."

"He's home, Jules. Call him."

Looking at the engagement ring again, I could call him. I'd rather be chicken shit and text him. I'll have my snack, and then I'm going home. I'll call him then.

"You're having normal feelings. It's normal to feel out of control." Gabriel steals my fucking cheese, asshole. I miss him.

"Do you think I'll be like her?" I can barely get the words out. I don't want to worry about that. Gabriel knew her. He would know. Not Aaron, not Quinn, not even Susan. Gabriel knew her.

"You're not a crazy bitch. She was a crazy bitch, Jules."

"I'm crazy."

"She did this shit to you. Her and that dumb fuck father of yours. They did this. You're not them."

"Are you sure?"

"I'm a hundred percent positive. I wouldn't lie to you. You know that. Ask Ricky, you know he'll tell you the truth." Gabriel gestures to the phone.

"He said it will be fine."

"Then believe him. You know he would not lie to you. Me, you, Ricky, we don't lie to each other, Jules. Now this Daniel guy, he's going to have to get used to us. We're family."

"I've missed you, Gabe."

*****

It's so quiet in my apartment. It's too quiet. In bed, I finally check all my missed messages. Forty-seven missed messages from a variety of people, Adam, Matt, Echo, and Kim, but none as important as Detective Fernandez. His are the only ones I check.

Detective Fernandez: I'm sorry. I should have told you.
Detective Fernandez: I need you to call me. I need to talk to you.
Detective Fernandez: Nothing has changed.
Detective Fernandez: Don't take off that ring.
Detective Fernandez: To be clear, I want to marry you.
Detective Fernandez: Jules, call me.
Message to Detective Fernandez: I don't know what to say to you.
Detective Fernandez: We need to talk, Juliana.
Me: I know. I'm sorry Daniel.
Me: Give me a minute. Just give me a minute.

I have to fix this. I need to fix it. I don't know how to fix it.

Text message to Enrique Sanchez: Please call me. I need you, Ricky. I can't do this. Please, help me. I need you.

DANIEL
April 10

An incoming call from an unknown number, area code, 510, glows on my phone. 510? A quick search reveals it's from Oakland, CA. Oakland? I don't know anyone who lives in Oakland. It must be the wrong number.

Text message from an unknown number: Pick up the phone. It's Ricky.

Fucking Ricky Sanchez? Ricky Sanchez, who has a tattoo of my girlfriend's name on his fucking wrist? Who Matt Senior filed a restraining order against? Who Aaron called a fucking stalker?

Ricky Sanchez, who Juliana calls her best friend?

Jules must have told him to call me.

My phone buzzes again. Shit, I have to talk to him.

"Well, hi." I didn't know what I expected him to sound like. I guess I wanted him to sound hard and edgy. This guy sounds ordinary. He sounds like he's outside. The sounds of a TV, traffic, not sure which. It's noisy wherever he might be. "Daniel Fernandez, we have a problem. Juliana's stuck. You got to go get her unstuck. She's fucking terrified. Everyone is telling her what to do. She doesn't know what to do."

"She ran off."

"Don't let her run from you. She's dangerous when she runs off." He starts coughing, "Hold on."

The sound of a door slamming makes it easier to hear him suddenly. "Never let her run from you. She's impulsive. She's afraid."

"She locked us out. I couldn't."

"Dude, you don't know me. You don't have to do shit I say to you. If you want to fix this, go over there. You need to see it before she does. Start looking for her signs. Take care of her. She's just, that's just Jules. This is who she is. She gets twisted up in her head. But I guarantee you, she wants this."

"Aaron and Quinn," I start to say.

"She's pregnant with your baby. Who's more important?"

"She is."

"Quinn and Aaron don't know shit. They're too overprotective. They fucking hate me. It's not me. I know that. It's easier to blame me for the shit they think I did than to face facts. Facts, she's fucking bipolar. Gabe told you the fucking truth. I talked to him too."

Gabriel told me that she's bipolar. Hell, she practically told me. This is a weird conversation. I don't even know this guy. I do know she loves him, calls him her brother.

"She's doing that 'feel sorry for Juliana' shit she does. I just talked to her. She's by herself at home. Don't let her be alone right now. She's scared and can't ask for help. She doesn't know how. No one ever helped her as a kid. Now, she doesn't know she needs help. You have to just be there."

"Just be there?" It sounds so simple. Juliana Lopez has always been alone. She might have created a family, but I know she lived in the shadows. I've seen it. I'm friends with her family and had no idea she even existed.

"Daniel, just go over there. Take care of my girl. I mean it. Take care of my fucking sister."

"Okay. I'm going."

JULIANA
April 10

    Slit your wrist and die, that's the kind of music I like to listen to, nothing but the saddest love songs on Earth. Daniel likes to call me emo, but that's not true. What's true is that I love sappy ass love songs, especially anything from the 1970's although honestly, I wasn't there. I wasn't even born yet. Got that imaginary kid? That's what you're going to have to suffer through.

    I promise you that will be the extent of your suffering, crappy music. I've waited for you. I've waited a long time. First, I have to get my shit together. Then, I had to find the right guy. Unfortunately, there are too many to name, shitty men out there. Now, before you get here, I have to figure out how to fix this.

    I promise you, I'll fix this.

    Maybe I shouldn't say shit to you, or fuck. Maybe I should work on that too. I won't be one of those fake ass parents. Maybe I will? I can bake you any kind of cupcake. Cupcakes and cuss words. Yep, we got this kid. I'm going to fix this. I promise you.

    The light tapping on my door jostles me out of the brain fog I was falling into. At this hour, it can only be Aaron, or Quinn. I think Gabe and Sam have left by now. He said he was going to stay with his mom while he's here.

    Daniel Fernandez is standing at my door with a bouquet of flowers, orange flowers. He hands me a milkshake. My heart does a flip.

Oh god, he came back.

"I'm not leaving, whether you like it or not. Call the cops, I've got their number. Call me a stalker, cool. I'm cool with Ricky now too. You're not going to push me away. I'm here. Do you still think I'm dangerous?"

My heart does a somersault. "Completely dangerous."

"I made a mistake. I'm sorry. I'm not leaving Juliana. I won't build you a dog house, no, but you better start looking for a house. I don't even give a shit if it's here, in the Tower District. I fucking hate the Tower District. You're moving in with me. We're getting married."

I just throw my arms around him. He came back. He sees me.

"I'm sorry for being, for acting crazy earlier. I didn't mean it." Leaning against him on my couch, I'm so relieved he came back. I'm humiliated. I can't believe I acted like that. I'm so embarrassed.

"I'm sorry too. I'm sorry for telling them. I should have told you. I meant to tell you. Just promise me, next time, we talk. You can get mad at me, just promise you'll talk to me too."

"Daniel, are we really okay?" I whisper to him.

"We are." He whispers back, "Yeah, we need to learn how to talk, but we're okay. I guess I finally figured out what you're good for."

"It can't be this simple. It's not okay. Something is wrong."

"It's this simple. Real life is this simple sometimes. Why didn't you tell me it was your birthday? Happy birthday."

I'm still not sure this is real. Everything seems so normal. Maybe it's me. Maybe the only person not having a normal reaction is me? Maybe this is what life is supposed to feel like? It's not the earth shattering revelation I thought it was going to be. People have babies. People fall in love. People argue about stuff. It's not the end of the world. It's okay. I'm having a baby too. I'm having a baby with Daniel. Oh my god. I'm really in love with Daniel.

"When are we having a baby?"

My fucking heart skips a beat, maybe two, "October, October 29th."

"More emo shit, huh?"

The bubble in my chest finally pops. I can breathe, he isn't leaving me. "Isn't that us?"

"I thought we were ride or die."

"We are not ride or die. What the hell? No, we are not ride or die."

"Are you sure about that, baby girl? Ride or die sounds pretty emo to me. I'm surprised there isn't an emo song called that. You know nothing has changed, right? I still want to marry you. I want to have five babies with you."

"Psht, five, that's excessive."

"Aren't we excessive? Isn't that who we are? We're all in, all the time."

Another wave of panic hits, this is so freaking bizarre. It can't be this easy. This is not how things happen in my life. My life is a colossal fuck up. I'm going to be sick. I'm nauseated.

"Daniel, I'm terrified. I'm so scared."

He gets up, taking my hand, "Let's go for a walk."

Outside it is quiet, the music from inside is still playing. It's no longer crashing against my brain. It's one of those things. I didn't even notice how loud it was until we went outside. I am a little more stable. It is better to be walking than to just sit. There is so much I need to get straight. I need a minute, just a minute.

"I owe you an apology. I'm sorry," he says, taking my hand in his, kissing it right under my ring he put on my finger. "I told them, yeah, I told them all about the 5150. I didn't know you then. I'm sorry. I knew from the first day I met you. That's when I found it. You're right, I looked you up. I'm sorry."

I still remember that day. It was not anyone's fault. I just didn't want to be here anymore. Now I have Susan. Now I'm better. I want to say it's okay. It's not okay. It's not bad, I can live with it. Just walk and everything will be okay.

I need to tell him the truth. I need to say it. "I didn't go to rehab. I went to treatment." Psych ward sounds nuts. I hate that. I just needed help. I desperately needed help.

"It doesn't matter."

"It should. I'm more bipolar than mood disorder. I can't commit to bipolar. I have a hard time with that label. I'm working on it. I know that's what it is. I don't want to be that, but I am."

"It doesn't matter."

"It should matter. There is something totally fucked up with my brain." There is no one out right now, it's really quiet outside. It's got to be close to 4 am at this point.

"I'm positive. It's not who you are, it's a part of you."

"Sounds like the same thing to me."

"It is, and it's not." He stops walking, "Baby girl, are you going to have my baby?"

I have to breathe. I have to keep breathing. Oh my god, I'm totally pregnant. My eyes fill with tears, how can I have any tears left to cry? I'm so sick of crying. Just breathe, Susan said to just breathe. "That's my favorite house, right there, that yellow one."

"A long time ago, I had to babysit a girl in a car there. She was hiding in her boyfriend's car. She wouldn't tell me her name. She ignored me, ignored my dad. It is funny now. At the time, it wasn't. It was cold and raining."

A cop car blocked me in. Ricky said not to talk to them, "A rusted red Mustang?"

He looks at me, "No fucking way."

"That was Ricky's car. Aaron called the cops on him. He thought we got into a fight. It wasn't Ricky. I hurt myself. I don't do that anymore. I have Susan now."

He smiles and pushes up his glasses. "You met my dad."

"I did?"

"Technically, you refused to talk to him, but you did. I can't remember what he said. I just remember the whole babysitting thing. The girl refused to talk. Wouldn't talk to me, wouldn't talk to Officer Fernandez either."

"Officer Fernandez?"

"My dad was always a patrol guy."

"Do you believe in fate, destiny?"

"No."

"Good, me either." I don't remember the cops. I remember there were two. Ricky said not to talk to them. Ricky said they would lock me up. "It's good we didn't meet then. I wasn't who I am now. I might have had some issues."

He's quiet for a moment, "Eric was still here, JC was still here, and my life was different then."

"You have no idea what I was hiding that day."

"You can tell me if you want. You don't have to. I believe you. I don't judge you. I see you, Juliana. I see you."

"Is this real?" I need him to keep saying it.

"I am not pretending. I mean that. It's you and me, ride or die, emo shit, all in, hashtag 100, whatever you want to call it."

"You and me and chocolate milkshakes, I'm starving."

He takes my hand and we walk back. It's nice to be quiet. I'm going to be okay. We're going to be okay.

Early in the morning, my phone starts buzzing.

Text from Aaron Johnston: Birthday brunch at 11. Do not be late Jules.

Wow, it's my birthday brunch, and I'm chastised not to be late. Nice.

"We have brunch in an hour."

"Do we have to go?" Daniel is all cozy in my bed, with messed up, sloppy hair. He's hella cute. I like this one. Daniel is home. I know that. That's what is so scary. He's dangerous.

"I guess so. I'm the guest of honor. Call your mom. Maybe she wants to come?"

"She's going to lose her shit, baby girl. She's going to do all kinds of weird shit to you, make you wear safety pins and shit like that. She's going to be overprotective of you. Sorry."

People will know? I can do this. I can totally do this.

"No more techno," Aaron says, changing the music to slow oldies. "Awful music, it's giving me a headache."

"Hey, it's her birthday," Gabriel says, grabbing pancake supplies. "She likes techno."

"No, she likes that stupid emo shit," Quinn laughs, "Change the music to that depressing emo shit, it is her birthday."

It's a weird moment for sure. We got up, and went to see Daniel's mom. He was right, Rosie burst into tears. Even now, she keeps watching me. It's freaking me the fuck out. I'm trying to be cool. I've got to be cool.

"No emo," I say, "Siri, play disco, 1976." Dance music pours out.

"Now that is good music," Quinn says. "That's wedding reception music."

"Oh, someone should have a wedding," Rosie sings. She gives me that look again. She glances at the ring. I kept it on. I haven't been asked, I haven't said yes. Oh shit, Daniel is going to ask me. Oh shit. He leans against me, just barely.

Breathe.

We're sitting on the couch. He's leaning against me. Everyone knows. Everyone is cool. If they're cool, I can be cool too.

"*Mija*, do you need more water, more orange juice?"

"Mom, you're going to make her nervous. She's fine. You're fine right?"

"I'm fine." I'm more than fine. I don't tell them that right now. I want to shout it out, fucking Daniel Fernandez got me pregnant. I don't want him to catch me looking at my ring, so I pretend to stretch my arms over my head instead. "Everything is perfect."

"I need to tell you something," Daniel says quietly, even though he's speaking to me, everyone is listening, "When we first met, I had to talk to some kid involved with some sexting case. I used parts of your story to reach him. It's not cool, I know that. We got the information we needed from him. He trusted me enough to tell me, to get him some help. But, during our conversation, he asked me, do you forgive her? Do you forgive her for letting it happen?"

"Do you? Do you forgive me?"

"I told the kid it wasn't her fault. It was never her fault. Of course, I forgive her, but I don't need to forgive her because there is nothing to forgive. You know what else I told that kid?"

"What?"

"I told him I was going to marry you. There's some emo kid running around Fresno who knows I was planning to marry you, even back then. It's about time you knew too. Will you marry me, Juliana Lopez? I mean it, for real, no pretending."

Twist the ring on my finger, I want to say yes. Yes is in my soul. This is it. He is picking me. Someone, someone worth it, someone finally picked me.

Gabriel throws a cushion at me. "Answer the man, Jules. Or I'll marry him."

"Yes."

"Let's go to Vegas." Gabriel sings, "Birthday road trip."

"No," Quinn directs, shutting Gabriel down instantly, "My girl gets a wedding."

"No wedding," I said adamantly, "No."

"You are fire, Juliana," Quinn says, looking right at me, "You get a wedding."

"My mom wants a wedding, baby girl," Daniel nudged me. "I am her favorite child."

"A big wedding Juliana, you went to Lily's. One like that," Rosie says, showing Aaron pictures of that night on her phone.

I have to get married. The thought of all those people, I can't do it. I cannot have a wedding. I can be married, but I don't want a wedding. But maybe I do. I want a pretty white dress and a cake with an umbrella. I want a Jedi wedding. I want to marry Daniel. I love him. Oh shit. He is dangerous.

I want to say it to him. I want to say it out loud. I haven't said it for so long. For so long, I didn't understand what it meant, but now I do. I finally get it. Well, I got it for a while now. I didn't believe it. I finally believe it. "I love you Daniel."

"I love you too. Baby girl, nothing has ever been pretending. It's all real. All of it, everything, we are not pretending." He pulls me closer, "I see you."

"Juliana, you need to marry that one."

I do, I need to marry this one. Oh shit, this is real.

Daniel Fernandez is fucking dangerous.

I am fucking fire.

EPILOGUE
Juliana
14 Years Later
May

"Mom, why can I have it?" She's exhausting sometimes. She doesn't need to know that. ADHD, that's my fault. Claudia Marie is named after one of her grandfather's moms, definitely Aaron's favorite grandchild.

"Hey, what did we already tell you?" Daniel only has to give her that tone to get her to knock it off. "Go get ready. Your grandmother will be here in ten minutes to pick you up. No phone. Grounded means no phone."

"Ugh! Fine!" She stomps off, still furious with me.

"Dad, what time are you picking us up tomorrow?" Eric holds his phone in his hand, waiting for a response.

"By ten."

"Cool," he rushes out.

Those two have been exhausting since the moment they were conceived. But I love them. Twins, twin flames, exhausting but beautiful, Claudia Marie and Eric, the two most perfectly flawed children ever. I'm lucky to have them. After that, it never happened again. We tried. We saw doctors. We only have the twins.

I have to hold my hand against that spot on my forehead. I can feel the pounding building deep in my brain, another migraine.

"You don't have to do this Juliana, Susan would understand."

"I need to do this. She saved my life, Daniel. I owe her this."

Susan. My heart hurts thinking about her. She's been gone a month now. Today is her memorial. Today I have to testify about her in front of her friends. I want to share stories about her with them. I loved her. She loved me too. It took me a long time to figure that out. People love me. I never believed it then. I do now.

"My name is Juliana Fernandez and Susan saved my life."

Matt and Adam are the brothers I never realized I needed. Sounds stupid, I lived a whole life without them, but now that they're part of it, I need them. I can call them for stupid shit and they'll help me, and vice versa. I made a beautiful white, floral nightmare cake for Matt's daughter's *quinceanera*. Adam has three daughters and one boy. Great, three more white cakes I have to make. I'll complain about it, but I love it.

Gabriel and I are cool now. He never came back. He told me he could never come back. I get it. How I can't leave, he can't come back. But he calls me and I pick up his calls. We talk again. His kids are my niece and nephew. We're one big happy family. His kids and my kids are all cousins. It's funny.

Daniel bought me a house. As soon as we agreed to get married, he bought me a craftsman-style home, right in the heart of Tower District, within walking distance from Aaron and Quinn. Close to the yellow one, my favorite one. It's one block from Fresno City College. He knew I couldn't leave. I could never leave Aaron and Quinn. It brought us half a town closer to his mom. We're only a 15-minute drive from her.

Our wedding was small and directed by Quinn. It was way more than I wanted. It was a perfect disco party. I made my own damn cake, with an umbrella on top.

Matt senior came. At least, I hear he came. I never saw him. He didn't stay long. He gave Daniel a check for $20,000 and said that's what he gave Matt and Adam. We never cashed it. I don't need shit from him. I never wanted that from him. He could never be what I wanted. I let that go. I have dads. Aaron and Quinn gave me away. And I got married to Far Behind. Emo shit. No, "Here Comes the Bride" for me. Fuck that.

We are not perfect people. We don't have a perfect life, but I'm the happiest I've ever been. Daniel has never needed me to prove things to him. He just believes me. He believes in me. I believe in him too. He can tell me anything. He tells me everything. This is home. We are not pretending.

And I have one more tattoo, just one more. A dandelion, right on my hip, Quinn doesn't know.

Text message from Enrique: don't die.

Me: You don't die either.

Daniel understands me. He knows I need Ricky too.

And we still play Fortnite, a lot.

ACKNOWLEDGEMENTS

Thank you to my family and friends for understanding my obsession with those people who live inside my brain, even ChGa. He's one pain in the ass! I love him and just adore every wrong thing he does. He's my boy. Thank you for listening when RiSa became more than I planned for and tried to take control of everything. Even when I didn't believe in myself, you all stood by me and helped me push forward. All my texts, questions, and tears, you sat with me through all of this.

Aida Landaverde, why yes, that plant story might be a story you once told me. You were my first reader! Thank you for asking hard questions. DaFe is a better name! Remember when we went looking for E-40 at the Warriors game? LOL! Of course the night we were there, he wasn't.

Anne Marie Sanneh, thank you for loving DaFe the way I love him (and refusing to forgive ChGa) and for sharing hot cop memes with me. Your reaction to RiSa is just what I needed-damn girl, me too. I love the story of how you saw an IRL ChGa on the subway. LOL! Thank you, cousin! I wish you all the best all the time, you know that!

Beth Stoddard and Becky Layman, thank you for listening to my dark moments. There's a lot of them… dark.

Celia Martinez, thank you for loving them as much as I do. It sounds silly, but I am glad it made you sad to get to the end. I'm proud of you for following your dreams! It might get harder at first but it will get better. Your story about the Bad Bunny DJ will always bring me a smile-you go! I appreciate your friendship, Mrs. Martinez (sing to the tune of "that song!")

Katherine Gibson, thank you for understanding my E-40 obsession and for telling me about those three things way back, once upon a time. Number two will always be a mystery! I think it was snake a drain? Who knows? I do know that was a good list.

Kristina Wyatt, thank you for taking stick drawings, song snippets, and random pictures and creating art. You are a talented artist. Your work is amazing. I love all the moody bitch vibes. You need "moody bitch nana," on a t-shirt.

Sandra Andersen, thank you for sticking with it and asking those questions that forced me to be clearer (what does he look like?). The day you walked into my space and screamed, "What the fuck is going on in your brain," is one of my favorite moments!

Big thanks to my mom and my brothers, Rosa, Robert, and Jose Aleman. Without you, I wouldn't be a very exciting person. Although this story is not true, some details are real. We shared a house with JuLo and had friends that hung out on the roof. Good times, good times.

Mom, thanks for being a great role model. I am who I am because of you. I'm defiant, bossy, and a know it all. That's all you. Just for the record, none of these people are real. No mom, you don't know them

The biggest thanks go to my favorite husband, Cesar. You believe in my story even though you haven't read it. You're still not allowed to. I am grateful for your unwavering support and love. You are the best parts of DaFe, ChGa, and RiSa in one real person. I even love that you don't like the Tower District.

Also, many thanks to my son, Diego, who is all in and wants to write a companion guide.

Lastly, I have to thank E-40, Too Short, and the 2 Live Crew. Your music helped me get through those tough spots! Music is my life.

ABOUT THE AUTHOR

Dori Aleman-Medina currently lives in Southern California with her favorite husband, son, cat, and dog who are not allowed to read the stories she writes. She grew up in Fresno, California, in a house that was near Vons and Holmes Playground but she did not go to Roosevelt either. She will always love the Tower District and Fresno City College. She loves emo music, alternative music, and E-40.

Made in the USA
Monee, IL
04 December 2022